"George Wallace with the capable aid of Don Keith has created a novel that is all to close to reality. . . . If you can still feel the roll of a submarine at periscope depth . . . if you still enjoy action-packed adventure and the surprises a good piece of fiction can bring to your easy chair, you'll love this."

—*Naval Submarine League*

"Achieves real power."

—*Booklist*

"The story gives us the full impact of submarine and Navy life . . . putting the reader in the middle of the action on every page."

—*Harrison News Herald*

FINAL
BEARING

GEORGE WALLACE

AND DON KEITH

A TOM DOHERTY ASSOCIATES BOOK
NEW YORK

NOTE: If you purchased this book without a cover, you should be aware that this book is stolen property. It was reported as "unsold and destroyed" to the publisher, and neither the author nor the publisher has received any payment for this "stripped book."

This is a work of fiction. All the characters and events portrayed in this book are either products of the author's imagination or are used fictitiously.

FINAL BEARING

Copyright © 2003 by George Wallace and Don Keith

All rights reserved, including the right to reproduce this book, or portions thereof, in any form.

A Forge Book
Published by Tom Doherty Associates, LLC
175 Fifth Avenue
New York, NY 10010

www.tor.com

Forge® is a registered trademark of Tom Doherty Associates, LLC.

ISBN 0-765-34317-7
EAN 978-0765-34317-8

First Forge edition: April 2003
First mass market edition: April 2004

Printed in the United States of America

0   9   8   7   6   5   4   3   2   1

Dedicated to my father, Edgar Allen Wallace,
6 August 1923–15 September 2002

GEORGE ALLEN WALLACE

and

To my wife, Charlene, who still pretends
that she doesn't mind my maddening compulsion
to make up stories for other folks to read.

DON KEITH

Interior Layout of USS *Spadefish* SSN 637

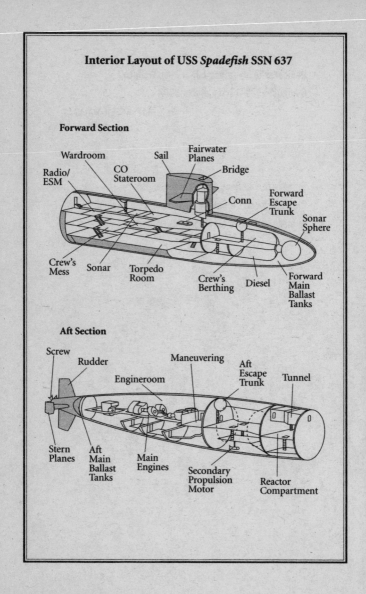

Forward Section

Wardroom
Sail
Fairwater Planes
Radio/ESM
CO Stateroom
Bridge
Conn
Forward Escape Trunk
Sonar Sphere
Crew's Mess
Sonar
Torpedo Room
Crew's Berthing
Diesel
Forward Main Ballast Tanks

Aft Section

Screw
Rudder
Maneuvering
Aft Escape Trunk
Tunnel
Engineroom
Stern Planes
Aft Main Ballast Tanks
Main Engines
Main Engines
Secondary Propulsion Motor
Reactor Compartment

Caribbean Sea

PANAMA

Santa
Marta
Barranquilla
Cartagena

Montería

VENEZUELA

Cúcuta

Bucaramanga

Pacific
Ocean

Medellín

Bogotá

COLOMBIA

Buenaventura

Cali
Neiva

Florencia

San José del Guaviare

Pasto

Mitú

Quito

BRAZIL

ECUADOR

PERU

**Beaman's Trek
Through Colombia**

1 Beaman's route ••••••••
2 Drug factory
3 Ambush
4 Cocaine valley
5 De Santiago's secret lab

© 2003, Mark Sarin Studios

N
W — E
S

miles
0 _____ 200
kilometers
0 _____ 325

The sea, washing the equator and the poles, offers its perilous aid, and the power and empire that follow it. "Beware of me," it says, "but if you can hold me, I am the key to all the lands."
—Ralph Waldo Emerson

Sandy Holmes

prologue

SANDY HOLMES'S NOSE WAS PRACTICALLY TOUCHING THE VW'S fogged-up windshield. She furiously wiped at the glass with the back of her hand and squinted into the wet darkness, struggling to make out the street signs as they slipped by. The address she was looking for should be right around the next corner if she had her directions right.

Damn the Seattle traffic! Why was every-damn-body out on this Friday night? And why wouldn't the jerk with the blinding, bright headlights behind her just go on around?

Okay, so the Lake Washington area was unfamiliar territory. But she owed it to herself to finally break some barriers, to explore some new ground, and tonight was the night. The computer-programming job over in Bellevue was all right, she supposed. But since the day she had been assigned her cubicle and issued her desktop box and her own copy of the company employee manual, work had soaked up every drop of what little life she had. Fun was a trip to an all-night grocery for salad-in-a-bag and a pint of pistachio ice cream.

A date? Forget about it!

The rain dwindled now to little more than an aggravating mist. Seattle sunshine. Sandy snorted in spite of herself. What did the Seattle Chamber of Commerce say? About the same annual rainfall per year here as they had in Washington, D.C.? Yes, but D.C. got theirs in occasional gulps. Seattle's precipitation was insistent, constant, and seemingly never-ending. A fitting metaphor, she often thought, for her job.

The roadway stretching out in front of her glistened black beneath the streetlights. Sandy tried not to envy the happy couples that walked hand in hand up and down the sidewalk, oblivious of the weather. They were likely heading for the cozy little restaurants that lined the street and backed up to Lake Washington. Lights and fancy neon flickered invitingly in their windows. She could smell grilled fish and alder-wood smoke through the Bug's cracked open window. Those were happy aromas, associated with dates and friends and a life. She rolled the window up.

Sandy was glad that Linda Farragut convinced her to give up an evening, to slip off work early for a change and enjoy herself. Linda was the only one at CedarTech who seemed to be any fun at all. She told her about this party, so it had to be worth the drive. And not a second too soon. Sandy's social life was for shit. It had been that way ever since she graduated head of her class from Iowa City Community College. "Number one nerd!" the yearbook had dubbed her beneath a horrid photo from back when she wore black-rimmed glasses and her hair in a tight, prim bun. So be it. The associate degree in computer science was supposed to be her ticket to success in high-techdom. So far, though, it had been nothing but a drag.

"Stock options! Stock options!" the screen saver on the computer monitor in her cubicle shrieked at her all day, a constant reminder of why she did what she did.

Now it was finally time for this nerd to let her hair down. The hormones had been hemmed up for too long. Nobody knew her here. Linda had even begged off at the last minute. Sandy would be as anonymous as she had ever been in her life.

There it was! Lake Street. She made the turn abruptly, with no signal, and the guy with the bright headlights angrily blew his horn at her. At least his high beams were gone from her mirror and she could see much more clearly as she searched for the house.

Now, what was it? Two blocks up, large brick on the left.

Okay, that was it. Cars in the drive and parked up and down both sides of the street. There was obviously a party there. Good to have a VW. Slide it right in there in that half-a-parking-space, behind the Lexus. She felt her heart beat a notch faster. Time to party.

Maybe there would be a nice guy there that Mom would like. Better still, maybe one she would absolutely hate.

She slammed the car door behind her. Sandy noticed for the first time in a while how fragrant the air was. One good thing about all the rain, the way the air always smelled clean and electric here. In the dark she could see that the aspen leaves had gone golden while she wasn't looking and the maple leaves burning scarlet just behind them seemed to color the gray night. She was convinced she could even smell the sea, feel the fresh salt air, even though it was many miles to the west.

Sandy Holmes felt as alive as she had in months as she boldly strode up the walkway to the neat Victorian house. She punched the doorbell. Someone cracked it open it a couple of inches, as far as the chain would allow. She could see only one eye and a deeply black face, topped with wildly spiked blond hair. There was a dog collar around the man's neck.

"Yes?" he hissed.

"I . . . ummm . . . am Sandy, Linda's friend," she answered. He looked like plenty of other twenty-somethings she saw around Seattle. This one scared her, though.

"Linda?"

"Linda Farragut."

He eyed her up and down through the crack in the door. She checked the house number again without backing off the little porch to make sure this was the right place.

"Yeah, I know Linda. But I don't know you."

There was someone else behind him, someone with an easy, friendly voice, soft but still audible over the sound of a party that drifted out from somewhere toward the back of the house.

"Wait a minute, Jason. Where are your manners? Let the little lady in. She says she's Linda's friend. That's good enough for me."

Jason obeyed immediately, unchaining the door and opening it wide, beckoning her in with a regal sweep of his hand and a demented grin that showed chapped lips and bad teeth.

The disembodied voice behind him turned out to be a young, dark man with big, sad, brown eyes. He had a welcoming demeanor, a handsome smoothness that instantly had her weak-kneed. He took Sandy's hand, nodded slightly, and welcomed her to his party.

"I'm glad you could make it, 'Sandy-Linda's-friend.' Please, make yourself at home. I'm Carlos . . . Carlos Ramirez . . . and I'm delighted to meet you. Come on back and let me show you off to the other guests."

There was something almost hypnotic about the man. He made her feel as if he was, indeed, profoundly happy that she had come. He held her hand in his, his other arm around her shoulders as he gently guided her through the expensively but tastefully decorated home.

They reached the source of all the noise. There were at least a hundred other people milling about the big room at the rear of the house, but Carlos seemed to be playing host only to her now. For that moment, the pretty blond computer programmer from Iowa City was the most important guest at Carlos Ramirez's party.

He led her down the steps into the big open room. The other guests fell silent and looked his way.

"Everyone, welcome Sandy!"

They all raised their cocktails to her in a friendly enough gesture. After a polite pause, they resumed their chatter. Sandy couldn't believe the crowd. It was as if someone had called Central Casting and asked them to send over a hundred "beautiful people" to populate the most glamorous party Sandy Holmes had ever seen.

A drink appeared in her hand from nowhere. She put it to her lips and took a sip. It tasted sweet, strangely cool on her tongue, but warm and spicy as it went down. Carlos ushered her into the midst of the guests and soon she was talking to someone tall and dark-haired and wearing a suit that cost as much as her VW Bug.

Thank you, Linda, she thought. *Thank you for delivering me right into heaven!*

She soon lost track of Carlos Ramirez. He was standing on the party's fringes, occasionally acknowledging one of his guests, but mostly watching this new arrival with a small smile playing at his lips.

His dark eyes were no longer sad. They had gone stone cold evil.

Beautiful white trash, he thought. *Look how shyly she flirts. How innocent she tries to look. Soon she'll be snorting with the rest of them. And taking back word of the delights available here to the others, just as her friend has done for her.*

I may have her before she is too wasted to appreciate it. Maybe not. Maybe I'll allow Jason to enjoy her first. These blondes are especially good, his favorites, and he deserves the perks of the job.

Carlos watched her as she laughed. He watched as her self-consciousness left her as she sipped the last few drops of her second drink. She was deeply involved in conversation, cozying up to one of those prancing, WASP, captain-of-industry types that he so despised. Despised even after they inevitably became his best customers. He observed the way the slight, pink flush was spreading its way up her throat now, coloring in her cheeks, adding starlight to her eyes as the alcohol did its work on her.

That was nothing. He would soon have another refreshment to serve her and the rest of his guests. And it truly was magical.

The plan is going precisely as Juan de Santiago promised it would, he thought.

"Give them a taste of the new powder," de Santiago had urged. "Once they have tasted, they are yours from now on. Yours and ours, Carlos."

And if the new powder worked as predicted, it would be gold.

A snort or two and hooked for life! How was such a thing possible?

Carlos didn't care about the specifics. The scope of what de Santiago and the others were doing was much too big for him to comprehend. He only knew how it affected him. Basic supply and demand. This new product would take care of the demand and de Santiago swore he and the others would soon have the supply problem solved.

It's finally my time, Carlos thought.

After the struggles of the last few years, the small-time marijuana business, the minuscule-margin cocaine distribution, he was ready to reap the bounty this new, powerful powder of de Santiago's promised.

The noise level in the room confirmed that his party guests were ready, too. Carlos stepped through the double doors and signaled to Jason.

It was time to bring in the new refreshment.

1

JUAN DE SANTIAGO WAS A MAN WHO INSISTED THAT HIS WORLD ROtate smoothly on a well-oiled axis, that his organization operate as a properly maintained machine. He knew how the tiniest overlooked detail could derail an operation. The smallest unobserved defect in a propeller could crack a bearing and seize up a perfectly good engine. A minor flaw in an otherwise perfect plan could doom the efforts of hundreds.

And Juan de Santiago was not a man who would tolerate imperfection.

Now, on this beautiful morning here in his beloved mountains, he could only watch helplessly as the awful result of some unknown minor flaw in an otherwise faultless plan played out below him.

"Bastard Americans!" he spat, his hot, angry words barely audible over the strident buzzing of the giant black insects that danced above the mountain field below him. "And that son of a dog, El Presidente Guitteriz!"

The smaller man standing beside him took a short, strategic step backward. He wanted to be out of his leader's reach. He could feel the heat of the man's fury. He knew only too well how that rage could sometimes manifest itself.

Roaring flames raced through Juan de Santiago's best coca fields. The crop, mere weeks from harvest, was now little more than a fog of thick, black smoke being shoved up the mountain slopes and into the jungle by a gentle tropical breeze. That breeze would usually bring him the fragrance of the wild orchids that grew among the trees below the field.

Not today. There was the foul odor of the imperialists' destruction.

The fragrance was one reason de Santiago loved to make the long, treacherous hike through the mountains over the ancient Inca trail from his base camp. This was his boyhood home. It rejuvenated him to come here.

He would often trek to this high clearing just before the harvest. He could see for himself the bounty God had sent him to help him free his people. He could watch some of those people as they worked below. He would go down and join the peons, walk among them, honor them with his presence, embrace each of them, thank them for their sacrifice and loyalty.

He now watched as a half-dozen Black Hawk helicopters reloaded the Colombian troops and their American advisors. Their morning's work was completed. There was no mistaking where the choppers came from. The U.S. flag unashamedly marked each of them. Four Apache copters still buzzed overhead. Guarding the men below, they scouted about in the surrounding jungle for any rebel troops that still lurked there.

Most of de Santiago's men had fled at the first thumping of the approaching helicopters. They had taken to the thick underbrush. Their loyalty to the Marxist cause and to their leader had given way to self-preservation. Their leader angrily kicked at the dirt. His perfectly polished boots now covered with dust, he spouted a continuous litany of deep-throated oaths. His swarthy face grew even darker with rage as a tic contorted his right cheek and eye.

That was not merely a cash crop going up in smoke down there. The fields represented the financing he needed to continue the revolution. It was a war that he was convinced would eventually return this beautiful land to him, to his people.

The Americans and their "war on drugs" had taken on a ferocious new intensity in the last year. It seemed El Presidente had unlimited resources. With the help of the *yanqui* military and their fancy machines, the president seemed to have the strength to break both of de Santiago's backbones, his revolution and the coca fields that financed it.

He had received the reports from Cartagena. He had heard the breathless reports from the mouths of those who had seen it for themselves. The Americans filled every wharf with their heavily laden ships, unloading more troops, more weapons, and more supplies every day. In only a few months, their advisors had transformed El Presidente's ragtag troops into an effective fighting force, putting the rebels on the run as they torched the coca fields. Even more disheartening was the word of the surveillance satellites overhead that were now trained on de Santiago's precious jungle mountains, never blinking, never missing anything.

De Santiago would build a processing factory. Build it even in the most remote jungle clearing, and the government troops would be there before the first shipment of silvery powder was prepared. Government troops and their American advisors met many truckloads of ammunition as if they had been sent an invitation. Or if the rebels sowed a field in some remote mountain valley and carefully nurtured it, they would soon see the fine coca devoured by flames when it was so tantalizingly close to harvest.

His people in Bogotá whispered of some new organization

he had never heard of. Something called the Joint Drug Interdiction Agency, a seamless coalition of the imperialists who had finally come together to fight those who would use the coca to win the righteous war of the people. Beyond the name, little was known about this alliance. If it weren't so obvious that the Americans and their allies were doing something radically different, de Santiago would have dismissed this JDIA as simply a myth. If one could not see it, feel it, smell it, it likely did not exist.

Juan de Santiago stared at the choppers. He felt the heat of the flames they had set loose. He smelled the stench of the smoldering revolution this JDIA seemed hell-sent to destroy.

"JDIA must be stopped! But how?" de Santiago muttered to himself.

They had no idea where its headquarters might be, its communications facilities, or its leadership.

De Santiago had been certain this series of fields, high in the Colombian Andes and down a narrow mountain valley, was safely hidden. No roads approached here. Only a steep path over the mountains that he and his bodyguard and a small cadre of his men had just hiked. Even the damned satellites should not have been able to find these fields. They were almost always shrouded in clouds.

De Santiago's experts had told him that the ridge was too high for a helicopter to cross. The only way one could approach these high fields, they had maintained, was to wind their way up the narrow valley. That's why the lookouts were deployed down that way. That's why the thin but strong cables had been stretched across to snare them like a spider's web should they venture up to the high fields. But the helicopters had unquestionably flown over the ridge three hours ago, dead certain of their target. They had come in fast, over the high ridge to the northeast, as surely as the sun had topped the mountains that morning.

De Santiago's proudest venture had been caught completely off-guard. That was not the mark of a flawless operation.

The surprise and the overwhelming firepower had been too much for the rebel peons who had been working in the fields. Most of them took to the jungle. The few who stayed to fight quickly gave their lives to the cause. The firefight was short and intense. The Apaches scurried back and forth across the valley, their 20mm chain guns beating out a staccato tattoo aimed at anything that moved.

El Presidente's troops fast-roped out of the Black Hawks into the fields below, showing more professionalism than de Santiago had ever seen from them before. On the ground, the government soldiers fanned out smartly and efficiently to establish protected landing zones for the choppers that were still hovering overhead. By the time the first Black Hawk flared out to land, the fight was over. They set to torching the crop, shouting to each other and laughing like truant schoolboys up to some kind of mischief.

"It is most difficult to kill a snake if its head cannot be severed," de Santiago said aloud but to himself.

Juan de Santiago and Guzmán, his trusted bodyguard, had been approaching the nearest mountainside that overlooked the field, a half-dozen troops close behind. They followed the narrow trail to this serene, beautiful overlook, to observe the crop, to watch the peons work, to maybe smell the perfume of the orchids. They heard the attack as it began. They knew immediately what the hellish racket was. There was no mistaking the yakking of those guns, the rhythmic flutter of the copter blades, the anguished screams of the brave peons. In awful frustration, he and the others had run to the overlook and watched most of the three-hour operation from the cover of jungle.

De Santiago knew he was the most hunted man in all of Colombia. If those bastards down there on the valley floor only knew he was here, on the side of this mountain, watching them the whole time, they would be in hot pursuit. They would not be laughing, boasting to each other of their victory. Now they climbed back into their helicopters and prepared to leave behind all the damage they had done. Not only to the crop, but to the people's struggle.

Spurred by their sniggering, de Santiago's anger reached a new pitch. He stomped the ground again. Guzmán could hear him grinding his teeth. He clenched his jaw even tighter as he spoke, forcing the words out one at a time as if he were biting them off and spitting them out.

"I will show these damned dogs that I do not scamper away and hide in fright like a rabbit!"

He spun on a heel and, in one quick motion, snatched the Starburst missile launcher from Guzmán's back before the bodyguard even realized what was happening. He locked the optical sight on a Black Hawk down below that was just lifting off and pulled the launch trigger. Flame shot out the back of the launch tube, scorching the dense vegetation on the slope behind him while the troops standing nearby scattered to get out of the way.

The British-made antiaircraft missile burst out the front of the tube and flew arrow-straight toward the hovering chopper. Despite his rage, de Santiago knew what he was doing. He kept the sight locked on to the chopper as it rose and banked, ready to climb and head back over the ridge. He kept the reticule locked on, the launcher sending tracking data down the thin copper filament that still connected him to the missile.

"*Madre de Dios!*" the startled Guzmán shouted.

His leader's sudden crazy move had caught the seasoned warrior totally by surprise. Guzmán—everyone knew him only by the one name—tended to always fight and defend using logic, and de Santiago's totally emotional and completely illogical response to what he had been watching had been unexpected. Now Guzmán was forced to react instinctively, impulsively.

He turned to see the scorched vegetation on the uphill slope smoldering, already sending up thin tendrils of smoke. He ripped off his campaign hat and began to beat out the flames before the Apache pilots with their infrared sights could spot the smoke and retaliate.

At Mach 1.5, only two seconds elapsed from launch of the Starburst to impact. The hapless Black Hawk in the Starburst's sights exploded with a deep *whoomph*, raining flaming wreckage down onto the still-smoking coca field.

"Justice!" de Santiago whooped. "Let *los diablos imperialistos* burn in their own hellfire!"

The two-second flight of the missile was more than enough for the Apaches. They were already facing that way and vectored in on the launch site. One of the choppers came roaring straight toward them. The chin turret, with its death-spitting twin chain guns, snapped back and forth like a cobra searching for its prey.

Guzmán didn't hesitate. He grabbed de Santiago by the collar of his starched khaki shirt and leaped off the trail, over the bluff and down the steep mountainside.

"Got to move!" he bellowed as they dropped into open space.

Projectiles zipped past them and over their heads as the two men fell a good twenty feet straight down, then began rolling and tumbling. The thickness of the vegetation was the only thing that kept them from falling much farther and much harder. They finally stopped rolling. They were in a thick tangle of vines. Chewed-up leaves and tree limbs peppered down on them.

De Santiago listened to the final screams of his slower-reacting troops, the continuous buzz saw of the chain gun, and the guttural rumble of the helicopter, now directly overhead.

It was finished. The patch of mountain where the rebel leader had been standing a moment before was now gnawed down to bare rock. What remained of four of his best men lay in bloody pieces amid the litter of the attack. Two others were cowering in the brush, checking their wounds. Down in the valley, the remains of the Black Hawk continued to burn fiercely while one of its brothers hovered above, checking for signs of life. Seeing none, it swooped up and followed the rest of the helicopters, which were already disappearing over the ridge.

"Damn them to hell," de Santiago grunted under his breath

as he shoved Guzmán off the top of him. He fought through the ferns and vines and climbed out of the small ravine where they had landed. He took stock of himself. Nothing broken. Cuts and contusions but nothing that would not stop bleeding on its own. A knot on his forehead from a tree trunk he had bounced off on the way down.

"You okay, El Jefe?" Guzmán asked as he emerged from the wall of green. The bodyguard limped slightly but seemed all right otherwise. He looked at his leader, tilted his head, and ventured an unsolicited opinion. "That was a very foolish thing to do, you know."

De Santiago's rage flared once again as he turned on his bodyguard.

"What would you have me to do? Would you have me run like a coward? Is that what you want? Look what those damned Americans have done. They will pay far more than one helicopter! I will make them pay!"

De Santiago stalked off, angrily slapping aside the vegetation. He followed the trail that led up from the field and over the mountain. Guzmán shook his head. It was difficult for him and the other rebel troops to keep pace with their leader. Years of fighting in these cloud jungles had toughened the man, given him the ability to endure pain and weariness without even appearing to be aware of it. He never noticed that his best fighters and his rock-hard bodyguard often struggled to keep up with him.

Guzmán tried to ignore his twisted ankle and hurried after de Santiago before he was too far gone.

"Catch up after you have buried the dead and bandaged the wounds of the others," the rebel leader called back to him.

The progress was slow. The two injured fighters lagged far behind. They climbed back up the mountain, beyond the tree line. Scrambling over rocks and scree, they came again to the pass over the mountain ridge.

De Santiago paused there for only a moment. He glanced over his shoulder, to the west, and a strange calm seemed to come over him. He knew that from up here, from this high trail first blazed by his Inca ancestors, if it weren't for the clouds, they could see the ocean over two hundred miles away. A realization struck him. He was disgusted with himself for not having seen it before. As much as he loved his mountains, the leader knew at that instant that the key to all that he must accomplish rested out there, with the sea.

He walked on, deep in thought.

They stopped for a short rest in the saddle of the pass. A stack of rocks left centuries before by the Indians marked this high point on the trail. The two troops caught up, falling in their tracks, exhausted from the brisk climb and gasping for breath in the thin air. They checked their crude bandages. Guzmán loosened the laces on his boot so the swollen ankle would have more room.

"Does he never rest?" one of the soldiers asked, nodding toward Juan de Santiago.

"No" was Guzmán's answer.

De Santiago paced back and forth, an odd look on his mud-smeared face, muttering crazily all the while. The other men tried not to look at him. They had never seen their leader in such a state.

Mountains on either side of this narrow pass soared to over eighteen thousand feet. The wind whistled through the cut. It was bitter cold at this altitude, driving snow and bits of sleet at them. The rough trail clung to the side of a near vertical rock face. It would take very sure steps and nerves of steel to descend without falling a thousand feet to certain death.

De Santiago turned and set off down the trail even faster than before. It was as if he had heard a call the others had missed. Guzmán groaned and followed him, favoring the ankle. The other two men looked at each other, then stood and obediently straggled along behind as best they could.

Headquarters was another twenty miles away. Worse, sunset would come in less than an hour. Trying to traverse this trail in the dark would be suicide. De Santiago charged on, unaware of the danger or of the misery of his men.

Guzmán yelled at his leader's disappearing back.

"Wait! Slow down. We can't keep up. It's not safe." His words echoed off the cliff faces.

The rebel leader seemed not to hear him. Guzmán struggled to keep pace. The others had given up. They lagged several hundred yards farther back up the trail, shuffling down the narrow path. Guzmán could no longer hear their ragged breathing or the scuffling of their feet on the scrabble rock path.

De Santiago stopped and turned, frustration in his voice.

"Keep up the best you can. Tell the other children behind you to camp at the pass tonight and hike in tomorrow. Join them if you must."

He turned and continued his determined downhill dash. Guzmán trudged on. It was his duty to stay with his commander, to protect him. That was difficult to do if he was out of sight on a narrow sliver of mountain trail.

They were crossing the face of the mountain, clinging to a path that was barely a foot wide. Below them, the mountain dropped away, nearly vertical for a thousand or more feet. Above them, it was straight up to a summit that was completely lost in the cloudy mist.

It was totally dark when the pair crossed a shoulder of the mountain and the path became a little wider. The drop below them was not nearly so plumb. Still, the loose rock and talus made the footing treacherous.

Guzmán slipped and grabbed for a handhold, stopping his slide just as his feet were at the edge. When he regained his breath, he yelled ahead again.

"El Jefe, what is so important that we stay out here like this? Even if we don't fall to our deaths, we can't make the camp until morning anyway."

Guzmán could hardly make out the dark figure of the most dangerous man in Colombia. De Santiago abruptly stopped on the trail and turned back to answer him. Guzmán later swore that he could see the sparks flashing in the leader's eyes as he spoke. His words were soft but determined. The wind carried them as it did the fine icy vapor.

"Guzmán, my friend, we must get back as soon as we can in order to continue what has already begun. There is much to do and many pieces to put in place. This will be a night you will tell your grandchildren about. This is the night the final victory begins."

2

COMMANDER JONATHAN WARD SLAPPED UP THE PERISCOPE HANDLES in exasperation. Reaching over his head, he grunted in disgust and snapped around the large red periscope lift ring, lowering the scope.

"Dammit, XO! That merch just won't move!" he complained to his executive officer. "He's still sitting up there and we can't shoot till he leaves. How much longer until the launch window closes?"

Ward wiped the sweat away from his forehead with the back of his hand, half dreading the answer he would get to his question. His blue poopie suit had long since wilted. Wide, dark streaks of sweat ran down its back. He paced across the side of the periscope stand, trying to walk off the nervous energy while he waited for his XO to finish checking figures.

Except for the skipper's footsteps on the deck, the crowded control room of the nuclear attack sub *Spadefish* was surprisingly quiet. The only other sound in the stifling air was the hum of the vent fans, straining to remove the body heat of twenty closely packed human beings.

Lieutenant Commander Joe Glass looked up from the chart table jammed into the forward starboard corner of the control room.

"Another five minutes, Skipper. Not enough time to shoot," he reluctantly reported.

A chart of the Southern California coastline was spread out on the table before him. It was crisscrossed with colored lines representing all the ship traffic in the area. Joe Glass was trying his best to find an open spot somewhere in the mess of tangled spaghetti surrounding a dot that represented *Spadefish*. There simply wasn't one.

Glass was the perfect counterpoint to Jonathan Ward in several ways, some obvious from appearance, others not. Where Ward was tall and razor slim, Glass was short, stocky, and prone to a paunch. Ward's thick shock of blond hair was a contrast to Glass's rapidly receding brush of dark hairline. Ward tended to assay a situation instantly, then moved quickly and decisively. Glass was more likely to ponder a problem studiously before moving toward the solution. The crew had long since dubbed them Mutt and Jeff, but only when they were for certain beyond earshot.

Lieutenant Steve Friedman turned from the computer console where he sat. He too had a complex picture before him, a mess of dots on the screen that he had been staring at for the last several minutes. Now that Glass had broken the silence, Friedman chimed in with his own report, speaking slowly, precisely, exactly as he had been trained to do, but in a thick Southern accent.

"Captain, I have tracking solutions on sierra four-five, sierra four-nine, and sierra five-four."

Ward acknowledged with little more than a nod.

"Skipper," came another voice from across the control room. It was Stan Guhl, the *Spadefish*'s weapons officer. He turned away from his launch panel to speak once the captain had looked his way. His accent was flat and nasal, "New Yawk" all the way, Queens or Brooklyn. "The torpedo room reports the Tomahawk in tube two has another ten minutes before we need to down-power it."

Ward absorbed all the information he had just garnered.

"Very well, Weps," he said. He stepped down from the raised periscope stand and looked over Friedman's shoulder. "Whadda you have, Steve?" he asked quietly.

Despite his youthful face, Steve Friedman was a master at operating the CCS Mark II fire-control system. He had an uncanny ability to extract the most information out of the least input, sometimes seeing things in the scrawl of figures and cryptic symbols on the CRT that Ward swore couldn't be represented there.

"Well, Skipper," he began in his slow Alabama drawl, "sierra four-five is the closest. He must be that merch y'all are looking at. Range four thousand. Speed ten. Course about zero-two-five. CPA in fifteen minutes at three thousand yards, bearing three-four-seven. I'm guessing he's headed into Long Beach."

CPA stood for "closest point of approach," the closest the contact would get to *Spadefish* if all the analysis was correct. Sub skippers start to get nervous when vessels come within a couple of thousand yards. There are too many collisions on record, caused when ships get too close and then unknowingly turn toward the submarine while the skipper is looking the other way.

And how many sugars is the merchant ship's captain having in his cup of coffee? Ward thought. It wouldn't have surprised him if the kid could tell him. He looked at the stick diagram that showed the computer's opinion on the more important matter at hand.

"Yeah, that looks about right. He might be a little broader in aspect. I could see across his main deck. The forward king posts were almost in line. That would bring his range in some and put him just about at CPA now."

Friedman twiddled a bit more with the push stick controls, moving the sight diagram slightly.

"Yeah, Skipper. I can make that work. The other two are farther out. CPAs at about eight thousand."

Ward let out a long breath and turned to the senior captain

who was standing quietly, observing from the back of the control room.

"Captain Hunsucker, we won't be able to launch in the time window. Too much interfering traffic in the area. I'm drafting a message to Pearl now to tell them. I'm also requesting a new launch basket. Just too damn much going on up there."

Mike Hunsucker appeared to be ignoring the captain as he studiously scribbled something in his steno pad, writing with such force his jowls bounded slightly. Now the scratching of his pen point on paper was the only sound in the room. The older man glanced up, looking at Ward over the top of his half glasses.

"Very well, Captain. Let's meet in your stateroom in five minutes."

"Yes, sir."

Mike Hunsucker eased himself into the little fold-down settee in the captain's stateroom. It had always been a running joke among submariners. The "stateroom" was hardly "stately," and not what the name might imply aboard a luxury cruise ship. About the only nod to grandeur was the dark walnut-colored Formica that covered the bulkheads. The stateroom was small and Spartan. Jon Ward preferred to call it compact and utilitarian.

The size of a small walk-in closest, the room contained everything that the captain needed in the way of a place to live and from which to command a nuclear attack submarine. The communications equipment next to the settee allowed him to talk with anyone throughout the sub. And, when he was patched to the sub's radios, his voice could reach to anywhere on the planet. The small course, speed, and depth repeater on the forward bulkhead enabled him to keep track of the sub's movements, too. Right now they told him that *Spadefish* was at periscope depth, and that they were heading slowly out to sea, farther away from the crowded California coast.

Hunsucker didn't even take a sip of the coffee from the cup in front of him before he began.

"Jon, I'll be direct. Your boat isn't doing very well. This is supposed to be a tactical-readiness examination. So far we haven't seen any tactics at all. My team is not impressed."

Ward slumped back in his chair but he met the senior captain's direct gaze.

"Mike, be fair for a moment. You just left command of *Topeka* a couple of months ago. You can't have already forgotten what it's like."

The JA phone buzzed before Hunsucker could respond. Ward instinctively reached to yank it out of its stainless-steel holder, then saw the senior captain's nod that the interruption was okay.

Ward held the handset to his ear and pinched the push-to-talk button in its grip.

"Captain."

"Captain, officer of the deck. Message sent to SUBPAC reporting the interference and asking for a new launch basket and launch window. Receipt acknowledged."

The ship's navigator, Lieutenant Earl Beasley, was standing watch as the OOD, controlling all of the operations of the sub.

"Very well. Tell me as soon as they answer. Meanwhile, stay at periscope depth. Continue on to the western boundary of our operations area. We'll bet on them giving us a new area farther out."

Beasley acknowledged and Ward replaced the phone. He turned back toward Hunsucker. The older man had raised the coffee cup to his lips. Ward spoke before the other man could swallow the thick, black liquid, hoping to make his point while he had the chance.

"Well, we asked. Don't know what they'll say. Anyway, back to what I was saying. You want us to do a Tomahawk launch simulating a wartime fight, but also following all the peacetime safety rules. All right, so far we're on the same wavelength. But then you put the launch basket close inshore off L.A. . . . so close we can keep score in the beach volley-ball games . . . and you give us a tiny operating area in one of the most heavily trafficked shipping lanes in the world. How do you expect us to show you anything except how damned proficient we are at not running into shiploads of Toyotas?"

Hunsucker set his cup back down deliberately. He leaned forward, a stern expression on his face. The sparkle in his beady eyes seemed gleeful.

"Jon, remember that you have the proud distinction of hav-ing the oldest boat in the fleet. This is the last *Sturgeon*-class left. Your reactor core is almost exhausted. We set this all up close to shore to save your core as much as possible." He grinned and smacked his lips. "And you still serve some damn fine coffee."

Ward finally breathed and let a small smile play across his face. He doubted he was out of the woods with Hunsucker yet. The tension that had gripped him for the last couple of hours was partially relieved.

"It's from Kauai. Good Hawaiian stuff. The supply officer gets it from a friend on a boat based in Pearl. I never ask what we're giving them in return." Ward could see Hunsucker was not impressed. "I know we have an old boat. We fight that every day. Talk to the engineer. That is if you can ever catch him with his head out of something else that's gone on the fritz." Ward sipped his own coffee. Hunsucker was right. Compared with most boats', the *Spadefish*'s brew was spec-tacular. "This boat is older than he is. She's still a class act, though. You know that, Mike. She does a lot of things that even those new *Virginia*-class boats won't be able to. Just give us a chance and we'll show you a few things."

"All right, Jon, but we need to talk about this next drill." Hunsucker's small eyes went steely and Ward felt a slight shiver climb up his spine. "I think we'll have an opportunity to see what you and *Spadefish* can do, all right."

Joe Glass stepped through the door that connected the cap-tain's stateroom with his own, separated only by a head that both men shared.

"Excuse me, Skipper. We've spun down the Tomahawk in tube two. Request permission to back-haul it from tube two and load an exercise ADCAP. We need the exercise fish in the tube for the torpedo shoot this afternoon."

Ward glanced in Hunsucker's direction. The senior captain could tell them to never mind, to wait for word from Pearl Harbor that the test was still a go. Hunsucker nodded his agreement that the crew could proceed getting ready, assuming an affirmative from the Pacific submarine command in Hawaii.

"XO, back-haul the Tomahawk in tube two and reload with an exercise ADCAP torpedo," Jonathan Ward ordered, then glanced back at the senior captain. There was something about the expression on the man's face that bothered him. He had a sudden thought. "And Joe, stick around for a few minutes. I want you to listen to the briefing for this next drill."

Glass didn't hesitate. He squeezed into a seat at the little settee.

Hunsucker began talking.

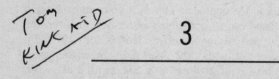

3

THIS WAS THE PART OF THE JOB TOM KINCAID MOST DREADED. BACK in D.C., the victims of those he warred against were anonymous and distant. Mere numbers on some government analyst's spreadsheet that they used for a kind of clinical, detached scorekeeping. Unlike the analysts, he saw firsthand the results of what the enemy was doing to real human beings. Saw the blank gaze in the lifeless eyes staring up at him in pointed accusation as he walked up. The innocent young face, now cold and gray, that seemed to scream at him: *Why didn't you protect me? Why did you fail me?*

All that before he had even had a chance to "meet" her. He preferred to call it "meeting" the victims, whether they were alive or dead when their paths ultimately crossed his. Such personalization made it easier for him to fan the embers of hate he kept permanently banked, ready to flame up once it came time. That made it easier for him to conquer discomfort, fear, red tape, or anything else that might hinder him in his battle against those who did this. Those who lured their victims with promises of forbidden pleasure, to draw them in, get them addicted, then steal from them all they had.

Victimless crime? Tom Kincaid knew better. He had seen too many lifeless eyes, too many cold, gray faces staring up at him, pleading for help that was much, much too late coming.

This one had been a lovely young lady not long ago. Probably no more than twenty-four years old. Blond hair still neatly combed but now peppered with dirt and debris and crawling alive with ants. The pretty silver clasp holding the curls back over her left ear so out of place and useless now. Nice complexion but already mottled and bluish. She could have been dead only a few hours. The rats would have gotten to her by now if she had been here longer than that.

How had she ended up here, beneath this bridge, lying on her side, fetuslike? There was no blood that he could see, no visible wounds or bruises, no sign of a struggle in the dust around where she lay so peacefully. It looked as if she might have just curled up to take a nap and never woken up. No doubt, it was an overdose. He would not have gotten the call otherwise. Too much of a party. Somebody panicked. Dropped her off here to be found by a wino or the cops. Nothing about her suggested "druggie." No needle tracks that he could see on the insides of her arms. None visible between her toes. Nice clothes. Relatively well groomed for somebody who had just turned up beneath a bridge.

She was simply dead.

Tom Kincaid closed his eyes and tried not to think about all the other blank young faces he had seen in the course of what he did for a living. Tried not to hear all the pleading screams for help that always seemed to come much too late. He wondered why he continued to give so much of his life to a war that showed no signs of ever being won. To a conflict whose casualties were so often youthful and full of life until they were sucked into something they were so ill equipped to survive.

Kincaid knew that simply closing his own eyes would not shut the pretty blond girl's stare. This was the very reason he continued to fight on. He knew the odds were against him. Even his own side seemed to conspire against him in the battle they all fought.

Kincaid cleared his throat hard and the noise startled the man who had been kneeling over the body. He jumped, then looked up. He was a beefy six-and-a-half-footer. The heavy badge dangling from his jacket pocket identified him as a member of the Seattle police. His wrinkled suit, soiled raincoat, and stained tie confirmed that he was a detective.

"Hey, Tom," he said.

"What you got, Ken?" Kincaid asked.

Lieutenant Ken Temple got up from his knee. It was a great struggle, his joints creaking noisily. He shook Kincaid's offered hand.

"Football knees. Sorry to call you out this late at night. Early in the morning. Whichever way you look at it. I know how you DEA cowboys like your beauty sleep. Thought you'd like to see this, though. Wanna take a look?"

Ken Temple had been a friend since the first time they met two years before. He had been one of the first contacts Kincaid developed with the locals when he was transferred in from Miami. They worked a couple of cases. Busted several small-time pushers. Mostly local kids growing pot in their backyards and selling it for car money. It was certainly a far cry from the anti-drug network Kincaid once headed for the Drug Enforcement Agency in South Florida. Down there he had a hundred agents fanned out all over Latin America. Each one fed him information on the top cartels, the multinational distributors, the twenty-first-century pirates who dealt in tons of cocaine and heroin.

It had been there in Miami, where he felt as if they might be turning a corner with this frustrating war, making a difference, closing some of those lifeless eyes. Now it was often only he and this affable over-the-hill detective fighting their war against junior-high-schoolers and their apartment-window flower boxes of recreational pot.

The rain beat down on the cordon of police cars behind them. Their blue and red lights flashed in the night. In the distance, Kincaid could hear the scream of the ambulance siren on the way to where they stood.

He can take his time, Kincaid could imagine the dead girl saying. *I'm in no rush anymore. Too late for me.*

Someone was stringing up the yellow tape that he had become so familiar with. Had to inform the innocent civilians that this was now unclean ground. A crime had happened here. Doesn't concern you, kind citizens of Seattle, so please stay away.

"Um-hum," he answered Temple's question.

"You okay, cowboy?"

"Hmmm? Oh, no. Just this weather. Kinda depresses me."

"You miss the beach, huh? All them supermodels in their bikinis gettin' their skinny little asses suntanned down on South Beach? Don't blame you. They say that Washington, D.C., gets more rain in a year than we do, though."

As he talked, Temple snapped on a pair of latex gloves and reached across the body to retrieve a small purse that was lying half underneath the young woman. He fished out a wallet from inside and flicked it open.

"Let me guess," Kincaid said. "Money's still in there."

"Yeah, I'd say fifty . . . sixty dollars. No robbery. Driver's license says she is Sandra Michelle Holmes. Age . . . uh . . . twenty-two, if my math's right. Couple of credit cards. Blue Cross Blue Shield. Won't be needin' that. Address over in

Bellevue. Employee ID card from one of those computer-geek places over there."

Kincaid examined their surroundings. They were in a warehouse district, surrounded mostly by industrial buildings, maybe warehouses. He could just make out the masts—king posts someone called them once—and a little of the hull of a freighter in a gap between two of the buildings. No one around except the cops. This place was really lonesome this time of night. How did she get over here? Long way from Bellevue. Not the normal stomping grounds for a young woman. Not on this side of town.

Temple answered Kincaid's thoughts.

"I'm guessing she was dumped here. No car or anything around that we can see. Looks like she had quite a party last night. Front of her dress is covered with what I'll bet are semen stains. No panties on. No sign she put up much of a fight, though. Musta been willing."

Kincaid winced and looked away again, studying the low buildings to the east that were already being silhouetted by the promise of the first light of a new day. It was getting brighter even through the filter of fog and drizzle. This girl lying here in the dirt was young enough to be his daughter. If he had ever taken the time to get married and have one. And not much older than his sister had been.

Too young to die. Too young to throw it all away. Where were you?

A cold gust of wind blew some of the thick mist beneath the shelter of the bridge. Kincaid shivered and pulled his raincoat more tightly around him. A uniformed officer threw a tarp over the body. The ambulance pulled to a stop and turned off the yelping siren and screaming red lights.

He hardly noticed that Temple now stood there right next to him.

"Come on, cowboy. Nothing more here until the forensics boys get done. Let's go get a cup of coffee. I know a good place just down the street. Open all night."

Kincaid stretched, glanced back at the pitiful form beneath the tarp. He stuck his hands into his raincoat pockets and looked up at the cop.

"Lead the way, big man."

Kincaid took a sip from the steaming cup and took pleasure from the way it burned his lips and tongue. He felt its warmth all the way down to his stomach.

"You're right, flatfoot. This is pretty good stuff."

Temple reached for a doughnut from the plate on the table between them.

"That's what I told you. You don't stay in the coffee business long in this town unless you got a pretty tasty cup." The doughnut was immediately gone, chewed and swallowed in one continuous move. "Now, you wanna know why I woke you up in the middle of that wet dream you were having just to come down here and watch me work a simple homicide? You've seen enough of these to know that kid ODed. And you know what else?" Kincaid had to wait for the answer to the detective's rhetorical question while he devoured another doughnut, then licked the sugary frosting off his fingers. "I've been hearing rumors of a new dealer in town. No hard info yet, just tidbits. Colombian connection, deals only in coke and heroin. High-end operation. This is the first real sign I've seen that it might be something." Another doughnut disappeared from the plate. "You've seen what this can do to a town more than I have. I don't want any more Sandra Michelle Holmeses dumped on my turf, Tom. I mean to find the son of a bitch that is killing people with this shit and bring him down, hard. And, 'Mr. DEA Hotshot,' I need your help."

Kincaid looked over the rim of his cup and squinted through the steam off the coffee.

"That really is a long speech for such an old man. You maybe want to go lie down for a minute, get your breath back?" The good-natured cop didn't even smile. He looked deadly serious. As serious as he could be with a big flake of doughnut sugar clinging to his chin. "Look, Kenny, it's my town now, too. You know I'll help. Let me check around a little. This isn't some kid dealing out of his trunk. He'll be cagey and very, very dangerous, especially if there's a Colombian connection. These guys play rough. The local guy has to have a source of supply and some backing and that leaves a trail. Maybe I can turn something up."

Temple's cell phone chirped loudly from his jacket pocket.

"Just a minute, let me answer this." He flipped it open, leaving sugar frosting where his fingers touched. "Temple." He listened for a few moments. "You sure?" A few minutes' pause. "Okay, thanks. Owe you one." He flipped the phone shut and pushed it back into an inside pocket of his suit coat. "Field toxicology report, OD all right. Massive dose. And he thinks it's semen on her dress, too."

Kincaid stood.

"Looks like we've got some work to do. I'll go make some calls. Where you going to be?"

"Office. Filling out paperwork. People knew how much paperwork it takes when they die nobody would ever get themselves murdered. Then I think I'll run out to where the girl worked, ask some questions. Good a place as any to start. Uniforms say she lived alone. Nobody there at her place."

"Maybe I'll join you there. What was the name of that place?"

Temple flipped open his field notebook.

"Hmmm, let's see. Here it is, CedarTech." He read off the address: 1035 112th Avenue Northeast. "Should be just off the four-oh-five at the Sixth Street exit. Meet you there at nine?"

Kincaid nodded and drew on his raincoat, dropping a five-spot on the table.

"Okay, see you at nine. And Kenny? Thanks for thinking of me."

The big man winked and hooked the last doughnut off the plate as he headed for the door.

Tom Kincaid stepped outside and into a steady mist of rain. The sun had struggled to back the rain clouds to the east with some light. It was going to be another blustery, rainy fall day. He turned and headed for where his car was still parked outside the yellow crime tape and amid several unmarked cars that belonged to the forensics people. The body was still there, anonymous beneath the tarp. That blond-haired girl had been someone. Someone's daughter, girlfriend, sister maybe. Kincaid knew what was next for them. There would be crying, sadness, a burial or cremation, another young life snuffed out while in pursuit of an illicit thrill.

He was uneasy. His gut told him that Temple was right about something being very wrong here. The detective had the typical good instincts of any longtime homicide cop. And besides, Kincaid had learned long ago to trust his own intuition in such matters. It had never failed him in all those years in Miami.

Well, once. It didn't give him fair warning that agency politics could be as powerful a threat to him and his career as any Colombian drug lord.

Twenty years he had spent down there on the front lines, building the best network in Latin America. Finally, with everything in place, nothing moved that he and the agency didn't know about. He was on top. There was even talk of moving him to D.C. to head the enforcement division. He resisted for all the right reasons. He was making headway. The war seemed winnable. The images of dull eyes and mottled skin were fading from his dreams once and for all.

Then Rick Taylor was appointed to head the DEA. It was a pure political appointment. Taylor had kissed the right asses, played the correct cards, and slurped martinis with the right politicians.

It was budget time and Taylor needed a bust to justify expanding his empire. Kincaid's current investigation was the ends to Taylor's means. Never mind that Kincaid was a full year into an investigation that promised to break the backs of Juan de Santiago and the Colombian connection once and for all. All he needed was another six months. All the pieces had been put together. Once he got his people clear his mighty hammer would fall and shatter the whole empire the South Americans had built along the ancient Inca trails.

Kincaid refused to make the show arrests Taylor demanded. The new boss was not understanding at all.

He transferred Kincaid to Seattle, to what was a relative backwater in the war against the major importers. Kincaid had not cleaned out his desk in Miami before Taylor had his own man in place. The bust happened the very next week. Over five tons of coke were seized. The table was piled high with some of the bounty for show at the press conference. Taylor and his new man smiled widely for the cameras, and the politicians approved the new budget. That bust ultimately cost six of Kincaid's best people their lives. And silenced a maze of informants for who knew how long.

Now Tom Kincaid was languishing in the "Siberia" of the DEA world. Nothing big ever happened up there in the Pacific Northwest. He certainly wouldn't get in the way of Rick Taylor and his featherbedding from way out there. And, as Kincaid often reminded himself, it was probably best he was in a quiet corner of the world, since he had no assets with which to go to war anyway.

Kincaid pulled up the collar of his raincoat and double-timed to his car. The pungent smell of dead, wet leaves hung in the air. The last streetlight flickered out overhead just as Kincaid unlocked his car door.

It was six o'clock now. That would be nine A.M. in Miami. Time to make some calls.

He pulled out his cell phone and punched in a number he had long since committed to memory. The number was ringing all the way across the country as he pulled away from the curb and out into the sparse early-morning traffic, leaving behind Sandy Holmes and her cold, staring eyes.

4

THE BROAD BLUE PACIFIC WAS HARDLY DISTURBED BY THE ZEPHYRS of the shore breeze. A few puffy clouds rode the wind in an otherwise azure sky. Off to the east, almost at the horizon, the beautiful blue of the sky paled, changing to an ugly tan-brown where it met the sea in the Los Angeles Basin. To the south, the gray-green silhouette of San Clemente Island was barely visible, riding low, guarding the Gulf of Santa Catalina. Beyond there lay the coast of Southern California north of San Diego.

The P-3C Orion aircraft circled slowly, hardly three hundred feet above the wave tops. Three of its four Pratt and Whitney turboprop engines easily drove their large propellers. That's all it took to keep the plane aloft and on the job. The fourth propeller windmilled slowly, feathered to conserve fuel. The crew of the Orion stared intently at their computer screens, searching for the "foe" they knew was below them, hidden beneath the glassy cobalt surface of the sea.

"Skipper!" the young petty officer sitting at the ISAR radar yelled excitedly. "Pop-up contact bearing two-one-seven, range seven miles. Signature of a periscope. Contact designate romeo two-six."

"Roger, Sheppard," Lieutenant Jim Pruitt answered. "Good work. Stay locked on to him." Shifting from the intercom to a voice radio frequency, Pruitt reported the contact with their quarry for this exercise. "Mission Control, Victor-Four-Tango. Pop-up contact on ISAR. Possible hostile sub. Going in for MAD run."

A disembodied voice from Mission Control, stationed in a

concrete bunker deep inside San Clemente Island, acknowledged Pruitt's transmission: "Roger ISAR contact. Good
hunting."

Pruitt banked the big bird sharply to the left and dropped
down to only about a hundred feet above the water's surface to
use the magnetic anomaly detection sensor. Simultaneously,
Randy Dalton, his copilot, reached up into the overhead between them and flicked a couple of switches. The number-
four engine coughed, spat smoke, and its propeller began to
turn with purpose. As it came up to speed, Dalton corrected
the propeller pitch so it would carry its share of the load.

Victor-Four-Tango was ready for battle.

Sheppard stared at his screen. The blip disappeared. It
didn't fade out. It simply went away.

"Skipper, romeo two-six went sinker."

Pruitt keyed his mike on the radio frequency and spoke.

"Mission Control, Victor-Four-Tango. Contact sinker."

"Roger, Victor-Four-Tango."

Pruitt keyed the intercom and spoke to the Orion's crew.

"Heads up, everybody. We're making a MAD run, then
we'll do a drop. Sensors, let me know what you get."

The P-3C was about to make use of the world's largest
metal detector. They weren't looking for lost change or jew-
elry on the beach. This mechanism was designed to detect a
far bigger and more deadly find in the ocean below.

Jess Carmon, riding in the sensor operator seat on the other
side of the bulkhead behind the copilot, heeded the skipper's
words, pressing the headset even more tightly to his ears with
both hands. His eyes never left the needle on the meter in
front of him as he watched for the smallest sign of movement.
All the way aft in the P-3C, a twenty-foot-long boom protruded from the tail of the aircraft. Inside the boom, extremely
sensitive coils sensed the earth's magnetic field. Those coils
were wired to the needle in front of Carmon. As long as the
plane flew over open ocean, the needle rested straight up. If
the coils passed near a large metal object, the needle would
swing wildly.

As Victor-Four-Tango roared over the spot where they had lost the radar contact, Carmon's eyes grew wide as he watched the needle swing all the way to the left peg, then to the right peg before again coming to rest in the middle of the dial.

He yelled, "Madman! Madman!"—the codeword that there was a submarine directly below where they had just flown.

Pruitt steeply banked the low-flying aircraft while he pulled back on the yoke to climb. Dalton reached for the throttle quadrants on the console between them and yanked all four down to full throttle. The Pratt and Whitneys responded, roaring with power as the P-3 climbed gracefully and turned back to retrace its route.

Pruitt keyed his mike and tried to keep his voice calm as he spoke.

"Confirmed hostile sub. Request weapons free."

The reply from Mission Control was instantaneous.

"Victor-Four-Tango, you are weapons free."

Pruitt leveled off at one thousand feet and yanked a handle on his left side. The bomb bay doors beneath the aircraft rumbled open. Next he keyed both the intercom and radio mikes simultaneously.

"Commence attack run. Drop on sensor's mark."

Carmon switched his gaze to the large computer screen in front of him. It recorded all the information from the encounter with the big, submerged metal object and did precise calculations at lightning speed. He watched as the little aircraft icon tracked toward the large X that marked for them the drop point where the MAD rig had detected the "enemy" sub.

"Standby," he called as the two blips converged on the screen. "Drop now. Now! NOW!"

Pruitt pressed the little red button on the right of his control yoke. The large plane lurched upward as 775 pounds of Mark 50 torpedo dropped out of the bomb bay and fell away. As the torpedo dropped free, a lanyard, still connected to the P-3, jerked taut, tearing open the chute pack on the back of the torpedo and deploying a small white parachute.

The weapon was away. The P-3 crew had done its job. Now they would see how well.

The submarine's periscope broke the surface. Commander Jonathan Ward jerked it around quickly, first with the crosshairs on the horizon to see if there were any ships close by. All clear. Nothing but light chop as far as he could see.

"Why couldn't we have had open water like this for the first test?" he said aloud. "We could have done one hell of a job for Hunsucker and his TRE team if we had only been given the opportunity."

He swung the scope around again. The crosshairs were elevated about forty-five degrees, scanning the sky for any threatening aircraft. He had almost completed his second 360-degree rotation when he saw it. There was no mistaking the P-3 that was bearing down on him. The aircraft filled his entire field of view.

It was close and the bomb bay was open! And it knew he was there. He had to get out of there and he had to do it fast!

He yelled, "Emergency deep! P-3 close aboard!"

The order "emergency deep" started an immediate and automatic chain reaction of carefully schooled responses by the watch standers. Chief Lyman, the diving officer, reached down to the engine order telegraph and spun the little dial to the Ahead Full mark. He punched a button that rang a buzzer by the throttleman, standing at his post in the engine room one hundred feet aft, telling him to open the throttles as fast as he could spin them.

"Cavitation be damned," Ward said. "We need speed!"

Seaman Cortez, standing watch as the fairwater planesman, was sitting directly in front of Chief Lyman. At the call, the young sailor pushed forward hard on his control yoke. Giant hydraulic cylinders pushed the huge winglike planes protruding from the sides of the sail, rotating them downward until they were in the full-dive position. The sub began to rapidly descend back into the deep.

Seaman MacNaughton, the stern planesman, was sitting right beside Cortez. He, too, shoved his control yoke forward. The stern planes, all the way aft on the sub, just in front of the huge bronze propeller, rotated upward, helping to push the sub's nose down toward the sea bottom. MacNaughton began with a seven-degree down angle. Too much slant and the screw would break the surface of the ocean, showing the world *Spadefish*'s tail, and telling the P-3 or anyone else above exactly where they were. He gradually pushed further forward as Chief Lyman called out the depth.

"Six-two feet. Seven-zero feet. Eight-zero feet. Nine-zero feet."

The chant was almost hypnotic, the chief's tone even and measured. By the time the sub passed through one hundred feet, the dive angle was at twenty degrees down and she was hitting twenty knots.

As these maneuvers were set into motion, Chief Ralston, the chief of the watch, reached above his head and yanked the red handle of the collision alarm. The piercing blast of the alarm told all the crew to immediately begin shutting every one of the watertight doors and ventilation dampers, to make the submarine as ready for flooding as possible. The COW reached for the large chrome joystick on the desk section of his panel. He pulled it toward him and watched as the meter for the depth-control tanks, located in the bilge two decks below him, as they began filling with seawater. The extra weight of all that water would do its part to pull the sub downward more quickly.

The USS *Spadefish* was sinking like an anvil, just as its commander intended.

The sub was doing what she was built to do, diving to the safety of the deep at the first sign of danger. Hiding in the black vastness beneath the ocean until it was once again safe to return to the surface and hunt. At 150 feet, both Cortez and MacNaughton pulled back on their control yokes. The sub rocketed ahead at over twenty knots forward speed, quickly vacating the area where the P-3 had spotted them.

Fifteen feet aft of the control room, in a small, narrow cubicle illuminated only by dim, bluish lights, Master Chief Sonarman Ray Mendoza searched the waters around *Spadefish*, trying to detect the sound of anything that might pose a threat to the boat. He watched the display of his discrete frequency analyzer as it showed him the four Pratt and Whitney turboprops as they passed overhead the first time, then again when the plane came back around.

There was another sound. There was no mistaking the splash of the Mark 50 torpedo when it hit the water. He heard the distinctive whine of the torpedo's Otto fuel-powered rocker plate engine as it came up to speed and sent the projectile plowing through the water, in pursuit of *Spadefish*.

Mendoza's broadband display began to show a depiction of the torpedo's noise on its screen. The sounds were unequivocal. Sweat poured from the sonarman's forehead and trickled down his back as he grabbed the 27MC microphone.

"Conn, Sonar. Torpedo in the water! Bearing zero-three-three!"

Ward grabbed the 1MC microphone and shouted, "Torpedo in the water!"

This announcement kicked off another automatic response from the crew. Chief Lyman rang up "Ahead Flank" on the engine order telegraph. Scott Frost, the throttleman, spun open the large, chrome ahead throttle as fast as he could manage, his breath rasping as he worked furiously. Steam roared into both of the massive main engines as they whined up to maximum speed. The seventeen-foot-diameter bronze screw at the rear of the boat, weighing better than thirty tons, was now spinning at over 250 revolutions per minute. *Spadefish* leaped ahead, accelerating her forty-seven hundred tons to almost thirty knots.

Chris Durgan jumped up from his small desk on the after bulkhead of the maneuvering room and stepped over between Frost and Bert Waters, the reactor operator. Durgan, the newest junior officer on board, had qualified to stand as engineering officer of the watch (EOOW) only the previous week. This was his third time supervising all the operations of *Spadefish*'s S3G reactor, and certainly his first full-speed tactical-readiness exam. The young redhead could feel his heart racing. The pulse pounding in his ears. He watched the reactor-power and steam-flow indicators climb up to one hundred percent. It was all happening so quickly, and for a moment it was more than he could watch at once.

Waters looked sharply over his shoulder at Durgan. When the young ensign didn't say anything, when he simply kept watching wide-eyed as the indicators climbed, Waters quickly reached down and pulled up on the handles for four of the six main coolant pumps. That move upped the pumps to fast speed an instant before the reactor power exceeded the safety limits for slow-speed pumps. The entire boat shuddered as the two-story-tall pumps shifted speed upward, slamming shut huge check valves and pouring massive amounts of cooling water through the reactor core to remove its rapidly increasing nuclear heat.

Durgan glanced at Waters. He realized he had been distracted by all the excitement and said, "Thanks. Too excited, I guess."

Waters only nodded. It was not the time to chat about the gaffe. There was more to do at the moment. He hoped no one else had noticed.

Spadefish raced through the depths as fast as she could go, attempting to outrun the onrushing torpedo. Mendoza watched the sonar track on the incoming Mark 50 and yelled out the bearing.

"Torpedo bears zero-three-three! No bearing change!"

The captain yelled to Chief Ralston, "Shoot the evasion device in the after signal ejector! Reload and shoot again!"

Spadefish raced along at a depth of three hundred feet. The cavitation, the tiny collapsing bubbles at the back edges of the fairwater planes, sounded for all the world like hail hammering on a tin roof.

Chief Ralston reached over and flipped a switch. The electric light indicator for the seawater hull valve for the signal ejector changed briefly from Shut to Open, then back to Shut. All the way aft, in the port side of the engine room, a small cylinder that looked very much like a miniature torpedo tube pushed its contents out into the sub's slipstream. The evasion device tumbled backward, past the screw, and generated a wall of noise in the water that was intended to hide the racing sub and its whirling propeller from the "ears" of the oncoming torpedo.

Mendoza shouted into the 27MC microphone, "Evasion device functioning. Torpedo bears zero-three-three." There was a pause. "It just blew right on past the device!"

The evasive device had not deterred the torpedo. The unflappable master chief was shaking as he watched on the sonar screen as the torpedo's trace merged with the one for *Spadefish*.

The Mark 50 raced beneath the submarine. Ward heard a deafening noise from somewhere below him, followed instantly by a report on the 4MC Emergency Report System: "Flooding! Flooding in the torpedo room!" The sound of the collision alarm was almost anticlimatic.

The lights blinked off for an instant, then back on. Over the 7MC, Ward heard, "Reactor scram! Loss of both turbine generators! Rig ship for reduced electrical! Answering 'All Stop'!"

What the hell is going on? Jon Ward thought. *This drill has gotten very damned real.*

This was the worst possible combination of casualties. It had been reported that water was rushing in to fill the torpedo room two decks below them. The reactor had automatically shut down, so they no longer had the power to maintain forward speed through the murky depths while supporting the extra weight of the seventy thousand pounds of seawater they had taken on when they needed to dive fast. With no reactor there was no forward propulsion and the boat would begin to sink quickly.

The normal peacetime response would be to emergency-blow the water out of the main ballast tanks and shoot the sub to the surface. But there was a "hostile" P-3 up there shooting at them. And God knows who else might have joined the party by now.

"Maneuvering, this is the captain. Answer 'Ahead two-thirds.' Report cause of scram."

He heard Chris Durgan answer, his voice little more than a high-pitched squeak.

"Captain, reactor scram due to loss of all pumps. Both turbine generator breakers tripped open by the shock . . . I guess. Restored one slow pump in each loop. Estimate ten minutes to reactor back on line. Reactor temperature too low to answer bells. Shifting propulsion to the emergency propulsion motor."

Commander Jon Ward clenched his jaw. He could guess how the breakers got tripped. He could not afford to let his anger tint his judgment. Things had just gone from bad to worse. If the nuclear reactor "scrammed," did an automatic shutdown, they could usually draw a little steam for propulsion by using some of the stored heat in the plant, cooling it down a little. But they had been driving at the reactor's limits when the torpedo "hit." They had used up all that stored heat in the first few seconds after the hafnium control rods dropped into the core, absorbing all the neutrons needed to sustain a nuclear reaction. There was nothing to drive the ship except a small electric motor powered by the ship's battery.

It wasn't enough. Not anywhere nearly enough.

"Skipper, depth three-five-zero and sinking," Chief Lyman yelled out. A heartbeat later, he reported, "Three-seven-five feet. Captain, I need speed or I can't hold her. We'll go to the bottom."

Ray Lawskowski, the Chief of the Boat, leaped from his seat in crews' mess at the first sound of the collision alarm. There was no doubt in his mind where the flooding was. He could hear the roar beneath his feet. Pointing at several members of the assembled damage-control party, he yelled, "You, you, you, and you, follow me." They chased after him as he dashed down the ladder to the torpedo room to face what had been reported as inrushing water.

Racing into the room, Lawskowski reached over and yanked the red emergency closure handle, shutting all the hull valves in the operations compartment.

Joe Glass was right on the heels of the COB and his damage-control team. He reached around and grabbed the red 4MC handset.

"Flooding has stopped in the torpedo room. Emergency closure has been actuated," he reported, out of breath.

The emergency closure system was used in an emergency to shut all the seawater valves in a compartment from one central location. It didn't use electricity, only hydraulic power, and that was supplied from several different sources to make sure it was always available. Shutting all the seawater valves in the operations compartment had stopped the "flooding." They still couldn't determine where the simulated damage was. And they couldn't reopen any seawater valves until they found the leak. Otherwise, they would only restart the flooding.

Looking forward, Glass spotted someone lying supine on the deck, not moving. It was Sam Benitez, the torpedoman who stood watch down here. Someone had placed a small card on his chest that read, "Unconscious, bleeding wound on forehead." The "injured" crewman helplessly gazed up at Glass, a "what can I do?" look on his face.

Outboard of the stowed torpedoes, up by number-four torpedo tube, two chiefs, wearing bright red hats with "TRE" in large letters on them, were standing there, one holding a heavy air hose, the other controlling the air valve. They had started throttling back on the air when the COB had actuated the emergency closure. It was barely a whisper now. It had been that air that had simulated the flooding of the torpedo room.

Glass spied a large card taped to a seawater pipe down below the torpedo tube. On it were the words "Double-ended rupture." Below that was another sign that read "Water in bilge to this level."

"COB, there's the problem," Glass yelled. "Get that pipe isolated, then get some people down there to fix it."

Isolating that pipe would allow them to reset the emergency closure without restarting the flooding. It meant locating all the ways that seawater could find into that particular stretch of piping and shutting the valves for those paths. Once that was done, the "damage" would be controlled and the boat once again would be secure.

Turning to two of the crewmen who had followed him down the ladder, Glass yelled, "Get Benitez up to the wardroom so Doc can take a look at him!"

The two carefully carried the "unconscious" Benitez up the ladder, the torpedoman doing his part to act like dead, lifeless weight. The corpsman, "Doc" Marston, was still setting up his emergency operating room in the officers' wardroom when they carried Benitez in and laid him on the table.

"Skipper, four hundred feet. I need speed!" Chief Lyman pleaded. There was no pretend in his plight. *Spadefish* was now in trouble for real.

"Captain, Maneuvering. Answering bells on the EPM. Answering 'Ahead two-thirds.' "

Durgan's team was turning the screw with the EPM, the emergency propulsion motor, and had it cranked to its maximum power. That was only producing three knots of forward speed. It wasn't nearly enough to stem the slide to the ocean floor. And even if it were, the electric motor would quickly drain the power from the battery, power they desperately needed to restart the reactor when it was ready to bring back on line.

Ralston turned to Ward.

"Skipper, the water we took on in the depth-control tanks

during the emergency deep is what's pulling us down. If we can reset the emergency closures, I can blow depth control in a heartbeat."

"Chief, I know that," Ward answered. "We need the flooding isolated first."

Ward heard a new sound coming over the WQC underwater telephone.

"Oscar, Oscar, Sierra. Oscar, Oscar, Sierra."

It was the signal that another submarine had detected them and was simulating shooting torpedoes in their direction.

Ward stole a glance over at Mike Hunsucker. The son of a bitch was calmly scribbling something in that damned notebook of his.

"Looks like he's taking notes in Physics 101 class back at the Academy," Ward muttered. Hunsucker didn't seem at all concerned with the mayhem he and his eight TRE team members had set loose on board *Spadefish*.

Master Chief Mendoza piped up, reporting, "Conn, Sonar. Contact coming out of our baffles. Submerged sub, close aboard. I think she's below us, Skipper! Definite near-field effect!"

Lyman turned to Ward, his face ashen.

"Skipper, depth four-five-zero and sinking. The EPM isn't doing it!"

Ward again looked over at Hunsucker as he continued to scratch notes in his pad. Hunsucker glanced up and casually said, "Captain, I suggest you don't let her go below four-seven-five feet. *Salt Lake City* is below you and you'd give them one hell of a headache."

Ward swore under his breath. That pompous ass had really put him in a no-win situation this time. Sinking like a rock, no propulsion, and another submarine just below him. He didn't dare risk sinking deeper. The possibility of a collision was too great and that could cause the loss of both boats. All so this bastard could watch him sweat!

He had no choice. The TRE had to be aborted.

He grabbed the 1MC microphone and said, "Secure from

the flooding drill. Emergency blowing to the surface." Ward turned to Chief Ralston and said, "Emergency blow all main ballast tanks."

Chief Ralston reached above his head without hesitation and grabbed the two emergency blow-valve actuators. He squeezed the spring catches and threw them both up. The thunder of high-pressure air in the control room was near deafening. Louder than the roar when the TRE team members had released a blast of compressed air a few minutes before to simulate a close-by torpedo explosion. The boat shuddered as the bow slowly started to rise.

Chief Ralston reached over to the diving alarm and pushed the green handle.

Aooogha! Aooogha! Aooogha!

The signal for an emergency surface sounded throughout the boat.

Chief Lyman shouted, trying to make himself heard above the roar of the pressurized air.

"Depth four-seven-five and holding." The boat's dive had thankfully leveled off. "Depth four-seven-zero and coming up."

The bow passed through level and the sub was climbing upward. The depth gauge stopped counting down and started to slowly count up. It whirled faster and still faster until it was only a blur. Cortez and MacNaughton watched the bow come up to a thirty-degree up angle; then they fought to keep it from going any higher.

Spadefish rocketed toward the light, everyone on board bracing himself.

Three hundred feet.

Two hundred.

One hundred.

She leapt out of the water like a gigantic trick porpoise, almost two-thirds of her bulk out of the water once she broke the surface. Then she splashed back down with a stomach-lurching jolt.

The proud sub bobbed helplessly on the frothy surface like a massive black cork.

Lieutenant Jim Pruitt watched out the cockpit window of his P-3, his mouth agape, as the submarine seemed to stand on its tail coming out of the water. He couldn't believe what he was watching down there.

"Wow! Randy, did you see that?" he exclaimed as *Spade-fish* leaped out of the water and splashed back down. He keyed his microphone. "Mission Control, Victor-Four-Tango. Sub on the surface, dead in the water. Looked like an emergency surface."

"Victor-Four-Tango, this is Mission Control. Remain on station. Try to make contact and see if they need any assistance."

Pruitt put the big bird in a lazy orbit a thousand feet above the motionless sub and waited to see if he could now help the sub he had, only a few minutes before, tried to "destroy."

"Man!" Pruitt said. "That had to be one wild ride!"

Commander Jonathan Ward was mad enough to bite a bolt in half.

"Captain Hunsucker, I need to see you in my stateroom right now."

There was no mistaking the barely controlled anger in the captain's voice, even though he tried to hide it from the crew who worked nearby. He turned and stalked aft to his tiny stateroom. Hunsucker watched him depart, closed his steno pad, and followed slowly behind him.

The senior captain stepped into the stateroom and shut the door behind him. Ward was standing against the after bulkhead watching him, his face crimson.

"Just what the hell were you trying to do out there! You damn near got us all killed. You didn't say anything about a scram or your guys tripping off the turbines when you briefed that drill. How dare you do something like that on my ship!"

Hunsucker backed up against the closed door. He really wasn't sure if Ward was going to come after him or not. The commander was plenty mad enough to do just that.

"Just a minute, Commander. I'm senior officer here and I—"

"Yes, and I'm in command," Ward shot back hotly. "I won't put up with any more of this bullshit. You know damned well that I'm responsible for the safety of my ship. That means I know beforehand and approve any drills aboard the boat. You and I are having a discussion with COMSUBPAC when we get back to port. As far as I'm concerned, this inspection is over."

The air hung heavy, neither man breathing at all, neither one speaking for a half minute.

There was a discreet knock at the door. When there was no answer, Lieutenant Commander Dave Kuhn, the engineer, stuck his head in anyway.

"Excuse me, Skipper. The reactor is critical, answering bells on the main engines. Request permission to line up for a battery charge. We really sucked it dry. Cells sixty-four and seventy-two were very near cell reversal."

Ward calmed visibly, now back on duty despite his anger.

"Eng, line up for a normal battery charge."

Kuhn nodded and went on with his report.

"We started a two-compressor air charge to bring the air banks back up. Number-one compressor crapped out again. We're out of parts until we get back to port. With one high-pressure air compressor, it'll be eight hours before we can dive again."

The high-pressure air compressor was just another of the many pieces of aged equipment that made the engineer's job a continual challenge. He had long since grown tired of spit-and-baling-wire jokes.

"Dave, we'll have you the parts you need a lot sooner than you expected." The engineer gave him a quizzical look. They weren't scheduled to return to port for weeks. Commander Jonathan Ward looked Captain Michael Hunsucker directly in the eyes when he explained to the engineer. "We're taking this boat home right now!"

5

TOM KINCAID EASED THE BLACK SUBURBAN INTO THE PARKING SPACE
and shoved the gearshift up into park. The day had turned
beautiful. Puffy clouds skidded across a blue sky. The brisk
sea breeze blew out the last remnants of early-morning rain.
The red alder and big-leaf maples someone had planted clung
to the last of this year's foliage. Piles of the gold and red
leaves, so brilliant in death, littered the corners of the shiny,
wet parking lot.

The CedarTech campus seemed to have been designed to
resemble a modern college. Its site spread over several acres
of unspoiled forest and well-kept grounds. He fully expected
to see students wandering about in their letter sweaters, frater-
nity houses, a football stadium. But there was something else
that bothered him about the well-ordered low, gray, modern
buildings, with their cold walls of reflective glass, and the too-
perfect rows of trees and shrubbery.

At first he couldn't place the feeling. Then it hit him. This
place reminded him more of some modern prisons he had seen,
institutions designed to look like anything else but what they actually were. No one could peek inside. The occupants of these
buildings, like prisoners, were surely being protected from the
disturbing view of the parking lots and passing traffic. The high,
grass-covered berms and liberal plantings of evergreen shrubs
were like unassailable walls. Only the razor wire was missing.
Kincaid suspected that someone wanted to make sure there were
no distractions for the drones who worked away in the hives of
cubicles he would find behind those unblinking windows.

He climbed out of the SUV and breathed deeply. The
earthy smell wafting from the Sitka spruce forests surround-

ing the campus mingled with the acrid exhaust the breeze was
bringing over from the adjacent freeway. Each aroma seemed
to affirm something good for Tom Kincaid. Sometimes it was
just good to be alive.

He hopped over a sodden mat of leaves deposited there by
the wind the night before, then stepped up to the sidewalk. He
followed with his eyes the winding path through the berms toward the largest of the glass-and-steel buildings. Discreet
wood posts along the way held small, engraved metal signs
that pointed toward various CedarTech facilities, but in a language that was foreign to him.

What was an "ASP Lab" or what did they do at "eCRM Development"? He was trying to figure it out when he heard a
car wheel to a stop behind him, its driver tapping the horn a
couple of times. It was Ken Temple in what looked like a new
dark blue Impala.

"Nice ride," Kincaid said jokingly as the big man spilled
out of the car. "Might as well paint it black and white and put
a bubble-gum machine on the top."

Temple wryly shook his head.

"Yeah, I know. Those bureaucrats over in Purchasing. The
thought process was, the more you buy of one model, the
cheaper they can get 'em. Everybody from patrol cops to us
have these. At least they let us have different colors. I asked
for a red one. This is what I got."

Kincaid pointed to one of the signs.

"You have any idea where to go?"

"Try 'Admin.'" Temple pointed to the tallest building.
"We're supposed to meet Mike Grey, head of security. He's
expecting us." Temple looked around warily. There were security cameras on the corners of every building they could
see. "Something tells me, we go to the wrong place, they zap
us with a death ray."

Mike Grey proved to be one of them, a retired Chicago cop.
A bear of a man with frosty hair and a developing paunch, he
seemed easygoing enough when he greeted the two. Temple
and Kincaid were both relieved.

"Not often I get to talk with my own anymore. Just these nerds around here. Come on in and have a cup of coffee."

He led them down a series of pastel-walled hallways and deeper into the interior of the building. The neutral walls were broken up every few feet with a large canvas liberally splattered with paint in random, bright colors. Each piece of artwork proudly bore the signature of the artist responsible for the mess. Each one looked like the result of some horrible accident at a paint factory. He kept his critique to himself.

Grey's office was a small interior room, hardly big enough for the three of them. It was littered with files, mementos of past triumphs back in Chicago, and the remnants of a McDonald's fast-food breakfast. The walls were unadorned. Two orange plastic-and-metal chairs were arranged in front of the desk. Off to the side, a coffeemaker sat on top of a miniature refrigerator. Grey poured three Styrofoam cups full of the brackish liquid and offered two of them to Kincaid and Temple. Waving to the chairs, he eased down into a plush, over-sized leather one behind the desk.

"Hemorrhoids. Ended more beat cops' careers than any other single cause," he said, explaining the one extravagance in his drab office. He turned toward Kincaid and Temple. "Now, I know you two aren't here for my fine coffee or an update on my anus."

His tone was crisp and his steel blue eyes confirmed that the pleasantries were over. It was time to get down to business.

Temple responded.

"As I mentioned on the phone, we're investigating the death of Sandra Holmes. Body found down by the waterfront this morning. About all we know about her is that she worked here at CedarTech. We'd like to talk with anyone here who knew her, worked with her, maybe heard her say where she was going last night and with who."

Grey looked hard at Temple then swung his eyes to Kincaid.

"That explains you, Lieutenant. What does DEA have to do with this?"

Temple shot back, "Probable cause of death is an OD on coke. Agent Kincaid is covering that angle."

Grey seemed to accept the explanation as he ruffled through the pile of paper on the cluttered desk, searching for something. The remains of his ketchup-soaked Egg McMuffin slid off onto the already-stained carpet.

"Have to do something someday about this filing system. Got it here somewhere." After some more digging, he pulled out a buff-colored folder. "Thought you might be wanting this. Copy of the Holmes personnel folder. It's yours. Don't know her myself. Not surprising. We've got over two thousand people here at any one time and a lot of them are perm-temps. Don't have detailed personnel records on those."

Temple took the folder. Perm-temps were programmers hired by large software companies as temporary employees but on a long-term basis. The practice saved the company the expense of all the benefits required for a full-time employee and made firing them easy once the project was completed.

Grey flipped through the pages.

"She was full-time, then?" Temple asked.

"Yeah. Went by 'Sandy,' by the way. Says she worked in 'gooey' development for the 'bee-to-bee' practice." Looking up, Grey noticed the quizzical look on both his visitors' faces. "Excuse me. Sometimes I catch myself talking like the rest of the gear heads around this place. In English, she worked at developing graphical user interfaces . . . GUI. Those are the screens the customer sees. And for the business-to-business practice. That department is over in one of the new buildings." Grey rose and handed the folder to Temple. "Come on. I'll walk you over there. Her manager is a lady named Ann Mershon. Has a reputation as a real slave driver, all business. Some of the kids call her 'Mush Mush' Mershon. You know, like sled dogs? You didn't hear that from me. I'll introduce you."

Grey pulled on a rain jacket and stalked for the door. Temple and Kincaid trailed behind.

They crossed the broad lawn that separated the buildings. Tom Kincaid couldn't help feeling as if they were the only three people on the planet. Despite the wide expanse of green and the beautiful sunshine, there was not another human being in sight.

Temple's cell phone buzzed annoyingly. Without breaking stride, he retrieved it from his pocket and flipped it open. The detective grunted acknowledgment a couple of times. The conversation was short and one-sided. He shut the phone in one quick move and without saying "good-bye" to whoever it was on the other end.

"Tom, we've got another one," he said through pursed lips. "Body found over in Bremerton, just outside the shipyard. Male, late twenties, well dressed. Initial ID is some computer whiz kid. Field toxicology shows coke. We average a couple of ODs a year and now we have two in the same night."

Kincaid nodded, his mind churning. Could be coincidence. As much money as there was in this town, and as many young people around with little life beyond their high-tech, high-pressure jobs, coke had to be a big temptation. And where there was a willing and moneyed clientele, someone usually found a way to meet the demands of the marketplace.

It was difficult to overdose on cocaine. Especially if the user was smart. These people were brighter than the typical cokehead or junkie. Something was going on. Kincaid could almost sense it. Smell it as surely as he could the aroma of the spruce trees being warmed by the bright, new sun.

Ann Mershon turned out to be an African-American woman in her early thirties. A hard-faced lady with a no-nonsense hairdo, dressed in a strictly-business suit. Grey's characterization was dead-on. She ruled over a warehouse-sized room crowded with tiny, close cubicles. The only sound in the big room was the chattering of fingers on computer keyboards. Tom Kincaid felt claustrophobic. He couldn't wait to finish up, get their information, and go back to where he could once again smell the spruce and feel the warmth of the sun.

No one imprisoned in this place could enjoy the views of nature. That is, except the senior employees, those blessed with windowed offices. Down here, in the bowels of this galley, they had to settle for harsh fluorescent sunshine. For clean but filtered and dehumidified air. Their only view of outside came courtesy of travel posters thumbtacked to their cubicle walls. Or by bright, flickering screen savers that danced invitingly on their computer monitors.

Kincaid glanced down the rows of programmers, bent over keyboards, faces frozen and bluish as they gazed at the screens a few inches from their noses. It reminded him of some Third World sweatshop.

Mershon never smiled but she invited the trio to follow her into one of the small, walled offices that ringed the big room. She glanced behind her, making sure the visitors had not disrupted the rhythm of her software machine in any way.

"I'd offer you gentlemen a seat, but I'm afraid there isn't any room," she said. "Now, what can I do for you? We're a little busy here so I'd appreciate keeping this short."

She spoke with a clipped but unmistakable New England accent, her hands on her hips, the clock running already. Temple and Kincaid both showed her their shields while Grey explained that they were investigating the death of Sandra Holmes. Temple added a few details.

Mershon's eyes widened only slightly as she listened to the story. Kincaid noticed she did breathe a bit faster and swallowed hard when Temple mentioned how they believed the young woman had died.

"I suspected something was wrong," she said when the detective finished. "Sandy . . . we called her Sandy in our work group . . . she was always quiet and withdrawn. A good worker, though. Really threw herself into the project. Didn't waste time like some of the others with all the gossip and silliness and carrying on. Never missed a day, until the last few days. No e-mail, no call or anything."

"How well did you know her?" Temple asked.

"Not very. Didn't talk with her much. Look, Lieutenant, I've got almost a hundred programmers here. And they come and go. I don't get to know them very well at all. Seems I remember she was from somewhere in the Midwest. Maybe I saw that on her résumé. Said something one time about having a mother back in Iowa, I think."

Temple was taking notes in a little pad he had pulled from his inside jacket pocket, scratching away with a stubby little pencil.

"She have any friends here at work that you know of? Somebody she might have gone out with after work?"

Mershon gazed thoughtfully at the ceiling for a few seconds.

"No, not really. She is . . . I mean was . . . pretty much a loner. I confess I like it like that. They don't cause me any trouble, that kind. Really, the only one I ever saw her talking with was Farragut. Linda Farragut. Bad actor, that one, though. Has a real wild reputation around here but I never thought they were exactly friends. Kind of ironic, I suppose. Nice girl like Sandy, talking with somebody like Farragut. Doesn't really make sense. You want to talk with her?"

Temple looked up from his pad, touched the end of his pencil to his tongue, and wrote down the name before he answered her.

"Yeah, that would be a good idea."

Mershon reached across her desk for the phone. She stabbed several buttons and waited, tapping her fingers on the desktop.

"Strange, no answer at her desk." She checked her watch. "Not break time yet for that team, either. She better not be slacking. . . ." Ann Mershon stood up, walked to the door, and spoke to someone in the first cubicle outside. "Cicelle, have you seen Farragut today?"

A disembodied female voice responded.

"Nope, she didn't show up this morning. Missed Friday, too. She may be working from home but she didn't call in. No answer there when I tried to call her about that unlock DLL problem, either."

Mershon hit a few keys on her computer keyboard, then scribbled something on a pink Post-it note and handed it to Temple.

"Here's Farragut's address and phone number. Find out who killed Sandy. She was a good kid."

The woman's voice broke slightly. It was the first real sign of any emotion he had seen from her. All three men headed toward the door on that cue, but the detective stepped back and handed her one of his business cards.

"We'll do our best. And let me know if you think of anything that might help us."

The woman nodded, then followed them back out into the massive room full of galley slaves. When Kincaid glanced back, "Mush Mush" Mershon was throwing a mean scowl at one of the programmers who had dared to look up from his monitor as the visitors passed by his cage.

Kincaid walked faster. He was dying for a breath of fresh, unfiltered air.

6

JUAN DE SANTIAGO KNEW HE WOULD HAVE TO PHRASE HIS WORDS very carefully, minding their slightest inflection, even the timbre of his voice. This could be the most important conversation he had conducted since he assumed command of the people's revolution. Neither he nor the people of his country could afford any misunderstanding at this point. He took a deep breath and listened to the metallic pops and the rattling, crackling static on the trans-Pacific telephone connection as he waited for the other man to answer.

Asians could be so difficult to negotiate with, much more

subtle and obtuse than the Americans. Every word and nuance
had gradations of meanings that required peeling away like
the layers of an onion in order to be understood. Juan de Santiago was a direct man and he preferred negotiating directly,
but for the next little while, he would have to yield to the style
of the man whose voice now spoke into a telephone mouthpiece half a world away.

"Good day, Mr. de Santiago, my friend," the voice said.

De Santiago expelled his held breath. The conversation
would be in English. No interpreter necessary. That would
make it much easier for him to make his points. And it was a
good omen that the Asian would be willing to negotiate on
common neutral ground, not insisting that each man use his
own tongue in some awkward discourse.

"Sui Kia Shun, my good friend. I trust that your family is
well and your sons prosper," de Santiago said into the cell
phone. His speech was deliberate as he enunciated the words
carefully. "And your daughter, too, of course."

According to reports, Sui now had his daughter in a place
of responsibility within his organization. De Santiago could
not imagine such a thing.

There was a short time delay while his greeting sought a
satellite and was relayed around the planet. When the most
powerful drug lord in Southeast Asia spoke again, there was a
faint Chinese lilt in his speech, magnified by a hollow, distant
echo that made his voice seem even more cold and brittle.

"Yes, yes. Thank you. And Juan, my good friend, my con-
dolences on your recent misfortune."

There it was. Before the pleasantries had been completed. It
was amazing how quickly the story of the raid on his fields
spread. The attack on his coca crop was only days old, the
black smoke hardly cleared from the mountain jungles. And
Sui knew of it. So did his peers in Amsterdam and Marseilles
and Miami.

De Santiago was a little taken aback that the Asian played
that card so early in their conversation. That changed the
complexion of the negotiation immediately. Sui had tried to

place him in a position of weakness. De Santiago knew he must parry in order to come back to an even basis.

"It was only a minor inconvenience. Nothing of concern. One field of many that will soon bear glorious fruit." He paused for a beat, then launched his own shot. "I hear that you too have been annoyed by the DEA. I trust the much-publicized loss of that shipment at Long Beach did not damage your enterprise. Mr. Taylor of the Drug Enforcement Agency can be so annoying on the American television when he boasts for the benefit of the taxpayers and bureaucrats."

Sui chuckled but there was no humor at all in the sound.

"*Mi amigo*, you are quite right. I too find his antics annoying. A mosquito that needs swatting . . . and soon."

De Santiago dived for the opening.

"Precisely. That's why I asked for this discussion today. I would like to talk with you about a mutually beneficial proposition that could permanently remove that annoying mosquito. And all others like him."

"I might be interested in your proposal," Sui responded quickly. The DEA seizure, and the publicity it generated, rankled the Asian as much as de Santiago had assumed it would. The man was eager to talk. "So, what might this proposition of yours entail?"

De Santiago outlined the general points of the plan, careful to only reveal enough to pique the Asian's interest until he could get his commitment. Previous turf wars would have to be forgotten now. Their futures might rest on the specifics of de Santiago's plan, and it would be far more likely to succeed if Sui was a part of it.

"I would suggest," de Santiago concluded, "that my most trusted lieutenant meet with your people as soon as possible to discuss the details. Might they plan such a gathering in Hong Kong in two days? I suggest the Mandarin Oriental Hotel. You know it?"

The group seated around the big mahogany conference table listening to de Santiago's end of the conversation could tell much from the smile that spread across their leader's face.

Sui agreed to the meeting. That meant he was willing to buy into their plan if the details were to his liking.

After the mandatory final small talk, Juan de Santiago punched the Stop button on the phone and flipped it shut with a flourish. He was still smiling.

"You all heard the conversation. Sui will participate. He can't afford not to. Antonio, pack your bag. You must be in Hong Kong tomorrow."

Sunlight poured in the window behind de Santiago. A flower-scented tropical breeze danced with the thin white curtains. The group erupted into excited applause. De Santiago stood and walked to the window. It was indeed a triumphant moment.

Below the window, in a large courtyard, his latest mistress and two of his children splashed and played in the sparkling swimming pool while several of his men stood watch nearby. They scanned the hills, the sky, looking for anything that might threaten them. El Jefe watched for a moment, his eyes drawn ultimately to the beautiful woman. Beautiful still, even after she had delivered to him the two little ones. He noticed the way the water played on her dark skin, how her full breasts bounced provocatively as she played some game with the laughing children, hopping into and out of the shallow end of the pool as they tried to catch her. Even from here, he could see her nipples, strong and erect against the filmy fabric of her bathing suit. The darkness at the nadir of her body where her long, slender legs met. The leader of the people's revolution felt a definite stirring.

The diplomatic flirtation he had just conducted with his Asian counterpart had gone well. As well as he could have ever hoped. And it left him with an odd feeling, one of unconsummated arousal. He felt an almost overpowering longing to call down to the woman, to beckon to her from where he watched her, to have her leave the children and their game and meet him in his quarters and to properly celebrate this powerful new alliance he had just arranged.

It was not to be. At least not now.

The group in the room behind him had quieted somewhat and would be looking to him for the next topic for the meeting. He shook his head slightly to clear away the thoughts that had come over him.

As he turned, Antonio de Fuka was still accepting the good wishes of the other men in the room. He would be their standard-bearer, the one who would bring home the final piece in their plan from his meetings in Hong Kong.

With a nod from the leader, Philippe Zurko rose to speak. He was a tall, slender man, but with enormous brown eyes that seemed on the verge of shedding tears at any moment. His dark beard was close-cropped and he spoke in the deliberate, calm manner of a seasoned diplomat. No one seemed to notice, though, the slight trembling of his hands when he set down the pen he had been using to make notes on the pad before him.

"El Jefe, I am pleased to report that we are progressing well with my project. The Russians demanded another ten million rubles for the plans as we anticipated they likely might. As you predicted, their hatred for the Americans is exceeded only by their insatiable greed. At any rate, the money is already deposited in the Swiss account, awaiting their arrival." He paused and took a long, thirsty drink of ice water. The ice cubes clinked softly against the glass as he raised it unsteadily to his lips. He swallowed, then went on. "They should arrive in Lima in three days. And, of course, we will be watching them for the entire trip."

De Santiago gazed at the tall, dark Latin for a few seconds. He and Zurko had been friends since boyhood, had grown up in adjacent haciendas, and he trusted the man implicitly. The room in which they were now meeting had once been Zurko's father's dining room, the walls covered with portraits of the man's family. The antique cabinets that had once lined the room had been filled with fine china and silver and the windows dressed with imported fabrics. De Santiago had memories of dinners he had enjoyed here, at this very table, and the stories Señor Zurko had spun for the boys as they lingered over dessert and strong coffee. But El Presidente stole the hacienda and had the elder Zurko put to death many years before. De Santiago's father had met much the same fate. The jungle had long since reclaimed not only his father's bones but also the burned-out ruins of de Santiago's boyhood home.

This was now rebel-held territory again. Juan de Santiago had taken back all he could of what the bastard and his imperialist allies had seized from him. And soon, revenge for everything else that had been stolen would be his.

"Where do they go from Lima?" he asked Zurko.

"Preparations are almost complete. We have contracted a small shipyard in Chiclayo for the modification of the freighter. The Russians go there first to check dimensions, then proceed to a small villa in the mountains outside Cajamarca. It is remote enough and the locals are sufficiently afraid that no one will ask any questions or mention the presence of strangers to anyone. Construction of the sections will happen there. The sections will then be trucked to the coast for assembly when all is ready."

De Santiago turned to the window again as he considered his friend's words, watching the woman and his children play. Beyond the wall that surrounded the pool were an expanse of green lawn, tall trees, and beautifully flowering shrubs. Emerald hummingbirds flitted about the flowers, doing a dance with the butterflies.

So very peaceful. So damned deceptive.

"Very well, Philippe. As usual, very complete and well done. Thank you." The tall man sat down. De Santiago turned next to a short, swarthy man sitting at the far end of the massive table. "Alvene, what of the scientists?"

The little man was sweating profusely, as always. Alvene Dura dabbed at his forehead and neck with a large handkerchief as he spoke.

"El Jefe, we have a slight problem on that count. Ramirez

has reported the trial shipment may have been a bit too strong. He has reported several cases of overdosing within the first week of use in our initial test market." Alvene Dura used the sodden handkerchief to swab at his upper lip and at the folds of skin beneath his chin. He had fought side by side with de Santiago and, despite his awkward appearance, hair-trigger temper, and tendency to perspire, he was one of the bravest, most loyal men the leader had ever seen. "We have the scientists already at work on a slightly milder mixture. Unfortunately, one of them, Señor Djenka, became homesick for his *puta* in Bucharest. He tried to escape down the mountains. His body is feeding the piranhas in the Rio Napo now. His work was key to making the milder dosage work, maintaining its addictive quality without the . . . shall we say . . . serious side effects? I am afraid his notes died with him. We still have much work to do."

De Santiago nodded.

"You acted correctly, Alvene. We have time to correct the formula of the mix while we dance with the Asians and complete the delivery mechanism. Meanwhile, make certain that we don't ship any more to Carlos. We can't risk the Americans sensing something new and finding out about our *producto especial* until all is ready."

Alvene Dura nodded vigorously, the perspiration dripping off his nose as he did. Next, de Santiago turned to the only Anglo in the room.

"Señor Holbrooke, what do you have to tell us?"

The dapper Donald Holbrooke was dressed immaculately. He wore a tropical-weight seersucker suit and a lavender silk shirt, with a conservative striped power tie perfectly knotted at his neck. He cleared his throat before he spoke and, when he did, the "Haavaad" accent was overdone.

"El Jefe, I am afraid that it is not good news. Our Swiss accounts are near empty. The American Treasury Service discovered the Liechtenstein accounts shortly after they found the ones in the Caymans. Both have been confiscated."

Angry murmuring broke out among the group. De Santiago raised his hand for silence.

"*Compadres*, please allow Señor Holbrooke to continue."

Holbrooke adjusted his tie. He had a tendency to smile, showing his perfect teeth, even when the news he delivered was not what the group wanted to hear.

"Thank you, Mr. de Santiago. As I was saying, both accounts were confiscated for a total loss of four hundred and fifty million dollars, U.S. On the bright side, our investments in the U.S. tobacco companies and the U.S. HMOs are showing better than fifteen per cent returns on a per annum basis. We will net about one hundred and fifty million dollars on those investments alone this year. Our landholdings in Miami, Los Angeles, and New York have appreciated by ten percent this year for a net gain of about seventy-five million."

Holbrooke paused to check his notes. The group squirmed uncomfortably. This pompous gringo had a tendency to drone on and on for hours about money and investments and amortization of bond debt.

"Pay no attention to the others," de Santiago urged. "We must manage the revolution as a business in order for us to realize its glorious potential."

The business end was why Holbrooke was there. He owed no allegiance to the people or their struggle against the capitalists. He was as pure a capitalist as there was.

"Yes, thank you. I must remind you, as I told you when we made them, that those investments I've just detailed are not liquid. It will take a year or more to unwind them without running the risk of being discovered. Meanwhile, gentlemen, we have ourselves a cash-flow problem."

Alvene Dura's well-known hot temper flared and he jumped to his feet, his face immediately livid.

"And just what is this cash-flow problem, gringo? Could it be that you have stolen more from us than even the American authorities?"

Dura made a move to reach for the wicked razor-sharp belt knife he always carried, but de Santiago was already holding up his hand, motioning impatiently for him to sit back down.

Holbrooke had taken an unconscious step backward, toward the door. Dura was closer to the truth than anyone in the room could imagine. He would gut him for sure if he had any suspicion that Holbrooke had been siphoning off large chunks of their money. He could feel the cold beads of sweat trickling down the back of his neck. He had to remind himself that the fat, sweaty little man had no way of learning about the Swiss bank accounts. De Santiago knew full well his financial expert was taking a stipend off the top. El Jefe just had no idea of the magnitude of that cut or he would have demanded more for his own kickback. Ten percent was a small price for him to charge for the risks he took on their behalf. Any good investment counselor would charge roughly the same fee for a like amount of work.

Still, if any of the other men around this table ever found out, Donald Holbrooke would be supper for the crows before that day's sunset. And he knew it only too well. The risk was worth it.

De Santiago slammed his fist down on the table when Dura continued to stand there, glaring at the American.

"Alvene, control your temper. Don't ever forget that Señor Holbrooke is one of us. If I killed everyone who brought me bad news, you would all have long since been with your ancestors in heaven. And especially you, *mi amigo*, with the report you have brought us today."

Alvene fell heavily back down into his chair, his face still crimson. With great difficulty he said, "Forgive me, El Jefe. We risk so much only to have our money stolen by the Americans." He shot a seething look at Holbrooke. "It angers me. That's all."

De Santiago waved his hand, acknowledging the half-hearted apology and signaling Holbrooke to continue.

"As I was saying, we have a cash-flow problem. With the current liquid assets and available revenues, we will not be able to meet payments as soon as next quarter. We need to either scale back our expenses or increase revenues."

De Fuka looked at de Santiago and spoke.

"Surely our friends in Iran and Pakistan will extend us credit? Are not our enemies also their enemies?"

De Santiago shook his head sadly. De Fuka was his most accomplished aide. The one man in this room to whom he would trust his own soul if need be.

"My friend, it is a cash-and-carry world. There is no credit there. But the timing is right. One of the first issues you will have to negotiate with Sui's people is the matter of a considerable cash payment to become a part of our alliance. Señor Holbrooke, how much do we need?"

Holbrooke thought for a few seconds. Forty million dollars would cover their expenses nicely at the current rate, and until they had the exportation of their new product well into the pipeline. Still, he could smell opportunity here. He did rapid calculations in his head, the smile never leaving his lips.

"El Jefe, we must have at least sixty million to cover the next quarter until shipment of the new product, fifty million if we scale back the efforts of the revolution until we have positive cash flow again."

The latter option would never be approved. Sixty million would be the figure.

De Santiago nodded slowly and turned again to de Fuka.

"You must get sixty million. That will be Sui's down payment to participate in this operation. We are too close to our goal to scale back now."

"I will do my best," de Fuka said.

"I am sure you will," the leader said, turning next to the three men who sat together at the far end of the conference table, the final three members of his inner circle. Each of them wore a camouflage uniform and had so far remained silent for the entire meeting. "Now we require a report from the jungles, from the front lines of the revolution, from the brave men who continue the fight even as we enjoy our cognac and shrimp cocktails here this morning. Colonel Abella?"

When the dark-skinned soldier stood, he uncoiled to over six feet tall and his bulk seemed to fill the room. He remained at attention as he spoke, his eyes steely and firmly focused on his leader.

"We have had a total of seven ambush assaults on government troops in the past ten days, all, I am pleased to report, with great success. We lost a dozen of our brave freedom fighters but we claimed the souls of over forty of El Presidente's traitors. It remains our mission to strike like a cobra, without warning, and to further demoralize the enemies of the people of our country until they are ultimately liberated by our leader, El Jefe."

There was enthusiastic applause from everyone around the table as the monstrous man sat back down. Applause from everyone except Donald Holbrooke. The American was studying his fingernails, considering his need for a manicure at the soonest opportunity.

"Colonel Marquez?" de Santiago said when the ovation died. "Your report on internal security?"

Marquez's most distinguishing feature was a long, pink scar that ran from the outside corner of his left eye, across the bridge of his nose, and to just below his right ear. Legend had it he had killed another dozen men in hand-to-hand combat even after having his face split open by the bayonet of an enemy of the revolution.

"Only one rat has been trapped since our last meeting, El Jefe. He was leaking word of the whereabouts of Colonel Abella's guerrillas and was directly responsible for the losses the colonel mentioned in his report. We cut the throats of his wife and each of his five children while he watched, then removed his limbs and ran his torso up the flagpole in the village square so his neighbors could see the results of his treason."

Another hearty round of applause and enthusiastic cheers greeted the graphic report. De Santiago's eyes now fell on the last soldier in the room, a small man with thick eyeglasses and a long beak of a nose that gave him an almost scholarly look.

"Finally, Colonel Fernandez."

Even when he stood, the man would have hardly been waist-high to Colonel Abella. He was known as "the Flea" by the elite band of saboteurs and explosive experts who worked with him.

"I believe you have heard already of our very successful sabotage attack on the barracks at Colón de Paso. We will have other rather explosive projects to report to you soon, with equal results, I assure you."

Again applause erupted among all the men gathered in the room as the diminutive rebel soldier sat back down. He almost disappeared behind the stack of papers on the table in front of him.

Several of those present had questions about the operations the men had mentioned but a discreet knock at the oak doors interrupted their discussion. It was Guzmán, de Santiago's bodyguard, who stuck his head inside.

"Excuse me, El Jefe. Your guest from Bogotá has arrived."

De Santiago waved his hand.

"By all means, bring our guest in, my friend." He looked at those sitting around the table and noted the quizzical looks on their faces. "This is someone I want you all to meet. A true hero of the revolution."

The short little man who accompanied Guzmán through the door hardly looked like a hero. He seemed to be trying to hide behind the bodyguard. His eyes were wide and nervous and his face pale and frightened. He was dressed in a rumpled, cheap suit and a yellowing white shirt. He most resembled a lower-level clerk, someone who was merely furniture in some government bureau somewhere.

De Santiago rose and walked over to embrace the little man, then kissed him on each cheek.

"Come my friends. Meet the greatest hero of the revolution! José Silveras is our eyes and ears in the heart of El Presidente Guitteriz's government. Without him, the people's war would have been lost already, I am afraid."

De Santiago placed his arm around the shorter man's shoulder. He led him to the table. Each of the others stood, walked over to the man, and solemnly shook his hand. The little clerk seemed on the verge of fainting dead away, his knees trembling as he stood there.

Finally, as they were seated, de Santiago asked, "Tell me, my friend, what is it that is so important that you journeyed all the way from Bogotá?"

Silveras began speaking slowly. A vein twitched in his left temple. Those assembled around the table had to listen hard to catch his words over the noise from outside, the songs of the birds and the children splashing in the pool.

"El Jefe, there are two things that I came to tell you and you alone. I had hoped that we could speak privately."

De Santiago smiled.

"Don't worry. These are my most trusted people. I trust them with my life. You can speak freely here."

Silveras glanced around the table, looking at each face, and began again, still reluctantly, still quietly.

"If you insist. The first matter is the Joint Drug Interdiction Agency, the JDIA. I have seen them with my own eyes. They are operating with El Presidente's military command. They have what they call an 'in-country command post' in the Ministry of Defense compound in Bogotá. They have much power. Very much power." Silveras swallowed hard and licked his lips. "El Jefe, I am very thirsty. Might I have some water?"

De Santiago waved at Guzmán, who poured a glassful of water from the crystal pitcher in the middle of the table. He handed it to the little man. Silveras took a big drink, then continued.

"This JDIA includes all the Americans' anti-drug organizations, including their military, but it does not include the DEA. I overheard two of their DEA agents talking about the JDIA. There is very great jealousy there. From what they said, their president is giving much money to the JDIA at a time when he is publicly cutting back the commitment to the DEA."

De Santiago stroked his chin thoughtfully. There was advantage to be had here. Maybe they could exploit this rift and tear the American machine apart. He would have to think on this situation some more, but this held interesting possibilities.

"There was a second matter?" the leader asked.

Silveras took another swallow of the cold water and again considered the faces looking at him from around the biggest and fanciest table he had ever seen. He grew even paler and his lower lip quivered.

"Are you certain it is safe for me to speak freely here?"

De Santiago waved impatiently and said, "Of course. Of course. Go on."

"Yes, thank you, El Jefe. This one worries me greatly. I am reluctant to report to you, sir, that you have a spy in your camp." All the air seemed to leave the room. Each man around the table stared at the clerk with obvious disbelief. "There is no doubt. I saw the report about the attack on your fields. Someone named El Falcone produced the information for the Security Police. The report said that it was this Falcone who gave the information to them. And it is of great distress to me to tell you that this traitor is someone very close to you, El Jefe. That is all that I know."

The room was deathly quiet. There was only the sound of the children squealing, the woman laughing happily as they played together in the pool outside the window.

No one needed to tell Silveras it was now time for him to go. He took one last drink of the water, then rose and left the room as quietly as he had come in, easing the door closed behind him.

Each man in the group looked about the room then, but carefully avoided eye contact with anyone else. The implication was clear. One of them was El Falcone! And whoever it was, that traitor was a serious threat to the new alliance that was being formed. To the daring secret plan that was about to unfold.

Juan de Santiago made a move to return to the window. To look out on the flowers and hummingbirds and distant cloud-draped mountains. On his beautiful, fertile woman and his happy children.

Somehow, just now, it didn't seem the right time to turn his back on anyone in this room.

7

JONATHAN WARD GAZED OUT OVER THE PEACEFUL BLUE WATERS OF the Pacific. From his perch at the top of *Spadefish*'s sail, more than twenty-five feet above the water, he could easily see the cliffs of Torrey Pines, just north of La Jolla. Farther south, the jutting projection of Point Loma marked the entrance to San Diego Harbor. It was partially hidden by a bank of low-lying clouds. The newer Coast Guard lighthouse, low down on the point, marked the end of land. The old Cabrillo Point Lighthouse up on the ridge was hiding in the mist.

Ward loved this time alone. He enjoyed working with the crew, appreciated the camaraderie and steadfastness of purpose almost every one of them demonstrated. Up here, he would permit the gentle motion of the sea and the balm of the damp wind on his face to work its calming magic on him. This was his only chance to be by himself, to put aside the constant cut-and-dried decisions it seemed he was always being called upon to make and simply allow his consciousness to drift away. No wonder men had always sought the sea. It held healing powers for whatever might ail a man's soul.

The commander was not totally alone. No one ever is on a submarine. The officer of the deck stood quietly nearby in the bridge cockpit. He knew the skipper well enough to sense that he now sought solitude. Especially now. Especially after how things had gone lately.

Ward was thinking of home. And, of course, of Ellen. He knew he had been away far too much over the last twenty years. He also knew that this homecoming would be bittersweet. Would he still have *Spadefish* after the meeting tonight with Admiral Donnegan? Or would Hunsucker do enough damage to send him straight to the bottom? After what had happened out there, Ward was more certain than ever that he couldn't trust that weasel. He was the type who conspired to get ahead with slick words and ingratiating smiles. A purely political animal. When it came time for him to step up to the next rung on the ladder, he would shove aside whoever was in his way, step right over him, and never look back.

Ward had to admit to himself the he was fed up with the politics of the senior command in today's navy. There didn't seem to be anyone left who would risk his butt to do what he knew was right. Nowadays, if anyone had his sights set on getting ahead, it was necessary to do a Pentagon tour. Everyone who came back from one of those seemed to have been emasculated, brainwashed. They were more concerned with "face time" and spin-doctoring and shoving aside competition for the next promotion than they were with the navy's mission.

Jon Ward sometimes found himself wishing he had the guts to chuck it. Maybe do like his old college roommate, Tom Kincaid, who risked a promising career in the DEA instead of knuckling under to the political pressure. Ward remembered the animated discussion they had over beers and dinner the last time he was in Seattle. It took real courage to stand up to that kind of pressure and say, "Hell, no!"

And that's what Ward had told his old friend. How proud he was of him for standing his ground, even when he knew the costs would be high. Ward had been surprised at Kincaid's response.

"Don't give me too much credit for guts, Jon," he said, his eyes almost closed as he quietly spoke. "Sometimes it takes something beyond guts or glory or even duty to drive a man."

The salmon steaks had arrived and Ward never got the opportunity to ask him what he was talking about.

Now, facing what he knew was likely coming that night, Ward had to admit that he still felt he was most useful when he commanded one of these graceful boats. When he saw the look of respect and dedication in the eyes of the men he led. When he knew that what he did made a real difference in keeping his country safe and free.

Sometimes, though, he had to work hard at remembering those things.

The splash of a gray whale, close off the starboard beam, broke his reverie. The giant tail fin flipped high in the air as the leviathan dove once more for the deep. Ward looked out toward the western horizon and, even without binoculars, he counted more than two dozen whales, blowing, frolicking, or just swimming, all headed south for the winter.

Not a bad life. Spend the entire winter cavorting off Baja. Nothing to do but eat fresh seafood and chase female whales. Then, when it suits you, swim back north and pass the summer cruising off Alaska. Not a bad life at all.

"Captain? JA."

Dave Kuhn was holding out the handset toward Ward. The commander knew that Kuhn enjoyed this time on the surface as much as he did. The engineer on the old girl had a hard life just keeping her running. Ward tried to make sure he got him on the bridge as much as possible as something of a small reward for all the dirty work the man did to keep the boat functioning.

Ward took the handset and put it to his ear. He gazed out toward San Clemente Island, tan and green, low on the western horizon. They weren't far from port now.

"Captain," he answered.

Thirty feet below, in the control room, Joe Glass reported, "Skipper, we have voice comms with Squadron. We have permission to enter port. Berth is north side of November Pier, inboard. The tug will meet us alongside the dry dock as usual."

Ward accepted the report.

"Very well, XO. Station the Maneuvering Watch when we are abreast Buoy Sierra Delta."

The Maneuvering Watch put the best people on board at all the key stations for the delicate operation of handling the sub in restricted waters. Although supremely graceful in the deep, *Spadefish*'s round keelless bottom and single screw made handling tricky in the shallow waters of a port. That was especially true at San Diego, where tidal currents could be downright treacherous. Regulations required that the watch be stationed before they were allowed past the first buoy that marked the entrance to San Diego Harbor. That marker was named "Buoy Sierra Delta."

"And," Glass continued, his voice now little more than a whisper, "Captain Hunsucker has been on the radio for the last ten minutes talking to the commodore. Chief Lyman tells me it has not been complimentary. Better rig for heavy weather, Skipper. Storms ahead."

"Thanks for the weather report, XO."

There was nothing he could do about that now. Better concentrate on getting *Spadefish* into port without putting any dents in her. He hoped Ellen wouldn't be waiting for him on the pier this time. As much as he longed to feel her close to him, feel her lips on his, that would have to wait.

He wouldn't be getting home until late tonight.

The traffic grew even thicker as they sailed closer to Point Loma. The large merchants and the squatty tugs with their barges in tow had been about all they had seen on the deep blue waters farther out. But now they gave way to a myriad of sailboats, sport fishermen, and runabouts. It seemed every weekend sailor in Southern California was out and that every one of them wanted to see a real, live submarine up close.

Kuhn was growing exasperated, doing his best to dodge the sightseers or try to warn them away. He had apparently invented a rather animated new hand signal to add to the Coast Guard's "Rules of the Nautical Road." It involved an upright digit on one hand accompanied by the vigorous waving of the other arm.

Ward caught the attention of the young engineer. He said, "Eng, smile while you're waving at the taxpayers. I don't want to have to answer some letter to the editor in the *San Diego Union-Tribune* from an irate citizen-sailor."

"Yes, sir," Kuhn replied a bit sheepishly, but he turned quickly to frantically wave another close-by launch out of their path.

Buoy Sierra Delta was festooned with the normal herd of sleeping sea lions as it passed down the starboard side. Kuhn reached for the 7MC mike and ordered, "Helm, left full rudder, steady course three-five-six." Both officers glanced over their shoulder to watch the rudder swing over, just to double-check.

They could now make out, through their binoculars, the range markers up on Shelter Island beside the entrance to the yacht basin. They were giant white signboards with a vertical orange stripe down the middle of each. The optical illusion presented by the markers enabled those entering the channel to see where they were in relation to the centerline. One marker was positioned a few hundred feet in front of and a little lower than the other. When a ship was in the center of the channel, the orange stripes lined up, one right above the other. If the ship was to the left of center, the upper stripe was to the left of the lower or, if it was to the right of center of the shipping channel, the upper stripe was to the right of the lower.

As *Spadefish* steadied up on the new course, they could see that they were just a little to the left of the center of channel. The ebbing tide was doing its best to push them over that way.

"Helm, Bridge. Steer three-five-five."

In the narrow confines of the shipping channel, barely a hundred yards wide, there wasn't room for any major course corrections. It was usually a slow, iterative process to correct for the tricky, ever-changing currents.

The 7MC speaker came alive again.

"Bridge, Navigator. We are in communication with a large

outbound 'ro-ro' just making the turn at North Island Point. We have agreed to a port-to-port passage. You may have to wait a little before turning in to the piers."

Ward could just see the giant "roll on, roll off" ship, designed to haul new automobiles from the Orient. It was now coming out from behind the *Nimitz*, where the massive aircraft carrier was tied up over at the North Island Navy Base. The cargo vessel was outbound from the San Diego Terminal down beyond the Coronado Bridge, headed back to Korea for another load of cars. Looked like the Nav was right. They should pass just beyond the dry dock at Ballast Point, when they needed to make the turn across the channel into the piers. The channel there was tight for such a big ship to pass them.

"Eng, slow to one-third. Let him pass us out here where the channel is wider. Get well over to the right side of the channel. He'll need a lot of room."

Kuhn nodded. "Aye, sir." He spoke into the mike. "Helm ahead one-third. Steer course three-five-six. Rig out the outboard, test and shift to remote. Make the anchor ready for letting go, snubbing scope thirty fathoms. Have line handlers lay topside."

That set of rapid-fire orders called a host of people into action. Down in the bowels of the auxiliary machinery room, just aft of the reactor compartment, an electrician used a series of controls to lower a small electric motor-driven outboard from the ballast tank. The little outboard, like a trolling motor on a bass boat, projected below the keel. The motor could be trained through 360 degrees to help nudge *Spadefish* in any direction. The electrician checked to make sure the equipment was operating and shifted control to the helmsman.

Seaman Cortez saw the remote control light come on and tested to verify he had control of the outboard.

"Bridge, Helm. Outboard lowered, tested, and shifted to remote."

All the way aft in the engine room, beside the massive spinning shaft, Bill Ralston struggled to make the anchor ready to drop. It was a piece of gear that was almost never used. In all his years on the boats, Ralston had never seen it dropped except when it was being tested alongside the pier. The anchor windlass on *Spadefish*, like a lot of her equipment, was old and cranky. Ralston muttered under his breath as he fought the stubborn gear.

"I hope this damn thing works if we ever need it," he growled, but no one heard him.

Finally, he had it lined up so that only the chain-brake had to be loosened and then the anchor would drop from its position in the ballast tank below him. He reached over and set the out-haul windlass so it would pay out only thirty fathoms of chain. Contrary to what most people believe, it isn't the anchor itself that holds a ship in place. The mass of chain lying on the bottom of the ocean does most of the work. With ten feet of water under the keel, they needed thirty fathoms of chain to hold *Spadefish* firmly in place.

Ralston grabbed the 7MC microphone.

"Bridge, Anchor. Anchor ready for letting go. Snubbing scope three-zero fathoms. Skipper, we need to lower the anchor and walk out the chain once we're in port this time so we can loosen her up. She's getting real sluggish."

"Okay, Chief," Ward answered. "We should have plenty of time to play with it this time."

"Skipper," the engineer was saying as he looked up at Ward. "Request permission to open the weapons shipping hatch and send men topside."

Ward acknowledged and looked back and down at the main deck, just behind the sail. He saw the large hatch swing up and the COB hop up onto the deck. He immediately attached a hook into a groove on the deck. That hook was attached to a harness he was wearing and connected him to the boat. The round deck was treacherously slick. Maneuvering the boat to rescue a man who slipped and fell overboard was dangerous in these tight waters. The COB watched as each man through the hatch attached his safety harness to the track before going to his assigned task.

Ward leaned over the side of the sail and called down,

"COB, rig out the cleats and both capstans. Take the tug alongside at the port number-three cleat to bring the pilot on board, then cast him off so he's clear before that 'ro-ro' gets here."

Master Chief Lawskowski yelled back up, "Aye, sir," and turned to his team of line handlers, telling them what the skipper had ordered. They were going to get the harbor pilot off his tug and aboard *Spadefish* before the hulking cargo ship and its wake got too close.

It was only a few moments before the large orange-and-mustard-yellow commercial tug pulled alongside and tossed over a light head line. The civilian pilot leaped over to the main deck of the submarine and scurried up the steel ladder rungs to the bridge.

"Afternoon, Captain! Glad to see you back," he said cheerfully, a warm smile on his face as he shook Ward's outstretched hand.

"Thanks, Captain. Always good to be home." Ward's voice was sincere. The pilot didn't know why they were back in port on such short notice. "Mr. Kuhn, have the navigator enter into the deck log that Mr. Sorensen is the pilot."

"Understand you're going to the north side of November Pier, inboard. Let's tie the tug up with split head lines to starboard cleats one and two, quarter line to four as soon as this 'ro-ro' is clear."

Ward nodded his agreement.

These new commercial tractor tugs were enormous and powerful, easily able to shove *Spadefish* where she needed to go. It would be lined up with its bow pointing right at the starboard side of the sail so that it could gently push or pull the sub toward the pier as need be.

As they were discussing the arrangement of the tug, both men looked up to see the outbound freighter bearing down on them, coming right down the very center of the shipping channel. Ward picked up the bridge-to-bridge radio.

"Outbound 'ro-ro' abreast Ballast Point, this is inbound submarine. Suggest a one-whistle passage. Captain, request you move a little to right of center channel. I need a little more room."

The "Rules of the Nautical Road" that all sailors obeyed were based on ships communicating with whistle signals. Ships still used their whistles, but the usual method nowadays was by bridge-to-bridge radio. A one-whistle passage meant that they agreed to pass port side to port side, like two cars meeting each other on an American roadway.

Ward watched closely as the giant wall of pale blue steel inched over to the far side of the channel, giving *Spadefish* a little more breathing space. Ward could read the name painted high up on the massive bow: *Inchon Moon*. The main deck was fifty feet above his perch, with the huge bridge another fifty feet higher. He could see his counterpart out on the ship's bridge wing, looking downward at the diminutive submarine. The two captains exchanged salutes as the giant passed on its way to meet the sea.

Sorensen spoke into his radio, then turned to Ward.

"Captain, looks like we'll be tying up at max ebb after all. Probably be close to a seven-knot current pushing toward the pier."

Ward shook his head. Seven knots of current pushing directly against the side of *Spadefish*, shoving her into the pier, was a lot of force, maybe even too much for this powerful tug to overcome.

Sorensen seemed to be reading Ward's mind.

"Don't worry, Captain. *Cherry Two* can handle a hell of a lot more than that. Just let her hold you off while the current pushes you toward the pier and it'll be like putting your honey to bed."

They passed the large floating dry dock at the south end of the submarine base. One of the *Los Angeles*–class boats was up on the blocks, being repaired. Must be *Houston*. Ward had been XO on her at one time. It had been nice to have a boat with all that speed and one that was so much easier to maintain than *Spadefish*. But this old girl really had a way of growing on a sailor, too.

A pair of F/A-18 Hornets roared off the end of the North Island runway just to the starboard, as if they were putting on a show for the sub crew. The planes were barely a hundred feet overhead as they turned out to sea and were quickly gone.

Nice welcoming party, Ward thought. And once again he felt a surge of pride at being a part of it all.

Spadefish eased past the three long piers of the sub base. It seemed empty somehow now that the huge gray mass of the sub tender no longer jutted out from the end of November Pier. All the tenders had fallen victims to Washington's budget cuts a couple of years before. They had likely been turned into razor blades by now. The functions that a tender once provided were now performed by shore-based facilities, usually manned by civilians.

"Captain," Kuhn shouted. "Time to turn."

They were now abreast of the old dolphin-training facility where the intelligent mammals had once been taught to do special, top-secret tasks. It was almost time to turn toward the pier, placing them broadside to the racing current. Ward looked over at the channel buoy. It was leaning over heavily, and the ebb tide made a large wake around it, pointing out to sea. It was really surging, probably more than the seven knots that Captain Sorensen predicted.

Ward yelled down to Kuhn.

"Just a few more minutes. Give us a little more room."

"Aye, sir."

The skipper could see that a sizable crowd had gathered on the pier, wives, kids, sweethearts, tourists, all there to welcome them. Some had already recognized the sub and were waving at them.

Ward waited until he guessed they had moved far enough up the channel to compensate for the racing ebb tide.

"Now, Mr. Kuhn, left full rudder."

The captain looked over his shoulder to see the rudder swing over then watched as the bow pivoted around to point toward land. He immediately felt the tide pushing the sub down onto the pier. He looked to see the foam churning under the stern of *Cherry Two* as the tugboat strained to pull the sub back, against the current. He could hear the groan of the lines as they protested the strain.

The sub and tug eased out of the channel and descended slowly toward the pier, everything going according to plan. Some of the crew on the sub's deck were looking toward the welcoming crowd, trying to pick out particular faces.

Suddenly there was an ugly gray-black belch of smoke from *Cherry Two*'s stack. At her stern, the frothy white churning stopped. The tug had lost power!

Ward braced himself. He could feel *Spadefish* picking up speed as she continued to slide toward the pier. Forty-seven hundred tons of steel being pushed inexorably toward the wood and concrete pier, crowded with families waiting to greet them.

It was too late to back out into the channel and there was not enough room to control the boat with that tug tied up alongside even if they could. Ward knew he had to somehow fight the racing current and prevent the mass of the sub from crashing into the pier. At this speed, it would crush the structure, killing or injuring those people who were standing there happily waving at them, unaware of the sudden danger they were in.

Ward grabbed the 7MC.

"Train the outboard to zero-nine-zero. Start the outboard. Let go the anchor."

"Outboard trained to zero-nine-zero and running," Cortez replied immediately.

Down below, Chief Ralston shook his head in disbelief. Had he heard that right? Had the skipper ordered him to let go the anchor? No, couldn't be. He grabbed the 7MC.

"Bridge, Anchor. Did you say 'Let go the anchor'?"

"Chief, let go the anchor now! I need to stop the ship!" Ward yelled, the urgency obvious in his voice.

Ralston didn't hesitate. He turned the gear to release the anchor brake.

Nothing happened!

He tried again. Still nothing.

"Skipper, it's stuck. I can't get it to let go!"

Ward heard the words and felt his stomach sink. They were rushing toward the pier now. He could see families smiling and waving, ready to greet loved ones on board, still not realizing the boat was about to slam into the pier.

"Sorensen. Drop every anchor you have on *Cherry Two*."

The pilot looked at him, his eyes wide.

"I can't. It'll damage her screw."

"I don't care if it rips her bottom out, drop those damn anchors!" Ward yelled back.

The pilot reluctantly obeyed. Ward could see the tug captain shaking his head as he waved to deckhands down on the main deck. The two huge anchors dropped into the brown water, splashing it high up on the sides of the tug.

Meanwhile, Chief Ralston beat on the recalcitrant anchor gear with the handle of a big wrench. Tears of frustration poured down his craggy, grease-streaked face.

Damn gear! Maintain the son of a bitch for years, but when you need the piece of shit, it won't work.

He took another swing of the wrench, this time with all the power he could muster.

Bang!

The brake sprang free and the windlass began spinning wildly. He could hear chain links clanging as they paid out from the chain locker below him.

"Skipper, she's loose! It's working! The anchor is dropped!"

Just in time. The combined restraint of the electric outboard, the tug's two anchors, and the sub's own obstinate anchor finally did their jobs. The boat eased up and gently kissed the inflatable camels alongside the pier in a near-perfect docking. None of the watching crowd noticed how close to disaster they had just come.

Jonathan Ward finally breathed again as he wiped his brow. He ignored his shaking hands.

Jesus, he thought, what else could possibly go wrong?

Fore and aft, lines were being passed to the pier and the U.S. flag was shifted from its "under way" position on the bridge to the "in port" position on the after part of the main deck. Ward scanned the pier, still looking for the beautiful, tall redhead who had met him at so many other homecomings. Thankfully, Ellen wasn't there.

Good. This particular landfall was different from any other he had ever had, and frankly, he didn't want to have to face her until he knew what the future held for them.

As he scanned the other happy, smiling faces, Jon Ward spotted a very familiar one. The commodore, Captain Desseaux, stood alone in a shadow, away from the others.

And he definitely was not smiling.

8

JUAN DE SANTIAGO STEPPED THROUGH THE DARK DOORWAY. IT LED into the dilapidated, rusting tin shed. The place looked like little more than a snake den, like any other abandoned plantation supply shed that the vines and weather were inevitably reclaiming. The leader of the revolution still wore a broad smile as he surveyed the place.

This shanty had once been in the center of some of the fiercest skirmishes of the revolution. On many nights inside this very shed, he and his staff had planned by candlelight the next glorious battles they would wage for the liberation of their people. And the blood of many of de Santiago's most loyal fighters was mixed with the red clay that anchored the surrounding jungle.

Now the fighting had moved far away from this sacred place. It was little more than a quiet, forgotten backwater. Not even the peasants came here anymore. They were afraid of the

ghosts still left from long ago. Frightened away by the anguished cries that rang out at night. By the bouncing, peculiar
lights that danced about in the dark, thick undergrowth. It was
only the scream of a jaguar at night, the luminescence given
off by rotting vegetation. The peasants had to wonder how so
many could die so violently without there being some restless
souls haunting this place. There were no crops grown here
now. There was no longer any reason for the peasants to come
here to this place. The ravenous jungle had long since swallowed the fields and the other buildings of the old hacienda
that once thrived in this spot.

And that was precisely the way Juan de Santiago wanted it.
This wasting, unimpressive shack in the midst of a desolate
jungle had a far more important role in the revolution he led.

He passed through the doorway, leaving the shadowy jungle
light and steamy heat behind him. He followed his guide down
a staircase that had been hidden by a well-concealed trapdoor
beneath the dirt of the shack's floor. The stairs led him downward into a truly amazing scene. The rough structure concealed a surprisingly modern chemical laboratory, glass and
stainless steel gleaming in the fluorescent light. The cool, dry
air in the big room sucked the moisture from de Santiago's
clammy, sweat-soaked camouflage shirt. It was more than the
chilly air-conditioning that brought goose bumps to the
leader's flesh. He had to pause for a moment for his eyes to
adjust to the illumination, but he had not lost his smile.

He surveyed with pride this huge room he had heard so
much about. It was truly a wonder. The American spy satellites
would never find this place. The nearest road was over five
miles away, the jungle nearly impenetrable. It was hardly more
than a rutted trail. The only reliable way in was by water, and
that was a grueling trip up a swift-flowing river. All the supplies, every piece of equipment, had been carried in by boat.
Then through the tangled rain forest on the backs of a few of
the local peasants. They only moved on dark, cloudy nights.
These men were intensely loyal to the revolution. And they
were sworn to secrecy on the threat of death to their families.

All precautions had been taken to assure the place would be nearly impossible to detect. The diesel generator that supplied the essential electricity was buried in the jungle a half-mile away. Even its exhaust pipe ended beneath the water of the river so the satellite infrared sensors would not be able to see its heat and raise suspicion.

Building this lab had taken many months and much money, but it was key to de Santiago's plan. The design was ingenious. Two-foot-thick insulation was hidden below the rusting roof inside of the shed to further defeat the infrared sensors. Ventilation piping ran underground for several hundred yards before exiting. Ninety percent of the lab was underground, protected from any sensing devices de Santiago or any of his advisors could imagine. A government patrol that might stumble upon the abandoned hacienda would be very lucky to find the lab. If they did, a carefully designed protective system would assure that their accidental discovery was a deadly one without doing serious damage to the wonder it was designed to defend.

Jorge Ortiez labored up the steep stairs to greet his most important visitor and, after pausing a moment to catch his breath, led him back down.

"El Jefe," the fat little man cried, still gasping for air. "It is a great honor to see you again. Señor Dura sends his apologies that he is not here to greet you himself. He was detained in Cartagena, where he is supervising the delivery of supplies."

De Santiago dismissed the apology with a wave of his hand.

"It is of no concern. Duty always calls." Placing an arm around the shorter man's shoulder, the leader continued, his tone congenial. "Now, come Jorge. Show me around this wonderful laboratory you have built. And I especially want to see this 'new product' with my own eyes."

A group of scientists, each clad in an immaculate white lab coat, waited nervously for them at the far end of the room. The antiseptic smell of the lab seemed cloying to de Santiago, almost too sweet after the dank, earthy scent of his beloved jungle. But he knew this sweet smell represented a crucial part of his plan and would ultimately lead to him finally regaining control of his own land. Or having that control returned to the people through him.

The rows of stainless-steel countertops reached back into the distance. He could not imagine the purpose of the over-flowing complex structures of glass tubing and odd-looking equipment. Colored liquids bubbled and dripped ominously in many of them, reminding him of some sorcerer's den where evil magic was being conjured. He knew, regardless of what spell the potions concocted here might cast on the un-suspecting for whom they were intended, they were ultimately for the good of the people here, his people.

De Santiago greeted the cluster of scientists with hearty handshakes and slaps on their backs. They responded timidly. The leader's reputation had preceded him. They seemed far less comfortable with the man who paid them their substantial income than they might have been with their beakers and test tubes and analysis machines. He hardly knew the scientists. He had mostly seen their photos and learned their reputations from dossiers supplied by Dura and the others. These were some of the "hired guns" of the operation. Lured to this high mountain jungle and its secret lab with the promise of a chance at winning their own sweet revenge against the Americans. And, incidentally, the promise of great wealth in the process.

De Santiago knew he could never truly accept them into his revolution. Each had his own agenda. They were merely tools of the struggle. Like his trucks or pack mules or weapons, to be used until they were no longer functional, then discarded if they could not be recycled.

The group represented a staggering accumulation of knowledge on a rather complicated subject: the microbiology of the interaction of dangerous drugs with the human body and the addiction process. Two of the men were graduates of the former Soviet Union's chemical-warfare labs, men who still held the United States responsible for the breakup of their great nation into tiny squabbling fiefdoms.

FINAL BEARING   83

Three others gained much of their experience in Iraq's chemical-warfare experiments prior to the Gulf War. Each had lost loved ones in the "surgical" bombing conducted by the Americans and had still been banished by Saddam as he sought to place blame for their country's ignoble defeat.

The final scientist was a refugee from the American tobacco industry. He had no political axe to grind. He was simply in it for the money.

All the men appeared to de Santiago to be weak, pasty-faced, bleary-eyed, unable or unwilling to hold his gaze or to adequately return his powerful handshake. They looked at the floor and mumbled to him in thick, heavy accents. Except for the American. De Santiago wondered if this one had not been conducting the experiments on himself. His eyes were watery and wild, his speech slurred, his hand damp and clammy when he shook it. But these men were not tucked away in this secret lab for their physical prowess or conversational abilities or even the soundness of their mental states. It was their brainpower he sought. With one exception, it appeared he had been getting his money's worth.

Ortiez politely steered the great leader on past the clot of scientists and down a row of lab benches. He stopped at a peculiarly twisted piece of glass tubing. The fat little man had a stricken look on his face.

"El Jefe, I am ashamed to report that this is our problem. Djenka, may his bones burn in hell, was working here." He pointed with a trembling finger to a tiny, intricate glass petcock that dripped a small amount of clear liquid into the mix. "This is a derivative of a hexanoic aldehyde. It was showing great promise in controlling the rate of addiction. Djenka was working on it before his *cojones* got the better of him and he left to find his *puta*."

De Santiago looked at the maze of tubing and listened to the meaningless words. He smiled toward Ortiez and placed his hand gently on the man's shoulder. The little man jumped as if the leader had stabbed him with a knife.

"Jorge, I am sure we didn't waste our time and money send-

ing you to MIT. Just make it work. Salvage what you can from
the bastard's work. I know you can do it. You have one month
to do so, my friend."

Ortiez stared at de Santiago's back as he quickly turned and
strode away. The smile was still on the leader's face. A shiver
of fear ran down the little man's spine.

El Jefe did not brook failure. Especially on a project that
was so crucial to his plans. Standing there trembling in the
cool, dry air of the hidden laboratory, Jorge Ortiez had absolutely no idea how he was going to avoid it.

"Come, Guzmán," de Santiago shouted impatiently. "We have
many miles to cover."

The visit to the jungle laboratory had energized the leader.
He was anxious to get back, to check on the progress of other
aspects of the plan. His bodyguard appeared from the thick
undergrowth around the shed and hustled to catch up to him.
The two men headed down the narrow jungle path at a trot.
The brutal midday sun was turning the humid jungle into a
steaming cauldron. Insects buzzed annoyingly about their
faces. The rustling of the undergrowth warned of the passage
of a tapir. They kept to the darkest shadows to avoid the heat.
Tripping on ensnaring vines and rotting logs seemed inevitable to Guzmán, but his boss kept the pace. He had no option but to follow.

As they rounded a sharp turn, the path dropped into the underbrush. The two of them followed it. They descended a slip-
pery, muddy bank to an oxbow lake hidden by the dense
growth and a canopy of vines and trees. Spectacular regalia
lilies, *Victoria amazonica*, the world's largest water lily, covered the little lake with huge fragrant blooms.

An unnamed, sluggish brown stream fed the lake and many
more like it before it joined the great Rio Napo many miles
downstream. Water from this lake then journeyed on to the
Amazon before finally reaching the Atlantic. It flowed over
two thousand miles.

De Santiago told his men that a ripple on the lake's surface here, far up in the mountain jungles of Colombia, would lap up on the shores of Europe and Africa and North America. The imagery was lost on them.

The small dugout canoe was tied where they had left it, hidden in the emergent grasses and reeds at the lake's edge. They carefully checked for signs that someone might have disturbed the boat. De Santiago jumped in front and Guzmán carefully pushed off from the bank and hopped in back. Dipping their paddles in the tepid brown water, the pair moved out of the lake and into the center of the channel. The lethargic current flowed more swiftly. They pointed the nose of the dugout downstream.

Juan de Santiago was reminded of many such trips he had made on this river during his boyhood. He enjoyed the quiet gurgling of the water slipping past the canoe. The welcome strain of his back muscles as he urged the boat along with his paddle. The many animals that came down to the bank to drink. Then there had been those times when his mission on this river was not so pleasurable. When he was stalking or fleeing the government troops. When the animals he watched for on the bank carried carbines and his death warrant.

No time for those memories now. He would have time to savor them later, when the job was done.

Toward midafternoon the pair passed the remains of a small, burned-out, and abandoned village. Villages that had stood since the time of the Incas, that had withstood the assault of the conquistadors. De Santiago could remember several villages along this stretch of the river. Now they were all gone, their residents having long since joined the other victims of the years of struggle, either in death or flight. They had finally fallen to their own traitorous countrymen, the henchmen of Guitteriz.

Soon, soon, I will bring back all those who still live, return the land to its rightful owners. Just as I will chase El Presidente to hell, he thought.

Downriver they drifted. They used their paddles to keep the dugout in the middle of the stream and away from the overhanging tree limbs where snakes might drop into the boat with them, or, almost as bad, the spider monkeys could shit on them. They were moving fast enough that the breeze cooled them. They could still hear the birds singing in the jungle, the chatter of the monkeys playing amid the vines. De Santiago could make out the distinct calls of the orange-bellied euphonia and the white-collared swift in the cacophony of singing. Hummingbirds and flycatchers flitted about the trees. This jungle was the home of more bird species than anywhere else on Earth, many not even named. He thought of all the times he had spent here with his father as the man pointed out each of them for his son, identifying them by song or by plumage.

Peaceful times like these were rare. De Santiago needed to get to the next inspection as quickly as he could. But he was hesitant to rush this particular part of the journey. The memories kept flooding back. He was thankful that they had no outboard motor, even if it was for a far more practical reason than merely to allow them to listen to the birds, the monkeys, the hissing of the dugout as it cut through the water. They had expended too much effort hiding the lab for it to be found out only because the revolution's leader might be in a hurry. Natives used dugouts with paddles here. Outboards drew attention. Might as well enjoy the quiet and listen to the jungle sounds.

They rounded a long sweeping bend in the river. De Santiago could just make out where the stream joined up with the Rio Napo a little farther down. Its broad brown mass stretched several hundred yards across to the verdant green bank on the other side. De Santiago relaxed. Even if someone spotted them now, he and Guzmán were far enough from the lab that there would be no way for anyone to backtrack through the maze of jungle streams behind them and find it.

There was a rustle from the left bank and several birds shot into the air, out over the broadening river. De Santiago felt the canoe rock as Guzmán turned, looked in that direction, then froze. He eyed the shore, spying what caused his bodyguard's reaction. The rifle muzzles were already spitting fire. He rolled the dugout to dump them into the dark water. He saw the slugs drill deep into the canoe bottom, where only a moment before he was sitting. He heard more sizzle as they pimpled the surface of the water.

He held his breath and went under briefly, then popped up again beside the canoe just as Guzmán broke the surface next to him, spluttering. The dugout shielded them from view, but bits and pieces of it were flying off as a flurry of bullets found their mark. It was hardly armor.

"You all right?" de Santiago shouted.

"I'm afraid I am hit in the arm," Guzmán answered, wincing. "But it is nothing."

Blood darkened the river water next to him.

There was an even more urgent danger. Bullets were flying at them from a new direction, from behind them, popping and singing as they struck the water near their heads. De Santiago could see the flicker of muzzle flashes from automatic weapons on the right bank now.

They were in a carefully planned crossfire. No way out and no way to fight back.

The service revolver on his hip was no match for this barrage. Their AK-47s had sunk to the bottom already.

He could hear the attackers shouting from the bank on both sides of the river.

"We have him now! Keep shooting! Ten thousand pesos to the man who brings me an ear of the bastard de Santiago!"

De Santiago pointed to the dugout. Guzmán nodded and dove, just before he did. They surfaced together inside the meager protection of the overturned wooden boat. He could already see daylight in many places where the bullets had chipped through.

De Santiago shouted, "We must dive deep and swim for the Rio Napo! It's our only chance. Stay under water until your lungs burst, my friend. For the revolution!"

Guzmán took several deep breaths and disappeared below the surface. De Santiago saw one of the bullets pop through the side of the dugout where his bodyguard had been.

"*Vaya con Dios*, my friend," de Santiago mumbled. He filled his lungs and dove to the bottom after him.

The leader of the revolution touched the muddy bottom with the toes of his boots. A tremendous explosion stunned him. The concussion left him senseless for a moment. He was aware enough not to try to breathe. He found himself floating helplessly toward the surface.

Something deep in his inner mind, some primal will to survive to fight again, shook him back to full consciousness just before he broke the surface. He could see the bright yellow sunlight filtering down through the mud brown water, tempting him to come to the surface for a brief gulp of cool, sweet air.

He fought the impulse mightily. He rolled over and dove back to the deep, taking long slow strokes to conserve the precious air still left in his lungs. He had to put as much distance between himself and the ambush as he could.

Only fifty yards to go. He could do it. Had to stay down. Don't think of the fire burning in the chest. Just keep swimming. Let the quickening current deliver him from the devils.

The searing in his lungs was near unendurable. Grayness started to slip in around the edges of his thoughts. He felt another blast now, behind him, not nearly as bad as the first, but disorienting nonetheless.

Grenades! They were using grenades to force them up!

And he knew he was fading, falling, losing the battle.

Then Juan de Santiago had the strangest series of sensations. First, he thought of his mistress, and he could almost feel the way she felt against him, hear her laugh, her cries when he entered her, the animal sounds she made as he took her. He heard the laughter of his latest children. The ones from her womb. He could feel their love for him like a glow in his heart. He could smell the flowers that grew around his compound. Hear the flutter of the wings of the hummingbirds.

At that instant, he felt a powerful inner force take hold of him, a sense of purpose that was so strong he almost swooned.

He realized what it was that he was truly placed on this earth to do. No longer was his goal merely to conquer the devils of El Presidente. To return the land to the people, to assure that he, as leader, would enjoy the lifestyle he had earned by reclaiming his land.

His purpose from God was far greater. The devil he must destroy was much bigger than the clown in Bogotá. El Presidente was merely the puppet. His strings pulled by an entity much farther north. A superdevil that would be far more difficult to defeat. A wonderful fact became so obvious to him. He already had the mechanism in place, in progress, to do that very bidding. He could see so clearly that the victory could be his.

El Jefe could free far more than the peasants of his own small country. Achieve revenge for the pillaging of his Inca ancestors. He would soon have the mechanism to free the entire world! What sort of a lifestyle would he earn for himself by such a massive liberation?

His body was at the point of forcing him to involuntarily inhale the thick muddy-brown river water. He felt the current shift noticeably, now hitting him from the side instead of shoving him from behind.

The Rio Napo! He had made it!

De Santiago bobbed to the surface, inhaling great gasps of pure, clean air, choking, gagging, but more or less breathing.

He felt the stronger current of the larger river pushing him along, farther away from the ambush. There was no way the soldiers could navigate the vine-clogged riverbank as quickly as the river's current was carrying him. It would take a while to launch boats if that was how they had stalked him to here. He was safe from the government assassins.

He took a few feeble strokes out toward the middle of the river. He bumped into an unmoving, lifeless shape. Guzmán, his bodyguard, floating facedown.

De Santiago grabbed his old friend by the collar and belt to roll him over. He struggled to hold Guzmán's head out of the water. He fought to stay afloat himself. A few strong strokes and they reached the far bank of the Rio Napo, shielded from view by overhanging undergrowth. Standing in neck-deep water, de Santiago felt Guzmán's throat for a pulse.

Yes, there it was. Very weak, but still there.

He couldn't allow Guzmán to slip away now. He had even greater need for the man now than ever before.

He pinched Guzmán's nose and floated him close enough that he could breathe into his mouth. He watched as Guzmán's chest rose and lowered with the breath he was giving him. Again he breathed life into his old friend. Once more and Guzmán started to spit and sputter. He vomited great gushes of brown water, then finally started to breathe on his own.

His eyes flickered open, his arms instinctively treading water as he realized he was not dead.

"Welcome back, old friend. Did you enjoy your nap?" de Santiago asked.

Before Guzmán could answer, de Santiago pulled him closer to the bank and up onto a small patch of dry ground until his bodyguard could regain his strength. They would have to move soon. Float farther down the river to a safe pullout he knew. He had no idea how they might do that undetected, and especially with his bodyguard wounded and half-drowned.

"What happened?" Guzmán asked, catching his breath.

"Later, we still need to get out of here. El Presidente's troops will soon figure out that they didn't get us. We need to be long gone by then."

"Ambush!" Guzmán spat, his words hoarse, as much from anger as from the muddy water he had swallowed. "You know what that means? El Falcone is real. There was no way for those troops to know we would be coming this way. No way unless they had ears in the meeting room at the hacienda."

"Of course, you are right, my friend. And I have an idea on that subject. Wait, I think I see our ride now," de Santiago said, pointing at a small tree floating downriver, uprooted by some storm far up in the Andes. De Santiago saw it as a gift from God, a sign that his revelation had, indeed, been a divine one. "Swim for it and hold on to the branches. Keep your head low."

He watched as Guzmán started out into the river, swimming mostly on his side like a wounded duck. The injured arm was hampering the bodyguard's already poor swimming stroke. He wouldn't be able to make it in the swift current. De Santiago dove in behind him, grabbed Guzmán by the collar once more, and took long, sure strokes, strong enough to propel both men. Aiming well ahead of the floating tree, he swam on until they met up with it in the middle of the river.

Safely hidden in the limbs, they allowed it to carry them downstream. De Santiago used his shirt to bandage the wound as best he could. At least he managed to stop the bleeding. Guzmán would make it. He was far too tough to be killed in some silly little ambush.

De Santiago began to make an eerie sound. A deep, guttural laugh that grew until it was almost dangerously loud. Guzmán was startled by the burning, intense look in his leader's eyes.

"What, El Jefe?" Guzmán asked him. "You have been almost shot, nearly drowned, you float down a river filled with crocodiles and water snakes, and still you laugh as if it is all a joke?"

The look on Juan de Santiago's face grew even more intense. As dark as the deepest rain forest. As cold as the Andean snow. It wasn't the waters of the Rio Napo that caused Guzmán to begin to shiver.

"I have realized our purpose, *mi amigo*," de Santiago said, his voice the growl of a primordial animal. "In the throes of death, God revealed it all to me. Listen now, and if the crocodiles don't devour us first, I will explain to you how we, you and I, shall soon destroy the American devil once and for all."

9

JONATHAN WARD CHARGED UP THE HILL, HEAD DOWN, FEET POUNDING the pavement, a sheen of sweat on his body signifying that he was doing some good already. Inhaling the clean sea air in big gulps felt wonderful after the canned stuff he had been breathing on *Spadefish*. He loved the solid feel of the ground beneath his feet, the warm sun shining down on his back as he ran. These were the sensations of being on land that he missed when he was at sea. It was impossible to run on a submarine, of course. No way to simply jog away from the demands and worries of the boat and allow the exertion to unclench the tense knots in his muscles.

He had to thank Joe Glass for this one. The XO insisted that Ward leave the boat for a bit, go out and run until he worked up a good sweat and a better attitude. Everything else would take care of itself. He still had a couple of hours to kill before Admiral Donnegan's plane was scheduled to land. Commodore Desseaux made it plain in their brief meeting at the pier that he didn't want to talk about the situation at hand until the admiral was there to hear all sides of the story. The greetings at the pier were mechanical at best, a quick exchange of forced pleasantries and little more. The commodore quickly departed, Hunsucker following closely behind, yipping at his heels like an eager-to-please puppy.

Ward's breath was already rasping a bit as he rounded the curves on the steep hill that made up McClelland Road, stretching to the Cabrillo Gate at the top. Despite the slight burn in his lungs, he felt good, the run already serving its purpose, purging his body and soul.

The XO was right, as usual. His captain needed this in the worst way.

Now a gentle breeze brought the scent of eucalyptus down the hill. The soft sandstone cliffs, sculpted smooth and round by eons of wind and rain, rose on his left, hiding little valleys filled with ice plant and sage. As he wound up the ever-steeper hill, Ward could gaze out on this side of Point Loma and down on Shelter Island. Whether it was the view, the freshened blood pumping through his veins, or the warm, fragrant air, Jon Ward felt a sudden burst of optimism about his situation and upped the pace to match his new disposition.

"Hell, they can't shoot me!" he said aloud as he picked up the pace. He was right on this one. What was it his dad always said? "Be sure you're right, then go ahead"? The man dutifully attributed the motto to Davy Crockett, but he still took it as a mantra he always lived by.

Ward was smiling now, thinking of his dad, and was startled by the gruff voice coming up the hill behind him.

"Hey, old man! Step it up or get out of the way!"

He instinctively moved aside. He looked quickly over his shoulder to see who it was that was so rudely challenging him. He felt the good mood he had jogged himself into fading. The sun behind the newcomer made his face hard to see, but the voice was familiar.

It was a tall, younger man striding easily up the hill toward him, not even breathing hard from the climb. Ward slowed a bit to allow him to catch up.

"You wanna race this 'old man,' I'll give you fifty meters and still beat you!" Ward said in mock seriousness. Bill Beaman pulled up alongside him and the two men slapped palms. "What's the deal, B.B.? The SEALs send you over this way for a real challenge?"

The two fell into the easy rhythm of two athletes who had run together many times before. Matching strides, they rounded the final turn and waved at the guard standing by the upper gate. They ran past the Navy Station firehouse and turned left onto Cabrillo Drive, neither man talking for a stretch as they set a pace.

Lieutenant Commander Bill Beaman commanded SEAL Team Three over at the Coronado Amphib Base. He and Ward had worked together on several operations. Theirs was a mutual respect that came from each man having seen the other perform at his best under pressure. The bond of friendship was further strengthened by their love for running. It was a camaraderie that was combined with a healthy dose of competition. Even now, as they ran along, each could feel the other pushing the pace slightly.

Beaman finally glanced over at Ward.

"Where you headed?"

"Thought I'd run out around the lighthouse and back. Think you can keep up that long?"

"Should I plan on stopping at the firehouse here and grabbing some oxygen for you?" the SEAL retorted.

Ward laughed easily.

"Missed these runs. Sure feels good to climb these hills again. You getting ready for the San Diego Marathon?"

Beaman picked up the pace a tiny bit more.

"Depends on when I get back from my next trip," he said. "Looks like JDIA has us slated for an op down south. Should be an in-and-out, but there is no way of telling with those guys."

"So you're playing the anti-drug game now?" Ward asked.

"Well, it's a combination anti-drug, anti-terrorist operation. Fine line with some of these bastards. Most likely we'll be training Colombian troops on spec-ops." He glanced over at Ward. "Say, you're back early, aren't you? Didn't expect to see you huffin' and puffin' along here for another couple of weeks."

The two were running along the ridgeline now. To their left, the expansive view of Coronado Island and San Diego stretched all the way down to the hills of Tijuana. To their right was the broad, blue Pacific, and nothing but water all the way past Hawaii to Micronesia. A hawk drifted lazily on the updrafts coming off the steep sea-cliff face. Both sides of the roadway were lined with white crosses. The manicured lawn of Fort Rosecrans National Military Cemetery stretched away in each direction. It was always a stark reminder of the sacrifice their chosen profession could possibly require.

Ward didn't answer until they had passed the cemetery. His words were carefully measured.

"Had a little problem. Came in to discuss it with SUBPAC."

Beaman knew his friend too well to not pick up the tone in Ward's voice.

"Take it you don't want to discuss it?"

"No, not really." Ward picked up the pace this time, striving for a level where elaboration would be more difficult. The two men ran in silence for a few more minutes.

Beaman pulled up and stopped unexpectedly. They were alongside a bunker burrowed into the hillside to seaward just before the Cabrillo Road turned off to drop down to the Coast Guard lighthouse. Ward recognized the structure for what it was, one of the remnants of the World War II coastal-defense gun system. These bunkers had served to house a multitude of tenants over the decades, most of them very highly classified. There was no sign at the guarded gate, but that was not unusual when whatever went on behind the cement walls was so top secret.

"Got to stop here, I'm afraid." Beaman waved a thumb toward the gate. "This is my office for a while. Welcome to JDIA Headquarters." Beaman offered Ward his hand. "Sorry I couldn't give you a decent workout this afternoon. Run tomorrow?"

Ward returned the handshake.

"Don't know. Give me a call at the boat."

Beaman looked his friend directly in the eye.

"Good luck with SUBPAC."

Ward winked and jogged away. Turning around at the entrance to the Lighthouse Park, he started back, increasing his already punishing gait until he was doing a brutally fast race-pace run. Sweat was pouring from his body and his breath was coming in great, raspy gulps as he finally pulled to a stop at the brow to *Spadefish*. His body felt good from the exercise, but as soon as he saw the outline of his boat at the pier, the trouble returned to his mind once again as if it had never left.

Ward crossed the brow to the round main deck of the boat he knew and loved so well. God, he would hate to have to give her up! And if it came to that, they might just as likely decommission the old girl at the same time. What a shame. What a damned shame that would be.

Acknowledging the salute of the Quarterdeck Watch with a nod, he walked to the weapons shipping hatch. He heard the 1MC blare "*Spadefish* returning" as he dropped through the hatch and slid down the ladder.

The ladder dropped to the deck in the passageway right outside the XO's stateroom. Joe Glass jumped up to greet Ward.

"There you are, Skipper. Just about ready to send the cavalry out to find you. Squadron Secretary just called. Admiral Donnegan's plane was early. Just touched down. You're to be in the commodore's office in half an hour. And, if you don't mind me saying so, you smell sorta like an army mule."

"Anything else?" Ward asked, grabbing the towel Glass handed to him.

"No, not really," the executive officer answered. "You know how they are over there nowadays. Very officious, solving all the navy's problems with paperwork and procedure."

Ward stepped down the passageway to his stateroom.

"Yeah, I know. And all those problems are caused by those of us out here on the boats. Their job would be a lot easier without us around to complicate things, wouldn't it, Joe?"

The XO shared his commander's laugh but Ward knew that was precisely the crux of the problem. He didn't even whistle as he usually did as he showered away the honest sweat of his fine afternoon run.

Jonathan Ward's timing was perfect. As he stepped up to the door of the Maintenance Facilities Building, he spied a black Chevy with blue flags flying from each front fender, just pulling up to the security gate. The guard snapped to attention, saluted, and immediately waved the car through. It rolled to a stop right beside the door Ward was about to enter.

He stopped and saluted the tall black man who climbed out of the back of the official car. Tom Donnegan returned the greeting smartly, stepped quickly to where Ward stood, then smiled and shook the commander's hand.

"Jon, good to see you. You and Ellen have been away from Pearl too long. Now what's this trouble you're in?"

He put a hand on Ward's shoulder and guided him through the door.

"Admiral, good to see you again, too. It's like my daddy used to say, 'If it was raining soup, I'd be the only son of a bitch with a fork.'"

Donnegan grinned broadly.

"You know how I felt about your father, Jon. And even some of those corny expressions of his."

"Well, I'm afraid that Mike Hunsucker and I had a little disagreement during my TRE."

The two of them walked side by side as they started to climb the metal stairs from the workshops on the first deck to the offices that were housed on the second.

Donnegan stopped halfway up and turned to Ward. He looked the commander directly in the eye.

"Not quite the way I heard it, Captain. Word I got was that you stopped the TRE prematurely, then wouldn't let Hunsucker back in Control." The admiral glanced around him, making sure no one else was within earshot. "I never have liked that twerp. He's been walking around like a damned war hero just because he lobbed a couple of missiles into Serbia and somebody gave him a medal for it." He looked directly at Ward once again and went on. "Now, let me give you a little advice, and you listen closely, Commander. When we get in there, you tell your story, tell it right, then shut up your cake hole. Try to keep that famous temper of yours under control. That's another thing you inherited from your old man. Let me handle this. Understand?"

Ward nodded, then kept quiet the rest of the way as the two walked on up the stairs to Commodore Desseaux's headquarters.

The office was richly appointed with a large walnut desk, overstuffed leather chairs and sofa, and hardwood paneling. Desseaux had worked hard to make the office appear to be the large stateroom he would have enjoyed if he still had a sub tender for a flagship. Even the brass lamps and wall brackets had been salvaged to enhance the atmosphere. Ward half expected the deck to rock gently beneath his feet any time he had an audience with the commodore, as if they might be afloat.

Both Desseaux and Hunsucker rose from their seats at the long conference table and walked over to greet Admiral Donnegan. Both men's eyes widened when they saw Ward step through the door behind the admiral and it was clear the two men had come in together. The air in the room seemed heavy, as if a thunderstorm lurked just over the horizon. Ward could only imagine what the two men had been discussing prior to their arrival.

Donnegan waved aside the formalities and dropped into the chair at the head of the table.

"All right, gentlemen, please tell me I didn't fly all the way here just to referee a spat between two little boys. I don't have the time or the patience for that kind of nonsense."

Desseaux took a deep breath and began.

"Admiral, it appears—"

"Appears?" Donnegan interrupted. "I would have assumed you would have sorted out whatever we have going on here to the extent that you would know for sure if we have an issue or not."

The commodore swallowed hard and started over.

"Admiral, we most certainly have a disagreement that has

arisen concerning the conduct of a TRE on board *Spadefish*. It raises concerns about the capabilities of the commander and the fitness of his crew. Captain Hunsucker was running a series of operational drills that had been approved by me as well as by your staff. He briefed the drills with Commander Ward prior to running them. It is my understanding that Commander Ward did not object to the proposed drills at that time. He only objected after his crew was not able to adequately respond to the TRE. From what I have learned, and from all appearances, it seems to me that Commander Ward has not trained his crew properly, and that he terminated a test when that fact was obvious to Captain Hunsucker and his TRE team. Clearly, this is a serious matter. We would not have involved you had it been anything less."

Jon Ward could not suppress a disgusted snort. Donnegan held up a warning hand in his direction.

"Just a minute, Commander. You will have your chance. Captain Hunsucker, what do you have to add?"

Hunsucker wiggled uncomfortably in his seat.

"Not much, Admiral. As the commodore said, I briefed Commander Ward completely, received his consent, then ran the drills. His boat was not performing well at all. I'm afraid that if we continued, they would have been 'Unsat.' He did not allow us that opportunity. He terminated the drill and refused to allow me in Control in one of the most blatant examples of insubordination I've witnessed in my twenty-four years in this man's navy."

Donnegan showed no emotion, no indication that he had heard a word Hunsucker had said. He turned to Ward.

"Okay, Commander, what do you have to say about this matter?"

Jon Ward's mouth felt as if he had been chewing steel wool. A strange calm came over him, the same steady hand on his shoulder that always mysteriously showed up when things got dicey. That dependable composure had gotten him through far more dismal situations than this. Besides, he had right on his side here. All he had to do was tell the truth. His voice was strong and sure when he spoke.

"Admiral, I'm sorry you had to be called here to straighten this out. Captain Hunsucker is correct on most points. The TRE was not going well, but it had nothing to do with my crew or their readiness. He had intentionally set the test up in a way that we couldn't possibly succeed. I could even live with that fact, but most certainly not when the safety of my ship and men was threatened. I had no choice but to act and that's exactly what I did."

Hunsucker was turning purple. The cords in his neck stood out like knotted rope.

"Go on, Commander," Donnegan said. "Explain yourself."

"As he stated, Captain Hunsucker briefed me, but it was on a relatively routine torpedo evasion and flooding drill. The precautions he briefed were appropriate for that drill. No mention was made about tripping the turbine generators or about another boat being in the area. My XO was present and can verify the scope of the briefing. There was no way I would have allowed a drill that dangerous to be run. That's why I stopped the drill and the TRE."

Hunsucker jumped up and shouted, "He's covering for his people's incompetence! It was a perfectly realistic situation!"

Ward looked hard at Hunsucker but went ahead and answered the interruption, unable to keep the sarcasm from his voice.

"Once again, the captain is correct on his final point. I agree that it was a perfectly realistic situation. It was so realistic that people almost got killed, just as they would have if it had been war-shot torpedoes. This was supposed to be an exercise and we don't usually kill people in exercises, at least not on purpose."

Ward sat back, hoping the anger he felt didn't show in his face.

Commodore Desseaux broke in.

"Admiral, *Spadefish* is an old boat. She's scheduled for de-comm in six months. This was to be her last TRE anyway.

Since Commander Ward doesn't think his boat is up to a TRE, I suggest we just accelerate the decommissioning schedule. Problem neatly solved."

Ward jumped to his feet.

"Now, just a second! I never said—"

Donnegan interrupted.

"Jon, sit down please. I know precisely what you said." The admiral re-crossed his long legs and took a leisurely sip of his coffee. The room was so quiet that the ticking of the old-fashioned brass ship's clock on the wall behind Desseaux's desk sounded like a time bomb. "Commodore, you've made no secret of your desire to get rid of the old boats that are eating up your limited resources. I can appreciate that. But with all the downsizing already, we're at a grand total of eighteen boats in the entire Pacific. They're even decommissioning the '688' boats now, for Pete's sake. Right this minute, I need every submarine I've got that'll float." Then he looked directly at Hunsucker. "Captain, I don't know just where you fit into this, but I have my suspicions. I think you and I will spend a little time with the chief of staff discussing what took place out there once you get back to Pearl."

If it was possible, Hunsucker's face grew even purpler. A private discussion with the admiral and his chief of staff would be neither pleasant nor an enhancement to his career. He glowered at Ward.

Donnegan seemed to take no notice and went on.

"Now, I think we need something to keep *Spadefish* occupied and to justify her existence for a while longer. And I think I have just the thing to keep her out of your hair, Commodore. JDIA needs a surveillance platform down off Colombia. Say a month to refit and do some workup exercises, then a nice leisurely transit down there. Jon, talk to Ops out in Pearl and make it happen." Admiral Donnegan abruptly pushed back his chair and rose to leave. "Now, if you gentlemen will excuse me, I have a plane to catch back to Pearl."

He walked out and closed the door.

Without a word, Mike Hunsucker stood, paused to give the

admiral a reasonable head start, then angrily stalked out of the room.

"Good day, Commodore," Jon said as he stood and started for the door himself.

"Just a second, Jon. Looks like you won that round. I know you and Mike don't get along. You should know that I have nothing personal against you. The admiral was right about resources. I barely have enough of what it takes to keep the seven '688s' that I have operational. Get with my materials officer and let him know what you need. Please keep it to the essentials. We'll do all we can. You have my assurance of that." He held out his hand. "No hard feelings?"

Ward took no measure of satisfaction in seeing Desseaux backpedal, and with so little grace. Still, he shook the offered hand. Desseaux's grip was loose and clammy.

"I appreciate your help, sir. No hard feelings," Ward said, and flashed the commodore a brilliant smile.

Unbelievable! He had come into this meeting fully expecting to lose his ship, maybe even have her funeral moved up six months. Now he was leaving with an actual mission, fuzzy as it was.

Streetlights were snapping on around the base as he stepped outside, the sun having already dropped below the high ridge of Point Loma. He was surprised to see the black Chevrolet still parked in the shadows of the building, almost lost in the gathering dusk. As he walked past, the rear door swung open.

"Get in, Jon. I'll give you a ride home," Admiral Donnegan ordered.

He joined Donnegan in the backseat and the car rolled away down Rosecrans. The driver unexpectedly turned up McClelland Road instead of driving straight on down Rosecrans.

"Jon, we need to make a stop up here first. Something that I want you to see, and it relates to what you're getting into. My real reason for flying over here."

The car passed through the Cabrillo Gate and turned left, heading out Cabrillo Drive toward the sea. The two rode in silence except for the jazz radio station playing from the speak-

ers behind them. The car turned in to the bunker where Ward
had already been once that day, the one Bill Beaman had
pointed out earlier as the headquarters of the Joint Drug Interdiction Agency. The metal gate obediently slid back to allow
the admiral's car into the cramped parking compound.

Donnegan led Ward to the giant blastproof metal door. It had
been designed to withstand bombardment from the sixteen-
inch guns of World War II battleships with their armor-piercing
shells the size of Volkswagens. The door eased open silently
when Donnegan swiped a small card across the optical scanner.
They descended the metal stairs into the brightly lit interior of
the bunker.

"Evening, Admiral." The man who greeted them was non-
descript in every way, middle-aged, medium height, medium
build, medium brown hair, someone who would never stand
out in a crowd. His eyes betrayed him. They burned brightly,
revealing an inner intensity that was impossible to hide. "So
this must be your submariner."

"Evening, John," Donnegan answered. "Allow me to introduce Commander Jonathan Ward, CO of *Spadefish*. Jon, meet
John Bethea, head of the Joint Drug Interdiction Agency, and
the worst nightmare of the bastards who would pollute our
people with their poison."

Bethea showed the slightest of smiles in reaction to Donnegan's compliment. He shook Ward's hand. His gaze was direct, powerful, almost hypnotic.

"I've heard good things about you, Commander. Please follow me. We're ready to start the briefing in the secure briefing
room."

Briefing?

He showed them the way down still more steps, past another optical scanner checkpoint, and further into the bowels
of the hillside.

Ward looked around curiously as they wound their way
downward.

"Interesting place you have here, Mr. Bethea."

"Yes, as a matter of fact, it is. This bunker was originally modified back in the sixties, during the Cold War . . . in your dad's time . . . to give the Pacific Command a secret emergency command post that could withstand a direct hit by a nuclear weapon." Ward glanced over at Bethea. If he knew about his father, what else did he know about him? Bethea didn't seem to notice the quizzical look on the commander's face. "It was modified again in the seventies when things got considerably more scientific. The NSA needed a place that couldn't be monitored by any kind of remote sensor that we knew of then. We were finding out how good technology could be for gathering information. Our satellites were having a field day with the Soviets. We needed a place here that was protected from that very kind of technology. We knew they would have it soon, too. Hell, this place probably shows up as a black hole!"

They had finally reached the bottom of the stairs. In front of them stood a metal door with a plaque that proclaimed the room on the other side to be the JDIA SECURE BRIEFING ROOM. Bethea led them inside.

"NSA used this place mostly to analyze all the information *Halibut* and *Parche* brought back from their cable taps."

Ward well remembered all the fallout after the disclosure of those highly secret missions. The subs penetrated deeply into the Sea of Okhotsk, in the icy waters between the Kamchatka Peninsula and Siberia, and were able to tap previously secure underwater cables that ran between Soviet command centers. That intelligence haul had been awesome. That is, until a spy tipped off the Soviets and the source was lost for good.

"Anyway, we inherited it last year when we and our allies formed the agency. Perfect for us. Very few people even know it's here. Even the communications are funneled through you submariners down at Ballast Point. We can stay as anonymous as is possible these days. And believe me, that's crucial with the enemy we're up against. It's amazing what degree of technology all that drug money can afford to buy."

The room they entered was small and brightly lit. It was dominated by a large, colorful map of South America that filled most of the far wall. Several chairs were arranged around a small conference table in the center of the room. Otherwise, the room was empty, undecorated, utilitarian.

Bethea walked across to the map.

"Captain, I'm going to keep this brief. I know you haven't been home since you came in port, so I won't keep you away from your wife any longer than necessary. We'll have a full set of briefing papers delivered by courier to *Spadefish* in the morning." He pointed to an area of blue, the Pacific Ocean just outside Colombian territorial waters. "We want you to patrol in this area here. For all intents and purposes, you are there to eavesdrop on any rebel radio communications. That will be the classified cover story." The man looked directly at Ward as he talked, his eyes even more intense. "The real mission is classified 'Top Secret, Special Category.' The code word is 'Inca Trail.' 'Inca' for 'Interdiction Colombia.' We'll have a team in there, making use of some of the trails the Incas first cut. That whole area was the northernmost part of the Inca Empire at one time. As you may know, we have been helping the Colombian government with military aid for some time to fight the drug trade down there, with admittedly mixed results.

"What you don't know is that we have been conducting covert operations against Juan de Santiago, the rebel leader who just happens to be the region's biggest drug kingpin. He's convinced a reasonable number of his people that the only way for them to win the revolution is by growing, processing, and exporting a staggering amount of cocaine and heroin. He's been very good at it, and we suspect he has quite a bit of assistance from some very shadowy folks who have even less ideological stake in this thing than de Santiago does. As I say, we've had some limited success so far. Trouble is, they have some very sophisticated intelligence. When we find a base, by the time the Colombians can mount a strike, the base or a fac-

tory has usually disappeared without a trace. We need a way
to secretly hit him, hard and quickly, before he can get wind
of the operation and disappear into the jungle. That's where
you and your boat fit in. You will be loaded out with Tomahawk missiles. When we locate the bases, you will be the
fangs of the snake that will strike de Santiago. Think you can
handle it?"

Ward nodded forcefully, then turned to Admiral Tom Donnegan. He couldn't suppress the smile. No more TREs. No
more keeping his boat afloat for little more than the amuse-
ment of the tourists when they pulled into port. As of ten seconds ago, *Spadefish* had a valid reason to continue her proud
existence.

"Sir, you got yourself a boat."

10

JUAN DE SANTIAGO STARED IN WONDER AT THE INCONGRUOUS SIGHT
before him. He was ten thousand feet up in the Andes, two
hundred miles from the Pacific Ocean, yet the shape before
him was unmistakably that of a submarine. At over thirty meters long, it filled the warehouse with its brooding, black
form.

"You have done well, Philippe," he said to the dapper businessman standing beside him. "When will it be ready?"

Philippe Zurko cleared his throat. He was one of de Santiago's closest friends and had marched with him from the beginning of the revolution. Like everyone else, he was cautious
when in the presence of the great man. He knew that de Santiago did not take bad news well and had become sensitive
since the latest attempted assassination. The matter of El Fal-

cone had driven a massive wedge between de Santiago and his lieutenants. He also knew the leader was distressed about the problems back at the laboratory. He knew the best way to deal with the man was to plunge ahead, giving him good news first, then the bad.

"El Jefe, the hull is near completion, as you can see," Zurko began. "The control systems and the navigation electronics will arrive next week. We have bought, through our sources in Pakistan, the control system directly from the Servdovinsk Shipyard. It was originally built for a Project 1832A Zibrus mini-sub and will fit our needs as precisely as if it had been designed exclusively for us."

De Santiago interjected, "I would expect nothing less. Our Russian guests designed that boat, after all." He nodded in the general direction of the three stolid Slavic men who were standing quietly to one side, smoking cigarettes and watching de Santiago warily. Their pallor and thick, heavy bodies were contrasted with the dark Latin features and muscled physique of de Santiago. And even Zurko, who, though tall and slender, was still well honed from his fighting days.

"El Jefe, the *Zibrus* was an inspired design," Zurko said. "A submarine that can crawl on the sea bottom. It is indeed unfortunate that the Swedes found its tracks outside Karlskrona."

The Russians in the room noticeably bristled when they heard the mention of "Karlskrona." That's where the Swedes had discovered the first attempted operational use of their mini-sub, even if quite by accident. If it hadn't been for the navigational error of the stupid captain of the archaic *Whiskey*-boat, if he had not foolishly run aground inside Swedish territorial waters, their prize would never have been discovered. Now they, not the captain who had made the unfortunate mistake, were the butt of all the jokes about "*Whiskey* on the rocks."

"Philippe, you have lectured me at length about the control system on this submarine. And you have described over and over the caterpillar tracks that allow it to be driven on the bottom of the sea. I know more than I would ever need to know about its navigation system." Juan de Santiago paused pointedly for breath, then looked at Zurko through his dark, bushy eyebrows. "What you have been carefully avoiding telling me about is the power plant. What drives this boat, my friend? What makes her go?"

Zurko sputtered, started to say something else, but bit his lower lip instead. Former Captain Third Rank Rudi Sergiovski, the middle one in the group of three Russian submariners, cleared his throat. In halting Spanish, he began, "*Perdóneme*, El Jefe, but I have thoughts on the subject. The *Zibrus* was designed for short missions with power to be supplied by the batteries. She is a boat with a quite limited range. You have demanded a much larger boat with much longer range. The batteries, of course, will not be enough."

De Santiago looked hard at the Russian then back out at the boat that was being assembled before him.

"Very well, El Capitán, what do you suggest? Do we equip her with a set of oars and row our way along? I remind you, we have already spent thirty million rubles on this boat and we would prefer that there be some way to propel her through the water."

The implied threat hung heavy in the air.

"El Jefe," Sergiovski answered, "the only solution is an air-independent propulsion system. We have three choices. The Swedes have a fuel cell technology. The Germans have adapted a liquid oxygen system to drive their 'type 209' diesel boat. And the Italians are using a liquid oxygen/hydrogen power plant." He paused for effect. "We merely have to acquire one of these."

"When we go shopping, which one of these devices do you propose?" de Santiago asked, the sarcasm heavy in his voice. "I should remind you, *Capitán*, our arrangement was for a delivered submarine, not for suppositions or a boat that runs on horse shit."

"Don't worry. We shall have our solution quite soon, I believe,' Sergiovski said with a conspiratorial wink. "Now, if you will only join my comrades and me for a glass of *wodka*, I will explain precisely how we will do it."

Lieutenant Yani Zurkoskovich silently broke the surface of the glassy, calm water. The midnight black was heavy, impenetrable.

What was it the American SEALs said? "The night is your friend."

Most of his life had been spent preparing himself to fight against the Americans in the Great War of Liberation. Years of SPETNAZ training had honed him. He was a fine, killing machine, one of the powerful weapons his nation would use against the capitalist devils when the time came to spread the revolution to the Americans. Now it had all fallen apart. His once-mighty country had been split up. Reduced to nothing more than a jigsaw puzzle on a confusing, demoralizing map. Here he was. No longer a weapon of the masses, but a prostitute mercenary, swimming his way through frigid Swedish waters in the black of the night. All for a few rubles so he could feed his wife and babushka and buy enough coal to keep their squalid little apartment from freezing over.

He shook off his rising depression. He still had skills that were in demand, if not by the Russian people, then at least by someone. Someone he didn't know and who he preferred remain anonymous. And tonight, he had a job to do. A job that would require his ultimate concentration.

The lights of the shipyard pierced the night a few hundred yards to his right. They danced and sparkled on the water's surface, guiding him toward shore. He could see the headlamps of the trucks barreling down the E-22 far off in the distance. His eyes adjusted. He could make out the tendrils of mist rising from the ice-cold water into the even colder air. Sea smoke, they called it.

Two more heads broke the surface on either side of him. The other two members of his team looked at Zurkoskovich questioningly. He pointed toward the pier. With hand signs, he told them to rendezvous there.

Lieutenant Zurkoskovich took a careful bearing on the pier and dropped below the surface. He hoped there was enough air in his rebreather to make it in and out again. They would be cutting it very close. The current farther out was stronger than he planned, the swim much harder and longer than anticipated.

The little fishing boat out of Riga was the best cover they could manage on short notice and limited budget. No submarine to sneak as close as possible inside the Karlskrona archipelago this time. The fishing grounds were farther out. The boat delivered them as close as they dared. He only hoped the sleazy Latvian fishermen he bribed would stay long enough to pick them up again. That the cold wouldn't cause them to decide to forfeit the rest of their money.

He swam silently. Zurkoskovich felt rather than heard the slow, heavy beat above him. It was from the screw of the patrol boat. It passed ten feet above his back as it finished another of its continuous circuits of the inner harbor. If his intelligence was correct, the Swedes hadn't changed the patrol cycle since he was last here. They had exactly forty-four minutes until the boat returned.

The three men surfaced next to the wooden pilings beneath the long pier. No light penetrated here. He checked his watch. They had forty-two minutes before the patrol boat returned with its probing searchlights. With a few more strokes, they could feel the sandy bottom under their feet. Sand and shells washed up against the headwall to form a narrow beach.

They tore off their rebreathers and dry suits. They wore Swedish Navy uniforms underneath. Zurkoskovich carried no weapons except the wickedly sharp fighting knife he always kept strapped to his back. If they needed other weapons, they had already failed this mission.

The diving gear was quickly buried in the soft sand.

Zurkoskovich peeked cautiously above the headwall. No one there. He lifted himself up the two-meter-high wall and looked around more carefully. Still no one.

Strangely quiet for the most important naval base in the Baltic, he thought. He knew that with his country now dismantled, the whole world had seemingly relaxed. A quick hand sign and the three men stood together at the head of the pier. They were merely three sailors taking a break from their duties for a smoke in the brisk night air.

They strolled along casually. It was as if they belonged in this place, sauntering over toward the large brick building across the road from the pier. Zurkoskovich translated the Swedish lettering on the little brass plaque next to the door. HEADQUARTERS, SUBMARINE DESIGN BUREAU. He walked through the door while his companions stepped a short distance to the right and left before blending into the landscape. They were his warning if any unpleasant surprise should appear. It was unlikely.

The guard inside the door was barely awake. Zurkoskovich passed his ID under the glass grille. Sleepy eyes gave it a cursory glance before it was slid back to him. The red light beside the door changed to green. The guard was back asleep before the door swung shut.

The long halls were empty. The glass doors he passed on each side opened into equally empty offices. Down one long hall, turn right, then down another, just as he had been briefed.

The lettering on the glass door read AIP SECTION. The door was locked, as expected. Zurkoskovich inspected it carefully. No telltale wires or contact pads. The Swedes weren't concerned enough about this section to install a security system.

He produced a little flexible plastic strip from his pocket. It made quick work of defeating the simple lock and Zurkoskovich was inside. He opened the door carefully, in case the Swedes had installed a more sophisticated alarm system. No bells or sirens. A good sign. He listened for armed troops who could be rushing his way without him knowing it, cued by some silent alarm. Nothing. His intelligence had proven to be correct. This highly sensitive area had surprisingly lax security. He went quickly to work.

Zurkoskovich booted up the computer at a desk marked

SVEN HARLINSON, CHIEF ENGINEER. A few seconds later and he was in. The passwords his employer supplied him worked the first time.

He copied the files he needed from the computer to a Zip disk he had brought with him. He noticed there was an icon on the desktop of the machine for a program labeled "Requisitions in Progress." He smiled as he double-clicked to open the file. He found the database for all the fuel-cell power plants now in production. Well, nothing ventured, nothing gained. Give it a try. It might well mean a bonus for him from his employer. A few keystrokes and one system ordered by the Royal Australian Navy and about to be shipped was now rerouted to a small Peruvian port. For good measure, he marked the invoice "paid in full."

While the computer was copying files to the Zip disk, Zurkoskovich searched for hard-copy files in the cabinets that lined the office wall. He pulled the miniature digital camera from a pocket and carefully photographed several papers and drawings; always keeping his senses tuned for any sign that someone might be coming.

Ten minutes at Harlinson's desk and he had the complete design for the fuel cell system on the disk. The pop-up window on the computer screen said, "All Files Copied." Nothing to be gained by searching any further here.

Zurkoskovich shut down the computer and carefully surveyed the office. No sign he had ever been there. He slipped out the door, locked it, and sauntered down the hallways. The door guard didn't even look up when he walked past him on his way out. He was sleeping soundly.

Outside, he gave a wave of his hand. His two sentries appeared from out of the shadows. They were three sailors, walking together down the street, a little unsteady, laughing and talking a bit too loudly, on their way back to their ship after a late night in town. No one who saw them would give them a second thought or even remember their passing.

They made their way to the headwall of the pier and

stopped for a smoke under the streetlight. Two cars drove by. There were no sirens, no screeching tires, no hail of bullets.

Karlskrona slept peacefully, completely unaware of their presence.

The last car turned and drove out of sight. They were alone with the night. With a slight wave of his hand, Zurkoskovich sent each of his companions over the edge. With a final glance around, he dropped to the little beach below. The three struggled clumsily back into their dry suits. They strapped the re-breathers on their backs. Zurkoskovich carefully put the disk and camera in a waterproof pouch, sealed it, and zipped it inside the dry suit.

He patted the bulge and smiled. It had been so easy. Almost too easy. He checked his watch. Still eight minutes before the patrol boat would come back past. They had made it with time to spare. All they had to do was swim back to the fishing boat and make their way home. In a day, he would have his money, and he could already smell his wife's cabbage and beef cooking on the stove, already feel her warmth next to him once again.

The three men slipped back into the water and quietly dropped out of sight. Not a ripple, not a bubble betrayed their passage under the icy cold water. Even if someone had been on the end of the pier, he would have never suspected that three swimmers moved along directly beneath him, quickly moving toward the mouth of the harbor.

They swam just below the surface on a bearing that took them beyond the small inshore islands. Little more than rocks breaking the surface of the inner harbor. Skirting the last of the rocks, Zurkoskovich changed course a few degrees to the south, aiming for the strait between Aspo and Tjurko islands. In mere moments, they would be safely away.

He didn't see the small transceiver floating just above the bottom of the harbor. He couldn't hear the eighty-five-kilohertz active sonar. It was far above the frequency range of any man's hearing. But the pinging painted a clear picture of his and his partners' passing for the harbor security control center.

The three had just entered the straits between Aspo and Tjurko when they heard the high-pitched whine of the patrol boat approaching from behind them. It was headed somewhere at deliberate high speed.

They heard another patrol boat coming from somewhere in front of them and it, too, was screaming through the water. The screw beat behind grew louder and more distinct, the one in front rose to a crescendo.

Zurkoskovich signaled and they quickly dove for the bottom. If they had somehow been discovered, they had no choice but to hide among the rocks and mud until the patrol boats gave up and stopped looking. The three swam with long powerful kicks of their flippers, moving quickly, just inches above the bottom. They were only a few hundred meters from the open waters of the Baltic now.

They could hear the two boats as they passed directly overhead. They wheeled around and raced by again. Zurkoskovich and his cohorts could not see the sailors on the deck of the two Type-80 *Tapper*-class patrol boats as they removed the safety locks from the ELMA ASW grenade launchers.

He heard multiple splashes all around him.

The grenades, similar to the Soviet RGB-60 depth-charge rockets, were meant to disable an intruding submarine. Each carried thirty kilos of high explosives. Even a single grenade detonating within fifty meters of a diver would be fatal. Six grenades from each of the two patrol boats sank in a rough ten-meter circle around the divers.

They detonated two meters from the bottom.

Yani Zurkoskovich felt the first fist slam of the concussion drive him hard into the muddy bottom and rip away his mask.

There was a blinding flash of white, then nothingness.

The diver lay motionless on the harbor floor. The computer disk and digital camera still formed a bulge inside the wet suit next to his lifeless body.

11

TOM KINCAID SLAMMED THE TELEPHONE DOWN IN FRUSTRATION. HE had spent the better part of the last week placing phone calls that had played out almost identically to this latest one. Phone numbers from his past, most not even answered. He had long ago grown tired of the much-too-sweet but officious mechanical voice: "The number you have dialed is no longer a working number." Even more tiring were the ones that did answer, then either pretended not to know who he was or slammed down the phone before he even had a chance to tell them why he was calling.

The most disturbing were those who alternately cried or cursed as they reported that the party he was calling was no longer among the living. And some even spat the blame right back at Kincaid himself.

"You promised him safety if he helped you," they said. "You may as well have pulled the trigger. You killed him! As surely as the *revolucionarios*. You killed him!"

He got the opportunity to explain himself to only a couple of the people he called and they feigned deafness or a bad line and quickly disconnected. He had drawn a total blank.

Rick Taylor's political grandstanding had completely destroyed the invaluable network he had spent so much time and personal capital wiring together. He was reaching the end of his contact database. Going through DEA channels was no option. If Taylor caught even the slightest whiff that Kincaid was doing more than "Just Say No" high-school-assembly presentations, that he was back in business and looking for information, he would drop a ton of bricks on him. Even worse, the bastard would likely have his storm troopers descend on the Pacific Northwest like a Vandal horde, accompanied by a mob of media types, all of them trampling into the mud any chance for a real investigation into what was going on.

There had already been six more ODs since the girl, Sandy Holmes, was found under the bridge. Smartly dressed young people, four women, two men, none with any record or signs of previous coke use, but with their systems loaded with enough of the stuff to kill a horse. There was another common thread. Each of the young women had been well used before they died or shortly afterward. There was none of the usual evidence of a rape. No torn clothes, no bruising from a struggle, no skin from their attackers beneath their fingernails. None was typical. Each was a mystery. A damned deadly mystery.

Kincaid checked the clock on his office wall and came close to calling it a night. It was almost midnight on the East Coast by then. His stomach was growling. He had forgotten to eat since a quick breakfast with Lieutenant Ken Temple in some cop café downtown.

There was one last number to try, one last hope. Might as well make it a clean sweep so he could say he had left no stone unturned. Kincaid punched in the number from memory, a South Florida area code. It rang twice, then went silent. He punched in another series of numbers from his mental database and listened to the faint click as several relays kicked in, the connection being rerouted to Cartagena on the Colombian coast.

It rang six, seven, eight times, and he was ready to drop the telephone and go looking for a cheeseburger and a cup of coffee.

Then someone on the other end picked up the call, fumbled with the instrument, and there was a faint, sleepy, *"Sí?"*

Kincaid hardly recognized the voice.

"Pepe, that you?"

There was a moment's silence, a sharp intake of breath. When the man spoke again, he was wide awake.

"Señor Kincaid. I do not wish to speak with you. Good-bye."

Kincaid spoke hurriedly before the man could slam down the telephone.

"Pepe, listen to me. It was not me who brought on the trouble. Taylor canned me and forced the investigation and in the process, he turned all of you. Please don't hang up. It's very important and I need your help." Tom Kincaid quickly played his ace card. "You know you owe it to me, Pepe."

Pepe Licciardi was the last name on the list of Kincaid's informants and most likely the one closest to the Colombian drug producers. Kincaid had saved him until last because he was certain he would no longer be among the living. But he was. Amazingly enough, he was. If anyone could find out for him what was happening, Pepe could.

When he finally spoke again, the distant voice was little more than a reluctant growl.

"Awwww, Señor Kincaid," Licciardi moaned. "What a remarkably inopportune time for you to try to collect on a debt, my friend."

There was a considerable obligation due Tom Kincaid. The American agent had risked his own life, pulling a wounded Licciardi from a blazing, shot-up car only seconds before it exploded. That was Cartagena, almost ten years before.

"I'm sorry, Pepe. I would not be asking if it was not important."

"Señor Kincaid, you must understand. It is *muy* dangerous now," the Colombian said in a raspy whisper. "Worse even than ten years ago. De Santiago is one bad hombre. The man is convinced in his own mind that he is chosen by God to save his people. And that he should do it with the coca. There is much going on, my friend. Maybe even more than when you were here last. The *revolucionarios* now control all the coca fields. No one is trusted anymore. They are desperate and moving on so many fronts." Licciardi's voice grew even quieter. "They are everywhere. The walls can hear my words. I think sometimes even my old cat is an informant."

"Listen, Pepe. Something is happening here that may be related to what you're telling me, something that has me very concerned. We have evidence of a particularly high grade of coke that has been introduced here in the States. And it's very powerful. It is killing folks. Common folks, not the usual addicts."

"I have heard rumors of such a new product."

"New product?"

"Awwww!" Licciardi groaned again. "I should keep my mouth shut. It is muy dangerous here, Señor Kincaid. So very dangerous. But yes, I have heard rumors. Rumors of a very powerful, very addictive powder. Something they have been testing in your country. That's all I've heard. I swear! If any of de Santiago's thugs suspected that I knew even that much . . ."

"This is de Santiago's way of increasing demand? Of reaching a new clientele? A strain of highly addictive cocaine. That would make sense."

"I do not know. *Madre de Dios!* I swear on my mother's eyes . . ."

"And how will he deliver his new product, Pepe? If this is a new thrust, he will have to have distribution for it to make any sense at all. We've only seen it here in Seattle so far and it appears to be coming through a new supplier that we don't know anything about. Do you know anything about that? Can you find out?" Kincaid paused for effect. "Remember. You have had ten more years of life because I was able to pull you from that inferno, Pepe."

The man on the other end of the phone line seemed on the edge of tears. His voice quavered when he answered.

"Yes. I owe you my life. And for that reason, I will try. For you, my friend, I will try. But don't expect much. Even for you, I can't do miracles. And now, I have a beautiful wife who loves me and a little daughter who draws pictures of birds and flowers *en la escuela* and brings them to me each day. For you . . . and for them . . . I will see what I can learn. The usual contact number?"

Kincaid breathed a sigh of relief.

"Yes. Taylor doesn't know all there is to know. And thank you, Pepe. You will save many lives if you can get me even the smallest bit of information. But, Pepe, be careful. I don't have many friends left, I'm afraid, and I don't want to lose you. I am now in your debt. And please kiss your wife and *nina bonita* for me."

Licciardi laughed, but there was no humor there.

"I will be careful, my friend."

The line went dead.

Kincaid was pulling his raincoat on when the phone rang. He almost ignored it, allowed the voice mail to get it, but something in its shrill chime urged him to answer.

He dropped his head and reached for the damned thing.

"So, let me explain once again. You have been asking the wrong questions of the wrong people, Señor Licciardi. That is why you have been brought here."

The brutal torture had begun hours ago. Juan de Santiago stood quietly behind the one-way mirror the entire time, watching with great interest. Guzmán was an artist at this. He almost never failed, but this time he was having little success. Still, de Santiago's pleasure in observing him work bordered on the sensual. It was almost like watching the matador working *el toro*, but this bull could resist only with willpower and defiance.

Tears streaked the tortured man's face. He tried to blank out the awful pain in his groin but it was impossible. The alligator clips attached to his scrotum hurt bad enough on their own, but when the swarthy man with the complacent expression on his face impassively flipped the switch on the box he held, the pain was excruciating.

"I swear I was only curious," he managed to squawk through parched lips. "I once worked with Señor de Santiago . . . in the early days of the revolution. I only wondered what—"

The red-hot bolt of fire seemed to rip his testicles apart, to explode inside his lower abdomen. He screeched, bawled, begged.

De Santiago paced back and forth behind the glass. He was rapidly losing patience. This was fruitless. This man, this Pepe Licciardi, was too strong. So far, what little information he had provided was worthless. Still, de Santiago wondered with grudging admiration how the man could withstand the pain. It was truly a wonder and most unfortunate that he had used that determination to betray his leader.

"You will tell me who ordered you to ask the questions. Who is paying you to be disloyal to your own people? You will tell me what you know of the JDIA."

"I . . . know . . . nothing . . . JDIA . . ."

His bladder was instantly filled with molten lava and his legs jerked spasmodically. He gagged and vomited hot bile.

De Santiago had seen enough. This was futile.

"It would be so much simpler for you, Señor Licciardi, if you—"

Pepe Licciardi heard the door crash open and someone else burst into the room, interrupting the interrogator's ominous but soft-spoken words. As he tried to turn his head to see who it was, he felt someone grab his hair and brutally jerk back his head. Something hot raked across his throat all the way from one ear to the other. Oddly there was little pain, but he thought he felt his own warm blood flowing down his chest.

"Good enough for him. He'll bleed dry in moments. And he'll never turn on his old boss again."

"But El Jefe, I was on the verge of learning—"

"This one would never tell you what you want to know. Take him home. Leave his corpse somewhere where others will see what happens to the traitors of the revolution."

"As you wish, El Jefe. As you wish."

Commander Jonathan Ward climbed down the long ladder into *Spadefish*'s engine room lower level. Dave Kuhn was just climbing up out of the bilge when he hopped off the last rung. The engineer's blue poopie suit was slimy with grease, water, and dirt.

"Bilge diving again, Eng?" Ward asked with a laugh.

The bilges in these old boats collected all the oil leaks, sea-water leak-off from the pumps, and anything else that might find its way down there. Working on the equipment down there was always a dirty, messy job, but there was no other way.

Ward remembered when he himself was the engineer of a boat. He was in the Officers' Club at the Royal Naval Base in Plymouth, England, comparing notes with the chief engineer of the HMS *Superb* over some very good Scotch. Ward was complaining about having to crawl through the bilges of his boat, making sure they were cleaned and painted. His Brit counterpart looked at him strangely.

"Blimey, mate," he said sardonically. "You crawl through your bilges? We shit in ours!"

Kuhn looked up when he heard the skipper's voice.

"Yeah, Chief Bechtold was showing me the packing gland on number two main seawater pump. Been running hot lately. Don't like the looks of it."

The equally grimy machinist mate chief stuck his head up from the bilge when he heard his name. His chin almost rested on the steel diamond treads of the deck plates. He grabbed a rag and began to smear the oil that coated his hands and face.

"I don't like it, Eng," he said. "She needs to be fixed. Means cracking the pump casing open and pulling the motor though."

The huge, three-speed electric motor stood six feet high and weighed at least a ton. Lifting it up off the casing was not a minor matter. In addition to its huge size and weight, a lot of piping and other equipment would be in their way, too.

Kuhn looked back up at Ward.

"Skipper, it means dry-docking to fix. No way to get all these leaky valves to hold while we have the pump lifted. I'd say at least two weeks."

Ward looked at the engineer, then over at the recalcitrant pump.

"That means a delay in 'under way.' How bad is it?"

"Well, sir, it might hold until decommissioning," Bechtold

reluctantly answered. "Then again, it might seize up next week. No way of telling." Bechtold had been the leading machinist on *Spadefish* for close to ten years. Both Ward and Kuhn deferred to his experience with her mechanical equipment. "But we still have the emergency flax packing, and if worse comes to worse, we can operate on one pump. It'll just limit our speed some."

Ward thought for a moment.

"Yeah, limit her speed to about twenty knots. Less when we get in warm water. It'll have to do, though. We simply don't have the time to go to dry dock and fix it now." He squatted down and handed Kuhn a fresh rag. "Eng, can you come forward to the wardroom in a few minutes? The XO and I want to sit down with the department heads and discuss the rest of this re-fit and the mission."

"Yes, sir. Need to check with Chief Hendrix first, though. The steam generator water level control system is acting up again. Needs an alignment. And Chief Lepke wants to show me the R-114 air-conditioning controller. Says it needs to be replaced. I'll be forward in half an hour if that's okay. Shouldn't take me any longer than that to tell them no in a real nice way."

Ward winked at him and started back up the ladder.

"Sure, Eng. See you in half an hour. And be gentle."

Jonathan Ward opened the heavy, watertight door and walked through the tunnel over the sealed reactor compartment. The tunnel was a shielded passageway connecting the living spaces forward with the engineering spaces aft. Below his feet, through two inches of steel, two feet of polyethylene, and six inches of lead, was the reactor compartment. Inside the compartment, the reactor core, a little over one hundred pounds of uranium 235, sat inside a three-inch-thick steel pressure vessel that, in turn, rested in the primary shield tank. The tank contained two feet of water to slow and reflect back any stray neutrons. Around the outside of the tank, more lead

absorbed gamma energy. All this shielding assured that Ward
and the rest of the sub's crew would receive more radiation
from the sun topside than they did from the reactor while
standing so close to it there in the tunnel. The watertight doors
at either end were always kept shut when *Spadefish* was in
port.

Stepping through the forward door, Ward entered the passageway down the center of the upper level of the operations
compartment. Just in front of him, the weapons shipping
hatch, the normal access to topside, allowed a shaft of sunlight into the interior of the boat. A metal ramp slanted down
from the hatch, through the missing deck, and on downward
through the mess deck below. From his vantage point, Ward
could look through the heart of *Spadefish*, all the way into the
torpedo room two decks below.

As he walked up, a long silver cylinder was gently sliding
down the ramp, restrained by cables from above. A clanging
bell and flashing yellow lights warned everyone that a Tomahawk missile was slowly working its way down the loading
ramp into the torpedo room in the lower-level operations
compartment.

Stan Guhl, the weapons officer, stood by the loading ramp,
wearing a white hard hat with large red letters reading
WEAPONS LOADING SUPERVISOR. He finally took his eyes off
the missile and noticed Ward standing behind him.

"This is the fourth one, Skipper. Sixteen more to go. Looks
like we're emptying the magazine of TLAM-Ds. You gonna
tell me what we need all these Roman candles for?"

"Later, Weps. As usual, you'll know when you need to
know," Ward answered. "Just make sure they all get aboard,
get tucked into bed all nice and neatly, and checked out 'sat.'"

"Yes, sir."

"And Weps, take a break in half an hour for a department-
head meeting in the wardroom," Ward added.

"This is the last bird on the truck. We'll have it stowed in
the room in twenty minutes. Then they have to go up to the

magazine to load more. That'll take at least an hour. I'll give the crew a break and see you in the wardroom."

Ward acknowledged with a nod then dropped down a ladder that deposited him just aft of the mess decks in the middle level. Just as in the upper level, the entire passageway was blocked, deck plates removed and the loading ramp angling steeply down to the torpedo room below. The silver cylinder containing the TLAM-D slid silently down the ramp as he watched.

Loading the weapons used by a modern submarine was a complex procedure. The behemoths weighed upward of four thousand pounds each and cost the taxpayers more than a million dollars per copy. The twenty-foot-long, twenty-one-inch-diameter cylindrical shapes were filled with delicate electronics, powerful explosives, and toxic fuels. There was no room for error, and obviously no hurry in loading them, despite how inconvenient the operation was for the crew.

Modern submarine design had placed the torpedo room on the lowest level of the operations compartment. Unlike on their predecessors, whose torpedo rooms took up the entire bow compartment and had tubes that shot straight out in front of the boat, on these submarines the precious space in the bow was filled with a large, very sensitive sonar dome. The torpedo tubes shot at an angle out of the midsection of the boat.

This design meant that the weapons needed to be lowered from the main deck topside to the very bottom of the boat, through the main working, living, and eating spaces. It completely disrupted normal activity on board the boat until the missiles were safely loaded and stowed.

It could be worse, Ward reflected. They didn't carry nuclear weapons anymore. Nukes complicated things even further. They required armed guards who got in the way even worse than the balky ramps did.

He stepped into the galley, the tiny domain of "Cookie" Dotson. Preparations for lunch were well under way and mouthwatering aromas filled the tiny space. The ship's cook, wearing a well-spotted apron, wiped the flour from his hands and grinned at his captain.

"Skipper, just passing through or looking for a handout?"

Cookie saw more officers in his galley during weapons loads than at any other time. It was the only route around the ramp without having to go all the way topside.

"Just passing through," Ward answered, working his way around the industrial-sized mixer and stainless-steel counter that filled the center of the space. "But something smells mighty good."

"It will be," Cookie called after him.

Carefully skirting the missile that was still slowly sliding down the loading ramp, Ward hopped into the wardroom pantry and finally found himself at his destination.

The wardroom on *Spadefish* was small, no more than ten feet by seven feet, dominated by a large table that was bolted to the deck. Dark, wood-grained Formica walls and brown Naugahyde covers on the chairs and the short built-in couch at the far end did their best to give the room a little of the air of a men's club. The neat row of reactor-plant manuals in the bookshelf above the couch and the three large double-lock safes beneath the serving buffet countered that first impression, though.

Ward poured himself a cup of coffee and settled down at the head of the table. He had hardly swallowed a sip before the duty radioman handed him three aluminum clipboards containing radio messages addressed to *Spadefish*. Each bore a legend in large letters across the front, telling the reader the security classification of the messages inside. Ward set aside the green "Confidential" board and the yellow "Secret" one. He opened the red "Top Secret" clipboard and signed the pink disclosure sheet resting on top of the lone message inside it.

The two-page communication was stamped "TOP SECRET, SPECAT SCI INCA TRAIL."

Ward read through the text carefully, absorbing every word. It instructed him to get under way by the end of the week and proceed south to a patrol box off South America, near the Colombian coast. They were to intercept and monitor all radio traffic possible, especially any signals that appeared to originate from Juan de Santiago's operations. It also tasked him with keeping surveillance on any shipping that might pass through the assigned area. Simple enough.

The commander's eyes grew a bit wider when he read the second page. The message described a covert operation being mounted by the SEALs high in the Colombian Andes. The SEALs would be pinpointing targets for him to take out. Looked like he and Bill Beaman would be working together again.

Still more interesting, JDIA was the operational commander for this mission, not SUBPAC. Ward whistled softly. John Bethea and his shadowy agency carried even more clout than he had imagined.

The ringing telephone interrupted his thoughts. He glanced over and confirmed that the light for his line was glowing. One of the basic things taught in Prospective Commanding Officers' School was to never answer the phone yourself. You could never be sure it wasn't *60 Minutes* calling.

Ward ignored the disturbance and reread the last few sentences of the message.

Joe Glass stuck his head in the door.

"Skipper, some guy named Tom Kincaid on the line. Wants to talk to you and he says you'd be glad to take the call."

Ward grabbed the phone. The gruff voice on the other end was unmistakable.

"Jon, you old seagoin' reprobate! How you doing?"

Ward felt the years drop away. Hearing Tom Kincaid's voice always transported him back to his college days once again. They had had their share of fun back then, partying, chasing the same girls, trying to work their way through the great beers of the world one brew at a time. They had also found time for serious discussions on the state of the world, the future of the universe, and whether or not Ohio State would beat Michigan.

Had it really been twenty years ago already?

"Tom, great to hear your voice. You still growing mold up in Seattle?"

"You know me. Perfect nose for finding the best beer and coffee in the world. Have 'em both here. You and Ellen need to take a break and come up here sometime. I've found a seafood restaurant down by the ferry landing that is out of this world."

Ward took a sip of coffee. His friend sounded ebullient, his voice full of excitement. The last time they had spoken, a good year before, he had been almost despondent, complaining of serving out a sentence at the far end of the drug-fighting cosmos.

"Tom, I think it's your turn to come down here. Little sunshine would do you good and we serve a pretty good cup of coffee at 'Casa de Ward.' Take a couple of days, hop a plane, and come on down here before we head out again. We might even break out the sticks and go lose some golf balls."

"I may just do that." Ward heard a very distinct shift in the tone of his friend's voice. He recognized it right away. The pleasantries were over. It would be all business now. Jon Ward was stunned by what his old friend said. "Jon, I've been talking to a friend of yours the last couple of days. John Bethea."

At that very moment, the commander was staring at the initials "JDIA" on the "Top Secret" message on the wardroom table before him. The message that had just confirmed that Bethea and JDIA owned *Spadefish*, its crew, and its captain for the next little while.

Ward caught his breath.

"A relatively new friend of mine, but a friend nonetheless."

Kincaid continued, "That's precisely what he told me. Jon, we've been having a problem up here. Losing too many people, young people who had no business dying. It's that damn white shit. Someone is bringing it in from down south and it's some nasty stuff. They've found some way to make it even more addictive, and you can imagine what that'll do with all the casual use the stuff gets already. Good people are going to get hurt, Jon. More good people."

Kincaid paused to swallow hard.

Ward knew exactly what was going through his friend's mind. A sister. A sister Kincaid had loved dearly, and that he had been unable to save from her own addiction.

"Look, Jon, I've been calling in every chit I've got on this thing and I'm running into a brick wall finding out any more about what's going on. And it's getting real ugly. I talked to my best informant down there a few days ago. Good guy. Name of Pepe Licciardi. Real careful type. Said he'd see what he could find." Ward clenched his jaw. Secure line or not, he was surprised Kincaid was mentioning out loud the name of so crucial an informant. He learned it no longer mattered. "They found him in an alley in Cartagena this morning. Throat slashed ear to ear. Not a drop of blood left in him. Left a wife, a seven-year-old daughter, and a cat."

Jonathan Ward felt a chill enter the wardroom.

"So, how do you hook up with Bethea?"

"He called me, right after I talked with Pepe. He had gotten wind . . . somehow . . . that I was asking questions about de Santiago and the new strain of coke. He did me two favors. First, he told me he was going to invoke some extraordinary measures to make sure Rick Taylor and the DEA didn't hear about me and my investigation so far. If JDIA knows about it, it's just a matter of time before Taylor and his clowns hear. Believe it or not, he knows how badly that son of a bitch could queer this whole deal. And secondly, he rather strongly suggested that I get down to San Diego and visit with my old college bud for a few days."

A dozen questions rattled around inside Jon Ward's head, but he decided to save them for a face-to-face with his friend.

"Tom, hop on that plane. Be here tomorrow if you can. We need to talk. Somewhere away from any ears."

"Put on the java pot, Jonny. And make it strong, strong, strong."

Tom Kincaid almost sang the words. He was clearly elated to be back in the game, back to somewhere where he could make a difference.

12

BRITISH AIRWAYS FLIGHT NUMBER BA025 CHECKED IN WITH HONG Kong Flight Control ten minutes early. The twelve-hour, nonstop trip from London was almost finished and Antonio de Fuka could not have been more grateful. He stretched his aching muscles by locking his ankles beneath the seat in front of him and lifting his legs upward as hard as he could. The Oriental lady in the seat next to him was too exhausted to even give him a hard stare anymore when he grunted with the effort.

Even traveling first class had not really helped. He had left Bogotá twenty-nine hours before. The five-hour layover in London had been beneficial, but only marginally. He had been able to walk a bit, but the bland British food had left him dyspeptic and the rain gave him a chill. Then there had been the cab ride from Gatwick Airport to Heathrow, through the fog and mist and during the height of the afternoon rush hour.

For some reason known only to the airlines of the world, there were no direct flights from anywhere in Latin America to Hong Kong. A traveler had to go through either the United States or London. De Fuka was simply not comfortable traveling through an American airport, even if he never left the international lounge. He remembered all too well the story of José Castillo. Because of the vagaries of the airlines, he was forced to fly an awkward zigzag from Nicaragua to Guatemala by way of Los Angeles. He was arrested by Immigration and Naturalization Service agents at LAX for smuggling illegal aliens. At least the British seemed more likely to respect the international part of Heathrow.

The layover in London had been without event except for the near misses during the cab ride. Once at Heathrow, he had tried to sleep in the First Class Club, but that proved futile. A group of giggling, squealing schoolgirls on some class trip from America combined with rude businessmen and their too-loud cell-phone conversations to make any nap impossible.

The Boeing 747 finally broke through the clouds that hid the giant Chek Lap Kok Airport. Jutting out into the South China Sea, the monstrous man-made island was the largest earthmoving project in history. The Chinese sheared the tops off two islands and filled in the sea with all that dirt and rock to make dry ground for the airport.

The smiling flight attendant, altogether too fresh and polite after such a long, grueling flight, handed de Fuka a steaming hot towel as they continued their descent.

"I hope you enjoyed your flight, Señor Silva. Hong Kong is such a vibrant city, don't you think?"

De Fuka muttered something polite but noncommittal and forced a smile. Part of his job was to remain as anonymous as possible, merely another Latin American businessman, a Mr. Silva, flying halfway around the world to seal some boring deal.

He hadn't been to Hong Kong since the Chinese had regained control or since the opening of the new airport. He certainly wouldn't miss the white-knuckle approach to the old Kai Tok Airport, even if he would no longer have the panoramic view of Hong Kong Island and Kowloon.

The one advantage of flying first class was being first off the plane. Despite wanting to blend with the crowd, de Fuka led the rest of his fellow passengers down the boarding ramp and out into the massive cavern of the terminal.

The scale of the building, even the soaring vaulted ceiling of the ultramodern terminal, was lost on de Fuka. He was sore, tired, and sleepy. Add the jostling crowds and the slow lines at customs and it all only contributed to his ill temper.

He didn't notice the neatly dressed Oriental gentleman

standing by the magazine stand, studying the racks of publications for some other reading matter to add to the newspaper he had already. Not even when the man half looked his way as he spoke into a cell phone, folded his paper under his arm, and walked away to be swallowed up by the milling crowd.

De Fuka stepped outside the mammoth building and breathed deeply. The warm, humid wind blowing in from the sea carried a faint scent of the New Territories of Mainland China, only twenty kilometers away across the water. The aroma mingled with the exhaust smoke from all the traffic that whizzed past. It was good to smell something besides the airline's canned air and his seatmate's cheap perfume.

A black Mercedes limousine pulled up to the curb, easing to a stop at his feet. A small white placard was stuck to the passenger side window. SILVA had been written on it in grease pencil. The driver hopped out, greeted him pleasantly in English, and placed his single bag in the trunk. De Fuka held on to his briefcase as he took one more whiff of the fragrant air and climbed into the backseat.

"Grand Hyatt Hotel on Gloucester Road in the Central District," he said, and the driver nodded.

"I know, Señor Silva," he said.

The Mercedes merged into the melee of buses and taxis leaving the airport. They eased past a shoeshine boy standing against the terminal building. The boy spoke a few words into a cell phone, then packed up his kit and trotted away.

The limo swung out onto Route 9 for the long drive to the Central District of Hong Kong Island. De Fuka watched the wild traffic ahead. His own feet subconsciously worked imaginary pedals in the floorboard as the driver negotiated the bedlam with seeming ease.

De Fuka continuously looked over his shoulder. He saw the various taxis that pulled in behind the limo for only a few minutes before giving way to another one. If he was being tailed, there was no way to differentiate these cabs from any of the others that herded around them, clogging the thoroughfare.

The route crossed over to Kowloon, then tunneled under the Inner Harbor to emerge on Hong Kong Island. The Mercedes joined several other vehicles pulling up into the long, sweeping drive to the Grand Hyatt. The scent of bougainvillea hung heavy in the air. Water splashed from the large rock fountain like a gentle rain on the mountain rocks back home. The Colombian thought how easy it would be to slip down into the seat and take a quick nap. He had time. He would not meet with Sui until the next day. Tonight, he could sleep and prepare.

De Fuka left the limo and stepped through the large glass doors into the cool grandeur of the hotel, his driver at his heels with his bag. Brass, black granite, and ornately carved furniture gleamed throughout the lobby. It was hard to imagine that he was now in a communist country. Hong Kong could still rival any great capitalist enclave in its opulence and splendor. Beijing had not yet tried to dim its bright lights. De Fuka couldn't help wondering if the Chinese would eventually gray it down to their customary drab utilitarianism. Or if this place might become the tail that wagged the Marxist dog that had now marked it as its own territory.

The hotel manager hastened to greet him halfway across the lobby. He insisted on escorting him directly to his suite without bothering with the formalities of checking in. The rosewood-and-glass elevator whisked them silently to the twenty-fifth floor, where the manager led de Fuka into an expansive suite whose all-glass exterior wall looked out over Hong Kong's bustling Inner Harbor.

The manager bowed his way out of the suite.

"I hope you enjoy your stay, Señor de Fuka. Mr. Sui asked me to tell you that he will see you for dinner in the Cheng Fui Room. It is on the second floor. Dinner will be served at eight o'clock."

De Fuka stared hard at the manager as he quietly shut the carved mahogany double doors. He had registered and traveled under the name of Silva. The limo and the room were for

"Mr. Silva." No one in Hong Kong should know his real name or purpose. Sui's people had been told to meet a Mr. Gómez at the Mandarin Oriental Hotel on Charter Road tomorrow evening.

As far as anyone was concerned, there was no Señor de Fuka on the island. But Sui knew he was there. The Chinese crime lord had enough time to change his accommodations from a business suite to the penthouse, arrange a private dining room, and move the meeting up one full day. Furthermore, he was now to meet with the mysterious Sui in person, not with some lieutenant. Sui was placing great importance on this meeting. He rarely traveled from his secluded home in the mountains on the Thai-China border.

He had gone to great trouble to gain the upper hand by forcing the meeting a day early. De Fuka considered sending the Oriental word that the meeting would take place at the time and venue previously determined. Sui was certainly welcome to take part in the discussion, but the proxy of Juan de Santiago would appreciate the courtesy of no more changes in the plan. That would allow him a day to rest, to regain his edge. It would put Sui back on the defensive.

He stood at the huge window and watched the choppy water of the harbor. The lights began to flick on in the buildings all around. He decided to play it Sui's way. He was about to ask for the man's partnership and a significant investment, even by major drug kingpin standards. Better to acquiesce on these points. He may have to be adamant on others.

That's why de Fuka had come instead of de Santiago himself. Something as insignificant as a change in the meeting plans, something as fully predictable as Sui being aware of his alias and his travel plans, could well have sent El Jefe into a rage. The chances of any accord with the Orientals would have been sunk to the bottom of the South China Sea.

With the recent discovery of the presence of a traitor, El Falcone, in their midst who knew what else Sui may know about de Santiago's operations and how they may have been compromised. It would be best to go ahead with the meeting.

Nothing to do now but wait and see what played out. De Fuka kicked off his shoes and stretched out on the king-sized bed to rest his travel-weary body.

The private dining room looked out over a small, walled-off garden. The shady green foliage and the artfully placed rocks gave a sense of isolation and tranquillity in the heart of the world's most bustling city. The gentle burbling of a small brook running though the garden added a further authentic touch of nature. Dense thickets of bamboo hid the high back wall. Small lanterns and soft overhead lighting illuminated the idyllic scene. Brilliantly plumed songbirds in cages hung from the limbs of a miniature ginkgo tree added even more to the illusion of being in a small, rural garden in the country, not just one floor above the lobby of a major international hotel.

The room was arranged with a small table that had already been set for two. The few pieces of antique Mandarin furniture along the two long sidewalls served as display stands for exquisite jade carvings. Two large Ming vases flanked the glass wall looking out into the garden. The effect was one of understated elegance.

De Fuka stepped into the room. A short, elderly man who had been gazing out the window turned and stepped briskly across to meet him.

"My dear Señor de Fuka. How very good of you to meet us so soon after your exhausting journey. I trust your accommodations are adequate."

The Oxford accent did not seem out of place at all, considering the Saville Row suit or the Italian silk tie the man wore. The hard, horny calluses on the extended hand, the iron grip, and the fierce light in the man's dark, Oriental eyes served notice of how thin the veneer was.

De Fuka bowed slightly at the greeting. He tried not to wince at the power of the man's grip.

"Mr. Sui, you do us honor by accepting our invitation to

meet and speak with this humble servant. But I must say, I was not expecting to meet with you. Juan de Santiago sends his greetings and highest respects."

Sui waved him toward a mahogany sideboard filled with shining crystal.

"May I offer you a drink?" A server appeared, as if summoned telepathically from behind the silk screen that shielded part of that wall from view. "We have an excellent fifty-year Laphroaig. That is your drink of choice?" De Fuka nervously agreed. The server poured several fingers of Scotch into a small snifter and handed it to de Fuka with a deep bow. Sui continued, "Although I never developed a taste for those earthy Islay malts. I much prefer a lighter Oban, myself."

As the two men strolled over to the window, they continued their small talk, discussing the virtues of various Scotches, the rigors of the half-a-world journey, the beauty of the garden, the changes in Hong Kong. The easy conversation continued over dinner, an excellent eight-course meal of Cantonese cuisine.

When the last of the dinner had finally been cleared away, the coffee and brandy served, and the cigars lit, Sui opened the next phase of the discussion. De Fuka fought to stay alert, his fatigue giving way to a sleepy mellowness after the fine fare.

"Señor de Fuka, now I hope you will please explain this proposition that Señor de Santiago wishes to implement, and tell me how I and my organization fit into his plans."

De Fuka looked quickly around the room, the question obvious on his face.

"Is it safe . . . ?"

"Do not worry, señor," Sui reassured him. "The only ears these walls have belong to me. These people all work for me. As do the ones who have watched over you since you landed in London. And their mission was not merely to track your progress, my friend, but to make certain that none of our mutual enemies deterred you."

De Fuka looked at the little man with a new respect. His reach was indeed a long one.

Carefully, de Santiago's lieutenant began an explanation of the smuggling and distribution system that de Santiago was already implementing. Sui leaned forward slightly. He sipped his drink, listening intently to every word de Fuka uttered. When the Colombian described the miniature submarine and how it would work, the man's eyes lit up and a smile flitted across his face.

"Ah, that is exquisite. How brilliant!"

De Fuka explained the additive being developed to increase the addictive properties of the cocaine they would be distributing. When he mentioned that an early version had already been shipped to America, Sui's eyes grew wide.

"Then it has been tested? It works?"

"We have already placed prototype shipments in test markets. The additive was one hundred percent successful in developing a strong addiction in our customers within the first two uses. Once they have tried it, they must have more and more."

"It is ready to ship in quantity?"

"We are entering the production phase now. We expect to be able to ship adequate stocks within two months, which should coincide with the final implementation of the first phase of the submarine delivery system. We believe the entire operation is on schedule and proceeding according to plan."

De Fuka hoped the Oriental had not heard of the slight problem they had encountered with the test. The discovery that the product was so addictive that users could not get enough of the stuff and that some had accidentally overdosed.

Sui leaned back and contemplated the glowing embers on the end of his cigar for a second. "Excellent, most excellent," he said, almost to himself. "A plot worthy of Sun Tsu." He looked up and his eyes were brighter than the burning ash on the cigar when he spoke. "This is all quite exciting, Señor de Fuka. But one thing puzzles me. Why do you need my participation? It seems you and Señor de Santiago have all the pieces in place to achieve domination of this lucrative import/export enterprise without having to bring in partners to share in the bounty."

De Fuka paused, ostensibly to sip his dark coffee, but actually to order his thoughts. The pitch had been made. It was now time to close the deal.

"That is quite true, Mr. Sui. But it is important for you to recognize that, unlike yours, our organization must work on two fronts. We are not strictly in the import/export business. We must also continue the revolution of our people as we attempt to overthrow the oppressive, corrupt regime that has its boot heel on our throats. As you are aware, the Americans, as they are so eager to do, have meddled in our own country's affairs at a great cost of money and heroic lives." De Fuka was pleased to see Sui's head nodding slightly. He was all too familiar with the havoc the Americans could set loose with their self-righteous interference. Even here, on the far side of the planet. He would be equally aware of the potential of profiting from such chaos. Sui was a living example of the possibilities, after all.

De Fuka leaned forward. "Were we merely in this business for profit, we would seek to be your most formidable competitor. And I say this with all respect, our goal would be to remove you from our mutual business. But since we also are seeking the liberation of our people, we must recover the monetary loss we have suffered at the hands of the imperialists and their cohorts in order for our initiative to continue and to prosper. We have no problem with allowing you to share in our eventual enormous profits in exchange for your investment at this juncture."

"Yes. Yes, that I can understand," Sui was saying, his head still nodding.

De Fuka felt like a salesman, looking for "buying signals." Sui had just shown him a basket full of them.

"The laboratory, the submarine, and the other facilities are not without expense. We have already bought the services of the world's foremost authorities in each area. They are not inexpensive. As you well know, the price of silence is considerable indeed." De Fuka paused for effect. Sui was waiting breathlessly for the figure that would allow him to partake. "Our proposition to you is for a seventy-million-dollar investment now and a ten percent cut on your gross revenue on the product you supply for the operation."

The big gantry crane gingerly lifted the pallet upward and out of the hold of the freighter. The shipping labels were stamped in large letters: KOCKUMS SHIPBUILDING AB, HOWALDTSWERKE-DEUTSCHE WERFT AG, KARLSKRONAVARVET. The yellow cross on the blue field of the Swedish flag was stenciled boldly over the names.

Philippe Zurko looked on in amazement. He had not believed it when Sergiovski called to tell him about the telex he had received. It reported the departure of the shipment from Karlskronavarvet and predicted a delivery date. Zurko and Sergiovski had been feverishly developing alternative approaches to power the mini-sub ever since the SPETNAZ team had failed to return to the fishing boat. Without the vital fuel cells, the mini-sub was little more than a large and very expensive toy.

Neither the Russians nor the Chinese seemed to have any technology that they could make work. The Italians and the Germans were guarding theirs too closely for them to attempt to steal the plans, though they were still considering the possibilities.

Zurko was already steeling himself, trying to conjure up the words he would use to tell El Jefe of their plight. That's when Sergiovski told him of the strange telex.

It didn't seem real, not possible. During the month while the freighter transited from Karlskronavarvet, Sweden, to Tumbes, Peru, they waited. They kept their fingers crossed, hoping that it was not some horrible hoax, maybe a trap set when the divers had been captured or killed.

The journey down the mountains from Cajamarca to the

port was filled with anxiety. The closer they came to the wharves at Tumbes, the surer Zurko was that it was all an elaborate ambush. When they tried to take possession of the shipment, Guitteriz's goons would certainly surround them, laughing uncontrollably at their naivete as they gunned them down.

The shipping agent routinely confirmed the freighter's arrival, along with the pallet-load of material. Sergiovski signed the documents.

No troops. No ambush. No spray of bullets.

They now smiled and toasted each other with warm beers as they watched the crates being lowered onto the flatbed trailer behind their truck. Its suspension groaned in protest as the ten tons settled down on its bed.

They drove out the gate with their new power plant and headed up the highway, back to Cajamarca.

Juan de Santiago replaced the phone in its cradle. He grinned broadly.

"Good news, El Jefe?" Guzmán asked, but the answer was obvious. There had been so much bad news lately, when something good finally happened it was clear in his leader's face.

"My friend, this is a great day in the revolution! A greater day even than when we routed El Presidente's troops from the field in the battle at Los Llanos and I slit the throat of Colonel Blanco with my own knife blade." De Santiago stood and stretched his cramping back muscles. He seemed energized and the bodyguard would not have been surprised to see him leap for joy. "Come, Guzmán. The horses. Let's ride. Saddle that new Arabian stallion, El Cid, for me."

El Falcone cursed quietly and replaced the listening device in its hiding place. De Santiago was about to leave the perimeter of the sensitive eavesdropping network, just as it appeared he was to tell Guzmán of some new triumph of the revolution, something that might be of great interest to the government and the JDIA.

Patience was a virtue with which El Falcone was well acquainted. De Santiago loved to boast. He had done so only the day before about the location of the new, remote coca fields. That boasting uncovered far more than the leader would ever divulge if he was aware his every word could be heard. He would again brag about whatever this new success was. When he did, El Falcone would be listening.

Someday this bastard's crimes against the people of his country, committed in the holy name of freedom, would be revealed, avenged. How could so many be duped by his rhetoric? How could they so blindly follow someone who would steal from them and rape them just as surely as had the other revolutionaries, the other governments that had come and gone before him?

El Falcone stood behind the curtains and watched with a seething hatred as de Santiago and Guzmán rode away from the estate, off toward the jungle in the distance.

The two men charged out of the hacienda at a gallop, flying across the fields and down the rough jungle roads. The miles melted behind them. At last they reined in the lathered horses.

They had arrived at a ridge top, looking out over a large valley below.

"Guzmán, at one time my family owned this valley, as far as the eye can see. And before that, it was all part of the kingdom of the Incas. El Presidente stole it all in the name of 'reform.' Today we are infinitely closer to taking it all back. It will be mine again, and soon." Reaching down, he patted affectionately the neck of the large black horse he straddled. "Today, Sui agreed to join us and is forwarding his down payment to our accounts in Macao. That is great news. Better still, the power plant for the submarine arrived today and is on its way to the mountains. We have all the weapons to kill the dragon, my friend. And soon . . . very soon . . . we will still its hot breath, once and for all." Three or four hummingbirds darted past them and disappeared into the trees. "Lastly, I have given much consideration to the identity of El Falcone. Guzman, I am convinced I have narrowed the possibilities and I have a plan to deal with the traitorous bastard. If you are horseman enough to catch me, I may just reveal it to you!"

With that, he spurred his mount and galloped off into the jungle again, yelping and crowing with unabashed joy.

Guzmán shook his head then urged his own horse to follow after the leader of the revolution.

13

TOM KINCAID WALKED STIFFLY DOWN THE JETWAY, FAVORING THE KNEE he had wrenched in some long-ago-forgotten tussle. The warm, golden glow of the California sunshine spilled through the broad glass windows of the terminal as he emerged from the blue-gray steel tube. It was good to see sunshine again. Seattle's sunny days could be spectacular, but they seemed to have been few and far between lately, serving to match the dour mood in which he so often found himself. The San Diego weather was already having a therapeutic effect on him. He could feel his spirits rise.

It wasn't only the sunny weather. Tom Kincaid had a purpose again, a quest, and he was a happier man for it.

"Hey, you lost?"

The sound of Jon Ward's voice was as heartening as the sunlight. There he was, standing off to his left, Ellen next to him, waving excitedly.

"Lord, I've been looking forward to seeing you guys!" he said.

The two of them made as handsome a couple as ever. A quick montage of memories of shared college days flashed through Kincaid's mind. Competing with Jon for Ellen's affections when the two of them first met the pert redhead. The late-night discussions, the parties, the ball games. Then there had been the awful year when Tom's sister died. Of course, Ellen and Jon had been there the whole way, helping him through that darkest time of his life. He would not have made it without their firm, solid friendship. He had served as Jon's best man at their wedding, accepting the inevitable when Ellen chose Jon.

All that seemed to have happened only a few years ago, but he noticed the gray just beginning to streak her hair, the crow's-feet around Jon's eyes. Had it really been twenty years already?

Kincaid boldly pulled Ellen close to him, hugging her warmly before kissing her on the cheek. She didn't resist and embraced him tightly. Then the two men hugged and clapped each other on the back.

Kincaid said, "It's sure good to see you two!"

"Yeah, it's been far too long," Ward replied warmly. "We got a lot of catching up to do. Come on. Let's get your bag and head out to the house. Ellen's making the best carnitas you've ever tasted and I've had the margaritas on ice all day."

"You sure you don't want to just drop me off at a hotel? Maybe let me grab a sandwich at McDonald's?" Kincaid asked, trying to keep a straight face.

"Well, that could be arranged if—"

"Shut up and lead the way to baggage claim!" Kincaid laughed. "I can taste that jet fuel you call a margarita already!"

Ellen laughed with him, then grabbed Tom's right arm and Jon's left. Both men noticed how natural it felt, having her there in her usual position between them, dead center in the middle of their close friendship. So did she. Together they marched in almost perfect lockstep through the terminal, the strikingly beautiful, shapely redhead flanked by the two tall, handsome, clear-eyed men.

"All right, Tom. Fill me in."

The two men lounged in comfortable chairs arranged side

by side on the redwood deck behind Ward's house on Point Loma. They could hear Ellen inside in the kitchen, putting the final touches on dinner. Both men knew she had finished preparing the meal already, that she was staying purposely out of their way. She intuitively knew that the real purpose for their old friend's visit was business, and that both men wanted to get to the point as soon as possible.

Kincaid touched his tongue to the salted rim of his margarita glass. He couldn't remember when he had been so relaxed. The Wards' backyard was lush, neatly tended. No doubt Ellen spent many hours here while Jon was off protecting the oceans. The scent of star jasmine and bougainvillea drifted over from the huge trellis of large red and tiny white blooms that entirely filled one garden wall and climbed the side of the stucco bungalow. The aroma blended with the meal Ellen was finishing up in the kitchen. The sun was dipping below the horizon, the garden filling with shadows. The gentle breeze was warm, soothing. Point Loma's flock of wild parrots cried raucously as they flew overhead, likely bound for their nightly roost somewhere up on the ridge.

"How can you ever climb aboard some smelly old submarine and leave this place?" Tom asked. Both men knew it was more than the "place." They could hear Ellen inside singing.

"Same reason you get up and go to work every day," Jon replied. "Because we're both deluded enough to think that we can still make a difference in this damned cockeyed world."

"I suppose so." Kincaid took a sip of the drink. His shift in gears was almost audible. It was time to get down to the business at hand. "Jon, it's like I told you over the phone. A couple of weeks ago, a body turned up under a bridge down by the waterfront in Seattle. Young girl named Sandy Holmes. Pretty. Apparently smart. Very dead." Even in the gathering twilight, Ward could see the look in his friend's eyes, hear the strain in his voice. Tom Kincaid saw his sister in this girl. He knew that. The wound was still as open and raw as ever, even after all these years. "This was not something I would usually get a call about, but I've got a detective friend up there with a good nose. Ken Temple sensed something and gave me a heads-up. Sandy was an OD, but things didn't add up on this one. She was not just another stiff." Kincaid paused to take another sip of the margarita. "Boy, these are good. You have this recipe down pat."

"It's all in the tequila," Ward answered. "That's El Tesoro *añejo*. It's handmade in a *fábrica* that doesn't even have electricity."

Kincaid smacked his lips appreciatively before he continued.

"Anyway, she had none of the signs of a hardcore user. No history according to everybody we talked to. In fact, it looked like she was a first-time binge user." Kincaid now took a long, thirsty drink and seemed stuck for a moment on what to say next. He gazed out over the sunset for a long time. Ward knew his friend was not even seeing the Technicolor show the falling sun was putting on for them. He was seeing another young girl dying during a drug binge twenty years ago.

"I wouldn't think that would be unusual," Ward said, trying to get Kincaid out of his reverie. "I'm sure it happens. Somebody gives the stuff a try at a party. Likes it too much. Boyfriend pushing it on her so she'll show him the proper appreciation for supplying the snacks."

"No, it's not that unusual, not even in Seattle," Kincaid went on. "At least, not every once in a while. Something was out of kilter on this one. Temple smelled a rat. So did I. Then, we had five more just like her within a week. Bodies just turning up in out-of-the-way places. All young and reasonably well-to-do. All seemingly smart enough not to do something stupid like this. All of them looking like first-timers with plenty to live for. All with enough coke in their systems to bring down a bull elephant. It could have just been some greedy bastard of a dealer cutting the stuff with something poisonous. Forensics confirmed it was simply cocaine . . . but lots of it. No poison. And there were far too many of them too close together for a little place like Seattle. Jon! We aren't talking about New York here!"

"Okay, Tom. That still doesn't tell me why Bethea and the JDIA got interested. Or why he called you. Or, for that matter, how my name came up."

Kincaid paused for a long minute and shifted in his chair. The wind chimes hanging from the eave of the bungalow tinkled softly in the breeze. The happy sound was a direct counterpoint to the conversation the two men were having.

"We started to see a pattern. After Sandy Holmes. I began to make some calls. I thought I might be overreacting, looking for something just to justify my existence up there. But the bodies kept turning up. The more I talked with Temple, the surer I was that I was on to something. Somebody was dumping some superpowerful stuff on my town and I had to find out who it was and how the hell they were getting it in. I tried to call most of my old contacts. Not a whole lot of them left, though. Taylor really did a wonderful job of screwing that up. Anyway, I convinced the old friend in Cartagena I told you about to sniff around for me and he reluctantly agreed. The only time we talked he said that he had heard rumors that a drug lord named Juan de Santiago had some new additive that caused almost instant addiction. You know what that means? The shit he's been smuggling in already was dangerous enough. Now, if he can just get people to try this new strain, look out!"

The color had drained from Ward's face already.

"You told me that the other day. I can't even begin to imagine what the ramifications of that might be. Ready-made customers who simply have to have the stuff! Talk about taking the schoolyard pusher to a new level! Are you sure, though? You know some of the things you hear about these drug lords are half truth and half myth. They want it that way, too. They want people to think they're omnipotent, bigger than God. How reliable was this guy? This informant of yours?"

"He was the best," Kincaid answered quickly. "He turned up with his throat cut. That confirmed that what he told me was real. They don't knock off somebody and send that kind of message unless they are serious about keeping something big under wraps. Oh, and there's one other thing I've learned about this de Santiago."

Ward looked across the rim of his glass at his friend.

"He can leap tall buildings in a single bound?"

"Just about. He's not just a drug lord. And he's not just a rebel leader. He's a zealot. I hear he's convinced that God put him on this earth to win the revolution and make him rich at the same time. And he doesn't care who or how many have to die in the process. He's smart. He's dangerous. And he's crazy as a loon."

Jonathan Ward studied the toes of his running shoes for a moment. With the sun now gone, the breeze carried a hint of chill.

Ellen stuck her head through the door.

"You two old war dogs done sniffing? Decided who is the alpha male?"

Kincaid laughed.

"Yep. All decided, and looks like I win again. Now, these war dogs are hungry as a couple of stray curs."

"That's good. I've fixed enough to feed a pack of hounds. Let's eat out here. It looks like such a beautiful night. Everything's in the kitchen. Fix a tray and we're in business."

The two friends didn't need another invitation. They jostled for position as they went through the door. Ellen laughed at the two of them.

"Just like the old days, fighting to see who gets to the food first."

"Yeah, some things never change," Ward agreed.

Kincaid stuck his finger in the guacamole and sampled a big dollop of it.

"Yeah, like Ellen's cooking. Answer a question for me. What did you ever see in this ugly old sailor anyway? Sneak away with me and I'll make you the 'Queen of the North.'"

Ellen poked him in the ribs.

"Now, stop that," she said with a giggle. "You just want me for my cooking."

He glanced coyly at her trim body, only half-hidden by the sweat pants and T-shirt she wore.

"Is that a problem?"

Ward shoved him aside with a well-placed hip.

"Bad enough you come down here and drink up all my liquor and eat up my food. Now you're trying to steal my woman right out from under my nose!"

" '*My* woman'?" Ellen yelped and tossed a pot holder in her husband's general direction.

The three of them settled into the banter of old friends. Comfortable riposte. The meal was consumed with gusto. The night sky darkened. Low lights snapped on, illuminating the path that wound through the garden. Stars appeared one by one over their heads. An occasional jet taking off from Lindbergh Field nearby roared overhead, causing what the locals had termed "the Point Loma pause" in their conversation until it was gone.

Ellen hustled to clear away the remnants of dinner and brought out a tray of coffee and port.

"Jon, I have to run over to Sally Desseaux's house to pick up the program for the Submarine Birthday Ball," she announced. "Be back in an hour. You two capable of independent steaming for that long?"

They both nodded. They knew she was making herself scarce once again.

"Well, maybe for a bit, hon. Hurry back, though. Never can tell when the neighbors might call the cops," Ward answered.

They waited for the sound of the car starting and pulling out of the drive.

"Damn, Jon. Has anybody ever told you what a lucky son of a bitch you are? Wish I could find a woman like that."

Ward glanced over at his friend.

"I'll have to agree with you on that one. God knows she puts up with a lot. Raised two great kids while I was off floating a boat somewhere. You'd find yourself somebody if you only made an effort to look."

Kincaid poured some port into a glass.

"Where are the kids anyway? Let's see, Linda is sixteen and Jim is fourteen by now, huh?"

Ward laughed and took the bottle from his friend to pour his own drink.

"You're a little behind the times. Linda is nineteen and a junior at William and Mary. Jim is seventeen and a plebe at the Naval Academy."

Tom Kincaid whistled softly and settled back into the lounge chair.

"Damn, time flies! Last time I saw Jim, he was worrying about making the Little League team and Linda was studying for the driver's-license test."

Ward laughed again.

"Seems like that to me, too. The house sure is a whole lot quieter now."

Kincaid took a sip of the port, inspected the liquid, and nodded approvingly.

"Those old Brit sailors knew a thing or two about living. Nothing like a little port after a great meal." He set the glass down on the little patio table beside his chair and leaned back again. He looked up at the stars before continuing, his voice so low that Ward had to strain to hear him. "Back to our friend, John Bethea. I was still ruminating what Pepe had told me about what de Santiago was up to when Bethea called."

Ward looked over at his friend.

"That's what you said. John called you. I'm still not sure why. Nobody at that level would have been aware of what was happening with the ODs there in Seattle yet, would they?"

"I wouldn't have thought so. But I think Bethea and his guys know when de Santiago takes a dump. I knew a little bit about the JDIA, just bits and pieces I'd picked up from being the nosy prick that I am. I'd heard about how they were kicking Taylor's ass for one thing so I like the guy already. Anyway, Bethea said he'd heard I was sniffing around, wanted to know what I was on to. And listen to this. He wanted to know if he could help. That tell you how much different he operates than Taylor?"

Ward shook his head.

"I just met him the other day but Bethea seems like an all-right guy. So you told him your story. How does that connect with him telling you to call me?"

Kincaid picked up his wineglass again and sipped. Ward could hardly see him in the dim glow from the garden lights. His eyes seemed almost luminescent. He heard the excitement in his old friend's voice.

Tom Kincaid was on a mission.

"I don't know how he knows, but he knows you and I are friends. And he thinks we can work together on this thing." He leaned forward and tapped Ward on the knee. "Now, old buddy, tell me what you're up to."

"You know I can't tell you everything because . . ."

Kincaid pointedly reached into his shirt pocket and pulled out a folded piece of paper. Ward took it and leaned back to catch a sliver of light from the kitchen window so he could see what it was.

"Now, once again," Tom Kincaid said with renewed emphasis. "Tell me what you're up to."

Lieutenant Commander Bill Beaman looked out the tiny airplane window. The little glass circle reflected nothing more than the dark of the night.

Should be about twenty minutes out now, he thought. He glanced at the luminous dial of his large diver's watch. Twenty-two minutes. Four minutes since the last time he looked. They were nearing the end of a long flight. Seven hours since leaving North Island Naval Air Station.

He glanced around the cabin of the C-17. The lights had been darkened hours before, both to allow the men to sleep and to dark-adapt their vision. The only illumination was a few small red bulbs down low, near the deck. Most of his SEAL team had found sleep. They leaned back in the uncomfortable canvas folding seats that lined the two bulkheads. In the semidarkness, the cargo compartment seemed cavernous.

Chief Johnston was up, back at the rear of the plane talking quietly with the air force jumpmaster. He finished his conversation and walked back down to where Beaman was seated. Johnston was huge and black, his voice like mountain thunder.

"Commander, the zoomie says the weather over the drop zone is socked in. Solid overcast to twenty thousand feet. No way of knowing if we'll break through or if it goes all the way to the ground."

Beaman nodded and pursed his lips.

"Thanks, Chief. Better wake the boys. Quick brief, then it'll be time to saddle up."

Johnston was already shaking shoulders and kicking outstretched feet, bringing the resting warriors back to the real world.

"Okay, listen up, toads," he growled, his voice loud and husky to be heard over the thunder of the airplane's engines. "Almost time to go. Give your gear a final check, make sure your timers and altimeters are working. We'll be jumping into pea soup, so you'll be trusting them."

He continued to review the jump, the rendezvous, and the thousand other details for the operation. As they listened, the team of eighteen SEALs was busy strapping on equipment. They looked like space warriors, clad in black jump suits with black helmets, oxygen masks dangling from their chests.

"Okay toads, radio check," Johnston barked.

Each of the eighteen checked in.

Johnston barked out, "Okay, we are ten minutes from the jump point. We will jump forty-seven miles from the landing zone. Course is one-nine-seven. Winds at altitude are one-two-one knots from zero-four-seven. Set that in your jump computers. Landing zone coordinates are seven-five degrees, three-one point two-two minutes longitude, zero-six degrees, four-eight point three-six minutes latitude. Elevation is four-seven-five-zero meters. All checked?"

Seventeen times he heard, "Yes, Chief." He was number eighteen.

The jumpmaster gave Johnston a thumbs-up sign. He stood and balanced himself against the slight bucking of the airplane.

"All right, toads. Up and at 'em."

The copilot's voice came through their radios.

"Door coming open in two minutes. Everyone on oxygen."

At fifty-two thousand feet, anyone without oxygen would suffocate in seconds. The jumpmaster pulled on a heavy fur-lined parka and Arctic mittens. Air temperature outside the giant plane was seventy-two degrees below zero. It was going to be cold outside.

"One minute to drop. Door coming open."

The big ramp across the back of the plane rumbled downward like a giant mouth in a slow yawn. A small red light at the upper left of the door blinked on. The plane shuddered as the flaps extended. The SEALs would be jumping with the C-17 flying at just above its stall speed, but that was still over one hundred and fifty knots. Even then, the flaps were needed for lift to allow the plane to fly so slowly.

"Thirty seconds to drop. Good luck, gentlemen."

No one spoke. They all stared at the toes of their boots.

"Ten seconds."

The red light died out and a green one flashed on. The jumpmaster gave the SEALs a hearty thumbs-up.

Beaman strolled casually out the back of the plane and dropped away into the night as gravity jerked him downward. Johnston and the others followed him out into the cold darkness.

The SEALS had developed this technique years ago to allow them to jump into hostile territory without the dangerous necessity of having their mother plane fly low over the landing zone, making it and its cargo of jumpers an easy target for ground fire. Instead, they jumped from a high-flying plane and did a long free fall in the direction of the landing zone. This particular maneuver was called a HALO jump. It was possible to cover over a hundred miles this way. This was the "HA," or "high altitude," part of it. It required very specialized survival equipment for the harsh, frigid environment they had to endure during the initial portion of the jump. Still, the "LO," or "low opening," was the most dangerous part of the procedure. To limit the amount of time any radar had a chance of detecting the large aerodynamic parachutes, they didn't open them until they were within fifteen hundred feet of the ground. That meant over fifty thousand feet of free fall, ten minutes of dropping all alone through an icy, pitch-black sky.

A HALO jump took extraordinary nerves and discipline. Even on a clear night, when the jumper could see the ground below and the stars above, the urge to pull the cord became nearly unbearable. Jumping into a thick cloud cover notched up the stress level to an entirely different plateau. Up, down, left, right, it all became meaningless. There was no reference point to use. The SEALs had to rely entirely on the instruments strapped to their arms. A compass for direction, an altimeter, and a timer were all on one forearm. On the other were a small GPS receiver and the jump computer.

As they fell earthward, the thick clouds enveloped each of them. Nothing visible. No stars, no ground, no friends in sight dropping through the night with them.

Watch the compass. Make the course corrections that the computer and GPS called for. Listen for the beep of the altimeter and try not to remember that the lowest bidder manufactured it.

Beaman heard the telltale chirp from his own forearm. He gratefully yanked the lanyard. He could still see only thick clouds all about him. No sign of the ground yet.

He felt the hard jerk as the chute opened and slowed his drop. Only a second later, he dropped through the bottom of the cloud cover. He was only seven or eight hundred feet above the ground. To his left, barely a half-mile away, the Andes rose high. A sheer wall disappearing back into the clouds that had just spit him out like a hailstone. To his right, a steep rocky slope was even closer.

Off to his left a couple of degrees and about a thousand yards ahead was the tiny jungle clearing they were aiming at. He tugged gently on his left steering shroud and flared the chute out to drift that way, then dropped neatly into the center of the clearing as if drawn by some invisible magnetism. He had fallen almost ten miles through dense clouds and landed within a few feet of dead center of where he had been aiming.

Seconds later, Chief Johnston flared out to land gently beside him.

"Evening, sir. Thought I'd drop in for a chat. You don't have the coffee brewed yet?"

"Evening, Chief. I apologize. Nice night for a stroll, though."

"Yes, sir. Let me round up the toads. Mission profile calls for five miles tonight."

"Yes, and we're not sure who else might crash our little kaffeeklatsch, Chief."

Beaman glanced around at where they stood, pulling in their chutes. Darkness was their best friend. Still, he knew that these jungles had plenty of animals that could see all too well at night.

Some of those animals could be sighting down a rifle barrel at them at that very moment.

14

BILL BEAMAN STOPPED AT THE TOP OF THE RIDGE, WIPED THE SWEAT out of his eyes, and sucked in a deep breath. Four hours of hard travel and they had covered barely two miles so far. With the tangle of dense jungle growth and the near-vertical terrain, every labored step was a battle. At this rate they would be here until next year before they ever accomplished any of their mission.

The tropical rain poured down once again as if someone above them had opened a spigot in the clouds. It streamed off his campaign hat, dripped off the luxuriant foliage, and turned the gorge behind them into a river. The downpour made it impossible for them to see more than a few feet off the ridge. The splattering rain and roar of the water damped the normal jungle sounds until Beaman could hear nothing else. Juan de Santiago's rebel army could march right up and say "Good morning!" before he and his men would know they were there.

Chief Johnston broke through the undergrowth a few feet farther along the ridge. His camouflage uniform was soaked through with rain and sweat, streaked with black mud.

"Damn, Skipper! This place is a bitch! Map shows we got ourselves two more ridges yet to cross. Does this ever stop?"

He pointed to the skies as he slumped down on the wet ground. Beaman ignored his complaints and looked at his watch.

"Where's Sparks? Almost time to check in."

"He should be here any second if he ain't drowned. Just behind me."

Three more SEALs struggled up to the narrow ridgeline right on cue. They dumped their packs and swore at the heat and humidity. One of them got busy opening his backpack and unfolding a small satellite dish while the other two flopped down in the mud beside the chief.

Checking his GPS, the SEAL carefully aimed the dish at the swirling clouds as if he was trying to catch it full of rainwater.

"All set, Skipper. Soon as I plug in the transceiver."

Johnston glared at the two exhausted SEALs.

"All right, O'Brien, Alvarez, you two lazy toads get off your butts and scoot down the hill. I want you two ten meters out. Split up and keep your eyes open. Don't let any nasty surprises get past you."

The two slowly rose, reluctantly reassuming the weight of their packs.

"Aw, come on, Chief. We're beat. Ain't nobody out here but us and the damn monkeys," the shorter, Hispanic SEAL groused.

"Alvarez, quit giving me lip and get movin'. Plenty of time to rest when you cash in. I'm the only one allowed to gripe out here."

The two disappeared into the green, lost in the torrent. More SEALs breasted the ridge. Johnston set them up around the impromptu ridgetop command post.

Sparks handed Beaman the handset for the satellite transceiver.

"All set. You're up on the freq. Solid signal strength. Crypto is in sync."

Beaman set aside the map he had been studying and squeezed the push-to-talk key.

"White Shadow, this is South Station, over."

Through the hissing static, Beaman heard a disembodied voice quickly respond. He had obviously been sitting right there, waiting for the call.

"South Station, this is White Shadow. Go ahead."

"White Shadow, reporting location coordinates golf-victor-seven, zulu-bravo-four. Progress five hours behind profile. Request next drop at coordinates golf-lima-four, alpha-hotel-three. Profile time plus three. Nothing to report in areas covered. Over."

"South Station, roger drop position and time. New search area ten-klick circle . . . say again, ten-klick circle . . . centered at golf-lima-four, alpha-hotel-three. How copy? Over."

Beaman nodded at Johnston before he answered.

"Copy new mission. Estimate three days in area to complete. South Station, out."

There was nothing but hiss on the radio and the sibilant sound of rain falling hard through the dense jungle.

John Bethea replaced the microphone on its hook. The JDIA command center was brightly lit, wide-awake. The air-conditioning hummed slightly, sending a cool, dry draft through the underground room. The communications equipment filled the entire corner of the room. Five large flat-panel display screens covered the two adjacent walls.

Bethea stood and stepped to the map of Colombia on the wall and drew a large red X through one block. Turning to Jon Ward, he said, "Well, you can see what your friend Beaman is up to. We have him searching down here in the southwest mountains. Pretty sure that de Santiago has his major fields established there somewhere."

Ward stared at the colors on the map where the X was.

"That has to be some vacation spot there," he muttered.

Bethea was refilling his coffee cup.

"Real rough terrain. Makes for slow going. You know if those guys are having a tough time navigating, it's no walk in the park."

Ward sipped his own coffee and hardly noticed it had gone lukewarm. He pushed back his chair, rose, and walked over to get a closer look at the map.

"He's working pretty close to the Peruvian border, isn't he?"

"Yeah, but that border is really open," Bethea answered. "De Santiago controls most of the Colombian territory near there and the Shining Path guerrillas in Peru control their side."

"Convenient," Ward commented dryly.

"Makes things a little interesting," Bethea explained. "The two groups pretty much leave each other alone. No known co-operation, but no open hostility either."

Sitting down in front of a computer console, Bethea used his forefingers to type in a series of commands. One of the flat screens on the bunker wall flicked alive to reveal a large-scale map of northwest South America and the nearby Pacific.

"Jon, this will be your patrol box." Bethea drew a roughly rectangular box about four hundred miles by fifty miles on a side. He guided the computer mouse to orient the box parallel to the coastline and placed it right against a red line that marked the boundary of the Colombian territorial waters.

"We want you to stay in the bottom half of the box most of the time, though. Stay ready to shoot your Tomahawks on a one-hour notice."

Ward looked over the map with a quizzical look on his face.

"Where Bill is operating, looks to me we should be a couple of hundred miles farther south for a direct flight."

Bethea nodded.

"Yeah, that would work if we had overflight permission from Ecuador and Peru. For security, we didn't even bother to ask."

Ward nodded his understanding, already calculating the added distance and its effect on his missiles.

Bethea punched a few more keys, and another flat panel blinked and lit up. A flowchart appeared.

"General scheme is this: Beaman finds a target and datalinks a location and picture to us. We plan the missile flight here and send you the data. You reprogram the birds and send them on their way. Figure the whole operation from geolocation to bird in the air at about ninety minutes."

He looked at the neat, sterile blocks on the chart. Commander Jonathan Ward was trying to imagine how it might feel to hurl a Tomahawk into the sky with actual living people likely waiting where it would dive back to earth. He ran through his mind some of what Tom Kincaid had told him about de Santiago and his army. The happy, beautiful, smiling face of another Kincaid flashed across his consciousness.

He couldn't wait to light the first fuse.

José Silveras stared at the yellow sheet of paper lying there on top of the stack of other yellow papers piled on his desk. It looked just like a thousand others that crossed his desk every day. The routine stream of bureaucratic gobbledygook flowed past him in endless torrents. That assured he would keep his cushy government office job and not have to ever return to the coffee plantation. So long as he kept his nose clean, his allegiances flexible. And his true allegiance a total secret, of course.

This particular sheet of yellow paper had attracted his attention at once.

The Americans wanted to control the airspace over the provinces near Camal for five days, starting the day after tomorrow. That was in the heart of de Santiago's territory. Dangerously near some of El Jefe's best, most productive coca fields.

Perhaps it was only a drill, to be blindly staged in a very sensitive region. It had happened before. Too much reaction from the rebels would cue the Americans that they had stepped too close to a coiled snake.

Silveras reached to unlock a lower desk drawer. Glancing around the tiny office to make sure he was alone, he slid out a thin folder and opened it before him. No scheduled government operations anywhere near there. That meant this was something the Americans were doing on their own. Something very secret. Something Juan de Santiago would pay well to know about.

Silveras returned the folder, closed and locked the drawer. He stood, stretched, and left the office for an early lunch. Whistling tunelessly, he nodded at a few of his coworkers who were still bent over their desks.

Two blocks up and one over, near the park, he stopped and bent to tie his shoe, using the opportunity to see if anyone was following him. There was no one there at all. The streets were still empty before the lunch rush. He stepped around another corner and lifted the receiver on a pay phone.

Dropping in a coin, he dialed a well-remembered number.

Juan de Santiago asked Antonio de Fuka the same question for a third time.

"Your fighters are in place, my friend?"

The two men sat beneath a giant stand of bamboo halfway up the eastern slope of a mountain ridge. Below them, the hillside dropped steeply to a small stream rambling through the cleft between ridges. Both sides were densely covered with jungle growth. They were perfectly hidden there.

"Juan, I have a hundred of my best men on either side of the stream. The Americans must come this way and cross this stream. They will be dead before they have time to ask for forgiveness of their sins." He broke a branch from a small tree and began drawing lines and circles in the black dirt. "The Americans are coming this way. We have intentionally left a hole in our line to let them through. When they pass, my men will close the hole, drawing tight the noose." Scratching out three more circles in the loam, he continued, pointing with the sharp end of the stick. "We have heavy machine guns here, here, and here. I have RPG gunners here and here. There will be a crossfire from which no one can escape." Looking boldly, directly at de Santiago, he concluded. "For once, we will take them by surprise. They will not enjoy protection from the air. Not from government troops. We have determined they move alone. They are ours, El Jefe."

There was no mistaking the broad smile on the leader's face.

Bill Beaman felt uneasy. He couldn't put his finger on it. Something in his gut just didn't feel right. The rain stopped. The terrain was not quite so formidable. They had made good time the last couple of hours. Down this slope, then they would have one more ridgeline to climb to get to the drop zone.

They hadn't seen any sign of human habitation in days. If de Santiago had any facilities in this area, they certainly had not found any evidence of them yet. Just empty jungle. Beautiful, wild, and unspoiled. It would be fun to hike these mountains as tourists rather than warriors, he thought.

He stopped for a moment to watch his men carefully move down the slope. Out here in the wilds, they had no reason to expect to see anyone. Still they were vigilantly and silently sliding through the jungle. A monkey occasionally squawked in protest or a bird exploded in flight at their approach. Still nothing else.

Chief Johnston eased up to a stop beside Beaman.

"Skipper, I don't like this. Things are going too well. My gut tells me something is wrong."

"Yeah, Chief. Mine's saying the same thing. It's been too quiet. Make sure the guys are alert."

They slipped down the slope toward the small, unnamed stream that awaited them at its bottom. The eighteen SEALs were spread out over a fifty-yard front. They moved silently forward, doing precisely as they had been trained to do. They kept their M-16s locked and loaded, ready for instant use. The two SAWS gunners stayed on either flank while the M-60 machine-gun team remained in the center of the line. In case of an attack, this group would meet a hail of machine-gun fire from the center and grenades launched from either side. Add in the automatic fire from fifteen expert marksmen with M-16s and any force short of one with armor or aircraft was well matched.

The SEALs passed through de Santiago's line unnoticed. Neither side saw or was even aware of the other.

A bird fluttered noisily into flight yards ahead of the SEALs. Beaman looked up with a start. What caused that? His people weren't anywhere near. Wild animal? Or did they have company? Again, his every instinct screamed to be ready for trouble.

He checked his M-16 one more time. Ready to go. The M-1911 A1 Colt .45 on his hip was also ready to rock and roll if need be. Nothing to do but move forward carefully and be ready for whatever while keeping an eye on their backsides.

Alvarez was the first to arrive at the stream bank. He stopped and hid in the undergrowth at the edge, waiting to see if anything out of the ordinary happened. Just like the training exercises. The open ground of the streambed was an ideal killing ground if someone meant to ambush them. He repeated the mantra he had learned: "Make sure you own it before you venture out into it."

He hunkered down to wait for the others to catch up before he entered the open ground.

Sparks Smith was next. He lay at the edge of the stream, mostly covered by vines. One by one, the SEAL team took their places along the bank. Twenty feet of rocky streambed separated them from the cover of the jungle on the other side. They lay there, watching, listening, all senses running at maximum.

Nothing moved. Not a sound.

That was not normal. Where was the sound of birds twittering around, the rustle of wildlife venturing to the stream bank, the jungle sounds they had become accustomed to on this long march?

Another bird burst into the air from somewhere farther along the bank to their right. Instinctively, all the SEALs turned as one to look that way.

There was the unmistakable glint of sunlight off polished metal. Immediately there was a burst of gunfire from the left. Both banks erupted, the still of the jungle trampled by an explosion of ordnance. Volleys of automatic fire rippled from the far side, controlled bursts of aimed fire came from the SEALs, aimed at the muzzle flashes. The heavy rumble of AK-47s mixed with the higher-pitched notes of the M-16s. Screams and moans from wounded fighters broke the short stillness between shots.

The heavy machine guns on the flanks opened fire at the SEALs, pinning them down under a storm of bullets as incessant as the earlier rain shower. Sparks screamed as one of the bullets found its mark. He rolled down the bank to the water's edge and lay there, deathly still. Blood seeped out into the stream and left a reddish pink trail in the clear water.

Alvarez looked aghast as his buddy died right there in front of him, a few feet away. They had been together since BUD-S training. They had shared Hell Week. Now Sparks was dying, the life bleeding out of him into some little stream in some godforsaken jungle.

Alvarez aimed the grenade launcher of his SAWS at the nearest machine gun and pulled the trigger. A two-pound

grenade arched across the stream and detonated directly over
the gun. It was out of action, the barrel pointing skyward and
the gunners slumped over it.

O'Brien, in the center of the SEAL line, opened fire with
the M-60 machine gun. The 7.62mm NATO rounds stitched
across the foliage. At 750 rounds a minute, the belt-fed M-60
didn't have the stopping power of a 23mm heavy machine gun,
but O'Brien more than made up for that with his accurate fire.

Beaman watched as his men fought whoever was assuring
they didn't make it across this insignificant little stream. His
team wasn't equipped for extended combat. They were a
shock force. Hit hard and fast, then get out before anyone
could pin them down.

That was exactly what they were now. Pinned down in the
sights of some heavy-duty ambush. They would need to pull out
and soon. The random shots were beginning to find their marks.

He started to signal Chief Johnston to pull everyone back
up the hill. Shooting started up behind them.

Pinned down! Trapped by the simplest of pincer movements! The rebels had closed off their only escape route.

O'Brien's M-60 went silent. Beaman looked over and saw
the young SEAL fall back against a tree and slide down to lay
in a lifeless lump. His men were being torn up. They had to
get out of here.

Alvarez fell to a burst from behind him, the AK-47 rounds
tracing a bloody line across his back.

Beaman gritted his teeth and rushed forward. He grabbed
the silent M-60 and opened fire. Shooting from the hip, he ran
across the shallow stream, hopping nimbly from rock to rock.
Bullets zinged past him. Water splashed up in miniature geysers at his feet. He felt the tug of rounds tearing at his clothes.

Twenty feet, less than five seconds. Seemed like a damned
marathon.

For a brief, fleeting instant Beaman saw himself and Jon
Ward, charging in tandem to the finish line at last year's San
Diego Marathon, neither man willing to give quarter. He beat
Ward by less than a step. This was another race he had to win.

Across the stream, Beaman dove into the cover of the underbrush. He was across. Tossing the empty M-60 aside, he pulled out the Colt and his fighting knife.

Had to break this attack. His team was pinned down.

Beaman ran down the line, parallel to the stream, shooting, screaming, and fighting all the way. He felt an odd exhilaration when he saw the shocked look on the faces of the rebels he jumped.

He imagined their thoughts. Who was this crazy man, slashing, shooting, screaming at them?

"I'm the last son of a bitch you'll ever see!" he screamed.

The rebel troops vanished in front of him. After what seemed a frenzied eternity, the shooting stopped.

Beaman stopped and leaned against a tree, breathing hard, looking for his men.

Chief Johnston tiptoed carefully across the stream, scanning the jungle for stragglers, followed by half a dozen of his men. They climbed the bank cautiously and made their way toward him.

No more shooting, no more loud explosions. Everything was deathly quiet.

"Skipper, you okay?"

"Yeah, Chief. How are the men?" Beaman was all out of breath and dead tired.

"That was the dumbest thing I have ever seen, sir. You workin' to be a dead hero?" The chief asked, still wide-eyed.

"No. Seemed to me that was the only way to break out before they chopped us to pieces. Now get the men together and let's see what we have. Set up a defense perimeter in case they decide to reattack. Fix the wounded."

Beaman wasn't ready yet to face the fact that he had now lost troops in combat. He simply couldn't say it. And he already dreaded that communication to Bethea.

"Yessir. Looks like they left at a run. You got a good half-dozen of 'em, looks like. I'll set up the SATCOM radio. Sparks bought it." Johnston shook his head sadly. When he looked up, there was a flash of anger in his eyes. "Sure would like to know how they knew we were coming. That wasn't an accident. That was a set piece ambush."

Beaman knew he was right. Right now, though, he was still breathing too hard to ponder the question.

Juan de Santiago watched it all from his perch high above the fighting. His men closed the trap on the Americans just as planned. It shouldn't have taken more than a few minutes to annihilate the outmanned and outgunned Americans. He saw the first several of the invaders fall, then his jaw dropped as the large *Americano loco* charged across the stream like an enraged bull. He seemed impervious to the rebel bullets. The lone soldier had broken the entire line of his men and sent them running like frightened children into the jungle. Even those closing the trapdoor from behind the Americans had fled when they saw their *compadres* on the run.

De Santiago had to watch the whole thing play out with grudging admiration. That was a fighting man. Worthy of being his adversary.

He turned away and marched up the mountain. No doubt about it. They would meet again. And oddly, de Santiago eagerly looked forward to that encounter, no matter when it might happen.

15

BETHEA COULDN'T BELIEVE THE WORDS HE WAS HEARING OVER THE scrambled radio circuit. He had lost people before. Lost good people in a violent way in the previous wars he had fought. Who hadn't in the never-ending war he waged with the drug trade? This was much different. This time it felt intensely personal.

His first reaction was to blame himself. De Santiago had penetrated his operation. The revolutionary-turned-drug-lord would have to have known about the SEALs' mission for several days. It would have taken him that long to set up the elaborate ambush he had sprung on Beaman and his men.

He had to find and plug the leak.

He leaned heavily against the bunker wall. Bethea was mentally reviewing his organization, top to bottom. Nothing leaped up at him. He had not expected that anyway. De Santiago had the money and power to reach deep into the heart of any organization. He had operatives at every level of President Guitteriz's government. It would take work to find where the flaw in the plan had developed. He would have to play everything even closer to the vest. Right now, the only people he was certain he could trust could be counted on three fingers: Bill Beaman, Jon Ward, and himself.

If Bethea had dropped anyone less capable than Bill Beaman's SEALs into those Colombian mountains, the surprise ambush would have been a total slaughter. Beaman was reporting six dead and four wounded. The whole operation, two years of painstaking preparation, was in jeopardy. The SEALs' presence in sensitive territory was common knowledge among the rebels.

Those were the tough decisions John Bethea was well equipped to handle. They were also the kind of decisions he relied on his best men to help him make. He seized the microphone once again and felt the detached coolness of its metal grille against his lips as he spoke.

"South Station, this is White Shadow. Arranging rendezvous in two days to evacuate your wounded. Should we bring you all out? Bill, it's your call."

Beaman looked through squinted eyes at the six shapeless lumps coldly lined up at the edge of the small clearing, like dirty laundry or so much garbage. He tried not to see Alvarez, Smith, O'Brien, or the others. They were gone. The SEALs had never in their history left one of their own lying on the

battlefield. These brave young men would soon go home for
the last time. Even if there was any chance his answer to
Bethea's question might have been different a few minutes before, he had no doubt now.

This might be a war they had little chance of winning, but it
was one they had to fight.

"White Shadow, we're staying. Get my wounded and dead
out. You find the security leak. We'd like permission to continue the mission and kick de Santiago's ass."

He was not at all surprised at the curt, crisp answer that
bounced off satellites from thousands of miles away.

"This is White Shadow. Granted. Out."

Joe Glass slumped down into his chair and took a long slurp
of coffee.

"Skipper, everybody's here except the Eng. He's still head
down and ass up in the oxygen generator."

All the chairs around the wardroom table were filled. With
only ten seats and fifteen officers aboard *Spadefish*, even the
cramped standing room area was filled. The doors at both
ends of the room were shut. Large red signs were posted on
the outside: NO ENTRY. CLASSIFIED BRIEF IN PROGRESS.

Ward, seated at the head of the table, put down his own coffee cup and cleared his throat.

"Gentlemen, as soon as the Eng gets the oxygen generator
fixed, we get under way. If you aren't fully ready right now,
you're behind the curve." He picked up a thin brown book that
lay on the Naugahyde tabletop. "I've been reading through the
war patrol log from the old *Spadefish*, SS-411. If you haven't
read it, I suggest you do."

"Gonna be a test?" Stan Guhl wisecracked.

Ward chuckled.

"Maybe just for you, Weps. And if you don't pass, I'll give
you to the Eng for upgrading."

The large New Yorker feigned horror.

"No Skipper, please. Have mercy. Not the engineer. Anything but the Eng. He'll make me stand watch back aft."

Earl Beasley punched the Weps in the ribs.

"You think you can even find Maneuvering if you had to? Been a long time since you been back there."

Glass looked over the table at the two department heads with a fatherly indulgence.

"Okay, you two and the Eng do remind me of the Three Stooges."

Beasley proudly patted his receding hairline.

"I wanna be Curly."

Ward lost his smile and raised his hand.

"Okay, enough. Let's get back to business. What I was trying to say before these two clowns interrupted me was we have a proud tradition to uphold. First the old World War II *Spadefish* and now ours. This will be last patrol by a *Spadefish*. I want it to be a good one." Pointing over at Beasley, he continued. "Okay, Nav. You can brief the under-way and transit."

Beasley stood and pulled the cover off a large chart taped to the outboard bulkhead. The chart covered the eastern Pacific Ocean. A green line stretched from San Diego down the coast of Mexico, past Central America, to a box drawn off the coast of Colombia.

"This is our track. Pretty simple. We had planned a seven-knot PIM."

PIM, or planned intended movement, an acronym that only a navy planner could invent, was the average speed of advance they needed to make. Since submarines routinely operated independently and couldn't communicate continuously, they were given exclusive use of a box of water. No other submarines or any kind of underwater operations were allowed inside the box. The boat could be anywhere in the box, but had to be on the surface if they somehow found themselves outside it. The box moved forward at PIM speed along the expected track the submarine would follow if they were progressing to some predefined operations area.

"You said, 'had planned'?" Ward asked pointedly.

"The change in the op-ord we got this morning jumps that to twenty knots. I say again . . . twenty knots. That means we'll have to haul ass to stay up." The operational order, the "op-ord," was the detailed instructions that told them the route to take to get to Colombia and what to do when they got there. "With a twenty-four-hour broadcast schedule, we'll be doing a flank bell most of the way just to keep up and stay in the PIM box."

Ward studied the chart for a second.

"Listen, guys. This means you have to get to the front of the box and stay there. Don't fool around chasing contacts or clearing baffles. Just run south and run damned fast."

Ward read the query on each man's face. They were being sent somewhere in one hell of a hurry. And they wouldn't be running that fast for another drill. To a man, the officers of *Spadefish* leaned forward to listen intently to the rest of the brief.

Juan de Santiago watched as sweating loyalists loaded the huge trucks. It was all going together so well. First, the power plant had unexpectedly been shipped to them. Then Dura solved the additive problem they had with the cocaine processing. There had been the successful ambush of the *Americanos*.

De Santiago had taken special satisfaction in the latter event. It had taken him back to his own combat roots. It might have been him down there on his stomach in the jungle mud swapping gunfire with the enemy. He knew his mission was much greater now. He must oversee a crusade both holy and vast, one whose import grew even greater each day.

God was looking over his shoulder, giving His blessing to the cause. They would soon defeat the American devils. It almost seemed foreordained. He had no doubt the decimated American soldiers would be airlifted out to regroup and attempt their mission again some other time, after his fields had long since been harvested. Yes, they would leave this sacred land because God had ordained it and because they were soldiers of the modern time. He was certain that there was among today's soldiers a noticeable lack of a will to fight and die for their countries. He had no reason to suspect these troops would be any different now that they had felt his scorpionlike stinger.

They were only soft Americans, after all.

Except maybe for the one wild-eyed one, the one who had charged across the stream like a madman. He certainly wouldn't remain behind by himself.

He would be back, though. Of that de Santiago was sure. He was confident he would know about it and would be ready to welcome him properly.

Philippe Zurko nudged the leader and pointed to the operation that was proceeding before them.

The first of the ten-foot-diameter, thirty-foot-long sections swung gently from the cables as the giant crane lifted it high into the air and toward where the first truck waited. The crane rotated through a short arc to bring the cylinder directly over the cradle built on the bed of the transport. The crane operator expertly lowered the cylinder until it touched down on the cradle. The special heavy transport's suspension groaned as it spread out the fifty-ton load over the sixteen trailer wheels.

De Santiago turned to Zurko.

"You have done well, my friend."

Zurko nodded in response to his leader's praise, but there was still a furrow of worry on his brow.

"*Gracias*, but I will feel better when *el Zibrus* is assembled and under water, swimming north, El Jefe. We never know how much of our plan may have been compromised by this El Falcone."

De Santiago patted his friend on the back.

"You are always too pessimistic. All will go well. God ordains it. I have a plan for El Falcone as well. It will not be long in coming." De Santiago's mind seemed to shift gears. "Now, tell me, how long will assembly of the submarine take once we reach the sea?"

"El Capitán Sergiovski says it will take one week, no more. The freighter has already been finished and awaits us."

"Excellent! Very good!"

The leader's grin filled his face. He looked for all the world like a hungry man about to partake in a sumptuous banquet.

"Maneuvering, Bridge. Have the engineer pick up the JA phone."

Stan Guhl replaced the 7MC microphone into the clip on the bridge box. He and Ward were alone on the bridge. Line handlers stood ready to take in the lines that held *Spadefish* tied securely to the pier. The tugboat *Cherry Two* was lashed to *Spadefish*'s outboard side, ready to tow her out into the channel. Ward saw Captain Sorensen climbing off the big tug and aboard *Spadefish*. Underway was scheduled for less than a half hour away but there was a major snag.

Guhl handed Ward the JA handset.

"Skipper, the Eng is on the line."

Ward took the handset and placed it to his ear.

"Eng, how is the oxygen generator coming?"

Dave Kuhn was exhausted, the strain heavy in his voice. He and his team of experts had been working on the complex oxygen-making machine for forty-eight straight hours. Wryly called "the Bomb," the oxygen generator was simple in concept. All it did was take water and pass a direct current through it. Hydrogen bubbled up at the anode and oxygen at the cathode. Then, the oxygen was gathered up for storage and use and the hydrogen was pumped overboard.

That was the concept anyway. The reality was a little more complicated. To fit enough capacity into the confines of *Spadefish*'s hull, the generator had to operate at very high pressure. At those pressures, hydrogen was dangerously explosive. Pure oxygen would cause just about anything that might ignite to burn vigorously at very high temperatures, even steel.

The electrical control systems were complex and the piping specialized. It was a nightmare to work on.

"Skipper, we've replaced the wall seals in the four bad cells. Cleared up all the grounds. Still getting some carryover."

Ward could hear the exhaustion and exasperation in the engineer's words. Kuhn prided himself on always being able to get *Spadefish* under way on time. It was a very high standard for the tired old boat to maintain and that made Kuhn's accomplishments even more amazing.

"Eng, what do you think? Going to be able to make it work?"

Kuhn answered without hedging.

"Yes. Eventually. Don't know if it'll be today or next week though. Skipper, the oxygen banks are fully topped off. We wouldn't need this Rube Goldberg reject for at least a week or more."

As Ward listened to the engineer's report, Stan Guhl held up the bridge-to-bridge radio and said, "Skipper, commodore wants to talk to you."

Wonderful timing! Ward thought sarcastically. He told Kuhn he would get back to him and spoke into the radio microphone.

"*Spadefish*, Ward on line."

The radio crackled.

"Jon, this is Commodore Desseaux. What is your status for underway?"

"Commodore, ready to get underway with the exception of the oxygen generator."

There was a slight pause and Ward could almost imagine the smirk on Desseaux's face.

"Jon, you know that regulations require that the generator be operational before I can give you permission to get under way."

"But Commodore—"

"No but's, Jon. Call me when that thing is making gas."

Ward said, "Yes, sir," but the radio was already dead on the other end.

Underway time was now less than a half hour. They had to make the underway on time. There was simply no option. The transit didn't have any slack in it now. People's lives depended on them getting down to Colombia on time. The whole mission did.

"Mr. Guhl, get the engineer on the JA again," Ward directed. Ward put down the radio and picked up the JA handset again. "Eng, how's it coming since two minutes ago?"

"We are bringing it up to minimum amps now," Kuhn answered. "Still getting carryover. Hoping it'll dry out. If not, we'll have to tear out the high-pressure section and replace the wall seals again."

Ward asked, "Is it making gas?"

"Skipper, we're only at min amps. We can't come up to full pressure until the carryover stops and we pressure-check all the joints. That'll take another three hours."

"Eng, is . . . it . . . making . . . gas?" Ward asked, his words slow and deliberate.

"No sir. I need at least three hours. What about underway? We'll never make thirty minutes."

"Eng, I'll be coming back to talk to you in a minute," Ward snapped.

Stan Guhl looked oddly after the commander as he disappeared down the long ladder and off the bridge. Now what the hell was the skipper up to?

Ward trotted out of the control room and quickly headed aft. Earl Beasley looked up from his charts questioningly. Seeing the skipper in the control room during an underway was unusual. And he was in a hurry to get to somewhere.

Ward glanced over at the Nav as he went past and smiled.

"Just heading back to give the Eng a little command training."

Beasley shrugged and went back to his charts.

Ward passed through the tunnel and climbed down to the lower level of the auxiliary machinery room. The engineer was watching the needles on the generator control as his team carefully checked the incredibly complex piping systems inside the cubicle.

"Eng, is . . . it . . . making . . . gas?"

Kuhn turned around and looked wide-eyed at Ward. His expression was a mixture of frustration and exasperation. He couldn't understand why Ward was being so insistent. Was he rubbing it in that he was taking so long to fix this piece of crap oxygen generator this time?

Now, when the engineer spoke, there was an edge of anger in his voice.

"Skipper, I told you ten minutes ago that it would be at least three hours before this contraption would be able to make oxygen."

Ward looked directly at his engineer and gripped the man's shoulder.

"Eng, you aren't listening to me. The commodore told me he won't approve an underway until that thing is making gas. Now, is . . . it . . . making . . . gas?"

The light finally came on for Kuhn. He grinned broadly.

This question his skipper kept asking him over and over was being very carefully phrased. He knew without even looking that the oxygen pressure gauge needle was firmly resting on the "zero" peg. He quickly glanced over to the hydrogen pressure gauge, though. Sure enough, the hydrogen pressure registered just above zero.

Hydrogen was a gas, wasn't it?

"Yes, sir," he said with an exaggerated nod. "It's making gas, all right."

Ward cut him off right there with an upheld palm.

"That's precisely what I wanted to know."

He turned on his heel and scurried back up the ladder before Kuhn could say anything else. He made the long climb back up to the bridge.

Ward grabbed the bridge-to-bridge radio.

"Commodore, this is *Spadefish*. I've just confirmed the oxygen generator is now making gas. Request permission to get under way."

"Jon, confirm please. Did you say it was making gas?"

"Yes, sir. It is making gas."

Desseaux hesitated an instant. Ward held his breath.

"Very well, you have permission to get under way. Good hunting."

Ward turned to Stan Guhl.

"Officer of the Deck, take in all lines. Get the ship under way."

Guhl grinned, answered, "Aye, sir," and quickly gave the orders.

Down on the pier, line handlers lifted the four-inch hawser off the bollards and slipped them into the water. Line handlers on the main deck pulled the long lines on board and stowed them in line lockers built into the smooth deck.

As the last line slid off the bollard, the quartermaster blew a shrill whistle. The in-port ensign was lowered from a staff at the rear of the main deck and the underway colors broken out from a staff on the top of the sail.

The giant screw on *Cherry Two* churned as it pulled *Spadefish* away from the pier. Guhl yanked a lever and the huge air horn blasted one long signal, telling the entire world that *Spadefish* was under way again and happy about it.

The tug effortlessly pulled the boat out into the channel and lined her up, ready to head out to sea.

The harbor pilot, Captain Sorensen, offered Ward his hand.

"Have a good trip, Captain. I'll see you when you get back."

He climbed down off the bridge and hopped onto the waiting tug.

"Mr. Guhl, let's get out of here," Jon Ward said. "Ahead standard until everyone is off the main deck, then ahead full."

Spadefish leaped forward, anxious to return to her element once again.

"Aye, sir. Oh, and by the way, Eng wants to talk to you."

Ward took the JA handset.

"What is it, Eng?"

"Skipper, the oxygen generator is completely out of commission now," Kuhn reported. "The wall seals on three cells just blew out. The inner cabinet is full of caustic. At least a week's worth of work."

"Okay, Eng. Carefully research the problem, take your time, and make sure you have all your facts straight. I want the casualty report message ready to send . . . by noon tomorrow."

Jon Ward gave Stan Guhl a conspiratorial wink and turned to breathe in the fresh, clean sea air that blew in off the vast Pacific.

16

BILL BEAMAN CAUTIOUSLY RAISED HIS HEAD TO HAVE A LOOK OUT over the log he hid behind. The rough mountain trail blazed by the Incas stretched out below him. It cut narrowly into the steep side of the mountain slope. A mere foot to the downhill side, the earth dropped precipitously all the way down to a river, roaring and spraying foam a thousand feet below. A ramshackle truck emerged from the clouds farther up the road. It roared and backfired its way down toward where he lay hidden. He was only a few feet from the uphill side of the road but out of view of its driver and passenger.

This was the third truck to pass his position today. They had all come down the road from the south. Each was fully loaded with something bulky and heavy. The tightly drawn tarpaulins hid the trucks' burdens from view. Beaman had noticed the driver and passenger in each truck cab. The drivers had a look of terror on their faces as they struggled to hold the truck's wheels on the narrow roadway. The passengers were always holding an AK-47 in plain view. That was not abnormal, considering the commerce in which these men were engaged.

John Bethea sent the remnants of the team into this remote corner of Colombia. The trek over the uncharted mountains had been as arduous as their initial jaunt from the original drop zone. Until they had spotted the first of the trucks, Beaman was wondering if this whole thing might be a wild-goose chase. If the JDIA head was reaching for an alternative mission, hoping they might stumble upon something by accident or luck.

All Bethea would say was that his "intelligence source" suggested they be alert for rebel drug smuggling activity in this area. He wouldn't, or couldn't, expand on that tidbit of information.

Beaman was perplexed about where the trucks were coming from. He knew that this particular road snaked into Peru; the border was less than a mile farther up the mountain. The map showed this ancient roadway headed deeper into the Peruvian Andes, away from Colombia. If the trucks were loaded with cocaine, where were they coming from? His intelligence sources and the briefings back at JDIA headquarters proclaimed that the Peruvian Shining Path guerrillas and de Santiago's Colombian rebels barely tolerated each other so long as each stayed on its own side of the border. There had been several reports of armed clashes between the groups and no reports of any serious cooperation. Shining Path controlled all of this part of Peru.

The truck roared on past where Beaman lay hidden. The huge dual wheels kicked up a cloud of choking dust that settled like a red fog on his hiding place. Beaman allowed himself a fit of coughing and sneezing once the truck was safely past and had disappeared around the next curve. He slithered back up the slope. He was again shielded from view from the roadway by the thick jungle growth. He climbed fifty yards up the steep slope. That's where he broke through the undergrowth into a small, hidden campsite.

"Another truck?" Chief Johnston asked him.

"Yeah, still can't figure this out. They have to be coming across the border from Peru," Beaman answered, slumping down to have a seat on a tree root. "It has to be coke they're bringing up from down there so that means the fields are across the border. De Santiago either has them hidden from the Shining Path as well as he does from us, or the bastard is a better diplomat than we give him credit for. Chief, you feel like a little cross-border jaunt?"

"Why don't we just grab a truck and ask them?" Johnston asked. He handed over to Beaman a cup of thick, black coffee he had just brewed up on his little alcohol stove.

Beaman gladly accepted the drink and blew across the top of the steaming liquid to cool it a bit.

"Thanks." He took a sip as he pondered their situation. "That is one possibility. But it's still at least a week before *Spadefish* gets here. If we grab a truck now, the element of surprise would be lost. If we did away with the vehicle and the passengers, somebody would miss them and suspect we're still here. Right now, we're assuming that de Santiago's men think we pulled out after the ambush. The longer they operate under that assumption, the more likely we will be to get this thing done."

"Well, we could try to hit 'em hard and quick, the way we've been trained to do," Johnston offered. "All we've done so far is walk and climb and get our asses shot off."

"Well, Chief, let's suppose de Santiago has some kind of operation down there. We don't have enough ordnance to take out anything of any size ourselves. We need *Spadefish* and her Tomahawks to make any kind of big boom. And if we just cause smoke and a few sparks, he learns we're still futzing around in his territory and he would have everything moved long before we could get a weapon on target. And even then, we have to consider that we'd be shooting into Peru."

"Okay, what do we do then? Every load that passes us by down yonder is probably a ton of pure coke, and I'd bet a month's pay it's heading straight to the U.S."

Beaman stood up, swirled his cup, and tossed the remaining coffee grounds into the bushes nearby.

"Likely so. I admit I don't know the plan yet. Let's do a little scouting. Maybe we can figure something out. One thing's for damn sure. We can't do much sitting here on this mountainside. Saddle up the rest of the troops."

Beaman's orders did not authorize any action outside of Colombia. He had to be on the north side of the border. His team was there at the invitation of President Guitteriz and most of the fine citizens of Colombia. They enjoyed the protection of the legal government.

If they took a single step across the line, they were interlopers. The Peruvian government could look at them as illegal invaders. If they got into a fight with de Santiago's troops, Beaman knew they could not expect any support from the Peruvians. The Shining Path guerrillas wouldn't even make a distinction. The best they could expect if detected by the Peruvians was to end up in prison. They could be court-martialed in the United States for disobeying orders. The guerrillas had their own far less refined system of justice and punishment. No, they had even fewer friends across that invisible line just up this ancient mountain roadway than they did here in Colombia.

Johnston stood, put his forefinger and thumb to his lips, and whistled. As he was pulling his pack onto his back, six more SEALs emerged from the undergrowth. They shouldered their packs and headed down the hill. Following along parallel to the road, they remained in the cover of the jungle to the up-slope side, dutifully traipsing southward.

There was no official border crossing, not even a sign of any kind to mark the transition from Colombia to Peru. The only way the SEALs knew they were south of the border was by plotting their GPS position on the map that Beaman carried. There wasn't even the slightest hesitation as they crossed the invisible demarcation.

The road had stopped climbing as they walked through a high mountain pass. It began a twisting, turning descent, falling quickly into a valley far below.

They had made barely another mile's progress down the road when they heard the growl of another truck, laboring in low gear up the steep slope, coming their way. It appeared, followed by a cloud of blue smoke, straining around a turn just after the last SEAL had dived for cover. Like the others, this truck was heavily laden. Like the previous trucks, a steely-eyed armed guard rode in the cab beside the terrified driver.

Beaman waited until the truck disappeared around a curve.

He lay still another ten full minutes, just to be sure that no one in the truck had seen anything and came back to check it out. He signaled for his men to resume their trek along the road and farther down the mountain.

Night descended on the slopes. They found nothing except more of the rough road. With darkness to cover them, the SEALs donned their night-vision goggles and marched down the middle of the roadway. That made for easier going and a faster pace. Beaman figured that the loaded trucks would not be traversing this treacherous stretch of road in total darkness. Even if they did, their headlights would give the SEALs plenty of warning to hide in the thick underbrush at its side.

They descended through the darkness. The road twisted and turned even more wildly. They descended forever through the far northern reaches of the old Inca Empire into the very heart of Peru. Some of the men were already grousing about the inevitable march back up the roadway, back toward the clouds. There could be no pickup from a drop zone in Peru.

Beaman could see the valley far below and the mountains on the other side through his goggles. They were ghostly, greenish shapes. The night sounds of the high cloud forest surrounded them. Not far from where he and his team walked, unidentified prowlers of the night pursued their prey in an eternal, deadly battle for survival. The SEALs could hear the warning cries, the chase, and the screams of death.

Two more trucks passed them as they made their way down. Beaman learned that his assumption about any night driving was wrong. Their cargo was critical. They were willing to risk the treacherous driving or the possibility of a night ambush to get it to wherever it was destined. The darkness and the trucks' noise and distant headlights gave the team plenty of time to hide.

Just before dawn, they came to a fork in the road. The left bend descended through several more switchbacks toward the valley floor. The right fork crossed a shoulder of the mountain and disappeared through a narrow cut in the rock face. There was no way to tell where it might lead. The main road had played out on Beaman's map once it crossed the border.

Beaman didn't have enough men to divide and follow both trails. Following the wrong one could cost them vital days of fruitless searching. Beaman was a firm believer in the old military axiom "the fifty-fifty-ninety rule": when presented with a fifty-fifty choice, you'll choose wrong ninety per cent of the time.

He decided it would be better to stay there near the fork and wait. It went against his aggressive nature, but they would find out soon enough where the trucks were coming from.

Stationing Johnston under cover with a view of the crossroads, Beaman led the rest of the small team up the slope about fifty meters. He set up the SATCOM equipment as they built a rudimentary camp beneath the protection of several large boulders.

In fifteen minutes, Beaman was talking to John Bethea, who had been awaiting word from the team from deep beneath the seaside hill in San Diego.

"White Shadow, this is South Station. Current location seven four dot seven nine five one south, five dot nine seven nine nine west. Backtracking suspected drug traffic into Peru. Have seen eight trucks in the past twenty-four hours. Intend to find source. Over."

There was no blink in Bethea's voice when he answered.

"South Station, if you find source in Peru, we're unsure of our ability to get approval for strikes. You may have to find alternate means to stop delivery."

Bethea's meaning was clear. If Beaman was willing to risk the border crossing, he wasn't going to stand in his way. He would do everything he could, diplomatically and politically, to help. But blowing anything up? He was on his own.

"White Shadow, request latest ETA of Sea Snake."

Beaman wanted to know when *Spadefish*, code-named "Sea Snake," would be in position to complete the mission.

"Sea Snake will be in position in five days. Left home day before yesterday."

The two discussed coordination to resupply the SEALs and talked about the latest intelligence summaries. The entire conversation lasted less than ten minutes.

"Out," Beaman said, and broke the circuit.

The sun broke over the far ridge, bathing Beaman in a golden glow as he stowed the equipment. The night sounds of the jungle quieted. The day sounds had not yet started. Beaman found a soft spot to stretch out amid the thick foliage, his intention to enjoy the sunrise and the brilliant blue sky overhead.

He was asleep in an instant.

It seemed like only seconds later that someone was shaking him awake.

"Skipper, wake up. Truck coming." It was Cantrell, disturbing a most pleasant dream. Beaman groaned and rolled over. Cantrell was the one who was lugging O'Brien's M-60 now. "Chief said to get you. Truck coming up the right fork."

Beaman blinked open his eyes. The sun was high in the sky and beating down with a vengeance. He checked his watch. He had slept for over four hours.

"Felt like I slept ten minutes," Beaman said with a yawn.

"It's quarter past ten."

"I know."

Rubbing his eyes, Beaman said, "Okay, right road it is. Let's be ready to haul ass as soon as that truck has gone on by."

The dirt road to the right snaked around the mountain and through a narrow cut in the rock slope, finally opening into the next valley. It narrowed to a track hardly wide enough for the men to walk down if they traveled two abreast, let alone for the trucks to use. As they backtracked along the trucks' route, they found that the rough roadway clung to the near-vertical slope for long stretches. Above and below was little more than the open scar of active rockslides. Thousands of feet below the road, the scar disappeared into lush rain forest. Far above, the steep wall disappeared into the gray clouds.

They stopped. In the valley far below where they now perched, Beaman could make out the regular rows of a cultivated crop. It looked to be a thousand acres or more down in the narrow valley and even more stretching up terraced slopes on the mountainsides. The valley closed to a narrow defile at its lower end. A rushing, roaring river slamming between two high rock walls.

They were many miles from any human habitation, in truly wild and desolate country. So this is where de Santiago had hidden his death crop. Little wonder no one had been able to find it so far.

Beaman signaled Johnston to have the team take a rest here. Johnston slid up to where Beaman was staring down at the valley.

"Skipper, looks like your hunch paid off. There it is."

Beaman stared down into the valley, looking through powerful binoculars.

"Yeah, we found what we're looking for, but what do we do about it? You heard Bethea. We shoot, we shoot at our own peril. Besides, even if Sea Snake was in position to lob a Tomahawk over here, the strike wouldn't do much damage. No target big enough. Certainly no processing plant."

The low growl of another loaded truck reached their ears, coming their way from lower down the mountain. Johnston sent the team climbing up the mountain for meager cover among the boulders and what little scarred brush was left from what had obviously been a long series of earth slides. The truck belched smoke as it struggled up the steep slope, creeping along in its lowest gear. The driver had his hands full keeping it on the narrow, muddy track.

The vehicle disappeared around the bend. Beaman joined the rest of the team twenty yards up the slope. Chief Johnston had hidden the SEALs at intervals around the little area where he and Beaman sat. The two men sat on a small rock promontory, affording them an excellent view of the valley. Both carefully scanned the entire area, searching for lookouts that might spy them. They looked for a possible solution to the problem of how to deprive de Santiago of the bounty of this crop.

"Too wet to burn. Too much to cut," Johnston mumbled out loud, summing up both men's assessments. "We don't have any spray. Shame, too, 'cause it looks like they just started harvesting the stuff. Damn, don't know what we can come up with to do any real damage down there."

Beaman's gaze swept the whole valley; then he looked again, even more intently, before he lowered the binoculars and glanced sideways at Johnston.

"Chief, what do you see down there?"

Johnston looked at Beaman quizzically.

"Lots and lots of ready-to-harvest coca plants."

"That's what I see, too. Nothing else."

"What do you mean?"

"No village, no dormitory for workers, no factory, no processing facility, not even another access in or out of that valley. Looks like a few tents over near the river, probably for the poor sons of bitches who have to chop and load the goods. This is the only way in or out right here. My guess is de Santiago is growing his crop here where nobody is likely to stumble upon it—us or the Shining Path—and that he keeps just enough people down there to do the dirty work. He's bringing the raw coca leaves out of there on this road and trucking them somewhere else to do the processing. It's not like most of the operations we've torched all along, where the plant was near the fields. Bet if we stopped one of those trucks, we'll find it full of coca leaves, going across the mountains to get turned into nose candy and to add whatever secret goo that they're putting into it lately. There's nothing down there but coca fields. Not a thing for us to make go 'boom.'"

"Okay, I'll buy that. So what do we do, then?"

Beaman rolled over on his back and surveyed the mountain above them.

"If we cut this road, those fields are worthless, totally isolated. At least until de Santiago can rebuild it. And these rockslides are a perfect place to cut the road for a long, long time. If we could drop some of this rock on the fields themselves, all the better." Sitting up, he turned to Johnston. "Chief, set up the SATCOM. I need to talk to Bethea. Put some of the guys down alongside the road. I want to confirm what's in the next truck. If it's coffee beans, we were about to screw the goose!"

Beaman talked to Bethea for several minutes. He explained to the head of the JDIA about the hidden valley and its coca fields and his suspicions about what de Santiago was about.

Grabbing two of the backpacks they had lugged across a good stretch of Colombia, Beaman tossed one to Johnston and said, "Come on, we got work to do."

The two senior SEALs scurried much higher up the mountain, the loose rock and dirt making the go a tough one. Down below them, four of the SEALs set up to ambush the next truck. Cantrell dug a shallow hole in the center of the road and buried a small packet of C-4 plastic explosive. He strung thin wire from the detonator across the track and behind a large boulder, then connected the electronic firing mechanism. He sat back to wait, still holding O'Brien's M-60, happy to be doing something besides walking and ducking.

Broughton and Martinelli walked fifty feet farther down the road and took cover, one of them above and the other below the road. Dumkowski walked on up the road fifty feet and disappeared behind the trees on the uphill side. All was in readiness for the next truck that was unfortunate enough to grind its slow way up the mountain road.

Beaman and Johnston worked high above the road. The slope became steeper as they climbed. The overgrowth gave way to nothing more than a rocky talus field and the footing was now downright treacherous. One slip and the narrow road might not be enough to stop a fall all the way to the coca fields below.

Johnston slipped and kicked a rock free. It bounded and bounced down the slope. It stopped somewhere in the trees far below. Neither man saw it land from his perch. After an hour of difficult climbing, they emerged at the base of a huge rock outcropping hundreds of feet above the roadway.

Beaman opened his pack and started placing C-4 charges.

Several key rocks held a mass in place on its precarious spot. Moving slowly around to the right, he put in place a string of six charges, each with a radio-controlled detonator. Johnston moved to the left, doing the same. With the last charge securely in place, the two men scooted and slid back down the slope, the going much quicker but the hazard for a deadly fall still quite real.

Just as the two senior SEALs leaped from rock to rock, back down to the road, they could hear the approach of another truck. They scurried for cover.

Cantrell waited until the vehicle was a few yards from the buried C-4. He pushed the little red button on his firing mechanism. The C-4 erupted with a roar, showering the cab of the truck with dirt and debris but doing no other damage than to likely cause the driver and the armed guard to soil their trousers.

The frightened driver jammed on the brakes and skidded to a stop instead of trying to drive on. The truck skewed dangerously, stopping inches before it would have dropped right over the side. The guard, stunned by the blast directly in his face, sat for an instant before stepping through the open door and trying to jump free. Good that he did. Down between his legs was a thousand-foot vertical drop. He slid carefully back into the cab, slamming the door shut again. Then the two men jumped out the driver's-side door to face the barrel of an M-60 pointing directly at their chests.

The guard threw down his weapon. Both men raised their hands, their knees trembling visibly. Cantrell yelled at them in Spanish to lie facedown in the road. The two didn't hesitate.

Beaman and Johnston bounded onto the road as Broughton and Martinelli ran up from their hiding places. Martinelli yanked up the weatherworn tarpaulin covering the bed of the old truck. Under it lay a stack of moldering leaves, reaching eight feet high from the bed bottom. The stench of rotting vegetation was almost overpowering.

"Hey, Skipper. Look what I found."

Beaman looked at the stack of vegetation, then at the two peasants lying in the dust.

"Cantrell, kindly ask our friends where they are going on such a fine morning."

Cantrell pulled back the action on the M-60, noisily chambering a round.

"Gladly, Skipper. First let me get their attention." He pulled the trigger. The machine gun was on full auto. 7.62mm NATO rounds kicked up dust clouds all around the peasants at 750 rounds a minute. The two twitched and yelled in fear.

"Skipper, I believe I got their attention now." Cantrell started to talk to the two in passable Spanish. "*Mis compadres*, we know of de Santiago and the coca fields. Tell us where you are driving the truck, *por favor*."

Neither of the two seemed inclined to talk. They stared wide-eyed at each other but lay there silently in the middle of the muddy road.

Beaman looked up at Cantrell and spoke in Spanish.

"Tie them to the truck. When we are up the road a hundred meters, detonate the rockslide. It will carry the road, the truck and this scum all the way back down into the valley."

Cantrell answered, *"Sí mi capitán!"*

Beaman turned his back and started to walk up the road.

It was the truck driver who yelled first.

"Wait, wait! Don't kill us. I will tell you what you want to know."

"Quickly. I am losing patience."

The words spilled from the peasant's trembling lips.

"There is a huge factory, hidden in a deep valley many miles away, between here and Chorera. It is a two-day drive by truck. No city nearby. Only stops for fuel and spare parts."

When Beaman tried to have the man show him the factory's location on his map, it was evident the driver was completely illiterate.

Pointing at the truck, Beaman said, "You drive. Take us to the factory."

The SEALs cleared out the back of the truck. They climbed

up into the truck bed, glad to be riding now since much of the backtrack was seriously uphill. Beaman, wearing the guard's floppy straw hat and stinking jacket, rode up front in the cab with the driver. The frightened guard was in back with the others.

They cranked up and rounded the bend in the road. Beaman pulled a little transmitter from his pocket and pressed a button. High up on the slope, the charges of C-4 detonated in perfect order, lacing the rock outcropping, the explosions reverberating off the mountains across the valley.

One boulder bounded down the slope, striking a few more, then more, until soon the whole mountain seemed to be sliding down to the valley floor. Hundreds of meters of the old Inca roadway disappeared, dragged down the mountain by the tons of rock and dirt and gravity.

The slide expanded until it threatened to engulf the section of road where the truck sat. Beaman hit the driver hard in the shoulder.

"Vamoose, muchacho. We don't want to die here."

The terrified driver punched the truck's accelerator, popped the clutch, and they jumped ahead, just before another section of the road dropped away in the wake of the avalanche. They were a half-mile farther along the road before the rattle of the truck's engine washed out the continual roar of the ancient mountain collapsing behind them.

A three-man jazz combo played soft, pleasant dance music as the small riverboat rocked gently in the wake of a passing ferry. A gentle breeze wafted down from the nearby mountains and kept the mosquitoes and gnats at bay. A table on the deck was laden with a buffet while waiters circulated among the two dozen or so party guests with champagne glasses on trays hoisted over their shoulders. Strands of Oriental lamps and hanging baskets of fragrant flowers gave the deck a soft, dreamy feel as darkness fell.

Three men wearing their customary camouflage uniforms stood at the head of the table talking quietly. One, the man with a horrid scar across his face, seemed especially nervous, anxious to make a point.

"What could El Jefe be thinking, having all three of us here on this vessel at the same time?" Colonel Guillermo Marquez groused, shifting from one foot to the other. He nervously surveyed the other guests nearby and gulped his wine. "Only in the safety of the hacienda are we ever all together at once. I appreciate the gesture, but . . ."

Colonel Ricardo Abella leaned down closer so he would not have to talk too loudly to be heard over the music.

"Relax, *mi amigo*. We are in one of the safest towns in our most secure territory. We could not be more protected if we were home in our own beds. It is as he has told us. He wanted to give us a few moments of pleasure, to reward us for all we have done for the revolution." The tall, stocky guerrilla colonel took a sip of his wine and grinned broadly. "Look, the river is beautiful, the evening delightful, and we certainly do not want to offend our host, do we?" He nodded over his shoulder, toward the far side of the boat. "Besides, our wives seem to be enjoying themselves for a change."

Sure enough, the three women stood together at the railing, comparing their new party dresses, gifts from El Jefe. They watched the lights of the town that lay on the far side of the river, laughing at a shared comment as they swayed contentedly with the music, trying out a few rusty dance steps. These women had given much to the revolution as well. They stayed home while their men, Juan de Santiago's most trusted colonels, continued the struggle. De Santiago himself had told them how important they were to the revolution when he met them at the gangplank and welcomed them aboard. It was a wonderful thing to have this rare evening with their husbands, along with a select few of the other members of their staffs and their wives. They appreciated Juan de Santiago actually thinking of such a thing. It was so unlike El Jefe, but they would not complain.

Even now, de Santiago seemed to be having a wonderful time talking with the beautiful young wife of one of Abella's lieutenants. He excused himself, took another glass of champagne from a passing waiter's tray, and joined the three soldiers who were still huddled at the head of the buffet table.

"My brave friends, you are not over there with your lovely wives, watching the reflection of the stars in their eyes?"

"We're only visiting with each other for a few minutes, El Jefe," Enrique Fernandez assured him. "These days, we seem to only see each other for seconds at a time in a jungle clearing somewhere or during the meetings at your hacienda. We were just comparing notes."

De Santiago pursed his lips, cocked his head, and scolded gently.

"Ah, but tonight's for your relaxation, not for work. For celebrating the culmination of our plans as they finally come to glorious fruition. Enjoy a nice trip upriver and back and the plentiful food and drink."

Guillermo Marquez acknowledged the sentiment with a tip of his wineglass but clearly couldn't resist expressing his misgivings to his leader.

"Still, sir, what with the treachery of El Falcone, it seems—"

"Damn El Falcone!" de Santiago exploded, his voice thunderous and vicious, his face contorted with rage. The wives at the railing turned to see what had caused the outburst. Everyone on deck hushed. The combo lost its tempo for a moment then resumed the soft samba they were playing. "Soon . . . very soon . . . El Falcone will be no more," the leader growled, more quietly now, but his eyes were still wild. "The bastard will no longer threaten me or the revolution."

He seemed then to be studying each of the faces of his colonels, to be examining their eyes for some sort of reaction to his words as they all fell into an awkward silence. De Santiago hardly seemed to notice that Guzmán, his bodyguard, had stepped up behind him.

"El Jefe, if I may have a moment," Guzmán finally said, discreetly tapping de Santiago on his shoulder.

The leader tensed his jaws, then finally smiled again.

"Gentlemen, enjoy this evening with your beautiful wives and your brave *compadres*. The revolution will still be there in the morning, I assure you." His grin became almost wicked then. "I highly recommend the oysters, flown in fresh from Barranquilla today. They will temper the steel in your swords later in the evening when you are back in your suites with your ladies, if you know what I mean."

He clinked glasses with each of his three colonels in turn, winked knowingly, and followed Guzmán to the darkness at the far end of the boat.

The drinks, the music, the soft rocking of the boat on the river finally seemed to be working their magic. The three soldiers began to relax. They strafed the buffet once more, then strolled over to stand with their wives, watching as the boat's crew cast off the lines and eased the vessel out into the current. They even dared quick kisses and stiff hugs as the boat pulled away from the wharf. The wife of Enrique Fernandez had to bend down to meet his lips and the others allowed themselves polite laughter at the sight.

Marquez, the internal-security expert, could not shake the strong uneasiness that almost overpowered him since he had boarded the party boat. The feeling was there despite the rare glow on his lady's face or the perfection of the soft-lit, fragrant evening. He knew he should be obeying his leader's order, enjoying this rare time away from the stealth and intrigue and death of his typical day.

Of all the members of de Santiago's inner circle, he was the one who had the most difficulty dismissing the threat of El Falcone. He, of all de Santiago's staff, understood the nature of one who was privy to such sensitive information and was so willing to share it with the enemy. He only regretted that the leader had not allowed him to pursue the spy himself. It was his job after all. But de Santiago had been adamant on that subject.

Of one thing he was certain; El Falcone would know about

the party this night aboard the riverboat. If he did, so did the enemy.

Marquez again tried to dismiss his fears, smiled and kissed his wife again, then led her past the other guests to the stern of the boat. The big paddlewheel was pushing them upriver now, its splashes igniting soft phosphorescence in the water. The lights of the town were easing away, dimming in the soft mist of the warm evening. Now, away from the lights, the stars overhead were brilliant, the sky vast and dark.

Then Marquez saw something. Something that made his heart stop for a moment.

There, standing side by side on the wharf from which the boat had moved away a few moments before, were Juan de Santiago and Guzmán. They were quietly watching the boat steam upriver, not waving or hailing them to come back.

Why would the boat leave without the host of the party on board?

Guillermo Marquez realized the answer to his question only an instant before the deck buckled beneath his feet. Before the massive explosion ripped the doomed vessel apart. Before white, hot fire devoured the entire world.

"I hope you realize what you have done," Guzmán said sadly. Horrified people were running past them, trying to see what the tremendous explosion on the river had been. Some windows had shattered in the building behind them and there was the distant wailing of a siren, already headed their way.

"Oh, I know perfectly well, Guzmán. I have sacrificed the lives of true patriots to make certain I have sent the soul of one damned traitor to burn in hell."

The river's current brought bits of flaming wreckage past them, but there were no cries of survivors. The flickering fires lit the stony face of Juan de Santiago with an eerie light, revealing what appeared to be pure hate in his eyes.

"You have killed men who are valuable to you, to the revolution."

"There are a hundred more waiting to take their place."

"But how can you be certain that one of the colonels was El Falcone?"

"I cannot be certain, of course. But it was a gamble I was forced to take. Our plan is too critical to risk having him remain alive a moment longer. The process of elimination leaves no one else." He turned toward Guzmán. "Unless he is you, my friend."

Guzmán didn't give the leader time to ponder that possibility any longer. He ushered El Jefe back toward his car before someone in the panicked crowd recognized the leader of the revolution walking there among them.

17

SPADEFISH SLID ALMOST EFFORTLESSLY THROUGH THE DEEP, LITTLE more than a black shape in a world without light. Eight hundred feet above, the sun was setting in a glorious splash of red and orange painted over a turquoise blue sea. The brilliant light show never filtered through to this depth. The march of sun and moon across the sky was meaningless. Day and night were marked only by the changing of the watch aboard the submarine.

Since submerging a mile outbound from Buoy Sierra Delta, *Spadefish* had run steadily at twenty knots, heading southward. She was now cruising five hundred miles almost due west of Acapulco, Mexico.

Jon Ward sat at the desk in his tiny stateroom, flipping through the patrol order one more time. His executive officer, Joe Glass, sat across from him, both elbows resting on the table, looking at a fresh, empty page of his yellow legal pad.

"XO, the way I see it," Ward finally said, "we run down to the patrol box, look around, and see what we can turn up. Check on traffic, that sort of thing. But we need to be ready to shoot at a moment's notice. That's why we're there."

Joe Glass looked up from the pad. He began to hastily scribble notes from the random discussion that he and the skipper were having. Two years' experience as Ward's executive officer had taught him that these sessions were not nearly so random as he first imagined. What to the casual observer appeared to be the skipper stating the obvious, or unconnected thoughts spoken out loud, were, in reality, Ward's way of carefully weaving a complete and complex plan. Glass learned that if he missed noting any of the details, he would be in trouble later when he had to rely on little more than his memory.

"No threat down there that I know of," Ward went on, seemingly thinking out loud.

"No, except maybe accidentally slamming into a fishing boat," Glass agreed.

Ward looked up at his XO.

"I meant an ASW threat." The commander was talking about the likelihood of needing any of the sub's torpedoes. "Anyway, it's a fact that we need Tomahawks more than we need self-defense weapons. Have Stan load all four torpedo tubes with Tomahawks."

Normally, a submarine on patrol kept torpedoes loaded in all four torpedo tubes. If the captain expected to be shooting missiles, he would load three of the tubes with missiles beforehand, but keep one tube loaded with a torpedo for use in case the boat was attacked. That was true in peacetime as well as when at war.

Glass scribbled a couple of lines then asked, "Why don't we shift weapons stowage around so that four more Tomahawks are ready to load in all tubes, too?"

The torpedo room on Spadefish was completely full. All four torpedo tubes now contained Mk 48 ADCAP advanced-capability heavyweight torpedoes, ready to fire immediately if needed. The weapons stowage racks in the torpedo room contained two more ADCAPs, but on this mission, they also held twenty-two TLAM-D Tomahawk land-attack cruise missiles. The "D" variant of the missile contained a submunitions warhead with 160 bomblets, each loaded with 2.2 pounds of high explosives.

Back-hauling the four-thousand-pound ADCAPs to load each torpedo tube with TLAM-Ds was a carefully choreographed game of musical chairs. Removing the torpedoes and reloading each of the four tubes with missiles would keep Chief Bill Ralston and his men busy for at least four hours. Thankfully, *Spadefish* was equipped with hydraulic weapons-handling equipment, so the backbreaking labor of manually moving the behemoths with ropes and tackle, as was once the case, was now gone. Even so, it was difficult, tedious, and sometimes downright dangerous work.

The torpedo-room load plan was carefully set up well ahead of battle so that the torpedo tubes were ready with the weapons that would be needed. The ones most likely needed next were sitting there, conveniently ready to load. With a normal choice of Tomahawk land-attack missiles, Harpoon anti-ship missiles, or torpedoes, and with only four tubes to shoot them from, critical tactical planning was necessary. Suddenly needing to shoot a torpedo when only TLAMs were ready could, at best, mean having to break away from an attack. At worst, the sub would be unable to defend itself.

Late model *Los Angeles*-class boats and the new *Virginia*-class submarines bypassed some of this problem by having twelve external vertical launch tubes for Tomahawk missiles, freeing the torpedo tubes for other duties. *Spadefish* was much too long in the tooth for such a nicety.

Both Ward and Glass agreed to put all their eggs in one basket and have eight TLAM-Ds ready to go: four in the tubes, four right behind them, ready to load. If Bill Beaman and his SEAL team needed missiles to rain down on target, they would do their damnedest to have them ready for them.

Cookie Dotson knocked at the door and stepped in at

Ward's invitation. He carried a tray that contained a pot of coffee, two cups, and something that smelled wonderfully good.

"Excuse me Skipper, XO. I've got some fresh coffee." He carefully set the pot and cups on the little table, then put down a napkin-covered plate between the two men. "Thought you two would like some of these before those chow hounds in the wardroom ate them all."

Pulling off the napkin with a theatrical flourish, he revealed a plate heaped high with chocolate-chip cookies, still warm and gooey from the oven.

"Cookie, you read minds! If I didn't know better, I would say you're trying to boost your ranking in the chiefs' evals," Ward kidded good-naturedly as he reached for one of the cookies.

Glass nodded in agreement, unable to say anything above a grunt around one of the cookies, which was already disappearing into his mouth.

Dotson smiled appreciatively and wiped his hands on the always-present, greasy apron.

"Now, Skipper, you know I would never stoop to bribery or anything like that. Wouldn't be fair. I got too many weapons."

He winked and turned to head back to his galley.

Pouring himself a cup of the coffee, Ward idly chewed for a moment before he continued. He had shifted back into "skipper mode," and Glass doubted he even tasted the cookie he was munching.

"Joe, what really worries me is the reactor core. This high-speed run we're making means we're getting really near a max-peak xenon-precluded start-up. We're going to have to be very careful or we're going to be in a fix."

Spadefish's S3G nuclear reactor core contained a little over two hundred pounds of enriched uranium 235. Over the long life of the core, about half of that had been burned up, used to drive the boat. Most of the uranium that was left was needed to maintain a critical mass. This would be simple to do if the core only needed to supply enough neutrons to make up for those that escaped. But it was more complicated than that, because the fission process got in the way.

When a U^{235} atom fissioned, the result was energy, several neutrons, some assorted beta and gamma particles, and the nuclei of two new atoms. These new atoms had atomic weights distributed roughly around 88 and 134 atomic mass units.

One of the most common fission products was xenon. Its decay product, kyrpton, was a ravenous neutron absorber. When the reactor was critical, this was not a problem since the kyrpton burned up as rapidly as it was produced. The problem came when the reactor had been operated at high powers for a long time then was suddenly shut down. The xenon continued to decay to kyrpton for several hours afterward, and since the reactor was not producing neutrons anymore to burn the excess kyrpton, it built up to a high level.

If the reactor had to be restarted before the kyrpton decayed away, the core had to come up with enough neutrons to do both—to supply the fission process for energy and to burn away the poison. Through most of the life of the reactor, there was enough U^{235} supply the needed neutrons. This late in *Spadefish*'s life, though, there wasn't enough left even with the control rods all the way out of the core. The only choices were either to wait several hours while the xenon decayed away, or, if there was a chance the sub might need to be restarted soon after shutdown, simply not run at high power levels for several hours before shutting down.

The real problem came if the reactor was shut down at sea, either intentionally or through a fault. If the crew could not find the cause, fix it, and restart it within about fifteen minutes, they would be stuck, wallowing helplessly on the surface without the reactor for hours.

Glass grabbed another cookie as he pondered the skipper's words.

"Won't be a problem once we are in area. I don't see any need to run around much then. We'll just have to stay up at full power until we get there." Another cookie disappeared. "These are great. Better grab one before I eat them all, Skipper."

Ward looked over his reading glasses at the few remaining cookies.

"XO, if you reach for another one, you'll pull away a stump."

Ward tried to manage a grin but he was already considering what the next possible anomaly he might have to consider would be. The oxygen generator. The load of missiles. The reactor core.

That seemed to be the list for now.

Jonathan Ward couldn't shake the nagging feeling that almost anything could happen next on this old boat.

Anything.

Juan de Santiago was raving like a madman. Guzmán had not seen him like this since the day they had watched the American helicopters destroy the coca field over the mountains from the rebel headquarters. This fit seemed to be taking on even greater proportions. The man had been ranting for hours, his face contorted and purple, the veins in his neck bulging.

"I'll kill them all!" he threatened. "They'll learn to deal with me!"

His voice had grown strained and scratchy from the threats, the oaths, the groans. Guzmán remained out of reach, certain at times during the tirade that El Jefe would strangle any living thing he could get his hands on.

Guzmán glanced at the innocent-looking note on de Santiago's desk. This little slip of paper was the offending instrument, the catalyst that had set off the reaction that had resulted in several broken lamps and fractured furniture.

The note was from Antonio de Fuka. It informed de Santiago that the trucks had stopped departing from the vast coca fields in the hidden, high valley. His scouts there reported that a massive rockslide wiped out almost a kilometer of the roadway into and out of the valley. An explosion had set off the slide.

Those fields in Peru were de Santiago's most secret and

highly prized project. Nothing else in his glorious plan would work unless the product could be grown and processed. No one except de Fuka, Guzmán, and he, along with the handful of workers and drivers even knew where they were. The few peasants who worked there and those who drove and guarded the trucks were forbidden to associate with anyone else in his organization. They didn't even know they worked for de Santiago's rebels. Most of them assumed they were part of the Shining Path group. They were all too frightened, for their own lives as well as those of their wives and children, to ever speak of the fields to anyone.

"That road was built by our ancestors, Guzmán," De Santiago said. "It has stood for a thousand years. Now the damned Americans have destroyed it. They will die a horrible death."

Someone had broken the secret and the fields had been taken away from him in less than a minute. The road would take months to repair, if it could be repaired at all. He needed the coca now. The crop was ready. It would all rot before a new way out of the valley could be readied. All was waiting for delivery to his factory then for shipment north. There was only enough processed and stockpiled now for one lone shipment.

"Guzmán, double the guard on the new processing plant. We must protect it at all costs and there is a good chance this rat in our midst may have told them where to locate it also. And Guzmán, find the traitor. Bring him to me. I will kill him slowly with my own hands while his children watch."

"You are satisfied you did not end the regime of El Falcone on the party boat then?"

"The bastard still defies me, Guzmán. Find him!"

De Santiago's voice wheezed as he spoke. The bodyguard nodded glumly and left the room. The rebel leader angrily grabbed his cell phone and punched in a number so forcefully he twice dropped the instrument.

Philippe Zurko answered the incessant buzzing on the nightstand next to his bed. Who in hell would call at a time like this? It was siesta! Only an uncivilized lout would disturb someone at this hour of the afternoon. He rolled over and reached across the sleeping form of his newest mistress to grab the phone from the bedside table. She moaned sleepily and obligingly reached to hold him, to allow him to take her once again if he so wished, but he roughly pushed her away.

"Zurko," he barked.

De Santiago started right in.

"Philippe, have the *Zibrus* ready in one week. We must now move quickly."

"But El Jefe, we have not yet tested the systems," Zurko protested, trying to shake the spiderwebs from his head. He slept best after sex, and this latest woman had the ability to put him under deeply. "The boat has not even been in the water yet. We need time to check everything out and one week will not—"

De Santiago didn't appear to be hearing the arguments.

"One week, Philippe. The shipments will be ready and so must be the means to transport it. There is no room for error. You understand? No room for error!"

Zurko heard the connection break and he was listening to a humming, dismissing dial tone. That and the faint snore his mistress had resumed.

El Falcone was confused, frustrated. The leader's side of the conversation had been clear enough on the sensitive listening device, but its meaning was as clouded as an Andean peak.

What was this *Zibrus*? It was some means of transporting the cocaine, but how was it any different from the usual methods adopted by de Santiago and his smugglers?

There was a strong urge to report this bit of information to the contact at JDIA, but there was so little to go on, so many pieces missing from the puzzle. It was not worth the risk until there was more to tell.

At least the information about the coca fields had paid dividends. The JDIA had certainly struck a blow to de Santiago's plans. At the same time, the destruction of the road to the fields had apparently hastened whatever the next move was to be, a move that involved something called *"Zibrus."*

Maybe El Jefe would call someone else, say something to

reveal what this mystery might be. Despite the straining, the hush-breathed listening, all El Falcone could hear now on the earpiece was the pounding of the leader's boots as he paced rhythmically from one end of his study to the other.

Bill Ralston stood at the hydraulic control station. From here at the aft end of the torpedo room, he could, with the flip of a few levers, send the long green torpedoes or silver missile canisters scooting across the room. This had been his kingdom for fifteen years on three different subs, and nothing, but nothing, happened in his room without Bill Ralston knowing about it. He had trained every one of these boys himself, including the Weps, and he trusted them implicitly. When you were throwing around high explosives inside a sub eight hundred feet below the surface of the ocean, that faith was critical.

The brightly lit room hummed with activity now as they followed the XO's orders to reconfigure the weapons. A four-man team worked on each side of the room, unloading ADCAPs and reloading the torpedo tubes with Tomahawk missiles.

Stan Guhl sat at the torpedo launch control console, lodged between the two banks of huge bronze torpedo tubes at the forward end of the room. He quietly, proudly watched his team at work. Like Ralston, he knew enough about these men and how well they did their jobs that he would trust his life with them. As he observed, the silver-gray TLAM-D canister slid silently into the number-four torpedo tube. Number four was the lower tube on the port side.

Sam Benitez shut the tube door and rolled the huge bronze locking ring. That was the last one to load.

"All done, Chief," he sang, and slapped the locking ring. "Can I go outside and play now?"

"Not hardly, you slacker! We got one more little square dance for you goof-offs."

Benitez began an energetic dance routine around the cramped torpedo room, singing some song in loud, off-key Spanish. He grabbed Ralston on the way past and swept him up into the waltz. The chief broke away, trying not to laugh. Guhl and the other torpedo men cackled and clapped along.

"You dance divinely, Chief!" Benitez yelped, and pranced away, now without his rather rotund partner.

"You don't quit that foolishness, you'll be chipping paint for a year once we get home," Ralston growled.

Now they had the job of moving the weapons around so there was a TLAM-D behind each tube, ready to load in a hurry. With a full torpedo room, it was a shuffle. To get one weapon in the necessary position might mean moving three or four others in the right sequence. Just like those pocket number games, only on a grand scale.

Benitez waved off the chief's admonition. At least the tension in the room had been broken and they could move to the next job at hand. He bent low to line the skid-tray dogs on the ADCAP torpedo that they had just back-hauled. It had to be moved to the outboard stowage position. Each weapon was cradled on four heavy metal supports, called "trucks," which were mated to grooves in the deck with special dogs. Metal bands reached around and clutched the weapons firmly to the trucks. The dogs could be aligned to move the weapon sideways across the room or locked firmly in place to prevent any movement with the rocking and changing attitude of the sub.

Benitez carefully checked each dog on the ADCAP. He had to make sure they were rolled to the transverse position. He disappeared from view as he leaned across the torpedo so he could get a look at the outboard dogs.

Meanwhile, Bill Ralston pushed the lever for the lower travelers. Hydraulic oil flowed to move the chain drive. The dogs for the ADCAP, engaged with the chain, smoothly moved the dark green behemoth.

Benitez, lying over the torpedo, out of sight, didn't even have a chance to scurry out of the way. Three-thousand-pound-per-square-inch hydraulic oil moving a four-thousand-pound torpedo was far stronger than any man's rib cage.

The quiet hum of the room was rent by an agonized scream.

Ralston jerked the lever back to reverse the move. Stan Guhl leapt from his seat. Benitez lay sprawled over the AD-CAP, moaning awfully, a steady stream of blood dripping from his chin.

"Injured man in the torpedo room! Corpsman, lay to the torpedo room!"

The 1MC announcement jerked Doc Marston from an extremely realistic dream he was having, one that included two girls, a fast, red sports car, and some rather interesting anatomical studies.

Rubbing sleep from his eyes and grumbling about the XO running drills while he was dreaming, he zipped up his poopie suit, grabbed his medical bag, and ran out of the chiefs' quarters. He would fuss later. Right now, he had to carry out the drill just like it was the real thing.

Doc dropped down the ladder to find Guhl and Ralston trying their best to help a badly injured Benitez.

"Outta my way! Comin' through!" the corpsman shouted.

One glance at Benitez told Doc more than he wanted to know. There had to be massive internal injuries. And when Ralston described the accident, it removed all doubt. The man was barely breathing, each gasp an agony. Bright red blood still trickled from the corner of Benitez's lips and his face was ashen, his skin clammy. He was already in shock.

Marston was in way over his head and he knew it.

"Weps, I need a backboard to move Benitez to the wardroom. Help me keep his head lower than his feet. Tell the Skipper we need a medevac right away!"

Guhl was on the horn before the corpsman finished the sentence.

When he heard the 1MC, Ward ran directly to the control room, Joe Glass on his heels. The room was dark, illuminated only by several red fluorescent tubes.

When Ward stepped up on the conn, Steve Friedman, the

officer of the deck for this watch, reported, "Skipper, Doc says Benitez is hurt bad. We need medevac pronto. I've come up to one-five-zero feet and started a baffle clear. No contacts yet."

Spadefish was headed for the surface to get shallow enough that they could send a radio signal. They also had to make sure they weren't coming up beneath a ship. So far, the ocean above them was clear.

"Okay. Let's get up to periscope depth. Have Radio ready to send an urgent priority message the instant we get there. XO, get down there and find out what is going on."

Glass turned and rushed out of the control room.

Ward stepped over to the quartermaster's stand, dodging Cortez, who was rushing to man his own station. Earl Beasley had just arrived, zipping his poopie suit as he ran.

"Nav, what's the distance to the nearest port?" Ward asked, but he had a reasonable idea already.

"About five hundred miles, Skipper. Puerto Vallarta, Mexico."

"Damn, that's twenty hours!"

"We wouldn't have to run all the way. Helicopter might save us a hundred miles. That buys us four hours."

Friedman, holding a black JA phone handset, yelled, "Skipper, XO needs to talk to you."

"Tell him I'll be right there." Turning back to Beasley, he asked, "Any ships around that could help? Either with a medical capability or a chopper?"

Beasley shook his head mournfully.

"No, sorry. Nothing tracking anywhere close. We're too far out of the way for once."

All those drills in all that traffic, and now, when they needed help, not a tub in sight. Ward stepped back to the periscope stand.

"Steve, we about to get to PD?"

They could do nothing to summon help until they were at periscope depth.

"Yes, sir. Cleared baffles to port. No sonar contacts. Coming up on course zero-nine-zero, speed five knots. Request permission to come to periscope depth."

Ward looked at the BQQ-5 sonar display for a second, double-checking what Friedman had just told him. The waterfall display was an incoherent mishmash of dots, no cleanly drawn line of a ship contact. There was only the chaotic noise of an empty ocean above them.

"Officer of the deck, proceed to periscope depth."

Ward grabbed the JA handset then and started talking quietly to the XO.

"Aye, sir!" Friedman confirmed Ward's order. "Diving Officer, make your depth six-two feet."

The deck angled upward as the planesmen pulled back on their control yokes. Friedman reached over his head, grabbing the red ring encircling the scope.

"Number-two scope coming up."

Seaman Cortez opened his mouth to say something. MacNaughton kicked his shin.

"Shhh, we're coming to PD!" he whispered. Nobody talked now, unless it was either part of the procedure of coming to periscope depth or an emergency.

A jerk of the wrist on the control ring and the greased mast rose smoothly out of its well. Friedman squatted down and followed it upward. As the eyepiece rose out of the well, he snapped down the handles, pressed his eye to it, and started to step around in a slow circle.

Friedman rotated his right wrist counterclockwise until the handle wouldn't turn anymore. He was looking almost straight up toward the surface, although in the pitch-black ocean, he couldn't tell for sure.

Doug Lyman, the diving officer of the watch, yelled, "Depth one-two-five feet, coming up."

Bits of phosphorescence flashed by Friedman's field of view like jagged streaks of lightning. He rotated his wrist until he felt a slight detent and that lowered the elevation of his field of view. He continued to slowly walk a circle, moving the scope through repeated 360-degree rotations. "Dancing with the fat lady," submariners called it, the slow, vigilant rotation, looking all around trying desperately to see anything that might be in the way of the surfacing submarine.

"Depth one-zero-zero feet."

Still nothing but blackness save for the flashes. Rotate the wrist a little more; look down a little more.

"Nine-zero feet."

Black as sin out tonight. Another click. Still nothing to see. Dance around another circle.

"Eight-zero feet."

Darkness.

"Seven-zero feet."

Friedman felt the ship level out a little. Must be about a five-degree up angle by now. Just right for PD in this sea-state. Still pitch black.

"Six-five feet."

Friedman finally saw waves breaking over the scope. Between the splashes he could just make out the brilliantly bright stars in the black, moonless sky overhead.

"Six-two feet and holding."

They were at PD.

Friedman whipped the scope around, making two complete revolutions, looking at the horizon. No telltale hulking shadow blocking the horizon, no red or green running lights on some ship the sonar had missed hearing. They were all alone in this part of the ocean.

Friedman yelled out, "No close contacts."

Everyone breathed easier. They had been keyed for an "emergency deep" if someone was up there. Now, safely at the proper depth, they could go back to business.

Friedman continued to search the placid ocean all the same. The stars formed a speckled canopy overhead. Far off to the east, the red lights of a jet airplane blinked as it transported a load of satiated sun-worshippers returning northward from the beaches of Mexico. A cloud slid aside and allowed a sliver of a moon to send a silvery trail down sea from the southwest.

It was a calm, beautiful night up top.

Ward broke the mood.

"Steve, the message is ready in Radio. Raise the BRA-34 and transmit. As soon as you have receipt acknowledged, go to four hundred feet and flank, course zero-nine-zero."

They would head eastward, assuming help would come from the closest point of land.

"Aye, sir. Chief of the Watch, raise number-two BRA-34. Tell Radio to transmit the released message when ready."

Sam Bechtal, the chief of the watch, flipped a switch high up on the control panel he faced. A small green "housed" light flashed out and a red "up" light flashed on, indicating the antenna was out of its sheath and ready. "Number-two BRA-34 indicates 'up.'"

Friedman heard a quick burst of static from a speaker behind him, hooked to an intercept receiver on the periscope. Radio had sent the message.

Cortez listened on the phone headset he wore. Turning to Friedman, he reported, "Officer of the Deck, Radio reports message sent and acknowledged. No longer need the BRA-34."

"Chief of the Watch, lower all masts and antennas!" Friedman ordered crisply. "Diving Officer, make your depth four hundred feet."

He slapped up the handles on the scope and reached for the red control ring. The scope slid smoothly back down into the well.

Bechtal saw all the lights on his display panel light up with a green "housed" light.

"All masts and antennas indicate 'housed.'"

Friedman ordered, "All ahead flank!"

Spadefish dove back into the depths and leaped ahead.

Jonathan Ward stepped into the wardroom. It was transformed from the pleasant, paneled, clublike atmosphere he knew. Two huge operating room lights protruded from the overhead, illuminating the table with their harsh, white glare. The brown

Naugahyde was off the table, replaced with white cloth sheets and a green oxygen bottle. The serving buffet was littered with chrome pans of sterilized instruments.

Sam Benitez lay on the table, pale as death. Tubing ran from his nose to the oxygen regulator. There was a horrible, telling rattle every time he breathed in and out.

In all his years at sea, Ward had never seen anything quite so stark.

"How is he, Doc?"

Doc Marston looked up and answered as soon as he had finished checking Benitez's pulse.

"Not good, Skipper. He has internal injuries I can't handle. No telling what all he has crushed in there, but I know he has punctured both lungs. He needs that blood drained off, like, right now, but a surgeon would have to do that. I gave him two ampoules of morphine and have him on oxygen. Otherwise, he'd be struggling so bad for breath we couldn't hold him down. That's about all I can do." Marston shrugged helplessly and looked at Ward, pleading with his eyes. "Skipper, we got to get him to a hospital quick or we'll lose him for certain."

"Doc, we're doing everything we can."

Ward listened to the noise of the young submariner's distressed breathing, watched the jerky rise and fall of his injured chest.

Never had he felt so helpless. Here, in the midst of all this technology, all this whiz-bang gear and all these gizmos, there was no piece of equipment he or the doc could reach out and grab and make it better.

No, he and all these highly trained men could do nothing more than stand there, their hands in their pockets, and watch this brave young man die.

18

ADMIRAL TOM DONNEGAN LAID THE REPORT ASIDE SO HE COULD reach across the end table to grab the jangling phone before it woke his wife, sleeping in the bedroom next door. The blood-red telephone in his home study almost never rang. It was the only official outside line that came directly into his house on Ford Island. All the others were routed through his yeoman at COMSUBPAC headquarters. His heart quickened. It would have to be something important. Especially at this hour.

"Donnegan."

"Admiral, sorry to disturb you this late. This is John Bethea. Emergency message from *Spadefish*. They have an injured man. Ward says it's pretty bad. One of his crew was crushed handling weapons. It looks like it's touch-and-go for the guy. Corpsman says they need to medevac him ASAP or the guy won't make it. Can you help us expedite?"

Donnegan removed his reading glasses and looked out the window. The warm wind gently rustled through the palms and bougainvillea, barely visible in the faint light. The sweet scent of plumeria filtered in through the French doors that led out to the lanai and filled the room with its pleasant perfume.

"What's their position?" he asked.

"Ward reports they are five hundred miles west of Puerto Vallarta, Mexico, and heading that way at flank."

"Okay, John, we'll take it from here. We'll set up a mede-vac and give them the water in that direction. Nobody's down there anyway. If I know Jon Ward, he'll run at flank until he's close enough for a helo transfer, whether he owns the water or not."

Bethea acknowledged, said his quick thanks, and hung up.

Donnegan dropped the red instrument back into its cradle and quickly grabbed the regular telephone. This was one of the bad things about being the man-in-charge. The sudden, late-night emergency calls, the little bit of action as he quickly put all the parts into motion. Then the gut-wrenching anguish of waiting, knowing that one of his people out there was in trouble. And that he had done all he could do once he had pulled the levers necessary to set everything off. Nothing to do but wait and pray, hope the injured sailor could hold on until he could be medevacked.

Donnegan punched the speed dial number for the SUBPAC ops center. The watch officer answered on the first ring.

"Yes sir, Admiral."

"Commander, *Spadefish* needs an immediate medevac. Get CINCPAC on the phone. We need something with the legs to get to her quickly. She's five hundred miles off Puerto Vallarta, Mexico, heading that way at flank."

"Yes, sir!"

And that was that. Now, there was only the waiting. That and the praying.

Commander Jon Ward stepped into the chiefs' quarters. The quiet, dimly lighted space always reminded him of a small cave, like the ones he had played in as a kid when he spent summers with his father's kinfolk back in eastern Kentucky. Deep blue curtains hanging from the fore and aft bulkheads hid the darkened bunkrooms that were stacked along the walls. With the continuous watch rotation on a boat at sea, someone was always in there sleeping, and, sure enough, he could hear faint snores now.

The men were sleeping despite the sad scene in the middle of the room. Bill Ralston, tears streaming down his face, sat there at the table, his shoulders hunched and his body shaking with sobs. The Chief of the Boat, Master Chief Laskowski, and Master Chief Ray Mendoza sat on either side of the anguished man, each trying awkwardly, futilely, to give him some faint solace.

Ralston, his eyes red, his face contorted, looked up as Ward entered.

"I killed him, Skipper. I screwed up and killed him." More sobs. Laskowski put an arm across the man's shoulder. Ralston slumped down, head in hands, and stared at the deck. "I thought everyone was clear, so I hit the hydraulics. I didn't know anything was wrong till I heard Benitez scream. Oh, God, I still hear that scream! I know I always will!"

Ward looked down solemnly at the seated chief, wishing he could somehow find the words that might ease the man's pain.

"We're doing all we can for him, Bill. Doc is with him and we've got help on the way. He'll pull through. We've got to believe that. Just keep praying."

Ralston stifled another sob.

"I always trained them to be so careful. 'Follow the book,' I always preached to 'em till I know they got sick of hearing me say it. Skipper, they're the best bunch I ever had. And what happens? I'm the son of a bitch that screws up. How am I going to face them, Skipper? How am I going to look Benitez in the eye again?"

It was Laskowski who answered him.

"Bill, you aren't the first man in this navy to screw up and you aren't the first chief to accidentally hurt one of his guys, either. It's tough duty down there and you know it as well as anybody. Accidents happen. No matter how well trained you all are, or how careful you try to be." Laskowski gripped the chief's shoulder. "And if I know Bill Ralston, I know how you'll handle this thing. You'll carry on. You'll do your job. We got a mission and you and the rest of your guys are a big part of what we're going down there to do. Just do like the Skipper says and pray Benitez makes it. Otherwise, just do your job, Chief."

Ralston sighed and looked first at Laskowski then Ward.

"Okay, COB. I appreciate it, buddy. That's what I'll try to do."

Ward rose to leave.

"I couldn't have said it better, COB. I've got to get up to the conn. We need to get back up to PD. SUBPAC should have medevac instructions ready for us by now. We'll get Benitez off. I'll keep you posted on how he's doing."

The skipper patted Ralston on the forearm and turned away. He had seen Benitez, had seen the gray pallor of his skin, had heard the rattle in his shallow breathing. He suspected what that condition update would likely eventually be. And he already dreaded having to relay that news.

The hazy gray MV-22 Osprey roared across the open water. The Mexican coastline had disappeared astern half an hour before, and now both the pilot and the copilot strained to try to pick out the little black shape in the vastness of the open sea. The Osprey wasn't designed at all to try to find a tiny ship at sea. It had been designed and built to carry marines into combat. As such, there was no surface-search radar, only the eyes of the two men who flew her. Still it was faster than anything else available and had the range to meet up with the submarine to bring back the injured sailor.

The copilot yelled and pointed excitedly just to the right of straight ahead.

"There she is! On the horizon, bearing a little bit to the north of due west!"

It took the pilot another few seconds to see what the man in the right seat was pointing to. *Spadefish* was no more than a black dot with a long thin white tail trailing behind.

The Osprey banked slightly and headed directly for the surfaced sub. The copilot reached over to the radio on the panel between them and flicked the frequency selector. He keyed the microphone.

"Hotel-Bravo-Four this is Romeo-Six-Charlie. I hold you visually."

The reply was immediate.

"Roger Romeo-Six-Charlie. We see you. Surface winds

five knots from two-six-one. Sea-state zero. Coming to all-stop. Ready for transfer when you are."

In the sub's bridge cockpit, Jon Ward turned to Chris Durgan.

"Mr. Durgan, tell the COB to lay topside with the helo-transfer party."

Looking back over his shoulder, Ward saw the hatch swing open. A group of men, led by the Chief of the Boat, climbed out onto the rounded, wet main deck. Each sailor wore an orange safety harness over his blue poopie suit. They clipped their traveler to the deck track as they stepped out.

"Mr. Durgan, tell the XO to send the injured man topside," Ward ordered, then watched as several of the group on deck clustered around the hatch. They bent to gently lift a wire stretcher basket out through the opening from below decks. Benitez, still on the stretcher, was carefully strapped inside. Doc Marston came through the hatch right behind his patient and knelt down beside him, hovering like a mother hen watching over a wounded chick.

The Osprey swooped low over the submarine's deck. The roar of the massive turbines was near deafening. The huge engine nacelles at the ends of the stubby wings rotated from a horizontal position to a vertical one. In one smooth operation, the aircraft transitioned from a normal turboprop plane to a twin-rotor helicopter, able to float in midair a few feet above *Spadefish*. The huge propeller/rotors whipped a deluge of wind-driven spray, soon soaking everyone below. The clean smell of the ocean air was replaced with that of the exhaust from the Osprey's jet turbines.

The starboard side hatch on the hovering bird slid open and an airman leaned through the hatch to lower a cable to the deck. Laskowski grabbed the cable with a tool that resembled a clear, plastic shepherd's crook with a heavy copper wire in its center. The wire emerged from the butt end of the crook and clipped to the steel deck of the submarine. Static electricity crackled and arced where the crook touched the cable as the electric potential stored in the aircraft discharged through the hull of the sub to the sea. Without the grounding tool, anyone grabbing the steel cable would have received a shock powerful enough to knock him to his knees.

Doc Marston grabbed the hook that dangled from the cable's end and attached it securely to Benitez's basket. Looking up at the airman waiting in the Osprey's doorway, Doc gave an exaggerated thumbs-up sign. The basket rose off the deck as the Osprey climbed higher, putting more air between itself and the sub. Benitez still dangled below as the Osprey picked up forward speed and started to transition back to horizontal flight once again.

"Hotel-Bravo-Four, this is Romeo-Six-Charlie. We have your man aboard. The doctor is looking him over now. He'll be in the operating room at Guadalajara in an hour. I'll make sure they keep you posted on how he's doing."

"Romeo-Six-Charlie, roger. Can't tell you guys how much we appreciate your help. Call us when we get back. Drinks are on us for a long time."

"Hotel-Bravo-Four, we'll hold you to that. Even with the cheap hooch we normally drink down here, that could get expensive. Romeo-Six-Charlie, out."

Ward glanced back at the main deck just in time to see the hatch shut. Looking to the east, Ward watched the Osprey grow smaller as it raced for the eastern horizon. When it was nothing more than dim lights approaching the horizon, he spoke again.

"Mr. Durgan, come around to course two-zero-zero and ahead full. Rig the bridge for dive. I'm laying below."

Chris Durgan answered with a snappy "Aye, sir," but the skipper had already disappeared through the hatch.

Tom Kincaid pulled into the parking space the best he could manage. These damn SUVs were impossible to parallel park, but there just wasn't any other place nearby to leave the vehicle. Either these things were built too big or the parking spaces were too small. The thing maneuvered like a boat, but in this neighborhood and at night, he didn't want to park too far from where he was going. He was confident he could de-

fend himself from some mugger. It was just that he didn't nec-
essarily want to have to. Not tonight.

He had the "land yacht" far enough out of the street to be
safe, he figured. He ignored the fact that the back tire was up
on the curb and the front fender protruded a bit out into traffic.

He climbed from the car and surveyed his surroundings.
The pavement was wet and oily, reflecting the orange-yellow
glow of the old-fashioned streetlights that, at one time, had
been considered quaint, but were now ugly. The street itself
was lined with businesses that prospered a generation before.
By the looks of them, most had fallen on hard times now. Several of the brick buildings were boarded up. Those that
weren't had the unmistakable air of seedy futility and despair.
The establishments nested there now shut down and went to
roost when the sun went down. Feet protruded from doorways
where homeless derelicts found shelter for the night.

There were signs of life a half block away. Near the corner
at a cross street. A flashing neon sign beckoned him warmly.
HARRY'S NEIGHBORHOOD BAR AND GRILL, it advertised.
Sounded welcoming enough. He walked closer. It looked how
one expected a "neighborhood" establishment to look in this
neighborhood. He doubted he would find any grill in the
place.

Kincaid pushed through the heavy, rusted metal door and
into a hazy blue-gray cloud of cigarette smoke. Nobody here
would ever think of enforcing any sissy no-smoking ordi-
nance. Several mismatched tables were spread around the
cramped room. A couple of booths sat against the back wall.
A half-dozen stools were lined up in front of a bar. A glowing
Budweiser sign and a television set suspended over the end of
the bar were the closest things the place had in the way of
decoration.

A group of men, most with their names stitched over the
pockets of their denim work shirts, were clustered around a
couple of the tables near the front, having a few beers. They
were loudly arguing the merits of the Seahawks' team this

Ken Temple

season, questioning the sanity of their so-called coach and the general manager who didn't know his ass from his elbow. From the battalion of empty long-necks standing at attention on the tables, the discussion had been going on for a while.

In one of the booths, a blowsy middle-aged woman with poorly dyed blond hair was climbing all over a beefy man, both of them oblivious of anything or anybody else in the bar. She looked like a housewife out for a little excitement while hubby worked the night shift somewhere.

Through the smoke, he spied Ken Temple sitting alone on one of the stools at the bar, nursing a glass of some amber-colored poison. A mirror ran the full length behind the bar, giving an excellent view of the backside of bottles of cheap booze lined up on shelves there. A purple and gold University of Washington decal had been stuck below the flashing Olympia Beer light.

Kincaid liked having the mirror there. It made it easier to watch his back.

He pulled up a stool next to the detective and tapped him on one of his knees.

"Hey, stranger. Once again, you have invited me to what is one of the best drinking establishments in the Pacific Northwest."

"Well, damned if it ain't God's gift to the DEA!" The cop winked, then quickly looked around to see if anyone else might have heard him use those initials. The blue collars were still arguing football and the couple in the booth seemed determined to both try to occupy the same bit of space at the same time. Temple lowered his voice when he spoke again. "Save anybody from the evils of killer weed today?"

"Nope. I only do that on Tuesdays and Fridays. Today was glue sniffers and cough-medicine junkies. What's that you're drinking, flatfoot?"

"Old Turkey, neat."

Kincaid looked over at the bartender, who was slouched down at the far end of the bar. He had a cigarette hanging from one corner of his mouth, watching through a continual curl of smoke the game show that was flickering on the TV. He also kept an eye on the amorous couple.

Kincaid waved. He finally got the man's attention. He pointed at Temple's drink and held up two fingers. The barkeep nodded and slowly ambled over to refill Temple's glass and pour one for Kincaid.

Temple watched Kincaid over the rim of his glass.

"Reason I called, we found the Farragut woman, the best friend of all those dead people we been turning up."

"Oh, where?"

He half expected to hear, "Dead. Under a bridge. ODed. Where the hell you think, Dick Tracy?" But not so.

"She had run to Las Vegas, looks like. She got spooked when her friends started showing up dead. She got stopped doing eighty-five in a forty-five zone, started acting skittish and the trooper ran her."

Kincaid took a sip of his drink and made a face.

"Damn! This stuff tastes like battery acid. How come you don't ever want to meet me someplace that serves good booze? You got a thing for these dives, don't you?"

Temple squinted at his friend through the thickening smoke. The bar could be ablaze and no one would be able to tell. There was an amused twinkle in the policeman's eye.

"It's part of being an underpaid flatfoot. We search out these little-known locales. You overpaid glamour types only get to sip your brandies and liqueurs in your fern bars and gentlemen's clubs. You miss the chance to explore some of the finer things in life down here where the real people live."

"Like 'Old Turkey-shit'?"

"Goes straight to the liver. Passes right on by the gut and cuts out the middle man altogether."

Temple looked around the dive once again. The bartender had moved back to his leaning spot, still alternately watching the gyrations in the far booth and Regis Philbin trying to give away a million bucks on the television set. No one in the joint was paying attention to the two men talking with each other at the bar. Kincaid clung to his old habits, watching for any sign someone might recognize him, have a score to settle. He always would.

"Anyhow, like I said, Nevada Highway Patrol ran her ID," Temple went on. "Turned up our warrant. They called, God bless 'em."

Kincaid leaned back on the stool, finished. Kincaid bit.

"Okay. She talking?"

Temple stared into the mirror. A thousand-mile stare, Kincaid called it. It was the stare of a man who had seen more than his share of maimed people, broken lives, heartless bad guys.

"Yeah, some. Scared bitch. Talks about some bastard named Ramirez. Carlos Ramirez. Ring any bells for you?"

Kincaid searched his memory as he sipped at the drink.

"Never heard of him. What did she say about the guy?"

"This Ramirez has ties to some jerk down in Colombia named de Santiago."

"Him I may have heard of," Kincaid offered but said no more, even when Temple waited for elaboration. When it was clear there would be none, the cop proceeded to leave his own hanging remark, thick as the cigarette haze in the barroom.

"That's all we have on that tie-in except . . ."

Kincaid waited, but only for a beat or two.

"Okay, except what?"

"Except this Ramirez bastard likes to brag to the ladies about ruling the whole U.S. drug trade market before it's all over. Like he's about to start printing up stock like one of them . . . what you call it? IOPs? IPOs? Whatever. He has his sights set real high. Miss Farragut is convinced from what-all he told her that he has the ways and the means to do it."

"Like what?"

"For one thing, he has a bunch of real nasties that work for him. Real scum. Chief one is a big black guy named Rashad. Jason Rashad. Ever hear of him?" Kincaid nodded a no but filed away the name next to "Carlos Ramirez." "From what she says, this new stuff they've started importing leaves you

absolutely hooked from the first snort. You'll do anything for
the next fix once you've had a taste. She picked up on something about how the first batch might have been even stronger
than the scum thought it was. Hooked some of the lovely folks
Miss Farragut sent to Ramirez's parties so bad they couldn't
get enough of the stuff. Damned amateurs killed themselves."
Temple slurped the last of the drink. He looked at Kincaid, his
big head cocked sideways. "Oh, and she said it was their usual
practice for Rashad and the rest of his Sunday-school class to
take liberties with the female victims while they were higher
than the Space Needle. That was before they knew they were
gonna OD and turn up as flesh-and-blood evidence in an alley
somewhere." The detective's eyes grew steely. "Tom, it's up to
us, you know. We've got to tear out this weed patch!"

Kincaid set his half-empty glass down on the nicked and
scratched bar top.

"I hear you, Ken," he said, too quietly to be heard above the
professional football coaches solving all the Seahawks' problems over at the tables.

"Tommy, something else is going on now. It's been too
quiet. We had that spate of dead people a month ago. Then
nothing. Not a peep. They couldn't have wanted to kill those
people. Stiffs can't buy coke. I figured they must have wanted
to get their recipe right and then they would be coming back
and opening up shop again."

"*Been* quiet? Something new happening I don't know
about?"

Temple had a hard look in his eyes. He reached inside his
jacket and pulled out a brown envelope.

"I figure Ramirez needed a little spending money. Maybe
the car payment came due and he tapped the stock." The big
cop swallowed hard. "Or they've sent some more of the shit in
already and it's just now hitting the street."

The photos were eight-by-ten black-and-white crime-scene
prints. One showed a pretty, dark-haired girl, on her back in
the rear seat of a car. Except for what looked like thick blood

on her upper lip, she could easily have been peacefully sleeping. The others were of a man, in his mid-twenties, curled up on a rumpled bed, and an older woman, lying on her side in what appeared to be a bathroom floor.

"What makes you think they're our guys?"

"All three were confirmed cokeheads. They've been snorting for years. All three ODed all of a damn sudden. Lab says it was the same poison that was killing the amateurs before. They can't figure what's in it. What makes it so damned delicious. But even experienced users are getting hold of the stuff and snorting themselves to death."

"Jesus."

The bartender sauntered over, bottle in hand. He refilled Temple's glass, glared at Kincaid for not having finished his own drink already, then headed back to his corner. The couple in the booth was approaching an X rating. The dirty blonde was now astraddle the fat guy. The barkeep didn't want to miss any of the free show.

"I know," Temple said. "What if there's more of this killer dope out there? Or more headed this way? How we going to stop it, Tommy? What happens if it gets here and into the supply chain? You have any idea how many stiffs we're gonna have piled up in the morgue? Especially if this stuff is as addictive as it looks. Everything's been just peachy lately, but my gut is telling me the other shoe is about to drop. And it won't be pretty when it does, Mr. DEA Man."

Kincaid abruptly stood and tossed a twenty on the bar.

"My gut tells me the same thing, Lieutenant. The very same thing. We can't afford to lose this war now. No way. Gotta run. Talk to you tomorrow maybe."

He was off the stool and gone.

Temple ruefully shook his head. That was one high-strung bastard right there. One intense son of a bitch. He was also glad Tom Kincaid was on his side.

Damned glad.

Juan de Santiago, the leader of the revolution, paced the length of the dining room. Seventeen paces in one direction. Turn. Seventeen steps in the other.

"My dear friend, Sui, this is the plan," he cooed into the telephone mouthpiece. "We are ready to make the first delivery with your product. My transport ship meets your ship in the mid-Pacific and transfers your powder to our boat. Your transport heads back home. Mine steams toward the United States and the world's most lucrative market for what you produce."

The cordless telephone was a real godsend to de Santiago. It freed him to pace, to allow his physical motion to keep pace with his mental gymnastics. Antonio de Fuka had assured him no one could get close enough to the compound to intercept the phone's nine-hundred-megahertz signal.

The tinny voice in the phone's earpiece urged de Santiago to go on.

"My people will process your heroin with the additive during the transit so it will be as addictive as our cocaine. The ship will rendezvous with the new transport sub outside U.S. territorial waters to make the transfer. Finally, beneath the surface and completely undetectable, the sub takes your shipment in for unloading and distribution."

Sui Kia Shun sat on the stone terrace of his palace on the Thai-Chinese border. He looked out over his gardens, resplendent with vanda and paphiopedilum orchids growing among the teak and bamboo thickets. This palace had been constructed during the early Ming dynasty to cement Chinese dominance over the southern barbarians. It had been six hundred years since Emperor Ming Chen Zu dispatched Sui's ancestors here to rule this land. And from this palace, they watched kingdoms rise and fall, the Mongols, the Manchurians, Europeans, Japanese, and now the Communists.

"Señor de Santiago, you have a most interesting operation. Please explain to me the need for the mid-Pacific transfer."

"Mr. Sui, it is a simple logistics problem. Because we made the special hull modifications to the mother transport, she can only steam at a maximum speed of fifteen knots." De Santiago stopped at the huge fireplace at one end of the room, turned and headed toward the other end again at a quick march. He did not breathe hard at all and the exertion had cleared his mind of his earlier frustrations. "If we steam that ship all the way to Thailand and back, the submarine would have to wait for over a month on the bottom of the sea. It doesn't have the endurance. It would also delay getting your product to your customers. And our distribution network is most anxious to go to work for us."

Sui sipped from his cup of tea.

"I see. Hmmm. Couldn't the transport bring the sub with it, then launch it once it was in position off the U.S. coast?"

"That would be technically possible. However, we felt that would raise suspicions with the Americans, or with anyone else who might accidentally see the operation. A transport manifested for Thailand loitering off the Washington coast, doing something strange with a mini-submarine? No, it is better for us to steam out to the mid-Pacific and meet your transport halfway, make the transfer, then come back with the product. A little paint and it becomes another cargo ship, maybe heading toward South America from Siberia. Meanwhile, the mini-sub is delivering our cocaine first, then heading northward for the transfer of your product off the Pacific Northwest coast."

Sui stroked his chin thoughtfully.

"Yes, I see. Very well planned. Let us proceed. My ship is loaded already and prepared to depart this evening. There is one thing that I must insist on, my friend. With this significant portion of my whole year's production aboard one ship, prudence requires that some of my people accompany the delivery. I will have a team transfer to your transport and one will go with the mini-sub once the off-loading is done."

De Santiago stopped in front of the huge polished dark wood bar. The crystal decanters gleamed on their silver serving trays. The value of one of the trays roughly matched the annual wages of a banana-plantation worker in his country.

He smiled as he poured a healthy shot of cognac into a snifter and warmed it gently with his hand. There had been a time when he might well have exploded at such insolence as the Oriental had just displayed, at distrust from someone like Sui. Despite the setback with the destruction of the road to the coca fields, he was certain that his grandiose plan could still work. With Sui's product and money, he could still manage to finance his operation until he could reestablish a crop in fields elsewhere. Before the landslide, they had hauled from the remote valley enough coca to comprise one lucrative shipment once it was processed. They had overcome the unfortunate problem with the additive. The mini-sub was ready to sail, the transport refitted and set to steam westward. Sui's ship filled with quality product, prepared to head for the mid-ocean rendezvous. The plan was primed to succeed, despite all that the dogged Americans had thrown at him. There was no way they could stop him now. No way they could know of the clever delivery means he and his loyalists had devised. No way they could have gotten wind of his structured distribution team in Seattle. No way they could ever suspect that he would soon develop an insatiable clientele for his potent product.

"I think we can accommodate that, my friend. They will only report to you how well the plan works and what the potential is for our joint venture. I propose a toast to the inevitable success of our first efforts together, *mi amigo*."

De Santiago tipped his glass in the general direction of Asia, out there somewhere across the vast sea that already held the key to the lands they would soon, in tandem, conquer together.

Ten thousand miles away, Sui chuckled softly into the telephone and raised his teacup.

He still worried. Not for a moment did he trust this oily-haired despot. But the man had apparently assembled the men and the machines to give him a reasonable chance of pulling off this plan. He would risk a staggering quantity of his product because the reward seemed worth it. As he dipped his teacup to where the yellow sun rose each day, he was considering ways he would not have to be so dependent in the future on the ideas of such an irrational partner.

"To our mutual success," he said.

19

SERGE NOVSTAD STARED SULLENLY OUT FROM THE BRIDGE OF THE merchant ship *Helena K*. The yellow globes of the dock lights were haloed in the humid late-night mist. The light drizzle had one good effect; it washed out some of the stench of this squalid inner harbor. Enough of the smell reached his nostrils to remind him where he was, and to make him even more grateful he was leaving this godforsaken place behind.

He lit a cigarette, tossing the match in the general direction of the dingy water below.

Making the final preparations to leave port, Novstad's crew bustled around the cluttered main deck, thirty feet below his perch, working in the gray half-light. The dock was absent any of its normal activity. Even this far off the beaten path, even in this out-of-the-way port, there would be stevedores working, trucks coming and going, loading coffee and bananas, off-loading equipment. Not tonight. There was only the glow of an occasional cigarette in the shadows to show anyone was there.

Give Juan de Santiago credit. Only he had the power to declare a longshoreman's holiday anytime he wanted and on only a few hours' notice.

Novstad sucked on his smoke. A few more minutes and he could bid adieu to this pesthole. Philippe Zurko had insisted the *Helena K* be modified here in this backwater, that Novstad personally supervise every step of the revamping. The Swede hated the place from the start. He couldn't wait to feel the damp sea air on his face as they steamed out to the big water, as the clean salt breeze erased the stink of this hellhole.

Novstad could understand secrecy and the need for operating in a port safely controlled by de Santiago's rebels. There was no doubt that these primitives required supervision for the most menial task. But Novstad was a master mariner. He was the only person within a thousand miles with blond hair, a sandy beard, and an odd lilt to his Spanish accent. Surely Zurko could have found someone else. The modifications he ordered were simple enough to accomplish. Any competent naval engineer could have supervised all the hull and structural work. Zurko was insistent. He kept saying over and over how there was no room for error and the project had to be completed on time and correctly. And with no questions asked about why.

Bottom line: Zurko paid the bills. Paid them very handsomely. So Novstad did as he was told and tried not to let any of the Colombians hear him complain, even if he usually did it in Swedish.

Six months here was more than any civilized Scandinavian should have to endure. The hotel was repulsive. There was not a decent restaurant in town. The women were all dark and dirty and mostly unenthusiastic. There was no reasonable aquavit for a thousand miles. He licked his thick lips, imagining how good a swallow would taste right now.

The shipyard was even worse. The stone dry dock had to be at least a century old. The grimy wooden buildings were that ancient, too. The place was more suited to lashing together nineteenth-century fishing boats than to doing anything like this project.

The work was completed on schedule and it was masterfully accomplished. What had been a compartmentalized main cargo hold still looked the same, but in only a few minutes it could be transformed into one large open space. The three bulkheads that were once watertight lateral dividers, built to prevent any flooding that might occur in one compartment from spreading to adjacent ones, were now only clipped to the hull.

Novstad didn't worry about the loss of the three lateral strength members. By his calculations, it was only a ten-percent reduction in effectiveness. This old tub could still handle the Pacific in anything short of a typhoon.

The most interesting modification was not visible until the bulkheads were removed. Then the entire bottom of the *Helena K* became two gigantic doors, opening to the ocean below.

Novstad was proud of his work and anxious to see it in actual use, to watch how it fit into the ingenious scheme the rebel leader had concocted. That would come soon enough. He was supremely confident it would all work flawlessly. He felt a sense of disappointment, knowing how risk-free this whole venture would be, unlike most of the clandestine missions with which he had been associated in the past. Oh, well, it was time he was treated to a carefree cruise for a change.

They had quite a distance to steam, bobbing empty and high in the water. He flicked the butt of his cigarette over the side and turned to his first officer.

"It's time. Get the ship under way," he said impatiently.

"Yes, sir," the first officer answered, then spoke into the radio headset he wore. "Cast off all lines."

The disembodied glowing cigarettes on the pier started moving slowly toward the *Helena K*. Men walked into the radiance of the pier lights and moved to the bollards. The lines arcing down from the main deck to the pier went slack. Novstad's crew pulled the lines aboard, more than ready themselves to put this place off their stern.

The *Helena K* was freed from the bonds of land, ready to return to the sea.

The first officer reached over to the central control console. He flipped a pair of switches labeled "Fore Thruster" and "Aft

Thruster." Huge fanlike propellers at the front and rear ends of the ship pushed her smoothly away from the pier. The diesel main engines then drove the screw to back the *Helena K* into the tiny harbor's shipway.

The rust-streaked merchant ship turned and disappeared into the night. She would soon be on the ocean, steaming as fast as she could manage, headed just north of west.

Bill Beaman held on for dear life to the strap above the truck's window and gritted his teeth so hard he was sure they would crack. The rickety old rattletrap careened madly down the rutted, muddy mountain road, on the verge of being out of control. The peasant driver held to the whipping steering wheel with white-knuckled determination, his nose almost touching its spokes, his eyes wide in sheer terror. The acrid smell of white-hot brake material wafted up through the rusted-out holes in the floorboards; the laboring engine balked and backfired in protest. Beaman glanced out the side window and looked straight down into the abyss alongside this skinny trail that masqueraded as a roadway.

No doubt about it. Death was scant inches away.

The dirt-stained peasant jacket and floppy campaign hat Beaman had stolen from the truck's guard stank of body odor and tobacco smoke. Neither article of clothing had been washed in years, if ever. This disguise was less than perfect. It still might pass a very casual examination or retain the element of surprise long enough to serve his purpose. There had been no test so far. They had not met any returning trucks. The fuel stops were strategically placed. They were unmanned tanks hidden in the underbrush alongside the road.

Cantrell, bouncing around in the bed of the truck, stood and yelled through the broken-out rear window.

"Skipper, do we have to go so fast?"

Martinelli pushed back the tattered canvas top that covered him and the others. He stood beside Cantrell. "I feel the need for speed!" he whooped, and laughed wildly. He held on to the rails. The wind whipped at what little there was of his close-cropped hair.

"Easy, my friend. Not so fast, *por favor*," Beaman yelled at the driver above the noise of the truck's moaning motor.

The peasant pumped harder on the shuddering brake pedal and downshifted the floor-shift transmission to a lower gear. The truck backfired in protest once again but slowed as it bounced around another turn in the mountain road. The way seemed to level out for this stretch. Beaman yelled at the driver once again.

"How much farther?" The driver held up five fingers. "Five hours? *Cinco horas*?"

Beaman sat back. He relaxed as best he could on this short but smoother section of road. He dozed. He felt the driver shaking him.

"Señor, look!" he said, pointing down the road ahead.

Another truck, belching heavy black smoke into the clear mountain air, was coming into view around a curve a mile farther down. It was heading up the mountain, coming in their direction. Beaman turned and yelled back through the window.

"Guys, we got some more traffic on our little freeway. Lock and load, but get hidden under that tarp. Try to look as much like a load of coca as you can. We'll try to just drive right on by, but be ready to come up smoking if they smell a rat."

He started to tell Johnston to make sure the guard kept quiet but he saw the SEAL already had his knife at the scared peasant's throat. Martinelli pulled the tarp back in place as Cantrell yanked back the charging lever on his trusty M-60. A round slipped into the chamber and the action sprang forward with a satisfying click.

Turning to the driver, Beaman said, "Just drive past. If I hear anything more than 'Hello,' your wife will be a widow. *Comprende*?" He showed the driver the end of his AK-47's barrel.

"*Sí, señor. Comprendo!*"

Beaman slouched low in his seat, trying to look like a Peruvian peasant to the two men in the oncoming truck. He chambered a round in the AK-47 and held it ready.

The two trucks approached each other on the narrow road. There wouldn't be any room to pass. There was barely room for one of them to get between the boulders on the up side and the sheer drop on the other. The driver next to Beaman slowed his truck a bit more.

The oncoming vehicle was the twin of the one they were riding in. It was battered and beaten, caked with mud. A sun-faded green canvas hid the bed from view. It might hold food and supplies for the workers back at the coca field. The truck could have left on the return journey before news of the landslide reached de Santiago's people. Or it could be an ambush. There could be a squad of rebel troops hidden underneath, ready to spring at them right here in this tight squeeze where there was no retreat or cover.

Beaman had no way of knowing.

They grew closer. He could see the two people in the cab through the mud-streaked windshield. The driver whipped the steering wheel with both hands, keeping the truck on the road, missing the larger rocks. The passenger sat stoically, as if on a simple Sunday drive, but holding an AK-47 just as Beaman was doing.

Twenty yards to go. The approaching truck labored up the mountain. It eased over to the high side of the road to allow Beaman's transport to get past on the bluff side. The driver guided the truck's right wheels high up on the slope. He stopped there, leaning precariously, threatening to roll right over and block the road entirely. Beaman's finger twitched on the AK-47's trigger. The other driver impatiently waved them past.

The space left between the parked truck on the high side of the road and the steep drop on the other side didn't look wide enough for them to be able to pass. Beaman's driver carefully eased over as far as he dared, assuming the truck's bald tires could get traction in thin air. Beaman took a quick glance out his window. He wished he hadn't. He was looking directly down the steep rocky slope into nothingness. They were far out on the road's ragged edge. He didn't see any way more than half the right-side tires could still be in contact with earth. He caught a quick glimpse of rocks and gravel, knocked loose by the tires, falling away into space.

He blinked hard and turned to scrutinize the men in the other truck. They stared back at him. Beaman felt a trickle of sweat work its way down the back of his neck. The slightest bump would send them over the edge. He avoided eye contact. Not do anything that might tip them off. The guard in the other truck eyed him. Beaman gripped his rifle tighter.

One short burst at the driver and this truck would plunge right over the side before Beaman could even get off a round. No one would survive the crash.

Beaman tensed. His senses were at their keenest state of alert. He honed in on the man with the gun without appearing to do so. He hated being at such a disadvantage. There was no choice. The other truck was hours from getting to where the roadway had fallen away. They should have no reason to suspect this brother truck had had anything to do with it.

The truck inched slowly past.

Beaman ventured to wave a greeting, trying to look friendly as the two cabs came abreast, separated by only inches. An eternity passed. They were past the bed of the parked truck. They were off the lip of the mountain and back in the center of the road. There was no gunfire from behind them.

They had made it.

Beaman stole a look back. The other truck disappeared down the road. He smiled and clapped the driver on the shoulder.

"You did well. You drive like a master."

He grinned when he saw how white the driver's face was, his lower lip trembling, big tears rolling down each cheek. There was the distinct odor of human excrement in the truck's cab. Beaman had a frightening thought. One that wiped the smile off his face and made his stomach flip over.

"*Amigo*, if you were as loyal to Juan de Santiago as some, we would all be dead now," he told the driver.

The frightened man didn't answer. The driver could have yelled at his friends, telling them that he carried *Americanos*. Then he could have steered the truck over the cliff. That would have rather efficiently ended this threat to *El Jefe's* cocaine-processing plant and, with the witnesses in the other truck watching the whole thing, the man would have been an instant martyr.

Chief Johnston's face appeared at the rear window.

"Phew, that was close! Hope we don't see another one of those bastards."

Beaman looked back. The smile returned to his face.

"Chief, you don't have any idea what 'close' is!"

Commander Jon Ward looked hard at the chart spread out before him. The little X showing their location was marked with a time that was only five minutes old.

"Another twenty-four hours, Nav?" he asked.

Earl Beasley measured with a pair of dividers the distance between the X and the green box that had been drawn on the chart to the southwest.

"Yes, sir. At a twenty-two-knot speed of advance, we'll be in the area by noon tomorrow."

Ward nodded and said, "Good. Looks like we're a little ahead of schedule. Think we have time for the drills the XO planned?"

Beasley smiled.

"Yes, sir. About time we got some of these people qualified to stand watch. Otherwise, the only thing they're good for is to breathe the air."

Ward chuckled. One of the facts of submarine life was qualification. Everyone from the most junior, newly reported seaman to the most senior department head was constantly working on qualifying for the next duty. Fortunately, the drills that had been scheduled for today were simple and wouldn't take much time. The fast pace of this trip had made them cancel most of the hands-on training in favor of getting down south and on station. This drill wouldn't affect that timeline for more than five minutes.

Ward stood and stretched his back. Stan Guhl was leaning against the BPS-15 under-ice sonar console. He was carefully observing Bill Ralston, who was sitting in the diving officer chair. Ralston was standing his first watch as diving officer under instruction (UI), learning the intricacies of making *Spadefish* behave herself in this unforgiving underwater environment. Doug Lyman stood beside him, quietly discussing emergency procedures. Today's subject was called a "stern planes jam dive," or what to do if the giant planes at the aft of *Spadefish* ever stuck in the full dive position, sending the boat plummeting downward out of control.

Guhl relaxed. He had just finished a similar discussion with Chris Durgan, who was getting some instruction of his own, learning the art and science of being the officer of the deck. Durgan sat on the high stool in the corner behind the two periscopes, taking a last look at the casualty procedures (CPs), trying to commit every comma and semicolon to memory. Ward glanced over at Guhl.

"You think you're ready?"

"Yes, sir. We have UIs at officer of the deck, diving officer, chief of the watch, and engineering watch supervisor back aft. I covered the CPs with all of 'em."

Ward stepped over to stand beside the stern planesman. Seaman MacNaughton looked up at the skipper and smiled.

Ward reached down and pushed MacNaughton's control column all the way forward and leaned on it. The stern-planes angle indicator moved smoothly to thirty-five degrees down. *Spadefish*'s nose immediately and obediently started to drop toward the bottom of the Pacific Ocean.

MacNaughton pulled back on the control column. It wouldn't budge. The sub was at a ten-degree down angle and dropping fast. Sailors leaned back to keep from falling forward

with the boat's angle. MacNaughton reached over and flipped
the hydraulic control switch from Normal to Emergency.

Ward still held the column firmly in the full dive position.
Spadefish was now at a twenty-degree down angle. A coffee
cup skittered down the deck and shattered noisily when it
struck the forward bulkhead.

"Diving Officer, my planes are jammed on full dive!" Mac-
Naughton yelled at Ralston.

"Officer of the Deck, stern planes jammed on full dive!
Depth four hundred feet!" Ralston yelled over his shoulder.
Spadefish was at a thirty-degree down angle. Everyone held
on tightly to anything solid that they could grab to keep from
being hurled forward.

Chris Durgan leaped from his seat.

"Jam dive! Jam dive!" he sang.

Hearing the code word, the watchstanders sprang to action.
Ralston reached down and flipped the engine-order telegraph
to Back Emergency. He pushed the button at the side of the
telegraph and yelled, "Depth four-five-zero feet!"

Back in Maneuvering, Scott Frost saw the telegraph needle
go to Back Emergency and heard the bell ring. The officer of
the deck wanted to go backward, and he wanted to do it now!
Frost whipped the large chrome ahead throttle shut and flung
the smaller astern throttle open. Steam flow shot past one hundred percent on its indicator and the reactor power climbed
quickly toward one hundred percent as well. The roar of steam
and the scream of the giant turbines filled the engine room.
The whole ship shook as the massive screw stopped, and then
reversed direction, pulling the submarine backward instead of
pushing it forward. As reactor power climbed past ninety percent, Frost shut down a bit on the astern throttle. The reactor
power needle came to rest at exactly one hundred percent.

Ralston yelled, "Depth five hundred feet!"

Doc Marston, attempting to qualify to stand watch as the
chief of the watch, keyed the 1MC microphone and yelled,
"Jam dive! Jam dive!" He put his hands on the emergency

blow valves, ready if the officer of the deck wanted to go "on the roof" quickly.

Seaman Cortez pulled back on the fairwater planes column, moving them to Full Rise, and whipped the rudder back and forth, fishtailing it in order to further slow *Spadefish* in her plunge to the bottom.

"Depth five-five-zero feet!"

The sub slowed.

"Depth five-seven-zero feet!" The pit log, measuring the sub's speed through the water, passed through zero, and started to accelerate astern as the boat began to move backward. The down angle started to ease.

Durgan ordered, "All stop. Stand by to hover."

Frost spun the astern throttles shut. *Spadefish* coasted to a stop and hung there, with no forward or backward motion, stopped dead still in the warm Pacific waters.

Doc Marston flipped switches that pressurized one of the depth-control tanks with high-pressure air and vented the other one. The pressurized tank was kept nearly full of seawater and the vented one nearly empty. Marston could blow water from one tank if *Spadefish* started to sink or flood a little in if she started to rise. It was all a giant balancing act.

Marston turned to Durgan and reported, "Speed zero, depth five-eight-seven feet and sinking. Ready to hover."

"Commence hovering. Depth six hundred feet," Durgan ordered.

Bert Waters ran to the aft bulkhead of the engine room with Chief Bechtold right on his heels. Waters was working to qualify as engineering watch supervisor. Bechtold was his current teacher. Waters grabbed a JA handset and reported, "Ready to take local control of the stern planes with emergency positioning pumps." These pumps bypassed the ship's normal hydraulic system and operated the rudder or stern planes from a small separate system in case all the ship's hydraulic power was lost.

Ward smiled as he watched. This drill had gone well. He finally let go of the control column.

As he turned to congratulate his crew, he found himself face-to-face with a livid Cookie Dotson. The sub's cook was wiping dark brown cake batter from his face and angrily flinging it wherever it might fly.

"Dammit, Skipper! Can't you ever tell me when you're gonna do these things? I was just about to put the XO's birthday cake in the oven when you sent me ass-over-teakettle into the mixing bowl. The damned thing is splattered all over the galley now. It looks like a chocolate bomb went off in there!"

Ward couldn't help it. He burst out laughing. With all the tension of the last few weeks, with the near disasters out of San Diego, and with the tragic accident in the torpedo room, there had not been much chance for levity lately aboard *Spadefish*. The chocolate-covered sailor was, to tell the truth, one comical sight. Besides, all the crew members gathered around for the drill were doubled over with laughter as well.

"Cookie, I'm sorry," the skipper finally managed to gasp once he got his breath back. "I'll come down and help you mix up the next one as soon we get to PD to get the message traffic onboard." He paused a beat. "Yellow cake okay? Chocolate doesn't seem to be your color."

And that simple remark set the whole bunch of them off on another laughing jag.

Ward finally turned to Stan Guhl.

"Mr. Guhl, secure from stern-planes jam-dive drill. Make your depth one-five-zero feet and clear baffles to come to periscope depth."

"Yes, sir."

Ward, still chuckling, walked back to his stateroom. He yelled through the joining doors at Joe Glass.

"XO, you missed it. You wouldn't have believed Cookie, covered with chocolate batter, wiping it out of his eyes and mad as hell and blaming it all on me and the jam-dive drill. Tell you what. I'm appointing you my official food taster until he calms down a bit."

Glass stepped into the stateroom, both hands raised in defense.

"No way! Submarining may be hazardous duty, but that's suicidal," he laughed.

"Okay, I guess I'll subsist on crackers and cold cuts for a while. Changing subjects. We're almost in area. I want to test our systems one more time. Get the ESM party manned and run a full search this time at PD. I want to know that our electronic surveillance systems are at one hundred percent."

Glass nodded.

"No problem, Skipper. I'll sit with them and make sure myself."

The JA phone buzzed. Ward grabbed the handset and keyed the talk button.

"Captain."

"Captain, officer of the deck under instruction. Depth one-five-zero feet, speed six knots. Made a careful baffle clear to the left. No contacts. Request permission to come to periscope depth."

Ward smiled. Durgan would be all right.

"Thank you, Mr. Durgan. I'll be out in a second."

The skipper stood and turned to leave.

"You know, XO, Chris is going to make a damn fine OOD one of these days."

"Agreed," Glass said.

They were both thinking the same thing: *Not on this old boat, though.* Ward patted the bulkhead affectionately as he exited the stateroom. He couldn't help being sentimental. One last mission and *Spadefish* would be jerked right out of the ocean she seemed to love so much.

Ward resolved one more time to make this final operation as good as it could be. He owed the old girl at least that much.

20

"CONN, ESM, REQUEST YOU RAISE THE ESM MAST."

Joe Glass's voice was hollow and metallic as it spilled from the open mike speaker. Chris Durgan lifted his eye from the periscope eyepiece. He had been observing one of his favorite sights while he circled around, looking for anyone approaching *Spadefish*. Outside, the western sky was ablaze in the pinks, oranges, and golds of the departing sun. The heavens darkened to a deep indigo to the east. A few stars were already starting to twinkle through the gathering darkness. Venus rose bright and bold in the east, just below the sliver of the new moon. The darker blue sea was empty, calm.

Inside *Spadefish*'s control room, the quartermaster had already turned off the bright white fluorescent lights and switched on the dim red ones, "rigged control for red." Doc Marston was little more than a shadowy form, seated at the ballast control panel over to the port side of the control room.

In a quiet voice, his tone seemingly dictated by the half-light, Durgan ordered, "Raise the ESM mast."

Marston stood, reaching high up on the vertical section of the panel to flip a switch.

"ESM mast coming up," he confirmed.

One of the bars of green lights that were lined up in a row in front of him blinked out. Durgan knew that the light said "ESM Mast Housed," but he was too far away to read the tiny letters.

Now Durgan spun around to take a look aft and down at the faint phosphorescent wake of the scope. He was just in time to see a strangely shaped object break the dark surface of the sea. It looked like a black beer barrel with a flat hat and bent rods sticking out at odd angles.

"ESM mast breaking the water."

Joe Glass, sitting on a bench locker in the ESM bay forty feet aft, watched as Al Carlos and Dan Larson carefully adjusted their electronic equipment, like a couple of piano tuners trying to strike only perfect notes. Glass heard Chris Durgan's voice over the open microphone system, which had been installed years before. It picked up voices in the vicinity of the periscope so the ESM watch could hear what was going on. Likewise, the microphone above Glass's head allowed Durgan to just as clearly eavesdrop on conversations in ESM.

The ESM bay constituted the after half of the radio room. Even in the highly classified atmosphere of *Spadefish*, the radio room was special territory. It was the only room on board that was kept permanently locked. Only crew members with a special clearance and a "need to know" were given the seven-digit code necessary to open the cipher-locked door.

The real secrets of the room were in this back corner. *Spadefish* and her sisters of the *Sturgeon* class had been designed more as spy ships than as offensive weapons. With their endurance and stealth, they could sit off the coast of an unsuspecting country for months at a time without being detected. The sophisticated sensors housed in this room allowed her to sweep the electronic spectrum, gathering, decrypting, translating, and interpreting.

During the long years of the Cold War, several of these boats were always on station, just outside the territorial limits of the old USSR, hidden but listening attentively. It had been a very dangerous game of cat and mouse. The secrets that had been gathered in this room and others on boats like it had helped to win that war. The "Silent Service" had certainly lived up to its name, and even now, few knew of its contributions to the eventual fall of the Soviet Union.

Larson looked up from the tiny CRT. The squiggly lines on its green screen commanded his complete attention, despite the tight quarters. He faced a bulkhead crowded with a myriad of black boxes, barely inches away. Another bulkhead behind his crouched form was equally close and similarly cluttered with equipment. The blue overhead light gave the packed-out closet a surreal glow.

Dan Larson, his eyes shining, glanced over at Glass.

"Got a signal already, XO. Looks like the receivers are working."

Al Carlos sat on a bench locker, facing the other way. He wore a headset and fiddled with a tiny keyboard on the vertical face of one of the black boxes. His face was scrunched up, his mouth crooked as he listened hard. He finally glanced sideways at Larson.

"Dan, you may be gettin' sumthin', but I ain't got squat."

He punched some of the buttons in front of him once again.

"You sure, Al?" Larson asked.

"You think I'm deaf? Course I'm sure."

Larson looked over at the shorter, darker technician. The two had worked as a team for years and had the easy familiarity of an old married couple, but with the same tendency for nagging. These two men weren't part of the normal *Spadefish* crew. They were special hitchhikers. "Spooks," the crew called them, on loan from the Naval Intelligence Service. They were specially trained to operate this equipment and to analyze its output. Sometimes they rode the boats, sometimes they flew in specially equipped planes, and often they manned lonely listening posts on hilltops far from civilization.

"Okay, okay," Larson said with a wave of a hand. "Ain't nothing between you and me except for four feet of coaxial cable. Everything hooked up right?"

Carlos reached behind his black box and felt around for dangling connectors or nonplugged sockets.

"Yep, all hooked up over here."

"Time to go to the last line o' the troubleshootin' manual then, buddy."

Carlos looked at his friend, his brow furrowed.

"What that be?"

"It's highly technical," Larson said with a smile. "It says, 'Wiggle here, wiggle there, wiggle, wiggle everywhere.'"

Carlos laughed.

"You damn hillbilly! You fished me in again."

Larson reached behind the black box he was watching. Grabbing one of the cables attached to it, he gave it a vigorous shake and a sharp tug.

Carlos held his headset tightly to his ears.

"I could hear snatches of signal. The BNC connector must be bad. I'll swap the whole cable."

Carlos fished a new cable from a nearby locker and tied the faulty one into a knot so it wouldn't accidentally be reused before the bad twist-on connector could be resoldered.

"Ahh, much better," Carlos reported with a contented sigh, as if he was now hearing beautiful music through his headset. He perked up, interested in whatever he was receiving. Larson saw the signs. His friend was listening to something that had grabbed him. Something out of the ordinary.

"Whadda you got?"

"Damn, that shouldn't even be here," Carlos muttered. He punched some more buttons on the keyboard and listened intently. Then he stood and reached over to another nearby black box. He flipped a switch that caused the squiggly lines on the CRT on the box's face to start to dance; then he pushed a series of buttons on its keyboard. "I don't believe it." He reached over to a cassette deck and started a tape spinning, then turned to Joe Glass. "XO, you speak any Spanish?"

"Sí, studied it two years at the Academy and I've taken a few trips to Tijuana."

Carlos picked up a spare headset, plugged it in, then handed the other end to Glass.

"Good, listen to this."

Glass slid the headset over his ears and cupped them tightly with both hands. The Spanish was rapid-fire and Glass was rusty, but as best he could make out, someone was arranging a meeting somewhere. Didn't sound very exciting to him. A couple of merch captains in port trying to pick their brothel for the evening, maybe. He looked over at Carlos and raised an eyebrow as if to say, *So what?*

The spook chuckled.

"I see you don't appreciate my find, XO. Let me help you out. First off, the signal is coming in on an encrypted channel on a frequency reserved for deep-ocean weather buoys. That means these guys ain't up to anything good. Anyone hearing it without this li'l gizmo would just be getting static. Someone is going to a lot of trouble to hide what they're talking about." Carlos glanced over at Larson. "Hey, how's about gettin' off your dead ass and DF'n this sucka?"

Larson ignored his partner's jibe. He was already speaking into the open mike.

"Conn, request you lower all masts except the ESM. Need to cut a DF on a contact."

Durgan acknowledged, "ESM, number-two scope coming down. Tell me when you're done. I don't like flying blind."

Even as he spoke, Durgan reached over his head and rotated the red wheel. The greased silver scope barrel slid smoothly into the well at his feet.

Larson watched the mast position indicator above his head. As soon as the green light came on showing that the scope was down and out of the way of his direction-finding signal, he flipped a couple of switches on a black box to his left. In only a few seconds, a strip of paper that looked much like a cash-register receipt popped out of an opening on the front of the equipment.

Larson glanced at the printing on the slip and handed it over to Carlos. He spoke into the mike: "Conn, DF completed. You can raise the scope and get your eyes back now."

Carlos studied the output of the radio direction finder for a half minute.

"See, XO. Just like I guessed. This guy is almost due south of us. Bearing one-seven-five. No land that way till we see penguins. We got us a druggie lookin' to set up a shipment is what we got."

Glass considered the evidence. It was slim, circumstantial at best. But this wasn't a court-martial. Hunches counted here. And Carlos and Larson knew their business. They had both spent a good part of their navy careers eavesdropping on drug smugglers and their clandestine conversations.

Glass spoke in the direction of the mike.

"Mr. Durgan, ask the captain to come to ESM."

Glass heard a deeper voice when he relayed the message.

"XO, on my way," Jon Ward said.

John Bethea chewed on his lower lip as he listened to Ward talk.

"John, we've got tapes we're analyzing now, but it all holds together. Our crypies' estimates are a high-probability drug transfer. We've been getting intermittent hits for the last couple of hours. Direction finding lines of bearings puts them about six hundred miles south of us. The area of uncertainty is an ellipse with a hundred-mile-long major axis bearing one-seven-nine and a ten-mile minor axis."

Bethea tracked the mouse across his own computer screen, drawing the area Ward described.

"Jon, that's almost two thousand square miles of ocean. Can you narrow it down any more than that? Could be a dozen or more ships in that area and there's no way for you tell in a hurry which ones we want to make a call on."

"Sorry, that's the best I got right now," Ward shot back. "We're doing this with only our line of bearings. If you can get anyone else in position to try to grab the signal, maybe we can triangulate it."

Bethea looked around the room. The command center was strewn with maps and papers. The large-screen monitors were showing the progress of Bill Beaman and his SEAL team through Peru and southern Colombia. Several new satellite photos lay on the desk in front of him. They vividly pictured a mountainside with a raw, jagged scar of fresh rockslide down the face of it.

Bethea scratched the uncharacteristic stubble on his chin.

He had not had time to run his electric razor across his face lately. He had simply forgotten to shave. He had also forgotten to eat and sleep.

They were getting close to the payoff. Bethea could feel it.

"Don't know how much time we can give you to pursue this, Jon. Beaman is hot on the trail and should be getting close to a major processing plant. You have to be in position and ready to send over some Tomahawks when he gets the info. Otherwise, all this is wasted and we don't have any way to turn that plant into sawdust."

Ward looked down at the chart once again. The ellipse looked so small and so close to where *Spadefish* sat. Every instinct in his body told him that they shouldn't let this sleaze get away when they were so near. A quick sweep through, a few hours' diversion from the mission, that was all it would take.

He also knew Bethea was right to hesitate. *Spadefish*'s job was to be there for Bill Beaman. Together, they could destroy far more than a single boatload of contraband. It was tempting.

Ward finally pushed the talk button on the red handset.

"John, you're right, of course. It just sticks in my craw to let this guy loose when we're so close."

"Well, we don't even know for sure that he's a druggie, do we?"

"Have to go on what my people say. They're sure it's somebody up to no good, so I'm sure, too. These guys are good. If they say 'druggie,' you can write it down in the log."

Bethea leaned back in his chair. He rubbed his temples. The pressure was getting heavy now. They were near to breaking the back of de Santiago's operation. If the boat they had heard was part of de Santiago's fleet, if it held a load of that killer dope headed back for the States, it would be worth investigating. But *Spadefish* was not the posse he needed riding after the bad guys.

"If you're that sure, Jon, I can get somebody else to go out there to take a look."

Ward scrutinized the chart again. They still had to travel

four hundred miles to the southeast before they would be in
their assigned patrol area. The intercept with the mystery boat
would be six hundred miles almost due south. If they maintained their current twenty-five knots, they would only be able
to arrive in area in time. There was no leeway for diversions.

"I'm sure. We'll take a pass. Get anyone you've got out
there. We'll leave it to you, boss."

Serge Novstad was livid. That damn mini-sub was late. Rendezvous was in one hour and the bastards still had not left
port. This was going to screw up the whole schedule. He
could do nothing more than sit out here and bob around. Wait
for them to show up on their own sweet time. Secure channel
or not, he hated having to resort to all the radio transmissions
they had been slinging around already. There were some big
ears out there.

He stared out the bridge window of the *Helena K.* The
beautiful star-studded night sky was lost on him. Novstad slid
the side window open a bit to let the cool breeze in. It didn't
mollify his heated temper.

He spun around sharply to face the first officer, seated in a
corner at the rear of the bridge.

"Anything new?"

The short, dark man slid back the earphones and turned to
face his captain.

"No, señor. They report they are still working on the problem with the navigation system. *Zibrus* reports everything is
loaded. As soon as Señor Sergiovski gets it to work, they will
depart port and head our way."

"Damn Russians!" Novstad paced angrily across the
bridge, then turned and stomped back. "Never could trust the
lazy bastards! Probably forgot to turn the damn thing on."

He strode over to the GPS repeater. The screen showed a
chart of the waters off the northern part of South America. He
punched in the *Zibrus* location. A dot appeared on the screen
just north of Coji mi es, Ecuador. Moving the little black

roller ball, he connected the dot to the X marking the location of where the *Helena K* rode on the open Pacific. They were over two hundred kilometers due west of the small isolated Ecuadorian port.

Even if the *Zibrus* left port and sailed at its maximum underwater speed of seventeen kilometers per hour, it couldn't arrive at the rendezvous point before fifteen hours had passed. That would put them there in the middle of the afternoon, in full view of any satellites that were overhead. The choreographed plan was falling apart.

Novstad had no choice.

"Ahead full, steer course zero-nine-zero. If the stupid Russian can't come to us, we'll go to him."

Don Pasten was way south of exhausted. His boat, *Hurricane*, had been patrolling the Colombian coast without downtime for the past week. The young lieutenant commander had rarely left the bridge of his new command for the entire time either.

Hurricane was a patrol craft of the *Cyclone* class. It was designed to support the SEALs in their special warfare operations. Armed with two 25mm Mark 38 Bushmaster automatic cannons, numerous .50-caliber machine-gun hard mounts, and Stinger missiles, she could slug it out with much larger ships if it came to it. Her shallow draft, long legs, and thirty-five-knot speed made her ideal for operations where quickness and firepower were more important than stealth. *Hurricane* was large enough to support a very advanced communications and electronic surveillance capability. Her systems were almost on a par with the much larger *Aegis* destroyers.

Hurricane had been assigned to JDIA several months before, though even intense scrutiny of her paperwork back in San Diego would not confirm it. Technically, she was on a training mission, operating near Panama. It was listed as on-the-job training. She was in the same ocean but she was far from Panama. Patrolling the long Pacific coastline of Colombia with its many coves, bays, and river deltas had proved to be tiring, dangerous work. It was a task suited to *Hurricane*'s capabilities. That was why Bethea had requisitioned her in the first place.

Pasten watched as the haze-gray hull slipped soundlessly up the shallow river estuary. He had planned on spending the night in Manglares, a sizable regional center thirty miles up the coast. A real pier, restaurants, and bright lights would be a welcome change from the little fishing hamlets and the steaming jungle coast they had been nosing around for the last week. But today, Bethea had sent him farther down the coast to the tiny hamlet that awaited them around the next bend in this muddy, foul-smelling river. Pasten had never heard of Toma Co and he doubted if Bethea had either, but there was something there JDIA wanted him to check out, so he would.

The encrypted radio receiver on the aft bulkhead of the bridge crackled and Pasten leaned closer to hear.

"*Hurricane*, this is JDIA Command, over."

The lieutenant commander could make out John Bethea's distinctive voice through the distortion of the encryption system. He grabbed the handset and pushed the talk button.

"JDIA Command, this is *Hurricane*. Go ahead."

The speaker sputtered again.

"Don, this is John Bethea. Have a job for you. Possible drug rendezvous. Some ship named the *Helena K*. We don't know anything about it except some very good intercept information. Intelligence puts the location two hundred miles west-southwest of your current position. I need you to head that way at flank speed. Good hunting. Bethea out."

Pasten stood there, staring at the silent handset. He could already taste the cold beer. Or even a warm one in some seedy pierside village bar. "Damn!" That would have to wait now. There was a job to do.

"Helm, right full rudder. Steady course two-six-five. All ahead flank!"

He could see the look on several faces of his crew. The little ship spun around. The stern squatted down in the brackish water as the diesels came up to maximum speed and the boat's bow wave grew to a real "bone in the teeth."

Hurricane met the Pacific surge at the river's mouth at a full thirty-five knots.

Captain Third Rank Sergiovski turned to face Philippe Zurko. He bore the closest thing to a smile anyone had ever seen on the Russian's face.

"Señor Zurko, it is working now. The interface between the *Zibrus* antenna controller and the American GPS system was not compatible. We had to totally reprogram the frequency agile transceiver."

The two men stood close together. Their shoulders touched as they stooped over in the tiny control room. There was barely room for the two of them to stand together aft of the pilot's seat. The bulkheads of this tiny, brightly lit room were crammed with piping, valves, and electronic boxes of every description.

Zurko allowed his gaze to wander. He tried to put the thought out of his head that he would soon be beneath the ocean, surrounded by tons and tons of seawater. He had no idea what any of these boxes and gizmos did. His only previous shipboard experience had been sipping cocktails on the fantail of Juan de Santiago's yacht. On that trip, their shipmates had been a flock of beautiful fashion models. This thing was certainly no yacht and Sergiovski was as far from a fashion model as anyone could imagine.

Zurko shook his head. He still wasn't sure why he was even here in the first place. Surely he had some functions for the revolution that required his presence somewhere above the surface of the ocean. But De Santiago was adamant on the subject. He told Zurko that, in no uncertain terms, this was the most important mission to which he had ever been assigned.

The leader was clear on one other point. If the mission failed because he wasn't there to watch over every detail, Zurko might as well take a pistol to his forehead.

He looked over again at the sweating, swarthy Russian. The man's body odor filled the cramped quarters and Zurko could smell his foul breath.

"Very well. It is certainly about time." He bit his tongue and went on. "Let's get this thing out to sea. We are already very late."

Sergiovski nodded his approval. He rose from the tiny navigation table, and pushed past Zurko to sit heavily in the pilot's seat.

"Señor Zurko, if you would be so kind as to stick your head through the hatch and tell those filthy sons of bitches to cast us off, we will be on our way. And you may want to close the hatch afterward unless you want to invite in the fish."

The sub pulled away from the dilapidated wooden pier. A hundred yards away, Juan de Santiago's Mercedes sat in the dark shadows of a derelict fish processing plant. El Jefe watched quietly, proudly, as the submarine dropped lower in the water. It disappeared completely, leaving only a spot of dirty foam where it had been.

De Santiago had lit and was already smoking a very large victory cigar before the car pulled away and headed for the climb back toward his mountain headquarters.

21

NOVSTAD AWOKE FROM A SOUND SLEEP. THE INSISTENT BUZZING IN his ear had to be stopped somehow. He snatched the telephone from its cradle.

"*Ja*, what is it?"

The quiet of the ship slowly seeped into his sleep-drugged conscious. Where was the throb of the engines, the beat of the screw?

"*Capitán*, we have been ordered to stop and to stand by to be boarded," the first officer reported.

"What? Who?" Novstad stammered. Sleep dulled his brain. His initial thought was pirates.

The first officer's report quickly changed his mind. "It is an American. A gray ship. With a big cannon. They are sending a Zodiac boat to us now. It is full of American soldiers."

Novstad relaxed, brushed back his disheveled blond hair, and didn't even bother to stifle his yawn.

"Very well. Greet our visitors. Everything is ready for company, is it not?"

If they were going to have to be inspected, now was the best possible time. They had no connection with anything illegal. It would be a good test of their preparations. The delays caused by *Zibrus* would prove to be providential.

Novstad shrugged into his uniform. It would not be good form for the Americans to find the *Helena K*'s master napping in his bed. He stepped out of his cabin and onto the bridge. The pale light of the dawn illuminated the bridge with a pinkish golden glow. The mahogany trim around the instruments gleamed brightly. All of the charts and publications were neatly stowed on their shelves built into the after bulkhead. For an old scow like the *Helena K*, this was a bridge to be proud of.

The swarthy first officer scurried across the bridge to greet his captain.

"*Capitán*, the *Americanos* have ordered us to stop. They are approaching to board at the starboard accommodation ladder."

Sweat poured from the worried little man's face. He pointed down to the starboard side of the main deck. Novstad glanced down. He saw a small black craft disappear beneath the high overhang of the *Helena K*'s steep side. Two members of his crew were already operating the windlass to lower the accommodation ladder down to sea level.

Novstad stepped out to the bridge wing and looked down. He had a clear view into the little black boat. He had read that

these boats were called RHIBs, "rigid-hulled inflatable boats."
They were favored by most of the United States military's
special warfare groups. This one contained eight heavily
armed SEALs in full combat equipment.

Five hundred yards away, a small patrol boat lay still in the
water. Novstad read the large white "PC 3" painted on the bow
below the gunnel. An angry-looking pair of cannons was
pointed directly at him and his ship. He could look down the
length of the barrels to see the shells, waiting there to be shot
his way. Pairs of sailors, dressed similarly to the SEALs at the
bottom of the accommodation ladder, manned several machine guns along the rail and on the bridge of the little ship.

Novstad saw the captain of the other ship step out onto the
bridge wing. He held a loud hailer.

"*Helena K*, this is the U.S. Navy ship *Hurricane*. Captain,
come up on channel sixteen."

Novstad grabbed the walkie-talkie that was stored in the
locker under the rail. He checked the dial to make certain it
was set at sixteen, the universal bridge-to-bridge marine
channel.

"This is the *Helena K*. I am Serge Novstad, the master.
What is the meaning of this?"

Novstad heard the control in the American's voice as it
came over the radio. There was no doubt who was in charge
here.

"Good morning, Captain Novstad. This is the U.S. Navy
ship *Hurricane*, Commander Pasten in command. We are
boarding you for a routine drug interdiction search in cooperation with the Colombian government."

Novstad waited a few seconds before he responded. He had
to appear both innocent and outraged.

"Commander Pasten, I have to protest. This is a Greek-
flagged ship in international waters. You have no right to
board us."

Don Pasten read directly from the little index card provided
by the staff JAG officer back in San Diego.

"Captain Novstad, you are within the Colombian Exclusive Economic Zone. The Colombian government has requested our assistance in searches in these waters. Please cooperate and allow my men to board."

Novstad smiled and replied, "Commander, your men are welcome to come aboard peaceably. We have nothing to hide. If you have time, you are invited over to enjoy breakfast as my guest."

Pasten was surprised by the calm, easy manner of this master. This Novstad was very gracious once he had made the pro forma protest. The invitation to breakfast was appealing, but Pasten had other missions.

"Thank you, Captain. I'm afraid I will have to decline. Duty demands my presence here."

Novstad shook his head.

"But of course, Commander. I fully understand. Now, if you will excuse me, I will go down to greet your men personally."

Novstad put the walkie-talkie back in the locker and strode to the ladder aft of the bridge. He could feel the American captain's eyes as he watched him through his binoculars. He arrived on the main deck just as the lead SEAL hoisted himself over the rail. The SEAL dropped into a crouch, his M-16 at the ready. Two more of his companions followed, each covering a different section of the deck with their automatic weapons.

Novstad stepped toward them, a half smile on his face. He raised his hands to shoulder height so the SEALs could see he was not armed.

"Greetings. I am Captain Novstad, the master of the *Helena K.* You are welcome to search as much as you like. My crew will assist you in whatever way you want."

The palpable tension emanating from the group of SEALs eased. It did not disappear entirely. They were ready for anything. Novstad knew these men were professionals. They would stay on edge until they were back on board *Hurricane.* They would not be easy to fool.

The Swede smiled at the boarding party.

"I am thankful I do not have to tangle with you guys!"

Captain Third Rank Sergiovski brought the little *Zibrus* up to near the surface. They were at the new rendezvous point.

Both he and Zurko were very glad that Novstad had decided to bring the *Helena K* in closer to shore. Even that was not enough. The submarine had proven to be much slower than the design work predicted. They were making less than twelve kilometers per hour, not even seven knots. They had come only fifty kilometers since leaving Coji mi es.

Departing the port presaged the frustrating night. The tracks under *Zibrus* worked well, but the heavy, muddy sediment near the port wouldn't support the weight of the sub. It sank deeply into the muck. Zurko was certain that they would be entombed, sucked right down into the harbor floor forever, but Sergiovski pumped water from the trim tanks until *Zibrus* was several tons lighter than the surrounding water. The buoyancy force pulled the sub from the clutch of the mud. The Russian flooded enough water back in so that *Zibrus* rested, light as a feather, on the bottom.

He reached across the control panel to flip up a large blue lever. Zurko shook in fear as a heavy grinding noise reverberated through the five-centimeter-thick steel hull. *Zibrus* shuddered as the tracks dug in. It began to crawl across the bottom, slinking out to sea.

The little submarine started to angle downward. The river bottom had met the sharp drop-off to the ocean floor. They crawled on down the slope, deeper and deeper into the dark waters.

Zurko broke into a sweat as he watched the depth gauge slowly rotate. They were going ever deeper. He cursed de Santiago for forcing him to ride this coffin. He jumped when the hull started to pop and groan under the awesome pressure of the depths. Sergiovski chuckled quietly while he watched with undisguised glee as the suddenly pale Latin shook in his custom-made Italian boots. The tiny control room soon smelled of Zurko's fear.

At a depth of two hundred meters, two miles out in the Pacific, Sergiovski stopped the crawler and pumped water out until *Zibrus* floated free from the bottom. He engaged the drive to the screw at the aft of the mini-sub. It picked up speed.

The fuel cell was working well. Sergiovski glanced at the power meter on the panel he faced. The needle climbed up past fifty percent, then seventy-five percent. He looked over at the speed indicator. It stopped at twelve kilometers per hour.

"Señor Zurko, that is the maximum speed we will get. Any more and we will deplete the cells too fast to make it to the rendezvous."

The rest of the trip passed without event. Zurko slowly relaxed until boredom overtook him. He drowsed, seated at the periscope stand, his face contorted by whatever dream he was having. Sergiovski had to shake him awake when they reached their destination.

"We are at the rendezvous. Sonar has picked up the *Helena K*. There is an interesting development. It has detected another ship nearby. I don't know what it is. We will go up and take a look. We will do it very, very carefully."

The periscope broke the surface. The gray form of the *Hurricane* was seven hundred yards away. Beyond it, the *Helena K* bobbed peacefully, drifting with the current. He lowered the scope and turned to Zurko.

"Looks like our American friends arrived before we did. We will go a little deeper and wait there until they grow bored and leave."

He pulled one of the levers before him while Zurko tried to squeeze the sleep from his eyes. It dawned on de Santiago's lieutenant then that this mini-submarine idea was not a bad one after all. Not with over thirty tons of cocaine hiding here, a few feet below where the inquisitive Americans floated.

The petty officer leading the SEAL boarding party shook his head. He stood on the main deck of the *Helena K* and spoke to Commander Pasten over his radio.

"Skipper, this thing is clean. We've covered every inch. There ain't nothin' here."

Pasten looked across the short span of water at the merchant ship. He was confused. John Bethea was sure this ship was running drugs. He had been certain that his intelligence was good. Pasten knew that JDIA had access to the best sources, but it sure looked like they were wrong this time.

"Are you positive? What's her cargo?"

The answer came back immediately.

"Yes, sir. Totally sure. She's in ballast. The cargo holds are empty. The master says they just left a shipyard repair and are manifested to Vancouver, British Columbia, to pick up a load of grain. Request orders, sir."

"Come on home. We've got real work to do."

Twenty meters below the surface of the Pacific, Sergiovski listened as the four screws on the *Hurricane* began turning. He heard them pick up speed; then the sound receded. The Americans were leaving the area. When the sound faded into the background ocean noise, Sergiovski decided to wait a bit longer. He could hear the faint noises of the *Helena K* sitting idly on the surface. There was no screw beat from her, only the sound of her auxiliaries.

Sergiovski waited another full hour. Zurko sat over in the corner, fretting anxiously, his designer shirt soaked with sweat. The Russian nodded, satisfied they were alone.

"Señor Zurko, it is time. We will have to risk a daytime rendezvous."

The Colombian nodded his head in agreement.

"Anything to get out of this sewer pipe. I need to breathe real air again."

The little *Zibrus* rose closer to the surface. Sergiovski raised the periscope and looked around in all directions. Zurko stared at the diminutive television screen, seeing what the Russian was seeing through the scope. Except for the *Helena K*, they were alone in this part of the Pacific. The Americans had disappeared over the horizon, off to chase other prey.

Sergiovski reached for the microphone hanging by the periscope, but Zurko grabbed his arm.

"Don't. The Americans will intercept the radio signal. If not the little ship that was just here, then their satellites."

The swarthy Russian looked at him with irritation.

"Don't worry, my nervous friend. This is an underwater telephone, not a radio. No one but the *Helena K* will hear us."

He seized the microphone, pressed the talk button, and spoke.

"*Helena K*, this is *Zibrus*. We are ready to commence docking operations."

The tiny control was silent. Zurko was sure no one had heard them. He was opening his mouth to tell Sergiovski to try again when the gray speaker box squawked alive.

"*Zibrus*, this is *Helena K*. We are preparing for docking operations. Estimate one hour. Stand by. *Helena K* out."

Sergiovski glanced over at Zurko. The rebel lieutenant scowled, unsure about the reason for this delay. Sergiovski explained.

"They have to transform the hold to receive us. It takes some time and they thankfully didn't begin until they knew we were nearby. Otherwise, the Americans would have been very curious about what they saw. Watch that television and I will show you something unique."

The Russian engineer sat at the pilot's seat and pushed gently forward on the control yoke. Zurko jumped, startled. He saw the waves wash over the periscope window. The view on the television monitor's screen changed from puffy white clouds and pale blue sky to the darker turquoise of the deep ocean.

Sergiovski turned the wheel slowly. The compass showed a slow turn to starboard, but Zurko's view of empty ocean water didn't change. If he was not seeing the heading numbers change, he would not have known they were turning.

Slowly the dim shape of the *Helena K*'s hull came into view of the camera lens. Zurko watched a small dark line appear in the ship's hull right along the keel. The long crack grew larger until the entire bottom of the ship disappeared. Zurko stared up into the innards of the merchant vessel.

"*Zibrus*, this is *Helena K*. We are ready to receive you. Heading zero-nine-one-point-three. Speed zero."

Sergiovski looked up at the compass repeater. He turned the control column to the right.

"Roger, *Helena K*. On course. Coming up."

The speaker squawked, "We see you. Come right one degree."

"Roger, coming right one degree," Sergiovski answered.

The sub broke through the surface of the water and floated into the ship. Zurko breathed deeply. He had not been consciously aware of holding his breath. The tension was gone. He felt like a wrung-out dishrag.

Serge Novstad looked down into the bowels of the ship from the railing high up on the forward end of the giant cargo hold. What had been three spaces for holding cargo was now one large swimming pool. The black submarine completely filled it. There were only two feet of clearance on either side and five feet fore and aft.

Novstad nodded, satisfied all had gone smoothly. He looked over at the seaman manning the control panel that operated the equipment in the cargo hold.

"All right, shut the doors. Pump down the hold slowly. We need to make sure *Zibrus* is evenly on the keel blocks."

The seaman hit a control on the panel before him, starting the pumps below.

Don Holbrooke lay back on the bed. He was sure he was alone. The shower burbled cheerfully as his mistress washed away the perspiration, the result of their recent amorous activities.

He reached over to the bedside table and grabbed his cell phone. The quick-dial feature was a godsend. No need to dial the many digits for an overseas call. The phone buzzed twice. It crackled once and was answered, "*Ja*."

"Herr Schmidt? Holbrooke. Let's go encrypted."

"*Ja*."

Holbrooke pushed a small red button on the side of the phone. The phone beeped twice and a small, yellow LED lighted on the face of the phone. Schmidt's guttural voice changed to a tinny, electrical sound.

"Herr Holbrooke. How good to hear from you. What can we do for our favorite customer?"

Holbrooke smiled. These Swiss were so predictable. He controlled millions of dollars deposited in Schmidt's vaults in Zurich. He would remain a favorite customer, no matter how obnoxious he might be to the haughty Swiss banker.

"Herr Schmidt, I wanted to verify that sixty million U.S. dollars had been transferred to our accounts from the Bank of Hong Kong."

"It arrived by wire transfer yesterday."

"And you put fifty million U.S. dollars into the main account and ten million U.S. dollars into the 'special' account?" Holbrooke asked.

"*Ja.* It is as you directed," Schmidt answered.

Holbrooke smiled, pleased with himself. He was now ten million dollars richer. Juan de Santiago did not know of the "special" account. Holbrooke needed no passbook to know that the ledger now showed over forty million U.S. dollars deposited there. That account, combined with the ones in Liechtenstein, Grand Cayman, and Kuwait City, made his personal fortune over one hundred million dollars.

Holbrooke stretched the length of the bed and kicked the sheet off. He felt rejuvenated and craved an encore. He would join the young lady in the shower. Life was good. Very good, indeed.

"Thank you, Herr Schmidt. As always, we trust your discretion in these matters. I will transfer your normal fee and a bonus to the account we discussed."

"Thank you, Herr Holbrooke," the Swiss banker acknowledged. "It is always a pleasure doing business with you."

"No, no, Herr Schmidt. The pleasure is all mine," Holbrooke said.

He hit the END button on the cell phone, jumped from the bed, let out a whoop of glee, and headed for the bathroom, where he could hear his woman singing above the rush of the shower.

Margarita, the mistress of Juan de Santiago, smiled. She returned the tiny earpiece to its hiding place beneath the bed.

No one would dare look there for any spy device. Juan de Santiago's bed was off limits to everyone but her and El Jefe himself. She, the room, and the bed were beyond the suspicion of the most ambitious security expert.

The snippet of one-sided conversation she had heard had been quite interesting. It could prove very valuable in the future. Margarita decided she would keep this information to herself, only to be used if she needed to.

No, El Falcone would not pass the bit of treachery she had just heard along to the JDIA until it was most opportune. Her purposes would be better served at some point in sharing it with El Jefe himself.

Margarita pulled on her swimsuit, checked her form in the floor-to-ceiling mirror, then headed for the hallway, calling the children's names as she made her way down to the pool.

22

BILL BEAMAN RAISED HIS HEAD TO TAKE A LOOK. THE HALF-ROTTED log shielded his body from eyes in the broad valley below him that might be turned his way. The black and green camouflage paint and floppy bush hat effectively caused his face to blend in with the jungle growth. Only the whites of his staring eyes broke the perfect color scheme.

His eyes were wide because he was looking down on one amazing site. At treetop level and above there was only another stretch of jungle. Another green isolated valley. No different from a hundred others. Most of which he felt they had slogged through already on this mission. Below the treetops it was a completely different story.

He was gazing down in awe at a huge, complete drug-manufacturing factory built right there in the midst of this isolated jungle valley. Had they not had the truck driver and his guard to guide them, they would never have found the place.

He had a far higher opinion of Juan de Santiago and his men. They would have to be magicians to have brought in all the materials and built this facility without anyone catching wind of it. The work involved in building this complex, miles from the nearest town, was mind-boggling, and to do it all and keep something this size out of the watchful eye of the spy satellites made it even more remarkable. For some reason, Beaman thought of the Incas, the industrious tribe who built an empire to rule this mountainous realm before the Spanish brought their own version of civilization. The scale of de Santiago's accomplishment here was on par with their works, seven hundred years before. The enterprising spirit of the Incas, however misguided it now might be, was still present in this place.

Beaman lifted the powerful binoculars to his eyes. Twisting the focus ring, he brought the factory complex into clear view. This facility must be capable of producing tons of cocaine at a time. No wonder they had been running a constant stream of trucks from the fields across the Peruvian border. That plant would be gluttonous. He realized with a sinking feeling in his stomach the potential customers for the factory's output would be as well.

Raising his arm, the SEAL lieutenant commander waved for Chief Johnston to leave his hiding place and move up to the lookout point. Johnston snaked his way over the few yards of open ground on his belly, keeping low as he skittered across the mud road.

"Yeah, Skipper. What's the play?"

"Damn, Chief! Do you believe all that down there? Look at the size of that place! I think it's time we took a few pictures and called in some of our friends to join the party."

Johnston pulled his own 10¥50 binoculars out and looked over the valley.

"They're real proud of it, too, Skipper. Did you see the defenses down there? Looks like they have Stinger sites on the hills, every thousand yards or so. I count at least a dozen. Glad we ain't calling in an air strike!"

Beaman scanned the valley another time.

"Yeah, I saw those. No way we could've gone in there and planted explosives. Looks like hardened strong points at both ends of the valley, too. I see a checkpoint down at the end of this road. Lots of people walking around down there with ugly weapons, too. Good thing we stopped up here. Where did you hide the truck?"

Johnston grinned. The combination of the black and green camouflage paint and his pearly white teeth reminded Beaman of the Cheshire cat from *Alice's Adventures in Wonderland.*

"It's a mile back up the road, pulled into a clump o' trees. Be weeks before anyone finds it and I don't think it'll matter much then. We got the driver and the guard tied up in the cab so they won't make any racket."

"Okay, Chief. Let's get some pictures and talk to Bethea. I think we've found what we came for."

He glanced back over his shoulder. The remainder of his depleted team lay hidden in the foliage on the uphill side of the road. He could see the hard black metal of their gun barrels extending from behind rocks, trees, and various other hiding places. Anyone disturbing this little patch of jungle was in for a very nasty surprise.

"Yessir."

"Where's Dumkowski?" Beaman whispered. "Last time I looked, he had the camera."

Johnston whistled once, low and quick. Anyone hearing it would have assumed it was a jungle bird. The lumbering SEAL rose from behind a rock and raced across the road. He fell heavily beside Beaman.

"Here's the camera, Skipper. Time to rock and roll?"

Beaman chuckled. This bunch was always ready.

"Hold your horses, Dumbo. Only pictures for now. Get the camera ready."

Dumkowski rummaged in his backpack. He pulled out a small digital camera and a GPS receiver. He set them both on the log. He snapped a series of digital images of the factory, concentrating on the camouflaged buildings at the center of the complex.

Cantrell set up the radio. Within minutes, the impressive digital images were converted to data and were traveling at the speed of light to a satellite far out in space, on their way to John Bethea's underground command center in San Diego.

The head of the Joint Drug Interdiction Agency whistled sharply as he looked over the shoulder of his best photo analyst.

"Beaman sure as hell found it this time. How long will it take to get this into targeting data?"

The technician looked at him over the tops of her half-glasses.

"A lot quicker if you'd let me get to work on it. I'm almost done with the mensuration. Say another fifteen minutes."

Bethea held up his hands apologetically and backed off, leaving the woman to her task. It was hard not to get involved when they were so close, but she was right. Better for him to sit back and plan what to do next. Probably a good idea to call Donnegan over at SUBPAC to let him know what was happening. He'd welcome the news, too.

Bethea walked over to his desk and grabbed the secure phone. He pushed a speed-dial button. The phone rang only twice before he heard Admiral Donnegan's gruff greeting.

"Donnegan here. Go."

"Admiral, John Bethea. Let's go secure."

Bethea pushed a button on the face of his phone. In his office in Pearl Harbor, Donnegan pushed a similar button. There was a brief hiss and crackle; then both men saw green lights illuminate on their phones. Donnegan spoke first.

"Hold you secure. What do you have, John?"

His voice sounded distinctly metallic now.

"Thought you'd like to know we just received a set of imagery from our SEALs down south. Tom, they have found a
large factory facility. Biggest I've ever seen. This is what
we've been looking for. We are finishing the targeting now. As
soon as we get it done, we'll be sending it to Ward and *Spadefish*. Admiral, I want to fly the birds tonight so we can pull our
men out of there." Bethea glanced up at the chart of the
Colombian coast that was hanging in front of his desk.
"Ward's going to have to run hard to get in the basket in time,
though. The injured crewman cost us time, then he wasted too
much time on that wild-goose chase with the freighter."

Donnegan could hear the exasperation in the JDIA director's tone. He could empathize with him. He had been there
many times himself, sitting thousands of miles away from the
action, trying to maintain some sense of control and coordination of an operation he couldn't see, hear, or feel except
through the cryptic communications from his people on the
front line. It was trying on any man's nerves. The added diffi-
culties in conversing with the submarine and the SEALs only
made matters worse in an operation like this one. Communication was better now than it was a couple of decades before.
None of this would have been possible then.

Both Ward and Beaman were trained to take the initiative,
to trust their instincts and take action. It meant they didn't always follow the plan as scripted. Their line of work required
some ad-libbing. Donnegan knew Bethea would need to
learn to accept the divergence from the overall plan that
sometimes resulted. It was an important lesson for a senior
commander.

Donnegan recognized the excitement in Bethea's voice.
They had both been waiting a long time to be in a position to
strike this blow against de Santiago.

"When will *Spadefish* be in the launch basket?" Donnegan
asked.

"We haven't talked to them in almost eighteen hours,"
Bethea responded. "They can go another six hours without

talking, but if Ward stays true to character, we should hear from him in an hour or so. We'll know then when he can be ready."

Donnegan sat back and chewed on the stub of an unlit cigar. He spat out a bit of tobacco leaf and said, "Ward'll move heaven and earth to get him where you want him. I wager that if you have the targeting, he'll have the birds in the air when we need them. Let me know."

Then Bethea found himself listening to a dial tone.

"Nav, where we at in this big old ocean?" Dave Kuhn asked, looking over his shoulder. He returned to looking at the sonar display before he got his answer. He enjoyed standing officer-of-the-deck watch. Besides giving him a respite from keeping everything in the old engine room working, driving ships was what he joined the navy to do.

Earl Beasley laid the divider down on the chart before him and looked at Kuhn through his eyebrows.

"We're exactly two miles closer than we were the last time you asked." He looked back down and drew a diamond around the dot on the chart and wrote the time beside it. "You ready to go to PD yet?"

"Slowing now. Seen the captain?"

"Saw him heading aft a bit ago. Probably find him on the Life Cycle." Beasley looked at the digital readout for the cesium clock. "Better get a step on it. You only got ten minutes to get up."

Kuhn chuckled.

"Never taken me ten minutes to get up before."

Beasley gave him another sardonic look while Kuhn stepped around the periscopes and picked up the phone. He selected an engine room station that was near the boat's Life Cycle exercise machine and spun the growler.

Aft in the engine room, tucked into a narrow space beside the spinning main shaft, Ward was pedaling furiously, trying to sneak in his daily workout. He felt better now, since the good report on Seaman Benitez, the man injured in the torpedo room. He had broken every rib, had punctured both lungs, lacerated his liver, and had other internal injuries, but, despite all that, it appeared he would pull through. The quick medevac by the Osprey had likely saved his life.

The angrily buzzing growler broke his concentration. He snatched the handset and put it to his ear.

"Captain."

"Captain, officer of the deck," Kuhn said. "At depth one-five-zero feet, course one-five-five, speed four. Completed a baffle clear to the left. No contacts. Request permission to come to periscope depth for the twenty-hundred zulu broadcast."

"Okay, Eng. I'll be forward in a minute."

Ward grabbed the towel he had draped over a hydraulic pipe and wiped away the sweat as he strolled forward. The rest of the workout would have to wait. They were almost in the patrol area, a couple of hours away. This broadcast would almost certainly have their patrol instructions and the latest intelligence. He suspected it would finally mean a bit of action for *Spadefish*.

He strolled forward past the main engines that drove them and the turbine generators that gave them electrical power. He stepped into the auxiliary machinery room and, out of habit, stopped for an instant to glance at the instruments that monitored the nuclear reactor. Everything seemed to be operating the way it was supposed to. He ducked his head and stepped through the hatch into the reactor compartment tunnel, walking directly over the reactor. Heading through the operations compartment, he threw the sweat-soaked towel into his stateroom and headed on to the control room.

"Okay, Eng. Anything change?" Ward asked as he stepped up onto the short platform around the periscopes and looked at the sonar displays. Nothing there.

"No, sir. Still no contacts," Kuhn answered.

Ward nodded.

"All right. Proceed to periscope depth."

Standing beside the navigation plotting table, Earl Beasley nudged Stan Guhl and nodded toward where Kuhn was about to grab the periscope.

"Watch this, Weps," he whispered, an odd grin on his face.

Kuhn snapped the red overhead control ring to the raised position and squatted to wait for the eyepiece to clear the deck. He slapped down the control handles and glued his eye to the eyepiece.

"Dive, make your depth six-two feet."

Spadefish rose from the depths. Kuhn kept his eye pressed on the eyepiece and watched the deep blue of the depths slowly turn to lighter turquoise, then to sky blue. He spun the scope around in two complete circles.

"No close contacts."

"Thirty seconds to the twenty-two-hundred broadcast," Radio Chief Lyman reported over the 21MC. "Request you raise the BRA-34."

Kuhn stepped back from the scope for a second to give the order to raise the radio antenna.

"Chief of the Watch, raise the BRA-34," he said, and glanced toward the navigator.

Beasley and Guhl erupted into laughter.

"Nav, that's beautiful," Guhl said between guffaws. "Haven't seen the old shoe-polish-on-the-eyepiece trick in a long time. Old Davey looks like a one-eyed raccoon."

Doug Lyman's voice over the 21MC speaker interrupted the hilarity.

"Conn, Radio. In sync on the broadcast. We have traffic aboard and JDIA requests the skipper come up on secure voice."

Ward was studying the sonar display and had not noticed the practical joke that had been played on Kuhn. He grabbed the microphone and answered, "Patch it to the conn. I'll talk to him from out here."

Joe Glass stepped onto the conn and asked, "Skipper, anything on the broadcast?"

"Just a second, XO. Getting it now. Bethea is on secure voice. I'm getting ready to talk to him."

Just as Ward finished speaking, the 7MC speaker squawked. It was Chris Durgan, back in the maneuvering room.

"Conn, Maneuvering. We have loss of 'open indication' on the port main coolant valves. Request the engineer lay aft."

Ward grimaced as he handed the red handset to Glass. Was this old boat going to hold together long enough for them to complete this mission?

"XO, you talk to Bethea. I'll relieve the engineer since I have a better handle on what's happening out here." He turned to Guhl. "Okay, Eng, head aft and find out what's going on back there. I've got the conn."

Ward stepped up to the number-two periscope as Guhl disappeared out the back of the control room. He spun the scope around until he faced the eyepiece. As he leaned over to look out the scope, Earl Beasley shouted, "Skipper! Hold on a minute!"

Ward looked quizzically at his navigator.

"What is it, Nav?"

"Let me take the scope. You shouldn't have to do that."

"Okay, Nav. It's all yours. Just get over here and keep an eye peeled for anything up above us." Ward leaned over and said quietly, "You aren't worried about a little shoe polish, are you, Nav?"

Beasley grinned sheepishly and said, "Okay, Skipper, you got me." He was glad the skipper didn't seem mad about the trick.

Glass looked toward Ward and raised an eyebrow. He had the red handset firmly planted to his ear. He had been listening for several minutes. The pad of paper on which he had been taking notes was filled with scribbles.

"Skipper, we got work," he whispered, even though he was listening to Bethea. "New targeting being downloaded now. Have to launch tonight. Looks like an eight-bird mission."

Stan Guhl jumped over to the fire control system and started typing something on the keyboard. The computer screen in front of him began to scroll numbers and letters. What appeared to be gibberish was vital information to the missiles down in the torpedo room.

Ward stepped over and looked at the plot. He grabbed the pair of dividers Beasley had left lying on the chart and measured the distance between their current position and the launch basket. He shook his head and looked over his shoulder at Joe Glass.

"XO, you better tell Bethea if we're going to get there in time, we'll have to stop this chitchat and go deep and fast."

Guhl looked up and said, "I've got the targeting on board. Everything verified correct. I'm ready to go."

Ward laid down the dividers.

"Okay, people, let's get out of here. XO, say good-bye to Bethea. Nav, lower all masts and antennas." Then he remembered they had yet another problem with the old boat that was still pending. "Oh, and ask the Eng how fast we can go until he gets his little problem fixed. We need to move our butts."

When he glanced around the control room, Jonathan Ward couldn't help but notice the determined looks on the faces of his crew. They were on the way to strike a blow for what was good and right. And, even if his boat wasn't, his men were definitely ready.

Serge Novstad, Rudi Sergiovski, and Philippe Zurko sat around the dinner table in the captain's stateroom on the *Helena K.* The remains of the lobster dinner littered the table. The bottle of Chilean chardonnay was empty. The cognac snifters were charged with Napoleon brandy. The three leaned back and puffed on Havana cigars.

Novstad sighed deeply, contentedly.

"It's good to be back out to sea again. I feel cleaner already, being away from that pesthole of a port."

Sergiovski shook his head in agreement.

"*Da*, it is good. Now if we only had some vodka instead of this brandy. That is a man's drink."

Zurko merely sat back and listened to the banter. These hired mercenaries had no appreciation for his people or his homeland. The blood of Pizarro and the *conquistadores* flowed in his veins and mixed with that of the ancient Inca emperors. His ancestors had ruled vast empires while the fore-bears of these louts were still huddling around peat fires and chasing reindeer.

He held his tongue, sucked on the cigar, and let them carry on their foolishness. They were a necessary irritation. For the good of the revolution. For the security of his and his family's own future once El Jefe controlled all of their beloved country.

Sergiovski glanced at the ship speed repeater mounted on the bulkhead beside Novstad. The polished brass case gleamed against the dark teak paneling. The digital readout showed *Helena K*'s forward speed. The Russian sat up and squinted hard at the numbers.

"Captain Novstad, that says we are only making twelve knots. Shouldn't we be going faster?"

Novstad took another sip of his brandy before he answered.

"The underwater door mechanism has a small problem. They did not shut completely after we housed the *Zibrus*. An alignment problem, my engineer says. Until we get it repaired, this is as fast as we can go."

Zurko slammed down his snifter in exasperation.

"You bloody fool! Don't you understand this will set back the whole timetable? We must tell El Jefe at once."

Even before the words were out of his mouth, he was trying to figure a way to avoid making that call.

"Take it easy. Have a drink."

"Why can't just one thing go right?" Zurko sputtered. "Why must there always be complications that will only serve to ignite El Jefe's temper? Do you not understand? He has severed heads and hung them on stakes for less."

Zurko seized the snifter and drained the rest of the brandy in one burning gulp.

Why did these problems always seem to happen on his watch?

Was someone conspiring against him?

What had he done to anger God?

23

DAVE KUHN LEANED BACK EXHAUSTED. HE PROPPED HIMSELF AGAINST the instrument panel, easing his tired muscles. His neck throbbed and his back ached from bending awkwardly over Bert Waters's broad shoulders, trying to watch what the reactor operator was doing inside the drawer crammed full of electronic components. The narrow passage between the two rows of panels made viewing unwieldy. The oscilloscope and the digital voltmeter sitting on the deck between them were in the way. He didn't dare move away. He had to watch the operation in progress.

Waters looked back over his shoulder and spoke.

"Eng, the waveform on the scope looks good. What's the next step?"

Kuhn read from the heavy black technical manual he was holding in his sweating hands.

"Says here if the waveform is good, we have an open primary detector in the reactor compartment. It says we have to shift to the backup. You should see a red lead on terminal J-202 and a white lead on terminal J-203."

Waters squinted into the drawer through his rimless eyeglasses.

"Hmmm. Yeah. See 'em."

"Okay. Swap the red one to terminal J-207 and the white one over to terminal J-208."

Waters grabbed a nut driver from his pocket and reached into the panel. In a few seconds he leaned back on his heels and grunted, "Done."

"Okay. Let's check to make sure. The red one is now on J-207 and the white one on J-208?"

Waters looked in the panel and nodded. "Yeah, Eng, I can take direction." Neither took the banter seriously. This "reader/worker" technique and double-checking every step was a normal part of safely operating the reactor. They had both grown up in this environment and regarded it as a normal part of life.

Kuhn read the next paragraph in the manual, his lips moving slightly.

"Only thing left now is an alignment check next time we cycle the main coolant cutout valves. Button up the drawer and stow the test gear. I'll give the skipper a buzz and fill him in."

Kuhn groaned as he rose, rubbing his back. He reached over Waters to grab the sound-powered phone. It was mounted on a small recessed panel outboard of the after row of instruments, along with several other pieces of internal communications equipment. The passage between the two rows of instruments was so narrow there was no way to step around the kneeling Waters, so he had to ignore the painful cramp in the muscles in his lower back.

He selected the control room on the phone and spun the growler. Almost immediately he heard Ward's gravelly voice say, "Conn, Captain."

"Captain, Engineer," Kuhn said. "We have completed repairs to the valve position indication for the port main coolant cutout valves. We had to put the backup detector coils in service. If they go out, we'll have to scram reactor and do an emergency reactor compartment entry to replace them."

He could hear the captain groan on the other end of the phone. An emergency reactor compartment entry was a major and uncomfortable procedure. The reactor operated inside a locked space, the reactor compartment. With the reactor critical and supplying power, the radiation levels in the compartment were high enough to cause a slow painful death from radiation sickness for anyone who entered. However, the radiation died off quickly once the reactor was shut down, so there was little danger from that happening.

There were two real problems, though. For the people entering the compartment to work, the air temperature was equivalent to a very hot sauna and all the exposed metal was blistering hot to the touch. Contact with skin would cause instant and very painful burns. Just to make the job more uncomfortable, everyone had to wear heavy, protective yellow anticontamination suits and bulky emergency air-fed breathing masks, called EABs. Most people could only work for fifteen minutes before they had to come outside to cool off.

The other problem was also related to time. With the reactor shut down, the only sources of power were the battery and the emergency diesel. This meant that *Spadefish* would be stuck at periscope depth for the entire time the repairs took while the diesel sucked outside air, and their speed would be limited to about three knots. At the same time, the rocking and rolling of the sub near the ocean's surface added to the discomfort and danger for the people working in the reactor compartment.

Ward hesitated for a second, pondering the possibilities.

"All right, Eng. Get everything ready, just in case. Draw the parts from supply, write a repair procedure, brief everyone, but let's hope we won't need to do it before they finally cut this old girl up."

Kuhn answered smartly.

"Roger that, Skipper. We'll be ready if we need to do it. Reactor power limit now one hundred per cent."

Ward turned to Beasley and ordered, "Officer of the Deck, ahead flank. Let's get our asses on down the road. We've only got two hours to get into the box and I doubt those SEALs are interested in hearing our miseries."

Beasley winked and promptly got to work.

Bill Ralston was a busy man and would continue to be for the next couple of hours. He had over sixteen years' experience working in the torpedo rooms of various submarines and this was the first time he was going to shoot weapons in anger. And he was going to make damn sure they worked right.

The four missiles already in the torpedo tubes were wired to the fire control system. Brass signs hung from each torpedo tube breech door. Large red letters on the signs said, CAUTION! WAR SHOT TOMAHAWK MISSILE LOADED.

The fire control technicians were making sure the system was talking to the missiles in the tubes. One of the men sat next to Ralston at the launch control panel between the two banks of tubes. He watched the lights on the panel and talked over the phones to his coworker, sitting at the fire control panel up in the control room.

So far, these birds were checking out fine. More missiles waited patiently in line to be loaded after the first four were out of the tubes and on their way. Ralston watched as two more sailors on his team hooked up a test device to each of these birds. The test set checked out all the circuits in the birds, almost as if they were already in the torpedo tubes and talking to the fire control system.

Two of his torpedo men were checking out the emergency loading equipment, a simple but massive block-and-tackle system meant to move the behemoths by muscle power if the hydraulic missile-loading system failed for some reason. Ralston had personally checked the hydraulic system, though. Hand-over-hand, checking every pipe and every valve. He had done the same thing for the high-pressure air and seawater systems, too.

His team was ready. Ready to hurl one big handful of destructive might out those tubes and into the Pacific sky.

Ralston felt his pulse quicken as he sighed deeply and went on back to look at the hydraulics one more time.

Joe Glass stepped into the wardroom. His immediate thought was that this was not the wardroom he was accustomed to.

Stan Guhl sat at a position in the middle of the table in front of a laptop computer. He was surrounded by quartermasters and fire control technicians, some banging away on computer keyboards, others plotting courses on charts that covered all the available vertical space in the room. Piles of paper, open manuals, and half-empty coffee cups filled every square inch of the table's surface.

Glass glanced over Guhl's shoulder at the image on the computer's screen. It was a graphical simulation of a proposed missile flight plan.

"How is it going, Weps?"

Guhl looked up, rubbing his eyes as he answered.

"Almost there. Way I have it figured, we'll launch the first four birds and set up the flight plans so they all arrive on target almost simultaneously."

He hit a couple of keys. The screen shifted to a chart of the waters off Colombia with their launch basket outlined in red. The map continued over land to include the highland valley with its hidden factory. A dot marked the launch position for *Spadefish* while a large, ominous, black X marked the target.

Guhl turned his face back to the screen, the colors reflecting off his intent face as he continued.

"Watch this, XO. This is playing at times-ten speed now so every second of the simulation will be ten seconds of actual flight time."

As he spoke, he hit a key on the keyboard. A yellow line started from *Spadefish*'s launch position and made a large slow circle to the left. Three seconds later, a blue line started from the same point, then circled to the right, its arc just a little smaller than the first one's had been. Five seconds later, a green line started and traced its own small circle to the left. Three more seconds passed and then a purple line started, but it headed directly for the beach, the rough silhouette that marked the Colombian coast. Meanwhile, the other three colorful streaks had already stopped their circling and headed east, too, following the purple marker.

Guhl glanced up at Glass.

"I calculated a total of one hundred twenty seconds to get all four birds in the air."

All the lines crossed the beach at the same time and continued their relentless progress toward the east, as if they were dutifully heading off to intercept the rising sun out there somewhere beyond the South American continent.

"But this is an eight-bird mission," Glass said dryly.

"I know. There's no way we can get them all in the air together. The first four wouldn't have enough gas to reach the target if they had to stay around, circling to wait for the second four to get launched. I didn't figure target alertment was too much of a problem here anyway."

Glass rubbed the stubble on his chin.

"You've got a point there. All Beaman saw was a bunch of Stingers. Not much they can do with those babies once we light a fire under them. I'll go tell the skipper you're about ready. Only about half an hour now and we'll be on the spot."

The weapons officer turned back to the computer screen, hit the key again, and watched the rainbow-hued lines as they once again appeared, circled, and headed off into the night.

Ward glanced up when his executive officer appeared. He had been sitting on the stool at the back of the periscope stand reading through the Tomahawk launching procedures by the dim red light that was hanging there. He could recite most of the manual from memory, but one more review wouldn't hurt. The control room was dark except for a few muted red lights and the glow of the computer screens. Even those were covered with thick, dark red Plexiglas. It was important to protect both his and the officer of the deck's night vision, just in case.

Glass stepped up onto the stand next to him.

"Just crossed into the area, Skipper."

"All right, XO," Ward said with a quick smile.

Several times he had wondered if they would ever make it to where they were supposed to be. The old boat with her aging pains, the accident in the torpedo room, even the brief distraction of the odd transmissions they had intercepted seemed to all pile up. He had begun to consider the possibility of not being able to get to their assigned position in time to help

Beaman and his men take out the target before Bethea decided to pull them out. That would have been an ignominious way for *Spadefish* to end her life. And it would have given the likes of Mike Hunsucker and Pierre Desseaux a reason to crow. All that aside, it also would have meant de Santiago could have continued making the deadly product bound for the States. That would have been the real tragedy.

Looking to his left, Jon Ward spoke in a louder voice: "Officer of the Deck, man battle stations missile."

Beasley looked up from the chart he was reviewing and Ward imagined he could see a glimmer in the man's eyes.

"Man battle stations missile, aye, sir. Chief of the Watch, on the 1MC, 'Man battle stations missile.'"

Sam Bechtal jumped up from his seat and grabbed the yellow handle of the general alarm. When he pulled it through a short arc, the warning sounded loudly throughout the ship: *Bong! Bong! Bong! Bong!* He picked up the 1MC microphone and shouted, "Man battle stations missile!"

The alarm, of course, was almost an afterthought. Everyone was already at battle stations, readying *Spadefish* to shoot her load of Tomahawk missiles. Unlike launching torpedoes, shooting Tomahawks required careful planning and several hours of work. There was no one jumping from his bunk, running excitedly through the sub to hurry to his station the way the movies usually portrayed such a procedure.

Ward watched as his crew rolled into action. No wasted motion, no unnecessary talking, no missteps, simply professionals going quietly about their business, the way they had been drilled over and over.

The captain turned to Beasley and said softly, "Okay, Nav, let's go up and see what is on the roof. No sense in scaring the bejesus out of some poor fisherman."

"Yes, sir," Beasley answered. "We just completed a baffle clear. No sonar contacts. On course one-two-zero, depth one-five-zero feet, speed seven. Request permission to proceed to periscope depth for a look around."

Ward nodded and said, "Proceed to periscope depth for a look around."

"Diving Officer, make your depth six-two feet," Beasley ordered.

Spadefish's deck visibly angled up as Beasley squatted to raise the periscope. Ray Laskowski, sitting in the diving officer's chair, reeled off the depth changes in a calm monotone.

"One hundred feet. Nine-five feet. Nine-zero feet . . ."

Beasley gazed through the periscope as he stepped in a slow circle, "dancing with the fat lady." He could see nothing but black. Occasionally a streak of fluorescence would flash through his field of vision. It reminded Beasley of tracer fire he had once watched in the sky during a night exercise off San Diego. Still, it was mostly blackness he watched through the eyepiece. The only way he could tell which direction he was looking was by feeling what his butt was hitting as he circled.

As he heard Laskowski say, "Six-four feet," Beasley finally saw the darkness broken with streaks and splashes of dirty-gray white. He shouted "Scopes breaking!" The deep black of the ocean was replaced by a star-studded sky. The light of a glorious quarter moon caused the calm sea's surface to shimmer a deep, silvery gray. Beasley quickly whipped the scope around in a 360-degree arc and reported, "No close contacts!"

Normal conversation resumed in the control room as everyone went back to the business of preparing to shoot.

Beasley made several slow circles with the scope, carefully searching the sea surface for running lights, the sky overhead for aircraft, looking for any black shapes bobbing near enough to be in the way.

Finally he said, "Skipper, made a careful search around. No contacts. Ain't nobody out here but us fish."

Ward nodded.

"Okay, Nav. Make your depth one-five-zero feet. Get on launch course. Time to get this show on the road."

"Diving Officer, make your depth one-five-zero feet!" Beasley shouted. "Helm, come left to course one-zero-four."

The deck slanted downward again as Beasley snapped up the scope handles and lowered the scope into the well.

Spadefish leveled out on depth and steadied on a course that pointed her bow almost directly at the spot on the Colombian coast the missiles would first cross. It was called the "landfall waypoint."

Ward stepped to the front of the control room. He faced the assembled team and cleared his throat before speaking in a loud voice.

"Attention in the attack center. We will be launching a four-missile salvo, reloading, and launching a second salvo. We will then reload all tubes with Tomahawks and go to periscope depth. We'll stand by there to see if any further missions are required of us. If any missiles fail, we will reload and shoot that mission as a single missile shot. Carry on."

Everyone turned back to his station. The excitement in the room was palpable.

They were about to do what they had trained so thoroughly to do.

Ward turned to Joe Glass and asked, "XO, are we ready?"

Glass was standing between Stan Guhl, seated at the launch control panel, and Chris Durgan, seated at one of the fire control computers. Both of the young officers nodded their heads vigorously, but it was Glass who answered.

"We're ready, Skipper."

"Flood all tubes and make tubes one and two ready in all respects," Ward commanded.

Guhl passed the order down to Ralston in the torpedo room. There, he flooded seawater into the tubes, opened the outer doors for tubes one and two, then lined them up to be fired. *Spadefish* was equipped to fire only two of her four tubes nearly simultaneously. The outer doors on these two had to be closed before the other two tubes could be used.

"All tubes flooded. Tubes one and two ready in all respects," Ralston reported, fighting to keep his voice calm and businesslike, as if he shot off Tomahawks every morning before breakfast.

Ward nodded and pulled a preprinted three-by-five card from his breast pocket. Reading from the card, he said, "Firing point procedures for a four-missile salvo launch, tube one first."

Beasley made one final check to make sure the ship was at the proper launch depth, speed, and course. He replied, "Ship ready."

Guhl checked that the missiles were ready to go and said, "Weapons ready."

Glass checked once more that the right missions were in the computer and the manual plot on the navigation table was set up. Once satisfied, he said, "Solution ready."

The control was deadly silent. No one there had ever before fired a weapon that would blow up things and likely kill people. The muscles on Guhl's neck stood out as he tensed to "pull the trigger." Glass unconsciously clenched and unclenched his fists at his sides.

Seaman Cortez, the helmsman, belched loudly. The tension of the moment was broken and every man within earshot grinned.

Ward, too, had a smile on his face as he ordered, "Shoot tube one."

Guhl flung the large brass firing lever to STANDBY and shouted, "Stand by." He flung the lever to SHOOT as he shouted "Launch permissive!" to the people in the control room.

Nothing happened. The room was quiet.

The action had been set in motion. Down in tube one, the missile gyro came up to speed and the missile performed a series of internal checks, verifying that it was ready to fly the ordered mission. When the checks were completed, interlocks switched, lining high-pressure air to the torpedo-tube flushing cylinder. The 1500-psi air forced the flushing piston down the cylinder, pushing high-pressure water up into the after part of the torpedo tube. Meanwhile, in the tube itself, the missile canister had opened a series of ports around its after part. The high-pressure water literally flushed the missile out of the canister and torpedo tube. It accelerated rapidly out of the tube and clear of the submarine. A lanyard, attached at one end to the missile and at the other to the canister, yanked taut and ignited the rocket motor attached to the tail of the missile. The missile roared up, out of the water, and into the mostly dark sky. The fiery lance of the rocket lit up the night like a Roman candle as it kicked the missile high into the starry sky.

As the rocket engine burned out and dropped away, a sequence of events began that transformed the missile into what could best be described as a small robot airplane. An air scoop dropped open beneath the missile and two small, stubby wings scissored out from inside the missile's body. The turbo-fan engine, now supplied with air from the scoop and ignited by a small explosive squid, came up to speed to give the missile power. The bird then dropped down almost to wavetop height and flew to the north, now beginning its preprogrammed flight.

The bird in tube two quickly joined its mate in the air, circling instead to the south. The birds in tubes three and four followed a minute later. As the last missile transitioned to cruise flight, all four headed toward the Colombian coast, toward the landfall waypoint. Tiny antennas in their guidance systems locked in on NAVSTAR satellites in geosynchronous orbit twenty-three thousand miles overhead. The birds made minor course corrections in response to the continuous GPS positioning information.

They knew precisely where they were going. And there was no doubt what they would do once they got there.

Back in the bowels of *Spadefish*, Bill Ralston and his crew were hardly finished. He shouted instructions at his reload parties. They were in a race to get the tubes readied and reloaded for the next launch. The canisters remaining in the torpedo tubes were jettisoned, pushed out of the tubes through the muzzle doors to sink slowly into the depths of the Pacific. With all the hardware out of the torpedo tubes, they were drained of seawater and checked for any damage or debris. Finally, the missiles that had been lined up behind each tube were slid into place, their complicated electronics connected, and the thick bronze breech doors were shut and locked once again.

Ralston reported all four tubes loaded and ready. His team still didn't rest. They positioned the third group of four missiles behind the tubes, ready for the next salvo to be loaded for use if needed.

Four more Tomahawks were now ready to fly. The team on *Spadefish* once again stepped through the carefully choreographed sequence to send them winging toward de Santiago's evil factory far inland.

Not a man on board the submarine had any qualms about what he was doing. The cheers that erupted throughout the boat when the last four birds were away confirmed it.

The initial four missiles climbed steeply as they crossed the beach and headed purposefully inland. Using small downward-looking radars, each took a picture at predetermined points in the flight plan and compared the returns with the expected radar pictures that had been stored in their memories. Each made ever-so-slight course corrections to bring them precisely on the planned route they were supposed to be following.

As they flew deeper inland, two of the birds changed course to the south, while the other two veered more to the north. They soared through narrow mountain valleys and climbed over ridges as they climbed and dived to stay just above treetop level. Flying at a speed of Mach 0.82, they whistled over villages and around towns, but mostly zoomed just above desolate jungle. There was practically no advance warning when they finally arrived at the north and south ends of the target valley almost simultaneously.

And once there, they did not hesitate.

———

Lieutenant Commander Bill Beaman wearily lifted his head just above the rotten log that had been his mostly inadequate resting place for the past thirty uncomfortable hours. Nothing in the valley down there below him had changed.

He crawled over closer to Johnston and whispered, "What do you think, Chief? They should have had those birds here by now. Do we stay here and risk them catching wind of us or do we bag it?"

Johnston squinted in Beaman's direction.

"Aw, Skipper, we've come too far to bag it just yet. Why don't we give it till morning? We can get under way and out of their sights before daylight if it don't start raining fire and brimstone before then."

Beaman knew his chief had the right idea. The longer his men stayed in position, the greater the possibility de Santiago's men might stumble up on them. They had to have patrols wandering the jungle and his squad would be outnumbered. They were out of supplies as well as patience. They could not spend another day hunkered down here.

He didn't want to abandon the mission until they had seen it through. Not unless there was no other rational action. The price had been too high to quit now.

Night or not, they could see the factory at full production in the valley. They had been able to bring in a tremendous amount of raw coca before Beaman's men cut the supply route. Under the camouflage, dozens of men scurried between buildings as trucks backed up to loading docks to take on the newly manufactured product. Light poured through open doors. A radio was playing loudly. The irritating, tinkling music rose up the hillside. It was business as usual down there. Loads of coca leaves in one end, white death out the other.

The team was bone-weary tired. So was Beaman. They had been on this mission far longer than they had planned. They had traversed great distances through trackless mountain jungles. They had fought a battle and lost teammates. They had even brought down a mountain. It had all been to arrive at this

point. Now they were supposed to stay here to confirm that all
the complicated calculations had come out right and that all
the high-tech gizmos had worked correctly. If the missiles
ever showed up.

Bugs crawled all over him and the sweat stung his eyes. It
had been for nothing. Frustration, anger, and plain old exhaustion were getting the best of him. His men were feeling it, too.

Beaman cocked an ear toward the sky.

Nothing. Still as death. The tinkly music, the happy shouts
of some of the workmen in the factory jawing with each other,
the buzz of the night insects all around them.

LCDR Bill Beaman rolled over onto his back and watched
the moon being swallowed up by a dark cloud. The stars were
brighter, the moon mostly obscured.

Then they were so bright they bathed the whole world in
hot, white fire.

The leading Tomahawk missile, coming in through the pass at
the north end of the valley, snapped a picture of the terrain
ahead of it just before reaching its target. It matched the digital picture it had stored in memory. It compared both pictures
with a GPS plot in its memory bank. The missile's electronic
brain was satisfied. It had arrived over its correct target.

A cover blew off the warhead section of the missile. It
dropped hundreds of 2.2-pound bomblets as it flew over the
factory complex. The bomblets fell through the camouflage,
through the factory roof. They detonated with reverberating
booms, destroying everything and everybody within range.

The SEALs watched the last bomblet fall. The missile
dived into the factory on a suicide mission. Its remaining fuel
exploded, igniting a roaring fire that blazed out of control.

The first missile was less than halfway through its attack
when the second one, coming in low from the south, rolled in
to launch its own bombing run. The third and fourth missiles
arrived on the scene. The factory was a blazing, exploding inferno. A few of the workers ran wildly from the complex,
screaming, disappearing into the jungle.

The only other sounds were the continual explosions and the awful roar of the hellish conflagration.

Bill Beaman watched in awe. He had not seen the Tomahawks approach. He had been watching for them. He knew they would be coming. He had jumped when the first bomblet exploded and shook the ground beneath him. Fire seemed to erupt all around him. It had not been that great an explosion. But soon others followed, the combined effect of the hundreds of bomblets adding up to a boom that could be heard to wherever that bastard de Santiago slept.

The rebel gunners stationed at both ends of the valley began firing wildly into the night sky. Assuming they were under attack from the air, they fired at a silent airplane. Their tracery laced through the night sky, adding to the general bedlam.

Beaman grinned and nudged Johnston, then raised himself up to get a better look at the destruction Jon Ward and his boat wrought from the west in the Pacific Ocean.

"Do you believe that?" he whooped. "Whole damn thing is burning like crazy! Great!"

Johnston grabbed Beaman and pulled him back down behind the log.

"Skipper, get your ass back down. Wouldn't be good form to get hit by a stray bullet from one of those crazy bastards shooting up in the air."

He exchanged a high five with Beaman. Both men wore broad grins in the dancing light from the inferno that roared in front of them.

By the time the second flight of missiles arrived, the factory complex was completely engulfed in flames. Those birds had little to do but add their own dose of destruction.

Beaman whistled to his team to draw closer.

"Come on, guys. Time to head outta here. It's Miller time."

24

WARD SPUN THE SCOPE AROUND SLOWLY, STARING UPWARD AT THE dark night sky. They were alone in this part of the southern Pacific. The shipping traffic tended to remain closer to the mainland and the fishing in these waters was hardly good enough to entice boats out this far. It was a beautiful night, though. The moon hung low on the horizon, paving a silvery trail to the west. The southern stars shown through occasional spaces in the few clouds that bounced along on the far horizon.

Ward and *Spadefish* waited for some word on whether or not their mission was a success. And, if not, whether more of the Tomahawks waiting down in the torpedo room would need to be hurled toward de Santiago's deadly factory.

"XO, time to impact?" Ward asked, never removing his eye from the periscope's eyepiece.

Glass looked at the red LED readout from the cesium time standard, the atomic clock.

"Skipper, first salvo should be hitting right about now. Second one in twenty-three minutes."

"All right. What is the status of loading the restrike birds, Weps?"

Guhl eased back the earphones and pushed back from the fire control console on which he had been resting his elbows. He looked back over his shoulder, a perplexed look on his face.

"You say something, Skipper? Chief Ralston was just reporting."

A burst of scratchy static came from the intercept speaker on the bulkhead behind Ward's ear. It disrupted the quiet conversation of the control room and everyone looked at it, as if by doing so they could tell what had caused the noise. This speaker was designed to intercept extremely high-frequency signals, such as those used by fire control radars that might detect *Spadefish*'s periscope. The static gave them some semblance of early warning, even before any analysis was done on the signal.

Ward's brow was creased in question. With the frequency range of the intercept receiver, he should be seeing some warship up there topside. And that was especially true, given the loudness of the static. The ocean was empty. He had just given it a good look.

What was happening? That was much too strong a signal to be spurious background noise. He yelled into the open microphone above his head.

"ESM, Conn. What the hell are we hearing out here?"

It was Larson, the cryptotechnician, who answered.

"Skipper, I honestly don't know. We're analyzing now. Can we use the ESM mast?"

"ESM, Conn. ESM mast coming up," Ward ordered. "Give me an analysis as quickly as you can. There isn't anything up there that I can see." Ward looked back into the scope just to confirm his own words for himself. Nothing but moon, stars, and puffy clouds. "Don't ask for a DF. I can't lower the scope right now. We need to keep the radio mast up until we get a report on the mission."

The irritating pulse of static on the intercept speaker was a curious puzzle, maybe even a potentially dangerous one, but there was a mission yet to finish. They might need to send up some more birds toward the beach if the first flock had strayed. He looked away from the scope toward Stan Guhl.

"Weps, you were saying?"

"Chief Ralston was just reporting all tubes loaded for restrike, Skipper. We're doing continuity checks now. We'll be ready."

Ward set his mouth firmly. He expected nothing less. He

hoped the same would be true if that damned noise proved to be a threat.

John Bethea cheered loudly, shaking his fist in the air in triumph. The home team had just scored a crucial touchdown! The transcript of Bill Beaman's report of the attack lay on his desk and photos from far out in space confirmed what the SEAL commander had told him.

"This is great! Fabulous! We finally hit 'em where it hurts!" he yelped to absolutely no one. His office was empty. It was two o'clock in the morning.

He grabbed the telephone and punched the speed dial. First he had to get Beaman and his men out of there. They had been trekking the mountains of Colombia, chasing Juan de Santiago for too long. Time to bring them back to the States and to the heroes' welcome they deserved. Hell, these men should be paraded down Broadway, tickertape fluttering around them. He knew that would never happen. Their mission was so sensitive that few outside the JDIA would ever know it had even taken place.

Bethea arranged for the Colombian Army to pick the SEALs up from a drop zone a few miles from where the flames that engulfed de Santiago's factory still raged. A two-hour helicopter ride to Bogotá, a shower, a hot breakfast, and a change of clothes, then first-class tickets to San Diego's Lindbergh Field. He would have them home by tonight so he could shake each man's hand before he sent him off on well-deserved liberty.

Even with that happy chore completed, Bethea's brow was still knitted with worry. There were still a couple of missing elements that bothered him. A factory the size of the one they had just hit could produce tons of coke and had been in full operation for several weeks. The satellite photos showed burning buildings spread over several hectares. They couldn't account for where all the product they had turned out had gone. There were no warehouses on the property that anyone could see. The stuff had not shown up in the States yet. Tom Kincaid up in Seattle reported everything eerily quiet there. So quiet, his chief suspect in the distribution of the deadly recipe had not raised his ugly head since the first spate of lifeless bodies had turned up. And the DEA man, flying beneath the radar of his superiors, had set up a tight network of former pals in the agency to keep tabs on the import of the mixture in other parts of the country. It was possible de Santiago might move his desired point of entry once he had killed so many with the initial test.

Nothing. None of the potent stuff had turned up anywhere since that first murderous shipment.

De Santiago wasn't stupid enough to leave it lying around in the factory, no matter how hidden it was. The stuff had to still be in shipment. There was likely a good boatload ready to go by now. None of his eyes and ears along the coast had caught wind of it. And El Falcone had reported nothing.

Bethea had no choice but to depend on his network of informants, especially El Falcone, to uncover the trail. Or someone in de Santiago's group would get talkative. If that happened, he needed *Spadefish* to be in position to intercept the conversation. She was equipped to do that better than anything else he had anywhere in the area, and, judging from the satellite photos on his desk, she was now free for her next assignment.

So that was what had to be done. He would ask the informants to listen even harder. And he needed *Spadefish* to move closer and turn up her hearing aids to the max.

"God help us if that shit gets through," he said to himself, imagining how much damage that potent poison could do, even if it would be a long time before any more could follow it.

He stood and walked over to the communications center to talk to Ward, but as he did, he pondered the second problem, the location of the lab that was making that addictive additive. The factory was adding it into the mixture but it wasn't doing the actual manufacturing. The pictures he saw and Beaman's eyewitness accounts confirmed that this was merely a run-of-the-mill coke operation, albeit on a grand scale.

More work for El Falcone, he decided. *Sure wish he wasn't such a pain in the ass to contact.* Even in the best of times, communications were tenuous with the spy. Bethea had no way to directly contact him. He could only place a specially worded ad in a Cartagena newspaper and wait for El Falcone to check in.

He would need to put that into the works, too. That is, as soon as he had Ward and his sub on the way to their next job.

Bethea stepped into the comm center. The on-watch technician looked up from her keyboard and pushed back her headset, not at all surprised to see the boss in the bunker at this hour. She had never seen the man sleep.

"Evening, sir. Ward is on the secure voice circuit waiting for tasking. We have the strike results yet?"

Bethea nodded. The ear-to-ear grin told the story. He grabbed a headset and pulled it over his ears.

"Jon, great shooting! Just got the satellite pictures. Confirms Beaman's initial report. That whole valley is burning. We won't be needing any restrikes just yet."

Ward answered in a voice that was strong and clear over the secure radio circuit.

"Good, because we've got a new development down here. My guys just intercepted that same signal again. You remember? The one from that merchant, the *Helena K*, that we picked up on the weather-buoy frequency?"

Bethea closed his eyes and slowly shook his head. Even though Ward was three thousand miles south, he could sense the man's eagerness to go chase that will-o'-the-wisp.

"Jon, you know the story. We searched that ship, stem to stern. There isn't anything there. She's empty. Look, I've got something else I want you to do."

Ward wasn't buying it.

"John, that guy's a druggie! I know he is. I'm going to ease off down there and take a look for myself."

Bethea bit down hard. He was adamant.

"Skipper, I need *Spadefish* in close to the coast doing signal intercept. I need to know where the rest of de Santiago's coke is. It's got to come out of one of those ports over there and I want you in position to hear any communications that will tell us where. Then you can go chasing them down."

Ward was almost shouting when he answered.

"Damn it, John! That's what I've been telling you. Those drugs are on the *Helena K*. I know it and I mean to prove it!"

Bethea's face had turned a dark crimson. He knew the reputation of some of these sub commanders, but he had never had to deal with such a stubborn SOB as this one before. The on-watch technician found something interesting to study in the bottom of her empty coffee cup.

"Listen to me. That ship is empty. We searched it from one end to the other. There weren't any drugs aboard at all, let alone several tons of pure cocaine. Now, Captain, you will follow your orders and proceed to the coast to conduct signal-intercept operations! That is final!"

Thousands of miles away, beneath the surface of the southern Pacific Ocean, Jonathan Ward strategically held the red phone as far away from his ear as his right arm would stretch. When he spoke again, he said, "JDIA, this is *Spadefish*. Receiving you garbled. Unable to receive your last. Say again."

He reached over to the bulkhead and turned the receiver off before facing Ed Beasley.

"Officer of the Deck, lower all masts and antennas. Make your depth six hundred feet. Set a course for the *Helena K*. All ahead flank."

Beasley acknowledged, "Aye, Skipper," to Ward's departing back.

Joe Glass followed on Ward's heels. They walked into Ward's stateroom together. Glass slumped down onto the settee.

"Skipper, what the hell was that all about? We didn't lose communications out there and you know it."

Ward half smiled, and nodded.

"Joe, file this away for when you have your own boat.

Bethea's sitting on his ass in a snug bunker there on the beach in San Diego." Ward plopped down hard into his own chair and took a swig of what had to be ice-cold coffee. He didn't notice. "He doesn't understand what's happening out here at the pointy end of the spear. Now, Carlos and Larson are telling me that boat is a druggie. Those two are the best spooks I've ever dealt with. My gut tells me to trust them and I'm going with my gut."

Glass shook his head slowly.

"Okay, Skipper. You're putting it on the line for this. Why don't you just follow orders? No danger there."

Ward chuckled.

"XO, you've heard the old saying 'No balls, no blue chips'?" The executive officer shook his head. "No blue chips in taking the safe way out. Yeah, we could run over and sit on our butts listening to Radio Cartagena and a bunch of taxicab drivers for a few days. No muss, no fuss. Then we troop home with nothing. All JDIA's fault when a few tons of super co-caine turn up on American soil. Way I see it, that merchant is involved somehow and our job is to find out how. Just because Bethea doesn't understand that is no reason for us not to do our job."

He looked into the cup and realized how vile the liquid in it was. He stood and opened the door. "It's like my old man used to say. 'Better to ask forgiveness than permission.' Now get some rest. I have a feeling we're going to be busy when we catch up with the *Helena K*. I'll be out on the conn for a bit."

Ward walked on out to the control room. Joe Glass smiled wryly. He couldn't imagine anyone else he would rather go to war with than Jonathan Ward. He hoped that when he had his own boat, he could be half the skipper that man was.

He finished his coffee and headed back to his own stateroom.

John Bethea stared in disbelief at the dead receiver.

"I don't believe that son of a bitch! He hung up on me! I'll fry his worthless ass as soon as I get my hands on him."

He grabbed the secure phone and dialed Tom Donnegan's

number in Hawaii. The admiral answered. Bethea started talking, angry words pouring out in a torrent. He didn't quit until he had detailed Ward's mutiny.

Donnegan spat out the remnants of a well-chewed cigar. He took a deep breath and exhaled before he spoke.

"Calm down. Won't do any of us any good if you blow a gasket. There's nothing we can do until Ward wants to talk again. I suspect his communications problems will be corrected once he has looked over this merchant. We can deal with his insubordination when he gets back."

"But—"

"You want me to send somebody down there to arrest him and put him in the brig? Let him run on down and look in the hold of that merch and satisfy himself. Either he'll turn up your cocaine and all will be forgiven or he'll owe you and me and the people of the United States a big apology."

"But—"

"Just get your informants on the job, John. Let my man use his gut for a bit. His ass will be mine if he's guessed wrong. And I'll let you take a shot or two at him just for good measure. He's a good man. And he's got some smart guys riding with him. Frankly, I don't think we have a choice but to let him do what he thinks is right."

"But—"

"Good-bye, John."

The receiver went dead.

Lieutenant Commander Bill Beaman walked into the clearing when he heard the beat of the choppers. The two H-60s cleared the ridgeline. They flared out and settled onto the grass as the rest of the weary SEALs walked out of the trees.

The pilot of the lead helicopter saluted.

"Señor Beaman, El Presidente Guitteriz congratulates you," the pilot shouted. "I am to take you to the military barracks in Bogotá for a bath, then to the airport for your flight home." He nodded in the direction of where the fire lit up the night sky. "I don't know what you did there but El Presidente is most impressed."

Once the SEALs were aboard, the two choppers lifted off and climbed above the ridges. They circled around slowly and headed toward Bogotá.

"Skipper! Skipper, wake up."

Seaman Cortez hesitated a moment, then shook Jon Ward's shoulder.

The captain awoke with a start, not sure for a moment where he was or who was so rudely interrupting the dream about his wife and a Hawaiian beach and a mai-tai in a gallon glass. He sat up and swung his legs out, off the narrow bunk. He didn't remember lying down, let alone falling asleep. His wristwatch said he had slept for two hours. It felt more like two minutes.

Cortez backed up a step and stood at attention. He pulled a small card from his pocket and read, "Captain, the officer of the deck sends his respects. He reports that we have sonar contact on the *Helena K* at an estimated range of ten thousand yards. He requests you come to the conn."

Ward ran his hands through his hair and tried to shake the sleep from his eyes.

"Tell the officer of the deck I'll be there in a minute." Cortez turned and started to leave the cramped room. "Oh, and tell him I want him to come to one-five-zero feet and to clear baffles."

Ward walked toward the control room. He heard the quiet, intense conversation of the section tracking party gathering and evaluating all the information they could about the sonar contact. He also heard Ray Mendoza's voice come over the 21MC speaker.

"Conn, Sonar. Contact sierra-four-two making one-two-zero turns on one four-bladed screw. Equates to twelve knots."

Chris Durgan, sitting in front of the fire control computer, grabbed the microphone hanging above his head.

"Sonar, Conn. Aye. Our solution agrees." He tweaked a dial

on the desk section of the computer, fine-tuning the computer's best guess of what the *Helena K* might be doing. He glanced over his shoulder. "Officer of the Deck, we have a curve. Eklund range calculated at nine-seven-hundred yards. Recommend coming left to course three-one-zero."

Steve Friedman, standing on the far side of the periscope stand, listened to Durgan as he watched the trace develop on the sonar repeater. The stack of dots was the history of the noise detected by the large sonar dome in the bow of *Spadefish*. Friedman was trying to uncover every secret that stack of dots concealed.

He nodded his head and said, "Helm, left full rudder. Steady course three-one-zero."

The compass repeater spun counterclockwise. That was the only way anyone aboard knew that *Spadefish* was making a turn. As the sub swung to the new course, the stack of dots skewed rapidly to the right. *Spadefish* steadied on the new course. The dots started to build a new vertical stack, well to the right of the old one.

Ward stepped up onto the periscope stand and stood beside Friedman.

"What do you have, Steve?"

Friedman looked up briefly, then returned to staring at the sonar screen even as he answered.

"Skipper, we have a tracking solution on the *Helena K*. Range nine-five-hundred yards, course three-five-two, speed twelve. No other contacts."

Ward smiled to himself as he watched the sonar screen for a second. These people were good. The long days of training, the endless hours of practice were paying off once again.

"Well, Steve, if it's all right with you, why don't we go on up and take a look at her?"

Spadefish slid effortlessly up from the depths until the periscope broke through the ocean's surface. Ward watched the video screen, seeing just what Friedman was seeing as he spun around with the scope. The sun was just peeping over the horizon to the east. The *Helena K* was little more than a black dot on the horizon. They couldn't tell much about the ship from this view and distance. The merchant boat couldn't see them trailing her either.

Ward tapped Friedman on the shoulder.

"Steve, shift to twenty-four power."

The view on the screen changed dramatically. It looked as if they were alongside the merchant ship, close enough to catch the worst of it if the cook tossed over scraps from breakfast. The screen was filled with the picture of the after port quarter of a rather decrepit merchant ship struggling away from them. They could see everything from the tops of the king posts to just below the main deck. The view below that was hidden by the curvature of the earth.

Ward stared at the screen for a bit. He didn't see anything unusual about this ship.

"Steve, I want to see her all the way down to the waterline. Let's take a high look. Make your depth five-six feet."

Spadefish came shallower until only two feet of water concealed her black sail. The periscope now stuck almost fourteen feet out of the sea. The churning wake of the ship came into view now. They could just read the letters painted across her stern: HELENA K.

"Skipper, I don't see anything," Friedman muttered. "Just a fully-loaded merchant heading north."

A light came on for Ward.

Bethea had told him that the boarding party had not found anything. The *Helena K* was nothing more than a freighter in ballast. Empty, bound for Vancouver to take on a load of grain. One thing was obvious to him now. He wasn't looking at a freighter in ballast. This one was fully loaded, riding low in the water. Something wasn't right here. There had not been enough time since the inspection for the old freighter to slip into a port to load and get all the way back out here.

The freighter steamed away at twelve knots as *Spadefish* followed at three. The *Helena K* disappeared over the horizon.

Ward needed to talk to Bethea once again, despite the nature of how their previous communication had ended.

"Officer of the Deck, raise the BRA-34 and have radio patch the secure voice to the conn."

Within minutes Ward had the head of the JDIA on the other end of the circuit. Bethea was livid and he let Ward know it at the first sound of his voice.

"Captain, you are one stupid son of a bitch! You should be down there helping me find de Santiago's coke, but you're out on your own private crusade. I just hope you haven't screwed up and wasted all the sweat and blood we've spent with this wild-goose chase!"

Ward took a deep breath. He understood the man's anger. He just didn't have time to deal with it right now.

"Hold on, John. I think we've found your missing coke."

There was a pause on the other end and Ward could hear the sharp intake of breath.

"And just where did you do that?"

"We have been watching the *Helena K*. She is low in the water and steaming north. Didn't you say her holds were empty and she was heading to Vancouver to take on cargo?"

"Yeah, she was empty and riding high. There isn't any way she took on cargo. We've had continuous satellite coverage over her since we left her." Ward could hear Bethea shuffling papers, looking for something. "She hasn't been in port or rendezvoused with anyone. She's just been steaming right along. You have any ideas?"

Ward shook his head as if Bethea could see him.

"Don't know, but I mean to find out. I'll get back to you."

Bethea was only slightly mollified.

"You'd damn well better. Your ass is still in a sling for that 'loss of communications' caper."

Ward signed off and turned to Friedman.

"Steve, go to three hundred feet. Get out in front of that bastard. We'll go back up and get a good close look as he comes by."

Ward sat on a stool beside the navigation table as *Spadefish* raced out ahead of the freighter. At twenty-six knots, it didn't take them long to catch up and go past. He watched calmly as Steve Friedman brought the submarine back up to periscope depth.

The *Helena K* came into view. She was steaming toward where *Spadefish* waited. The freighter knifed through the water, her white bow wave curling back along her high, rust-streaked sides. Ward guessed she would pass a thousand yards away from where they watched. That would be close enough for him to clearly see her. She was riding low in the water all right. He could read the draft markings painted down the port side of her bow. The seawater lapped up above the full-load draft marks. For an "empty," she was carrying a lot of tonnage.

As the *Helena K* steamed past, Ward watched closely. He couldn't see anything else unusual. The only sign of life was up on the bridge. Two seamen were visible inside the wheelhouse. Looked like any freighter steaming innocently up the Pacific coast, full of coffee or bananas.

It didn't add up. The *Helena K* was fully loaded. There was no doubt about that. She had been empty just two days ago.

Ward turned to Friedman.

"How do you hide something like that on the open ocean? And under the vigilant gaze of the most sophisticated satellite surveillance ever conceived?"

He slapped his forehead hard. Again he checked the scope. Sometimes the answer was right there in front of your very own nose!

"Officer of the Deck, man battle stations. We are going to do an under-hull of that ship."

25

"BATTLE STATIONS MANNED AND READY," DOUG LYMAN REPORTED.

The chief radioman marked off the last entry on his checklist. He sat in front of the ballast control panel and watched as his crew bustled about, making their equipment ready for battle.

Ray Laskowski, the Chief of the Boat, was sitting in the diving officer's chair. He nodded and turned to the XO.

"All stations report 'manned and ready.' "

Joe Glass held the earpiece to his head, straining to hear the voice on the other end through the noise in the cramped room. He turned to Ward.

"Captain, all stations manned. Sonar reports one contact, the *Helena K*, currently held broadband on the sphere. Bearing zero-zero-five, signal-to-noise ratio plus-five."

She was a big target, close by, and hard for *Spadefish*'s equipment to ignore.

Ward looked around the control room. Members of his team were keyed—ready for anything the situation might throw at them. He waited a moment to allow time for their nerves to settle down a bit. And, in reality, to gather his own thoughts. He stepped to the front of the periscope stand and spoke.

"Attention in the attack center. We have a contact, the *Helena K*, on course three-five-three, bearing zero-zero-five, speed twelve, range three-five-hundred yards. I intend to close to one thousand yards astern of her, come to periscope depth again to verify our solution, then to conduct an under-hull surveillance using number-two periscope."

Ward looked around the room. The team was calmly listening, taking in every word. Not one of them revealed any sense of fear. They all knew that they were about to sneak underneath a freighter to within inches of her and ride along there for a bit while they looked at her bottom. The risk of a collision with the freighter was real and the results could be disastrous. A second's indecision, a slight wrong move, and the hardened steel bow of the *Helena K* could slice into *Spadefish*. Every man aboard the sub suspected what the outcome of such a collision would be, who would get the worst of that kind of bump. They had practiced this delicate maneuver in the trainers and with cooperating ships. This would be their first time doing it for real beneath an unsuspecting target.

Ward took a deep breath and continued.

"Gentlemen, it's just like we've practiced. Maintain a one-knot speed advantage until we can see her screw. Then slow incrementally until we are underneath her and matching her forward speed. Speed changes will be in one-turn increments and course changes by tenths of degrees. If she zigs, break off and try again. If we have any problems, same thing. We break off immediately."

Cookie Dotson handed Ward a cup of coffee without saying a word. Ward nodded his thanks, took the mug, and went on.

"If I call for an emergency break-off, Chief Lyman, I want you to immediately flood to the depth-control tanks until we have a downward acceleration. COB, maintain a zero bubble and ring up 'ahead two-thirds.' Come to a depth of one-five-zero feet. Helm, I want you to use a five-degree rudder to change course ninety degrees and get us out from underneath. Everybody understand? Any questions?"

Ward sipped from his coffee as he waited for everyone to absorb the instructions. There were no questions. He turned to Joe Glass.

"XO, secure the weapons-handling party. We won't be needing them. Secure the damage-control parties, too. Shouldn't be needing them either."

Glass talked into his headset for a second, then stepped over to stand next to Ward.

"Skipper, I have a good solution on the contact. You know we could go straight in from here if you wanted to."

Ward shook his head.

"No, XO. We'll do it the way we practiced and the way I briefed it. That way no one will be confused." Turning to Beasley, he said, "Officer of the Deck, lower the scope. Make your depth nine-zero feet. Make turns for fifteen knots."

Spadefish increased speed and slowly gained on the freighter. With a three-knot speed advantage, Ward calculated that it would take twenty minutes to close to within a thousand yards of the *Helena K*. They could do it faster for sure. Much faster. But this was a good time to allow everyone to settle in and get over the initial rush of nerves. The *Helena K* wasn't going to get away from them.

Ward sat back and watched as his team went about their work. It was hard to not feel like a proud father watching his sons turn a double play, or a football coach seeing his game plan perfectly executed by his players out there on the field.

The signal-to-noise ratio on the sonar increased as they drove closer to their unsuspecting prey. Ward sipped the last of his coffee. He watched the trace on the sonar repeater grow more dense. He stepped down off the periscope stand and leaned over the COB's shoulder. These three, the COB as diving officer, with Seaman Cortez at the helm and Seaman Mac-Naughton on the stern planes, were key players in this undersea ballet they were about to perform. They would have to act as one. No missed orders, no slight hesitation could be allowed. None of them wanted to think of the possible consequences should they misstep.

"You guys ready?" Ward asked quietly. "Stay on your toes. Just like we practiced. Slow and easy."

Cortez smiled reassuringly.

"Piece o' cake, Skipper."

"Yep, piece o' cake," MacNaughton chimed in, then

seemed to have another thought. "Hey, Skipper, speaking of food, if we pull this off, can we have a pizza night tonight?"

"Pretty pushy considering all you're doing is your job, doncha think?" Laskowski cuffed the young sailor playfully.

Ward laughed.

"Tell you what, MacNaughton. We pull this off, I'll have Cookie make your favorite. Deal?"

Beasley tapped Ward on the shoulder before MacNaughton could acknowledge.

"Skipper, it's time. We're there."

Ward nodded.

"Okay, slow to three knots and come up to six-two feet. Let's take a look at this old sow's belly."

Spadefish slowed and eased up to periscope depth. As the scope broke the surface, Ward saw what he expected to see. He was looking at the high stern of the freighter from directly behind her. She was still riding very low in the water. Her screw was completely submerged but furiously beating the water, struggling to maintain the speed she was making.

Spadefish's periscope was in the middle of the freighter's churning white wake. Time to get the show on the road.

Ward held his eye to the scope eyepiece. He quietly said, "Make your depth nine-five feet. Make turns for thirteen knots."

Water rushed over the periscope as *Spadefish* eased deeper. The bright blue of the sky was exchanged for the deeper blue of the tropical Pacific waters.

"Depth nine-five," Laskowski called out. "Making turns for one-three knots."

The scope shook in Ward's hands as the water coursed around it. The scope normally would be used only at very low speeds. It couldn't be employed if the sub was traveling above fifteen knots. At that speed there would be a real risk of the force of the rushing water bending it over. At thirteen knots the thing bucked forcefully, the eyepiece smacking into Ward's forehead, but he kept his eye in place. There was too much for him to watch out for.

He spun the scope around to look aft. He rotated the right handle clockwise to look downward. He needed a feel for the limits of visibility in these waters. If it was too murky, there was no point in sliding beneath the ship. They couldn't see anything anyway. A view down the back of *Spadefish* would give him some idea of how far he could see.

Beasley was watching the video monitor that showed what Ward was seeing.

"Skipper, I can see the after escape trunk and can make out the forward edge of the rudder."

Ward nodded.

"I see it, too. Make the visibility about two hundred feet. Way more than enough for what we're going to be doing."

The mission was on.

Joe Glass was standing between Chris Durgan at his computer console and Dave Kuhn, who was working at the navigation table.

"Skipper, we shifted to a close-in solution plot. Hold range at nine-two-five yards. Closing at one hundred yards a minute. You should start seeing the bubble trail soon."

The "bubble trail" was a stream of underwater bubbles, air entrained and pulled deep by the freighter's spiraling screw. The bubbles drifted behind the ship and slowly made their way back up to the surface. Seeing the bubble trail through the periscope was a sure sign they were driving closer and would be able to make out the screw itself.

"Not yet, XO. We need to get inside of five hundred yards for that. Is Chief Mendoza reporting the near-field effect yet?"

Near-field effect was a sonar phenomenon caused by very close range to a contact. The sonar would begin seeing the freighter as a number of different noise sources rather than as one composite source. The result was that they would begin to see many lower-noise-strength contacts on several different bearings. Before submariners figured out this occurrence, more than one skipper collided with the contact or broke off the approach in total confusion. Near-field effect started to be seen at about five hundred yards from the target.

"Sonar reports they are starting to see near-field now," Glass responded. "The contact is shifting to upper D/Es, now at plus six."

D/E, or depression/elevation angle, measured the angle between horizontal and the incoming sonar noise. The D/E was normally a negative number. A close contact above them would result in a positive D/E. This was also a good sign that they really were deeper than the *Helena K*'s keel. It was crucial that they remain so.

"Okay, I'm seeing the bubble trail," Ward called out. The little white dots flew by the scope. "Can't see any shapes yet."

Joe Glass reported, "Close-in solution, still tracking. Range six-five-zero yards. Better estimate of speed eleven-point-seven knots. Drifting slightly left. Recommend coming left a tenth."

Ward, his eye glued to the scope, said, "Helm, come left a tenth. XO, watch the drift. I don't want to overcompensate and start yo-yoing across her track."

Glass shook his head. Sometimes Ward could worry like a mother hen.

"Took that into account, Skipper. We'll slowly come back onto track."

"Possible contact zig. Bearings are tracking off," Durgan shouted.

Glass jumped over to look at the computer screen. If the *Helena K* was going to change course, this was the worst possible time. All their efforts would be wasted. They would have to plot the approach all over again once she had straightened out. At least they wouldn't have to worry about her dropping her anchor. That had happened to Glass once early in his career. He had been doing this very same maneuver "up north," looking at a Soviet ship, when the bastards had decided to drop anchor. Only luck had prevented one mammoth *clang* as the heavy anchor fell through the water only inches away from them.

"XO, these bearings are all over the place!" Kuhn yelled. "Looks like somebody shot at the plot. He hasn't zigged. Sonar is tracking off."

Glass glanced over at the paper plots. Kuhn was right. They were now seeing what near-field effect could do once they got close to a previously easily discernible target. No matter how well trained they were, sonarmen could get confused when their target seemed to go to pieces on them.

"Sonar, Coordinator, your trackers are tracking off."

"Sonar, aye." Mendoza's voice boomed over the speaker. "We'll do the best we can, but we're in too close now."

Beasley looked intently at the video monitor. There was only a hint of excitement in his voice when he spoke.

"Skipper, stop there for a second. Thought I saw something."

Ward had been panning the scope slowly back and forth across their intended path, looking for any signs of the *Helena K* besides her bubble trail. He slowly brought the scope back to the position where Beasley thought he had seen an image.

"Yeah, I can see it now. Screw tips, I think. I can just make it out through the bubbles. We're coming in closer now. Dive, drop down a foot."

"Down a foot, aye," Laskowski answered. "Depth nine-six feet."

Ward rotated the right handle on the scope up a click to keep the blade tips in view.

"Drop speed a turn." He wanted to slow the approach under the freighter. Better to take a little time out here than to rush underneath the cargo ship and try to slow the sub down. He was beginning to see the shadowy hull of the freighter through the curtain of bubbles. They were drawing damned close! "Dive, drop down another six inches."

"Down six inches, aye. Depth nine-six-point-five."

Now inches mattered.

Ward rotated the scope up another click. Then another one. He was looking straight up as the massive, spinning bronze screw blade passed a mere foot above the top of their periscope. He could only imagine the damage that thing could do if they so much as hiccuped.

They were under the freighter now. The crew held their collective breath.

"Drop speed another turn," Ward ordered, his voice far more calm than he felt.

Spadefish was moving faster than the freighter and was directly underneath her keel. Ward could see the rays of bright sunlight penetrating the depths on either side of the ship.

Underneath, she looked normal. Nothing there.

Ward watched as they moved forward slowly. Not a whole lot to see. Just the smooth bottom of a boat fresh out of the shipyard. No barnacles or sea growth on her hull. There was nothing to see under here after all. This risky maneuver was for naught. He had put his boat and crew in danger for nothing.

"Helm, come left a tenth," he said.

Cortez answered: "Come left a tenth, aye."

Ward watched more intently as his view changed to the port side of the freighter. They had almost drifted out from under her.

"Come right a tenth," he ordered. This slowly brought them back parallel with the freighter, but along her port side. *Spadefish* had advanced until they were now under the bow of the freighter. "Drop a turn."

They slowed until the sub's forward motion matched the speed of the *Helena K*.

They searched for some clue as to how the *Helena K* had taken on a heavy load of cocaine without making port or anybody seeing them take on the cargo. Everything looked normal under here.

"Ho! Skipper, as we were moving over, I thought I saw something," Earl Beasley called out.

"What was it?"

"It looked like a dark line parallel to the keel but out a bit. It might just be a sloppy weld or a paint line. I don't know. It was just a glimpse of something that didn't look right."

"Okay, Nav, we'll drift back and take a look. Helm, drop a turn." The freighter moved ahead. Ward strained his eyes, looking for the line the Nav had seen. Finally, there it was. Not paint or a sloppy weld. It was a mechanical feature of some kind. He couldn't make it out. They would have to move closer for him to be able to tell what it was. "Dive, up six inches."

"Up six, aye. Depth nine-six feet," Laskowski answered, hoping the skipper didn't see him swallow hard.

Ward still could not make it out.

"Up another six inches," he ordered. *Spadefish* moved up even closer to the freighter. Perilously closer. There was now less than a foot between the freighter's steel hull and the top of their periscope. "Nav, look at that. It's a door that's not fully shut. They must have a problem with it. If that thing were fully closed, we'd never have seen it. That flap you saw would cover the seam and look like just another hull weld."

Still running slower than the ship, *Spadefish* continued to slowly drift back. Over two-thirds of the way aft, the door seam stopped.

Ward shook his head in disbelief.

"That thing is huge. I make it out as over a hundred feet long. I'm going to match speed and move over to the starboard side. Let's see if they have the same thing over there. Helm, add a turn." With the order, the sub increased speed just enough to once again match *Helena K*'s pace. "Helm, right a tenth."

Ward and the team repeated the slow, careful maneuvering of the sub until they were under the freighter's starboard side. Ward scrutinized every inch of the freighter's underside as the sub hovered only a foot from the ship, even as both vessels continued moving forward. Intent on his search, Ward had forgotten how close to catastrophe they were.

"There it is!" he shouted. "We would never have seen it if we didn't know what to look for. Beautiful work. The whole bottom of that thing opens up like a sardine can."

It was time to go. They had seen what they needed to see.

"Dive, ease slowly down to nine-nine feet," Ward quietly ordered. "Helm, drop five turns. Right five degrees rudder." This would ease them down, back, and away from underneath the freighter. "Lowering the scope."

Ward slapped up the handles, reached over his head, and rotated the control ring to lower the scope. He was completely drained. He had not felt the crushing tension while they were maneuvering beneath the freighter. They were safely clear. The tension eased. He felt as if a ton of bricks had been lifted from his shoulders.

"Great work, everyone. That was the best under-hull I have ever seen. You did good. MacNaughton gets to pick the pizza tonight!"

"I hope Cookie's got some anchovies! I'm craving me some anchovies!" the happy sailor whooped to the groans of several little-salty-fish haters.

Glass stepped over to where Ward and Beasley stood and slapped each man on the back. He wiped the sweat from his forehead with a towel. Cookie Dotson appeared then with a stack of mugs and a pot of coffee.

"Here, Skipper. Figured you might be needing this right about now."

"Thanks, Cookie."

Ward grabbed the offered mug and took a swig. Glass looked over the rim of his own cup.

"Skipper, you were right. That was a balls move, but it paid off. What next?"

Ward leaned back against the sonar repeater and took another belt of the java before he spoke.

"Damn, my back is sore. I'm gettin' too old for this kind of stuff." He rubbed his lower back as he answered his XO's question. "Way I see it, we run out ahead of that rust bucket up there. We'll come up to periscope depth and tell Bethea what we found. We'll just wait while it passes us by. We'll fall in behind and trail it to wherever it's going."

Glass sipped from his cup.

"Think JDIA will buy that? Bethea was pretty pissed at you when you blew him off."

Ward slumped down on the stool, still rubbing his solar plexus.

"Don't see that he has much choice. We're here, ready to go. We're too far out for the patrol boat to intercept now. Nobody else's anywhere close. He can't easily track them any other way and we sure as hell can't afford to lose a load of killer cocaine. If he's calmed down, Bethea will see it our way. If he ain't, we'll just have to make him see it our way." Ward turned to Beasley. "Nav, get us out ten miles ahead of that freighter and a mile off her track. Don't lose sonar contact. She's noisy enough; you should be able to get up to twenty knots and still track her easily. When we get in position, clear baffles for coming to periscope depth. Have radio set up to be ready to talk to the home office."

Beasley nodded.

"Yes, sir."

"Now, I think I've developed a powerful taste for some pizza myself . . . anchovies or not," Ward said with a broad smile.

Serge Novstad proudly puffed on his third Cuban cigar of the day so far, toking until the fire at its end burned brightly and the smoke hid his face. Philippe Zurko snorted. This Hun didn't even appreciate fine tobacco. No wonder he had no empathy for de Santiago, his revolution, his beloved people. It was the money. Nothing more, nothing less. To Zurko, anyone who didn't share his zeal for freeing the people was a whore, a prostitute who thought only of the eventual payment once the act had been consummated.

"So, Señor Zurko," the Swede said. "I assume your leader has not dispatched his famed assassin squad swimming after us to cut off our heads because our little door will not properly seal and we've had to go slower than we intended."

"I have not told him yet," Zurko whispered.

"What?"

"I have not yet told him of the problem."

"You mean one of the architects of the revolution is too scared to deliver a bit of bad news to his leader? From eight hundred miles away in the middle of the Pacific Ocean, no less? Hah!"

"I fear he has received more disturbing news. The Americans have destroyed his new factory. They managed to bring in enough explosives to bring production to a halt. That makes our cargo even more precious. We must not fail. Do you understand?"

Novstad, his face expressionless, strode to the far side of the bridge and gazed out over the vast, empty Pacific.

"No worries, my friend. We have brought the mini-sub aboard successfully. With such good weather, we should stay on schedule. We'll fix the doors once the sub is away for its delivery." He put the stub of the cigar back into his mouth and swept his arm grandly, taking in with his broad gesture the un-inhabited surface of the sea all the way to the undisturbed horizon. "The ocean is all ours. We shall not fail, my revolutionary friend. We shall not fail."

Juan de Santiago threw the cell phone across the room with enough force that it crashed into the marble mantel and shattered, bits and pieces of plastic and electronics raining down onto the priceless Persian rug.

So the *Americanos* had destroyed his new factory. The cocaine that was there was consumed by the fire. He could not imagine how they had been able to find the factory in the first place, much less destroy it so completely. He had taken every precaution.

First, the fields. Then the hidden factory.

El Falcone.

He grabbed up the nearest cut-crystal goblet he could reach and flung it after the cell phone. That was the only way the *Americano* bastards could have accomplished what they had. He suspected that the soldier he had watched in the ambush had had something to do with it. He had led his men to the factory. He had called in the rain of rockets.

He figured the loss to the people of his country to be over two hundred million dollars. That would have been enough money to fund his revolution for several years. To give him, his mistress, his children the safety and accommodations the leader of the revolution deserved.

Juan de Santiago looked at the broader perspective through his red rage. The first shipment was safely loaded inside the submarine that was now resting in the womb of *Helena K*. Once it reached America, his enemies would learn that they could not trifle with him. They would learn that lesson very painfully indeed. Destroy his factories, cut off his fields, and he would still get product to the hungry American consumers. Customers who would soon be all the hungrier for his blend. They would soon be aware that even though their best punches had solidly landed, El Jefe was not staggered at all. There was no way they could see his next counterpunch coming.

The follow-up shipment of doctored heroin from Sui Kia Shun would be the coup de grâce.

He still owned the sea. And the sea was still the key to the lands he would soon conquer.

De Santiago almost smiled now as he sauntered into his bedroom and grabbed the bedside phone, the only one in the house that still worked after all the recent bad news. Don Holbrooke answered on the second ring. De Santiago started right in with no wasted pleasantries.

"Señor Holbrooke, we have suffered a setback. The *Americanos* have destroyed our new factory. We will need immediate capital to rebuild it, and to do so even better and more securely than before. That will be expensive. Contact Ramirez and tell him to demand a fifty-percent cash advance for this delivery."

Holbrooke smiled as he tightly cupped the breast of his mistress in his free hand. He would demand sixty percent in advance. He thumbed her nipple and felt it respond to his touch. The extra ten percent would be over thirty million dollars, enough to bring his bank balance to better than a hundred million total. The woman groaned slightly and moved her hand beneath the covers to stroke him. It would soon be time to disappear. Time to retire to some far more civilized place than these stinking, fetid jungles.

De Santiago was not finished.

"And Señor Holbrooke, you will return the ten million to me that you stole from Señor Shun, from me, from our people who struggle so valiantly for their freedom. Your greed has become too great for me to continue to turn a blind eye. If you try to steal anymore, you will be feeding the piranhas."

Holbrooke roughly shoved the woman's hand away, sat up in the bed, and began to scream a sincere denial into the mouthpiece. There was only an irritating dial tone on the other end of the phone line.

De Santiago dialed another number. He was too primed to initiate action to worry about whether or not the telephone line he was about to use was secure.

Jorge Ortiez had stepped away from the shack that hid the lab to take a piss in the nearby jungle. He tried to get outside, away from the smelly foreigners in the cramped laboratory, as often as he could. He had to cut off the stream to answer the buzz of his satellite phone. It could only be one person and he would not tolerate a man daring to complete a piss before answering.

"Sí, Señor de Santiago. It is Ortiez. What can I do for you?"

"Jorge, I will be visiting you in three days. I want you to have the procedures for the additive all documented and recorded on a computer diskette. I will require enough of the compound to doctor a thousand kilos of heroin all ready and packaged. I will bring it back with me."

De Santiago knew now that he had to spread the risk. This lab was the only place where the additive was being manufactured. It was the one place that had the formula, technology, and the people to do it. If the gringo bastards could locate and destroy his most hidden fields and his most highly guarded secret factory, they could find this place and throw a real kink in his grand design. He could not afford to have to notify Sui that there was no more of the additive for the treatment of his future shiploads of heroin. No, that was not an option. There would be no more alliance if the additive were not part of the deal. He had to make sure the whole operation was viable, even if the location of the lab was discovered and the American rockets fell on it, too.

He did not mention the reasons for this order to Ortiez. Better the man not know that he and the lab might be in danger. De Santiago couldn't afford for Ortiez and his chemists to go running into the jungle, screaming like frightened women at the first rustle of some nocturnal animal in the jungle underbrush.

Ortiez reached into his pocket, pulled out his note pad, and wrote down his leader's instructions.

"It shall happen as you order, El Jefe. That is only ten kilos. We will have it ready for you."

He had to wonder what had brought on this sudden change in the plan. He finished his piss, buttoned his trousers, and headed back for the lab.

Margarita slipped quietly back into the bedroom. Juan de Santiago was gone, off to eat and carouse with his lackeys and gloat over the latest brilliant move he was making to counter the setbacks he had recently suffered.

She eased the door shut behind her. She locked it. She reached underneath the bed and removed the miniature recorder. Juan had been using the bedside phone. He had destroyed all his cell phones, had ripped all the wall phones away from their cables in his fits of anger.

Everything he had said would be on the tape.

She looked at her face in the mirror, at her eyes. The hate she felt for the man with whom she slept smoldered in her eyes. It would be so easy to end his life now. To one night interrupt his grunting with the blade of her stiletto while he was on top of her, bragging of those he had killed even as he pushed and shoved himself into her. It was not the time. He would only become a martyr and his organization would be even stronger.

It would be better to help destroy all he had built first. Then, when the time was right, she could end his reign in a second.

That would be such a sweet day.

It was time for El Falcone to once again send more information to the JDIA, to drive one more nail into Juan de Santiago's coffin.

26

"YOU DID WHAT?" JOHN BETHEA WAS HAVING TROUBLE UNDERSTANDing what Jon Ward was trying to tell him. "You drove under that ship and took pictures? Isn't that a damn fool thing to do?"

"It has a few risks, but it's not that bad," Ward answered quietly. "We're trained for it. Besides, it was the only way of proving what I believed without boarding her again and looking in the hold."

Bethea was scrutinizing the picture on the computer screen in front of him. Ward had sent the images to him only a few minutes before and he wasn't sure what he was looking at.

"Jon, I'm no expert, so help me here. All I see is a picture of the underside of some ship. What should I be looking for?"

Ward stood on the periscope stand on *Spadefish*, holding a half-dozen photos in his hand, prints of the same pictures he had radioed to Bethea. He pulled one from the group and laid it on the top of the sonar repeater.

The bait was on the hook. He needed Bethea to take a nibble.

"Okay, first look at the image marked 'port side, outboard.' Got it?"

Bethea found the right file on his computer and opened it. He was seeing a dark, red hull with a long black line slashed down it.

"Yep, have it up now. So?"

"See that black line? Zoom in on it."

Bethea zoomed in to times-three power. The black line took shape. He gazed at it intently.

"It looks like some kind of flap hanging down. Seems to be a hinge or something under it."

"Good, you're starting to get it," Ward answered. It was time to give Bethea another sniff at the rest of the bait. "Now look at the one that's labeled 'aft midships.' Should be the next one in the file."

Bethea opened that one. Same red hull, but taken lower down on the ship. The keel was clearly visible.

"Okay, I have it, but I don't see any hinges."

"I know you won't. But see that faint line running across the hull, perpendicular to the keel, just forward of where the hull starts to taper in again?"

Bethea looked carefully. He zoomed in to the maximum capability of his powerful computer. He could just make out the bump that Ward was telling him about.

"Okay, I see it what you're talking about. Not much there."

"Right. Just remember what it looked like and where it was in relation to the hull. Now let's look at the 'starboard side outboard' one. You'll see the same faint line. And on the 'bow midships' one. I calculate those lines are approximately thirty-two feet across and one hundred twenty feet long. It's one big underwater door, John." Ward knew Bethea had swallowed the bait now. It was time to set the hook. "The reason you didn't see the *Helena K* take on her cargo is because she was loaded by submarine. Or more precisely, a mini-sub. I'm betting that sub is in there, right there in the hold of the ship. No real reason to use one at this end. They had plenty of places they could have put the stuff on board. But there will be a use for the mini-sub when she gets to where she's going."

Bethea shook his head. What Ward was telling him was just beyond belief. The evidence was right there in front of him, though. It all added up neatly. He whistled long and low.

"Damn, Jon, if this true, de Santiago works on an even grander scale than we thought. This is brilliant. Expensive!

And the planning this must have taken! Musta been working on this for years. Wow!"

Ward seized the opportunity to reel him in.

"Way I see it, we ought to tag along behind her and watch where she goes. Perfect job for *Spadefish*. We can give you a blow-by-blow on his entire trip. If the skipper of that tub decides to cheat at cards, we'll send you pictures of his hand."

There was only a moment's hesitation.

"All right, Jon. You've got yourself a mission. Stay with him. Don't spook him, whatever you do. We've wanted to find out where de Santiago's distribution network is on this end ever since the deaths drove them to ground. This could be the break we've been looking for. You track him to the beach and we'll root out the whole nest. He catches you, though, and you can bet that he'll run."

Ward chuckled.

"Don't worry. This old gal has snuck up on some of the finest anti-submarine warships in the world, grabbed pictures, and snuck back away again. I betcha we could pick his pocket and he'd never suspect a thing. We'll be careful not to let that trash hauler catch us."

"Just see that you do. I'll call SUBPAC and get the water cleared in front of you for your transit. Good luck and good hunting."

"Thanks, John. *Spadefish* out."

Juan de Santiago hopped out of the Land Rover before it even stopped and strode to the edge of the dirt road to gaze down into the valley. Smoke still drifted up from the remnants of the buildings that had been his prized cocaine-processing factory. The smell of burning wood and the sweet, sickening stench of charred flesh hung heavily in the humid jungle air. He reached down and grabbed a handful of black soil and let it dribble through his fingers, the dirt blown away by the light wind.

"Guzmán!" de Santiago yelled. "Come! Stand here next to me. See what they have done! Those American dogs!" Sincere tears gleamed in the man's eyes. He had suffered too many occasions like this one lately, standing on some jungle hillside, surveying the latest destruction wrought by the *diablos Americanos*. "They have destroyed it all. This factory took two years to plan and build. The lumber and equipment were transported to this spot on the tireless backs of my people. It was to be another of the weapons of their liberation. Now it is all gone, destroyed in a few seconds by those damned imperialists."

Guzmán wisely hung back a couple of steps from where El Jefe stood. With that legendary temper already at the boiling point, there was no telling in which direction he might lash out next.

"It is truly a tragedy," Guzmán said sincerely, shaking his head. "Our people have indeed suffered much."

De Santiago slapped his thigh in anger, the dirt on his hand streaking across the perfectly creased, light khaki, custom-made jodhpurs.

"I am not a vengeful man, Guzmán. You know that is true. But on behalf of our people, there must be a repayment for what the bastards have done. It is time to make them feel the sting of retribution. We must make them suffer, *mi amigo*. We must strike at their very hearts."

El Jefe surveyed the valley below him. His eyes were mere slits as he glared. It was as if he were engraving a picture in his mind of the destruction he saw. A picture he could feed on and draw strength from. A picture that would only serve to feed the fires of his blazing hatred. He turned.

"I am glad I came here to see this for myself, *mi amigo*." The words sounded like hail rattling on a tin roof. "God has brought me here to witness this for a purpose, to show me that I must fight back at those who attack and kill our people in such a cowardly way. Come, Guzmán. There is much work to do."

Even in the muggy air, Guzmán could not suppress a shiver.

Bill Beaman stepped out of the airport into the late-afternoon sunshine, the warm, dry Southern California air. It certainly was good to be back home. He drew a deep breath and stretched out his arms. Better find a cab and head down to his apartment in Imperial Beach. After a shower and a change of clothes he would be off to a good Mexican meal and a couple or three strong margaritas. He would be good as new by morning.

"Hey, Bill! Over here!"

Beaman turned to the voice. It was John Bethea waving from the driver's seat of a black Ford Expedition.

"Well, hey, boss. Didn't expect a welcome-home party."

Beaman waved as he walked over to the huge vehicle.

"Where's the rest of your team?" Bethea asked as he shook the SEAL's offered hand.

"John, it's good to see you. I hope you're not planning on a debrief this evening. I've got a hot date with a carnitas burrito and a bottle of tequila."

"No, no business tonight," Bethea said with a laugh. "I just wanted to come down here to greet you guys and haul anyone who wanted to come with me up to La Jolla for a thank-you dinner. I've reserved us a spot at the Marine Room, down on the beach at La Jolla Shores."

Beaman whistled.

"Either JDIA has a real big expense account or you really are grateful. That place ain't cheap and you've got to know that this bunch is real thirsty."

"I'll hear from the bean counters, no doubt," Bethea chuckled. "What are they going to do to me? Make me work overtime to pay for it?"

Chief Johnston led the six remaining SEALs out of the terminal door. They sauntered over to where Beaman stood.

"Got the bags, Skipper," he reported after a nod in Bethea's direction. "We're ready to roll. Dumkowski lost the last hand so he has to buy the first round."

"Well, Chief, you may have a better offer on the table," Beaman said with a grin. "JDIA is putting on the dog for us at the Marine Room. Any one of you guys interested in free booze?"

"Count me in!" Dumkowski was the first to bark. "I can't afford to pay for these lushes."

Bethea couldn't help but notice how close-knit the team of men was. They all seemed to move and talk and whoop it up as one. He was acutely aware of those who were missing.

These warriors were the remnants of a team he had sent out on a mission. A team that had fought and died under his command. The sense of failure and guilt had never really been lifted from his shoulders, despite their eventual success. He knew that no matter what happened, he would feel he failed these men.

It was one of those things he would never get accustomed to. He doubted others in his position ever did either. He put it out of his mind as the young men crawled into the Expedition, making bets on who would drink whom under the table at the Marine Room. The argument roared on as they pulled away from the terminal and merged into traffic.

Philippe Zurko stood in the after port corner of *Helena K's* wheelhouse. The night was pitch black, the stars obscured by thick clouds. The gunmetal gray sea was kicking up. A salty mist was sheared off the wavetops by a freshening wind that caused the old scow to rock and buck as a storm built off to the southwest. The long rollers were hitting the *Helena K* on her port quarter. Hard enough to be uncomfortable as she corkscrewed over each one. She groaned in protest every time.

Zurko backed himself tightly into a corner, trying to steady himself on the heaving deck. He wished he had not had so much sea bass for dinner. He would never understand why people went out on the sea like this by choice. There was nothing comfortable about it, with everything moving all the time. Nothing to do but hold on and stare out at the endless, seething water, trying to keep down dinner.

De Santiago's call was late. El Jefe had insisted they talk at this hour and demanded that no one else be able to hear the conversation. Novstad had been very annoyed at being forced off the bridge of his own ship, but he had put the *Helena K* on autopilot and stalked out to go sulk in his stateroom.

The speaker crackled and Zurko jumped at the noise of it.

"Philippe, this is Juan de Santiago."

"Yes, El Jefe, I am here."

"Philippe, is all as I directed?"

"Yes, El Jefe," Zurko said into the mouthpiece. "I am here alone. All the other radios are secured. No one can hear you but me. No one can hear my voice."

He cast his eyes about the darkened wheelhouse to make sure. He was alone. That was for certain.

"Good," de Santiago said. "What I have to tell you is for your ears only. No one else is to know about this. Not Novstad, not Ramirez, and certainly not that drunken Russian. Understand?"

"Yes, El Jefe. No one will ever hear of this discussion from me."

De Santiago began with a question.

"My *compadre*, you know we have an extra supply of the additive aboard the mini-submarine?"

"Yes."

They were shipping some of the recipe to Carlos Ramirez so he could enrich the mixture if it did not have the desired effect in the beginning. De Santiago did not want to leave anything to chance.

"Philippe, you will use that stock to double the concentration of the additive to the cargo on the *Zibrus*. You will do this without being detected by anyone else on the ship and you will not ask for the help of anyone else there. You will tell no one. Understand?"

Zurko was horrified. He protested without thinking.

"But we already know that much can kill anyone who uses it. Remember what happened with the trial shipment?"

He stepped back, deeper into the corner, appalled at what he was hearing. He was literally being ordered to murder thousands of people. Many of them youngsters. Some barely more than children.

Surely de Santiago was only testing his loyalty with this bizarre command. He wouldn't order that he do anything so cruel, so murderous.

"Philippe, do you really care so much for these *Norteamericanos*?" De Santiago snorted, his impatience obvious in his voice when he spoke. "Your concern is touching but misplaced. You should be so troubled for your own people. For the innocent souls of those who died horribly in the hail of fire when the *yanqui* bombs fell on our factory."

"You know I care nothing for the *Americanos*," Zurko protested. "They are weak and decadent. But they are our customers. If we kill them, we will destroy the market." He spoke quickly, emphatically. Maybe logic would dissuade de Santiago from this evil deed. "How will we sell our cocaine if all the users are dead? There will be no more money coming from the *Norteamericanos* to finance the revolution. Our people will starve in slavery."

Zurko was impressed with his own reasoning.

"Philippe, we will have no lack of customers in the future." De Santiago was having none of it. Zurko's arguments were being ignored. "First, we must destroy their will to fight or they will never back off. We must teach them not to trifle with us. We are not dirt under their feet. If they attack and kill our people, we will attack and kill theirs. We are at war, my dear friend. Now do as I say and increase the dosage." He paused for an awful beat, then added one more command as if it had just occurred to him. "And, Philippe, when Shun's heroin is on board, double the dosage on that, too."

Sui Kia Shun lowered the delicate porcelain teacup onto the granite tabletop. He templed his fingers and rested his elbows on the hard surface of the centuries-old table while he gazed at the misty mountains. The morning air was light and refreshing on the patio. The sun had risen already.

Sui found comfort in the sun's predictability. Much in this life defied prophecy. At least he could depend on the sun doing what it had done the day before, the year past, centuries back into history. If only people could be so dependable, so predictable.

He brought his thoughts back to the words of his most trusted lieutenant as she reported the latest on his cargo and its progress toward America.

"Our shipment is safely aboard the *Malay Messenger*. It departed Kwang Zhou two days ago. Manifested to deliver a cargo of toys and yard goods to Los Angeles. That cargo is on board and will pay for the trip with a ten-percent margin. The heroin is safely stored in several of the containers."

The woman paused for a second to verify something in her notes. Sui marveled at how adept she was at arranging these operations. A generation ago, a lovely woman like this would have been a concubine in his father's house. Now she ruled a worldwide multibillion-dollar drug-distribution system like the seasoned CEO of a major corporation.

"Yes, go on."

"The crew is made up of our people. As you have directed, our best security team will board the *Helena K* at the transfer point. They will have—"

Shun held up one hand to interrupt her briefing.

"What about the weapons?"

"Master Sui, as I was about to tell you, one of the containers is filled with weapons for the team. The South Americans have been told to expect three containers of deck cargo. The fastest way to transfer that much heroin on the open ocean is to transfer the whole container."

She punched a series of keys on the tiny laptop computer. A chart of the northern Pacific blossomed across the screen. A large cross marked a spot almost a thousand miles due west of Seattle.

Placing the computer on the table in front of Sui, she continued.

"The transfer will occur here. It is well away from normal shipping routes and away from the American coast. We can expect to be left alone there." She drew a deep breath. "Do you have any suggestions, my father?"

The sun was especially warm and pleasant on his upturned face. His smile confirmed that he was pleased with his daughter's report.

Tom Donnegan looked at the chart of the eastern Pacific and glowered with anger. The chart was divided into a maze of rectangular boxes, each identified with a letter-number combination. Several narrow columns slashed through the neatly stacked boxes at odd angles.

He stood in SUBPAC's underground operations center. The concrete-reinforced room had been constructed beneath the headquarters building during World War II. It was the heart of all submarine operations for the Pacific Ocean, with the exception of the eastern Pacific operating areas from the Mexican border north to the Gulf of Alaska. The San Diego submarine squadron controlled those areas.

An acetate sheet lay over the chart. It was covered with similar boxes, but these were crosshatched and each one had a label with a submarine's name in it. Although SUBPAC used a complicated computer scheduling system to keep all the subs operating in the eastern Pacific from running into each other, Donnegan preferred this anachronism. He maintained that he could see the big picture much better than having to scroll through the same information on a computer monitor.

It was normally a busy and complicated piece of paper. Right now, it was even more so. The Pacific Fleet was running a major exercise in the area and had invited all of the Pacific Rim allies to participate. Dozens of American, Japanese, Australian, Korean, and Canadian submarines filled the space, and the mess on the overlay sheet confirmed that many of the invitees were taking part.

One narrow column, outlined in red, crossed the area from

south to north, but with several zigs far to the west around other boxes. Those boxes contained the names of other subs. *"Spadefish"* was hand-lettered in the slim column that cut through the middle of the entanglement.

Donnegan grabbed the phone. Within seconds he was talking with Pierre Desseaux in San Diego. The submarine squadron commodore sat in front of a computer monitor in his own expansive office, on its screen an electronic version of the chart that had just spiked Donnegan's temper right off the scale.

The admiral didn't waste any time with pleasantries.

"Commodore, I want enough water for *Spadefish* to get through your operating area with no problems."

"Admiral, we are in the middle of the largest multinational exercise in years," Desseaux protested. "I've got over a dozen subs out there. We routed her through the area with all the water we can spare right now."

Donnegan spat out his cigar.

"Captain, I don't give two hoots about your exercise. *Spadefish* is doing something useful. Don't you think you can manage something a little better?"

"Admiral, the only way I can do that is to have the Japanese run on the surface. They won't like that and it will, of course, ruin the exercise."

Donnegan snorted.

"Make it happen. *Spadefish* will have an operating box fifty miles either side of that freighter and a hundred miles ahead and behind. Is that very clear?"

He didn't wait for confirmation or any more blather from Desseaux. He slammed the phone down and stormed out of the operations center. He stepped back through the door, winked at a couple of the men who had just watched him stomp out, picked up his cigar from where it had landed behind a chart table, and strolled upstairs once again into the Hawaiian sunshine.

27

"SHE STILL UP THERE AND AFLOAT?" JOE GLASS ASKED THE SKIPPER as he walked into the control room. He was still rubbing sleep from his eyes and stifling a yawn with the back of his hand. "About time I relieved you out here, isn't it?"

Jon Ward stood next to the fire control computer, watching the dots neatly stack in a vertical line. He nodded and handed Glass a cup of coffee.

"Here, you look like you need this. Yep, she's still there. She hasn't changed course or speed in the last twelve hours. Still course three-four-seven, speed twelve. Come over here to the plot and I'll show you what we're doing."

The plot, laid out on the navigation table, showed the history of the last six hours of following the *Helena K*. The freighter's course was dead-arrow straight, heading relentlessly to the north-northwest. Bright red lines were drawn parallel to its course but fifty miles to either side. *Spadefish*'s course snaked drunkenly every few thousand yards as she maneuvered back and forth around the freighter, gathering more sonar data.

"I see that we got the water," Glass observed, looking at the wide area in which they were cleared to operate.

"Yep," Ward confirmed. "The clearance was on the last broadcast. We got ourselves a big operating box. It's a hundred miles wide and two hundred miles deep, essentially centered on the *Helena K*. It moves at twelve knots. Good thing, too. Take a look at the SoCal op areas."

Ward flipped up a new chart, a larger scale one centered on the waters off the southern California coast. Glass whistled long and low.

"Man, I've never seen 'em that crowded."

"It's that RIMPAC exercise Desseaux had his pantyhose all in a knot about before we left. He's got to be boiling mad. We're steaming straight through the center of his little invitation-only party." Ward folded the chart and returned to the plot. "Anyway, we're out ahead of the *Helena K* right now. I ran out ten miles ahead and five miles off track so we could go up and talk and not risk being seen." He gave Glass an odd look. The XO wrinkled his brow. What dire message was Ward about to deliver? "By the way, the message boards are over on the conn. You might want to read them when you get a chance . . . Commander Joseph Glass."

The executive officer did a double take and stared hard at Ward, apparently sure he was still dreaming. Ward smiled broadly.

"Joe, the selection board results are out. Congratulations! They somehow lowered their standards enough to pick you up. Looks like you're in the first group to put the stripe on, too. You're out of uniform." Glass's mouth was open, his eyes disbelieving. Ward pulled a set of silver oak leaves from his pocket. "Here, put these on. We'll do it official and fancy when we get back."

He shook the XO's hand as he passed over to him the insignia for a full commander.

Glass grinned, his face flushed red as he pulled the gold oak leaves of a lieutenant commander off his collar and replaced them with the new silver ones. Everyone in the control room broke into loud cheering and sincere congratulations.

As the revelry died down, Ward finally continued his briefing.

"Joe, we're out here," he said, pointing at a dot on the chart. "Right now, we're steaming back in to close track. It'll be time to go up and take a look at him when you get back to within eight thousand yards. By the way, we deployed the towed array last night. We didn't want to risk losing sonar contact as we opened out. That guy is a real noisy trash bucket, though. We held him firm broadband on the sphere at thirty thousand yards. We really didn't need the towed array after all. Let's leave it out, though. It'll make life easier when we steam through the SoCal op areas. We can use it to sort out all that traffic up there, and—God bless Tom Donnegan—we certainly have the room."

The towed array was a very sensitive line of sonar hydrophones towed almost a mile behind *Spadefish*, like a thick sausage at the end of a long string. The reel for the cable was up in the forward port side of the bow compartment. The array, roughly four inches in diameter and two hundred feet long, was housed in a tube that snaked along the sub's hull and ended at the after edge of the port stabilizer when it was stowed. When in use, the array was far behind *Spadefish*'s own noise and that greatly increased its sensitivity. The hydrophones were tuned to detect very low-frequency sounds in the water, allowing for long-range work. The one drawback was the cable. If the submarine backed down while the array was deployed, her great bronze screw could easily slice right through it. Then a two-million-dollar piece of equipment would sink slowly to the bottom of the sea.

"Okay, Skipper. I have a handle on what's happening. Why don't you grab some chow and hit the rack? Cookie has some great sticky buns in the oven for breakfast."

Ward groaned as he answered.

"I've been smelling them baking all night. I can't wait to bite into one. Call me if you have any questions." He paused to take one more look at the new insignia on his XO's collar. "Looks damned natural there, Joe."

Then he shook Glass's hand one more time, walked out of the control room, and turned to disappear down the ladder to the submarine's middle level, following the enticing smell of cinnamon.

Juan de Santiago strode proudly into their bedroom. There was time for her to service him quickly before he moved to other matters. The hurt look on her face said otherwise.

"What is it? What have I done?" he asked pleadingly.

Margarita erupted into tears.

"I can't believe you would forget. Not after all these years. But you have. You've forgotten again," she sobbed.

She stalked into the bathroom and slammed the door hard behind her. The pictures of the children on the nearby vanity fell over on their faces.

De Santiago faced the wooden barrier, a perplexed look on his face.

"Forgotten what?" he muttered, but not loud enough to be heard beyond the mute divider separating them. "What is it that I have forgotten?"

He could control a rebel army, rouse a populace to revolt, call down the wrath of the most powerful nation on the earth on his humble country, but he had no hope of controlling this hot-blooded woman. He had to try to make amends for his transgression.

"Margarita, my sweet. I haven't forgotten. I've planned a picnic for us tomorrow. We'll ride down to the old hacienda ruins, just you and I. Guzmán is putting everything together now. I wanted to surprise you."

The door opened a crack. He could see one large brown eye, impossibly deep and luminous. She rushed out and fell into his arms.

"You didn't forget after all," she gushed. "I'm so sorry for doubting you. Can you ever forgive me?"

De Santiago laughed.

"But of course, my sweet. There is nothing to forgive."

"A whole day, just for us! Juan, when was the last time we had a whole day just for ourselves?"

With his free hand, he brushed her long, black hair from her beautiful face as he answered.

"Too long ago, my parakeet. Much too long ago. But . . ."

She heard the hesitation in his voice and pulled back away from him, the first flash of anger already returning to her eyes.

"But what?"

"I will have to leave late in the afternoon. I must meet some men at the old Alvarado hacienda ruins the next morning. We'll be on horseback instead of going by river, so . . ."

"But Juan, you will have to ride all night through the jungle to get there. Is it so important? Can't you postpone this meeting or send someone else in your place? Send Alvene Dura. He doesn't seem to do anything these days except hang around and harass the maids." She snuggled comfortably into his arms, rubbing her body against his. He became aroused. "It would be such a wonderful day for both of us if you did not have to hurry away."

He continued stroking her shining black hair as he felt her wonderful body melting into his.

"Yes, my love. But it is very important. I must attend to this myself, or else we could plan on a full day together. And Alvene will be accompanying me. Now, my sweet, I have a few things to attend to before we . . . hmmm . . . go to bed."

He playfully kneaded her bottom as he pulled away from her, then strode out of the room, shouting for Guzmán even before he slammed the door shut behind him.

Margarita Alvarado smiled. She should have listened to her uncle and become an actress. This performance merited some kind of an award. There was no date or event to be forgotten. He would never suspect she made up the whole thing.

El Jefe was riding to the old ruins, visiting that spot once again. They were going deep into the jungle. Far from anything she knew about that he was involved in. He had been in that area not long ago and Margarita's report had almost cost de Santiago his life in the government ambush.

A sudden all-night ride through dense jungle, all the way to that place of ghosts. It had to be something important. El Falcone would report it as quickly as possible.

John Bethea sat across the conference table from Bill Beaman and Chief Johnston. The remnants of a tray of breakfast pastries and several half-empty coffee cups littered the polished wood surface between them. They were deep in the JDIA

Command Bunker at the end of Cabrillo Point. The reinforced concrete walls were a sharp contrast to the modern walnut conference furniture and deep-piled, wine-colored carpeting. Brass and chrome halogen track lights brightly illuminated the room, but the charts on the wall behind Bethea dominated.

The biggest chart showed the track of the *Helena K* and *Spadefish* as they laboriously made their way northwestward. Alongside the chart hung several large-scale maps of Colombia. Each was covered with various markings that Beaman neither recognized nor cared to ask about. One thing he had learned: It was better not to know anything at all about things he didn't absolutely need to know about.

He downed the last of the strong coffee. One map did attract his curiosity. It showed a circle a few miles from a little known river that was labeled "Rio Napo." The circle jumped out at him. It was all by itself on the map, drawn in an area that Beaman knew held nothing more than nearly impenetrable jungle.

Bethea followed Beaman's gaze toward the map.

"Bill, I see your powers of observation weren't impaired by all the tequila you drank the other night. That circle that has so appropriately caught your attention is the reason for our little meeting this morning."

Beaman's head snapped around.

"Oh? I thought we were here to debrief from the mission," he said as he leaned back in the padded leather chair.

"That was my original intention when I set the meeting, but we just received some new intelligence."

He pointedly picked up a thick file from beneath an empty doughnut platter on the table. The legend across the file read TOP SECRET, HIGHLY SENSITIVE SOURCES in two-inch-tall red letters. Bethea put on a pair of half-rim glasses, opened the file, and began looking for something in its contents.

"Chief Johnston and I both recognize the code words for a 'spy,' " Beaman said. "I hope this particular spy is a good one. I'm too tired to go trekking through the jungle on some wild-goose chase. And, in case you haven't heard, they play pretty rough down there these days."

Bethea looked out over the top of his reading glasses. He fixed Beaman with a quizzical stare. Beaman felt like a rabbit caught in the glare of a hungry wolf.

"Oh, he's good all right. El Falcone seems to have access to very valid information. You might be interested in what he has to say here. It concerns your old friend Juan de Santiago."

Beaman perked up.

"Hardly an old friend."

"Seems he and one of his lieutenants rode on horseback though the jungle last night for an important meeting." Bethea turned to the map. "Right there in the middle of that circle. That meeting is happening as we speak. Unfortunately, El Falcone could not give us enough lead time to get any assets on the ground to observe the meeting more closely."

"You got a bird in the sky over them?" Johnston asked.

Bethea pulled a couple of aerial photos out of the file and scooted them across the table to both men.

"Funny you should ask. You can see from this that the area is pretty wild. That first one is visible-spectrum. Nothing but jungle and some old, burned-out ruins of some kind of plantation that's disappearing into the undergrowth. The second photo is near-infrared. Nothing there either. Not even a stray body. Those two were taken early this morning. These two were taken an hour later. You can see two riders and horses quite plainly on the IR shot. We're now keeping the site under near-constant satellite surveillance. If El Falcone is correct, something is going on, and that's a spot we need to investigate further."

Johnston carefully laid down the photograph he was scrutinizing. He looked across the table at Bethea and asked the question both SEALs were thinking.

"Why go there? Million miles from anywhere and nothing but some pretty tough jungle?"

Bethea smiled.

"Exactly, Chief. Why go there? De Santiago has a million

choices if he just wants a secure, hidden site for some kind of a strategy meeting. All easier to get to than this one is. If it was simply a meeting place, we think he would pick one of those, or just hold it right there in his own hacienda like he usually does. He's arrogant enough to think we don't have ears there. But we've seen his propensity for hiding major facilities in very out-of-the-way places. You guys certainly have, firsthand. I'm betting he has something important to him hidden near here. And as you might have suspected already, I want you to go in and find out what it is."

"But what could it be? You'd be sure to see another factory, fields."

"We don't know. We know it's important enough to send the leader of the revolution off on an all-night ride through rough territory. Secret enough that he didn't take his bodyguard with him. We've seen him in that area once before. When the government troops almost got the son of a bitch in an ambush down on the Rio Napo."

"Any background on the place?" Beaman asked. "Some history that would tie it back to de Santiago some way?"

Bethea pulled a small sheaf of papers out of the file and laid them on the table next to the folder.

"Good question, Bill. We're gathering information as fast as we can. It was once a hacienda owned by a wealthy family of cattle ranchers. The Alvarado family. The Alvarados were a very powerful family in the area, going all the way back to the original Spanish conquest and royal land grants. They got caught up sideways in the revolutionary politics. They died in some kind of massacre. All except one daughter that we've lost track of. Facts are hazy on what happened. The place was burned in what must have been a big showdown. It all happened years ago, back when de Santiago was beginning to gain power. Since then, the place has been deserted. The jungle's reclaiming what was a very sophisticated ranch at one time. The local Indians claim the place is haunted. Ghosts of the murdered family come out and wander about at night, and no one goes anywhere near there anymore, not even the Indians."

"Well, one thing's for certain," Bill Beaman said.

"What's that?"

"Those aren't ghosts on that IR photo."

Juan de Santiago rode out of the jungle into the small clearing, reining in his heavily lathered sorrel stallion. The animal wheezed from the hard ride and the jungle heat. Alvene Dura emerged into the clearing a few seconds after him. His horse was also near exhaustion.

De Santiago lowered himself to the ground, stretched, and began to remove the saddle from his mount.

"Alvene, we are here. Rest your horse. We will need them shortly for the trip back."

Dura walked about stiffly, rubbing his backside.

"I still do not understand why we had to come in on horseback. Would the river not have been more direct and an easier trip?"

"This mission is too important to risk another showdown on the Rio Napo. No one will know of our visit this way. Your ass will heal from saddle sores quicker than from a bullet."

Dura gazed around the clearing. He had been charged with designing this lab and hiding it in this remote location. He had not been to the spot since they started construction.

"Juan, nothing has changed since I was here last. Except for more jungle. The ruins of the old house are almost invisible." His eyes grew distant. "I still remember the battle we fought here. The one that set ablaze the people's revolution against Guitteriz. We were so young, so brave."

De Santiago chuckled as he, too, remembered one of the earliest battles of his youth.

"Yes, and damned foolish. We almost lost our entire revolution that day before it had begun. Guitteriz surprised us with that battalion of his best troops. If we were smarter, we would have run for the trees. Come back and fight another day when the odds were more in our favor. We were much too brave, too idealistic for that. We came away with a new set of martyrs to the revolution. Guitteriz emerged with his first victory and that set him up to become president."

"That was the day Guzmán was wounded, wasn't it?"

Dura had heard the story many times, had been there, but he knew how much his leader loved recounting it over and over.

"Yes. A squad had me cornered over there, near that hummock. It was the stable then. They set it afire and tried to burn me out. I was unconscious from the heat and smoke. Guzmán fought his way in and carried me out on his own shoulders. They shot him in the back but he ran on until we were safe. We almost lost him that day."

Dura pointed over toward the ruins of what had been the large main house.

"I was in the house when they tried to burn us out. The family hid in the wine cellar while we fought. All dead. Burned to death in the fire. It was sad."

De Santiago snorted.

"Sacrifices are always necessary. People must die for the cause. Old man Alvarado made a fatal mistake when he refused to take sides. He thought he, his family, and his hacienda would be safe if he straddled the fence. In the end, no one was there to help him and both sides used him. He and his indecision ultimately caused the death of his entire family."

The two old warriors left their horses to graze in the clearing and strode together toward the vine-covered remnants of the stable. The shed that had been at the end of the stable and had served as the tack room stood, but just barely. It threatened to tumble down and rot away along with the rest of the charred and overgrown ruins.

They approached the ramshackle structure. Jorge Ortiez emerged from inside and waved a greeting to them.

"El Jefe, it is so good to see you again!" he shouted as they neared. "*Y* Señor Dura. I hope your journey was not too arduous."

De Santiago leaned over and embraced the short, rotund scientist.

"Jorge, you have done well. The revolution benefits greatly from your sacrifice out here in the jungle. You are already a hero of our people and soon, they will know it."

Ortiez blushed at the praise de Santiago heaped on him. He was not accustomed to such compliments. He endured the insults hurled his way by the Russians and the Iraqis and the American, all in their odd, staccato tongues.

"You are too kind, El Jefe. I merely do my job. You order and I follow. All is ready as you directed."

He led the way through the open door into the hut, then down the hidden passage into the laboratory. De Santiago and Dura shivered from the blast of chilled air blowing up the stairs to greet them. It was a brisk and refreshing change from the cloying heat and humidity of the jungle.

The gleaming, clean facility was empty, save for the three men coming down the staircase. De Santiago raised an eyebrow as he looked about for his expensive scientific talent. Ortiez rushed to explain.

"I sent them all to work in the library for a few hours. From the nature of your instructions, I assumed it would be better if they were not aware of your visit."

De Santiago smiled and nodded.

"As usual, you are most discerning. It would be better if no one knew we had come here. That would only raise curiosity about the nature of our visit."

Ortiez fidgeted, then seemed to summon the courage to spit out a question on which he had been chewing.

"I must admit, I am curious why you want to take all the additive. To have the secret recipe leave this place. It is safe here."

"Of course it is! This place will never be discovered by the *Americanos* or Guitteriz's bastard army." De Santiago punched the man on his shoulder playfully. "We have a pressing need for the additive now. We are including it in a new batch from one of our most secret factories. We still can't trust the foreigners. Who knows when they might get homesick for their godforsaken homelands and try to flee our little paradise? They would die swiftly, but we cannot afford to have the recipe die with them. No, Jorge. This place is secure."

Ortiez seemed to accept his leader's explanation. He turned quickly and reached into a locker under one of the lab benches, retrieving a backpack. He handed it over to de Santiago.

"Here is everything, El Jefe. I have included all the procedures, both in printed hard copy and on a computer disk, as you asked. There is also sufficient additive here to enrich several tons of cocaine. It is all of our production for the last month. We have none left."

De Santiago took the offered backpack.

"But it is so light. It can't weigh more than ten kilos. Are you sure this is everything?"

"El Jefe, most of the weight is the paper for the formula printout. There are only four kilos of the additive. Remember, it is very concentrated."

De Santiago laughed and threw the backpack across his broad shoulders.

"So little will cause so much worry for our enemies." He jumped up the stairs, taking them two at a time. "Come, Alvene! We have far to ride before the sun sets."

Without a word, Dura chased after him.

Jorge Ortiez shivered slightly in the chill of the air-conditioning.

The satellite continued to process images of the scene, recording one every hour. It had successfully downloaded the images of two men crossing the small jungle clearing. A lone man emerged from the open space. He was coming from a small structure of some kind. It had sent down an image of the scene after they had all disappeared. It was processing an image showing two men saddling their horses.

John Bethea waited as the last image was painted on his computer screen.

No doubt about it now. There was something of definite interest in that lonely, remote part of the Colombian jungle.

Sophisticated and all-seeing as the satellite was, there was no way it could tell him what was going on there. There was only one way. The old-fashioned way.

He would have to wait for Bill Beaman to drop in there and find out.

28

DAVE KUHN SLIPPED OUT OF THE DARKENED STATEROOM ON TIPTOES. Steve Friedman and Stan Guhl waited for him in the narrow passageway. The dim red light illuminated the three as they huddled together, whispering conspiratorially.

"Get it done?" Friedman asked under his breath.

Guhl glanced over at him, an evil gleam shining in his eye, and nodded.

"Yeah, he'll never know what hit him. You ready?"

"Ready. All I have to do is turn the tape on. I recorded this 1MC announcement while we were running the casualty drills last week."

Joe Glass stepped into the passageway just then and spied the three submariners huddled together, murmuring to each other. He stepped up and grabbed Kuhn by the shoulder.

"All right, what mischief are you three derelicts up to? I'm not giving you enough work to keep you busy?"

Kuhn held his finger to his lips.

"Shhh! You'll spoil it, XO. You remember how particular the Nav is about always having his poopie suit ready to go, always hung up neatly on that middle hanger? Well, we switched poopie suits. We hung up Chris's suit on Beasley's hanger. We even changed the collar devices and dolphins so he won't notice anything. I figure the Nav is at least eight inches taller and fifty pounds heavier than Chris is." Kuhn wore a wide grin. "The fun is just about to begin."

Steve Friedman pulled out a small tape deck and held it just outside the door to Earl Beasley's stateroom. Kuhn and Guhl stepped into the wardroom with the XO.

"Watch this," Kuhn whispered as he signaled to Friedman, who hit the Play button on the recorder.

"Red sounding! Red sounding! Navigator, lay to control!"

The tiny machine blasted at a volume extraordinary for its size.

They could hear Earl Beasley as he bolted up in his bunk and bounded out in a state of near panic. A "red sounding" meant *Spadefish* was in very real danger of running aground immediately and that she was far from where she was supposed to be. They needed to take immediate and drastic action and the sub's navigator was the expert to tell them what to do.

Beasley grabbed the poopie suit from its customary center hook and stepped out into the passageway to pull it on. In one smooth move, he put one leg into the coveralls, then the other, and tried to pull them up and over his back. The suit wasn't coming up far enough. In his half-awake state, Beasley jerked hard on the sleeves to try to get the outfit on and zipped. He grunted as the poopie suit rode up tightly in his crotch and pulled his shoulders backward.

He jerked at the recalcitrant suit again, even harder this time. And that only resulted in considerably more discomfort.

His sleep-shrouded mind slowly registered that there were three officers standing at the end of the short passageway, laughing at him and his efforts to get dressed. Just behind them, the XO stood, shaking his head.

Beasley dropped his grip on the much-too-small uniform. It fell to the deck as he shook his fist at Kuhn.

"Eng, you son of a bitch! I'll get even with you for this! You scared me to death!" he yelped, but only half in anger.

Kuhn could barely speak, he was laughing so hard.

"Nav, that's payback for the shoe-polish trick. Way I have it figured, we're about even now," he was finally able to choke out.

Little Chris Durgan stepped into the passageway then.

"You children done playing now? I need my poopie suit back. I got work to do."

His words sent the three men into another fit of wild laughter when they saw the shorter man in Beasley's coveralls, the stride halfway to his knees, the legs puddled around his feet, and the sleeves long on his arms.

Even Joe Glass had to laugh.

Carlos Ramirez sat across the small wooden table from Jason Rashad, playing idly with a beer coaster. The bar was dark, almost empty. The cold Seattle drizzle had reduced the light weekday-evening traffic in this suburban watering hole even more. A brass wall lamp barely illuminated the two as they sat hidden in the back corner of the bar. They were removed from the late-evening customers seated around the bar, discussing the stock market or the latest hot IPO. The noise of the game show on the television set suspended over the far side of the bar masked the two men's conversation.

They stopped talking when the bartender placed two glasses of dark beer and a basket of pretzels on the table. They remained silent until the man scurried back to his haven behind the granite-topped bar.

"I have heard from our friends down south," Ramirez resumed quietly. "It's time to put everything in motion. The first shipment arrives in five days. Are we ready?"

The black man smiled and fingered his nose ring.

"Ready as we'll ever be. Our customers were balking at a fifty-percent-advance fee structure. I persuaded them of the advantages of the arrangement." He took a long swallow from his beer and smacked his lips. "There was one small problem. I'm afraid we are short one middleman now. Seems our distributor for Detroit had an acute attack of lead poisoning during the negotiations. It was fatal. The others were very eager to cover his action, though."

"Good, good," Ramirez nodded, not concerned by the murder. He was confident the task had been necessary, its execution accomplished properly.

"One thing, though," Rashad said. "I thought we were going to take it slow, get the product out here, make sure the additive was doing what it was supposed to do. Why are we bringing in all the distributors so soon?"

"Don't ask me. I just do what de Santiago tells me to do. If I didn't know better, I'd say El Jefe needs some cash in a hurry. Maybe he needs some curtains for the hacienda." Ramirez took his own swig of beer and chewed on a pretzel for a moment. "We make our dough quicker this way so who gives a shit? And we'll be back in business in no time." He winked and grinned at Rashad. Then he turned serious. "I know you had to rush up your plan. How's it going with the receipt and delivery operation?"

Rashad drained the beer from his glass before answering, then licked the foam from the rim.

"Got a handle on it, boss. We're gonna land everything down at that old navy testing facility on Carr Inlet. It hasn't been used for anything in years but a shithouse for the seagulls. Coupla big buildings there to hide the trucks in."

Ramirez nodded and studied the condensation from his beer mug that had pooled up on the table.

"Sounds okay. But one thing still worries me. How are we going to get that many trucks in and out of there without anybody noticing anything?"

"Figured we do it right under their noses in broad daylight. Trucks're all painted like UPS delivery trucks. Baby-shit brown. Nobody'll see one or two extra runnin' around out there."

Ramirez took a long pull on his beer.

"Start moving them in. Shipment arrives Monday. Make

sure the security is very tight. I don't want anything happening to this stuff. We've got too much invested in it. No slipups."

He gave Rashad a long, meaningful glare. There was no mistaking the message he was trying to impart. The big black man nodded slightly and hoped he had made his boss as confident as he was that everything would go according to plan.

Ramirez rose, tossed a crisp, new hundred-dollar bill on the table, turned on a heel, and walked out of the bar.

Rashad shook his head ruefully, picked up the hundred and left a wrinkled ten and two ones. Some things the boss would never learn. A bartender would remember two guys, off in a corner by themselves, talking quietly, then leaving a ninety-dollar tip for a couple of brews.

And Jason Rashad, of all people, knew how dangerous it could be to be remembered.

Jim Pruitt banked the P-3C hard left. The big four-engine airplane leveled out. He turned to Randy Dalton, his copilot.

"That damn Japanese sub has to be around here someplace. I feel like we've searched every square inch of water between SoCal and Hawaii. He has to be hiding in the noise of that freighter." He pointed downward at a darker gray silhouette that was pitching and bucking on a gray, rolling sea, struggling to the northwest. "Let's take a look. Sensors ready to drop another search pattern? We'll drop ten thousand yards in front of it and let it steam through the pattern."

Dalton looked over his shoulder, back down the passageway of the old plane. Jess Carmon gave him a thumbs-up.

"Yep, Skipper. Ready to drop in auto as soon as you arm the pickle. I'm sure glad we're up here and not down there in that crap."

Rain lashed across the windshield of the low-flying aircraft. It bumped and yawed with the wind. It was far rougher down there on the ocean's surface.

Pruitt lifted up the small red cover from over a switch on his right control handle, then flipped it on.

"Pickle is hot. Steady course two-seven-five."

Priutt heard Carmon's voice coming crisply over the headset.

"Stand by for auto-pattern drop. Stand by. Commencing drop now."

The P-3C flew on through the rain and clouds. Six sonobuoys were ejected from beneath the aircraft, one after another, in a computer-controlled sequence. The AN/SSQ-53 DIFAR sonobuoys parachuted to the water below, then dropped a hydrophone on a long wire to listen deep under the storm-tossed Pacific. The main body of the buoy stayed on the surface, bobbing about in the churning seas. A thin wire antenna shot out of the top of each one.

Carmen spoke into his microphone.

"Skipper, I have six live buoys on the link, but I don't know how long I can keep them in this sea-state."

"Just do the best you can, Jess. We'll go back upstairs to do an ISAR search. Shep, keep your eyes peeled. If that Japanese is shallow, he may get sucked to the surface in this sea-state. I'd like to catch him if he does."

Pruitt pulled back on the control yoke. The big gray bird climbed slowly until the low cloud layer swallowed it up. The sea disappeared from view. There was a light gray wall outside, exactly the same color as the P-3C.

Kevin Sheppard looked up from his screen and nodded.

"I'm ready, Skipper. Taking the radar from standby to ISAR search. Going to the two hundred-mile-range scale." He flipped a couple of switches. The large CRT screen in front of him developed into a picture of the seas below. "Skipper, we're radiating. Only return is that freighter and a lot of sea-return."

"Okay, keep your eyes peeled."

The crew sat back for the long wait. Hunting submarines was a game of strategy, guesswork, and waiting. Pruitt had once tried to explain the gratification of a successful sub hunt to his fighter-jock friends. He compared his game to chess, theirs to a kid's video arcade game. He had given up when he realized the jet pilots lived in a split-second world of instant gratification while his was a slower-paced one, a snail-paced competition. One where he could savor each gambit.

To each his own.

The airplane flew a large circle through an all-gray world. Three engines turned to keep her aloft. The operators watched their equipment, electronically slicing through the gray to search the sea beneath it for its hidden secrets.

"Skipper, buoy three is hot!" Carmen yelled. "Positive contact. Bearing two-four-three." He watched the information develop on his screen. "Hey, wait a minute! This ain't that Japanese boat! These lines equate to a *Sturgeon*-class. This has to be our old friends on *Spadefish*."

"Are you sure?" Pruitt shot back. "Any chance the Japanese are spoofing us?"

Carmen did not hesitate in his answer.

"Skipper, ain't no doubt. If you don't believe me, come back here and look for yourself."

Pruitt looked over at Dalton. He didn't need to go back and look at the display. If Carmen said there was a Spanish galleon down there, it damn sure would be.

"What the hell? *Spadefish* isn't playing in our little jamboree. What are they doing out here? Get on the horn and tell the TSC what we have. We'll let them sort it out."

The Tactical Support Center was located in a cinder-block building back on North Island. From there, the ASW area commander directed the airborne search for submarines, and that included Jim Pruitt's aircraft. From the relative comfort of a desk that didn't move about with the pitching of the sea or the eddy of upper air currents, they could see the big picture. That picture didn't include the broad red stripe through the area drawn for *Spadefish*'s safe transit. They couldn't help the air crew.

Dalton turned to Pruitt to report that fact.

"TSC doesn't have any report of *Spadefish* being out here."

"Then I guess we're just gonna have to ask her what she's doing ourselves. We don't want her running up on that Japanese sub before we do!"

Ward held on tightly to the chrome rail around the periscope stand. The rocking and pitching of the sub at periscope depth was worse than it had been the last time they came up to look and talk. The storm was building. It made these trips up to near the surface uncomfortable.

"What do you have, Mr. Durgan?"

"Looks to be a sea-state five, building to a six. I'm guessing these waves are twenty to thirty feet tall. I can't see the *Helena K* at all anymore. Visibility down to maybe four thousand yards in this rain."

Ray Mendoza spoke over the 21MC.

"Conn, Sonar. We're losing signal in this sea-state. I'm tracking now in manual, buzzing bearings. Not enough signal for ATF. Skipper, we'll never be able to keep it all sorted out when we get closer to where the fleets are playing."

Ward grabbed the swinging microphone. The nose of the sub pitched downward in a roller, slamming him hard into the sonar repeater. He managed to keep his feet.

"Do the best you can, Master Chief. We'll try to stay close."

Spadefish rolled sharply to starboard. A loud crash of broken pottery followed by a yelp and a string of curses from Cookie Dotson came from the galley, down in middle level. That foretold a disaster for lunch.

Dan Larson reported through the open microphone.

"Conn, ESM. I'm picking up an ISAR radar. Signal strength five. I'm guessing we have a P-3 pretty close."

Ward looked over at Bill Ralston, sitting in front of the BCP. The man was holding on with both hands and his skin had a peculiar green tinge to it. He clutched his legs around a trash can, mute indication of the submariner's weakness for seasickness. Ward felt sorry for the suffering chief, but times like these came with the job.

"Chief, raise the BRA-34."

Ralston nodded and let the trash can settle back onto the deck at his feet. He quickly rose, flipped the switch to raise the mast, and plopped back down hard. He dropped his face into the trash can, his shoulders heaving pitifully as he retched.

"Radio, put me on the freq for area ASW operations, secure voice," the skipper ordered.

After a minute, Doug Lyman answered.

"Conn, Radio. You're on the freq. Skipper, ESM reports picking up a sonobuoy uplink signal. There's for sure a P-3 out here looking for us. Or for somebody."

Ward scooted around Durgan and stumbled on the unsteady deck to the back of the periscope stand. He dropped onto the stool and grabbed the red radio handset. He grasped a pipe stanchion and held on as he jammed himself into the corner to fight the pitch and roll as he pushed the talk button.

"This is *Spadefish* calling P-3 in op area Charlie Three Delta, over."

"*Spadefish*, this is Papa-Victor-Four." The reply was almost instantaneous. "Thought that was you we had on the DIFARs. What are you doing out here? We haven't seen you since that emergency surface a couple of months ago."

"Papa-Victor-Four, glad to see you guys again. We're conducting a classified surveillance op and I need some assistance. Do you have contact on a freighter about five miles from me?"

Pruitt looked back at Sheppard, who nodded affirmatively.

"Yep. We're painting him now. Really getting tossed around in that crap down there."

Another wave slammed Ward back into the corner. He got himself steadied somewhat before he talked again.

"Yeah, tell me about it. Can you get an ISAR picture of him?"

The inverse synthetic aperture radar was designed to take detailed radar pictures of Soviet warships and do it while the P-3 was flying outside the warship's anti-aircraft missile range. It used radar imaging. It worked just as well at night or through clouds as it did on a bright, sunny day. The pictures were so good that details as small as a foot long could be seen. Papa-Victor-Four could snap a few pictures of the *Helena K* without anyone on the rogue freighter even knowing there was a plane flying above her through the soupy, thick cloudbank.

"No problem," Pruitt answered. "Just consider us your friendly neighborhood 'Fotomat.' Who do we deliver these to . . . or do you want to drive in and pick them up?"

"No, thanks! Can you get them to John Bethea at JDIA?"

Pruitt had heard of the agency. He just wasn't sure what it was or what it did or what *Spadefish*'s business might be with them. He did what the skipper requested.

"Sure. We'll downlink to the TSC and have them landline them. This Bethea guy should be looking at some nice shapshots of your freighter in an hour."

He couldn't help but wonder why the sub was tailing this particular boat so tightly. Or what interest the JDIA had in the freighter that necessitated *Spadefish* wallowing around down there in that mess. It wasn't his job to ask such questions.

"Much obliged."

"Just another satisfied customer."

Pruitt banked the big, ungainly bird and brought it on a course parallel to the *Helena K*. He looked over his right shoulder back to the radar operator.

"Shep, snap some pretty pictures of this guy as we fly by. I'll do a pass down his starboard, then across his stern, up his port side, then across the bow. Get as many shots as you can."

Kevin Sheppard glanced up from staring at his radar picture and flashed a grin and a thumbs-up.

"Tell 'em to smile and say, 'Sex!' I'm snappin' pictures for the yearbook."

Down below, Ward held on tightly as another wave washed over the scope and tossed the sub onto its side. The bubble inclinometer, mounted on a brass plate above the front of the periscope stand, read twenty degrees at the bottom of the roll. Durgan pitched back from the scope. His tight grip on the handles kept him from being thrown across the control room. He glanced at Ward and calmly said, "Scope's under."

Ward nodded and spoke into the handset.

"Papa-Victor-Four, can you stay on station and help us track this sucker through the op areas? I'm afraid in this weather we'll lose him and track off onto someone else we're not supposed to be following."

"Don't see why not," Pruitt answered. "We have seven more hours of on-station time. We're supposed to be finding some Japanese sub that's hiding out here but we don't show him anywhere nearby. I'd have to hit his sail with a buoy to find him in this crap now. Meteorological reports call for it to get progressively worse. Just don't expect us to be late for happy hour at the offices' club."

Ward looked around the control room. Ralston was head-down in his trash can. He was sharing it with Seaman Cortez. Master Chief Mendoza strapped himself in the diving officer's chair and was using every trick he knew to keep *Spadefish* at periscope depth and to keep the churning seas from sucking her to the surface. The helmsman and planesman were pushing and pulling their control yokes as the sub rose and fell inside the waves. The quartermaster and the fire control technician were sharing their own trash can over behind the plot table. The ventilation fans had the air moving just enough to keep the stench at a barely tolerable level.

The crew could put up with this for a few hours, but the constant pitching and yawing sapped their strength. It was near impossible for them to rest. The seas would toss them from their bunks. Cooking was impossible. That was just as well for most of the crew. Food was the very last thing they wanted to think about. There was the ever-present danger of a wave catching someone off balance and tossing him into a piece of equipment or a sharp edge, or sending someone plummeting down a ladder.

They had had enough injuries for one run. They had to get deep, where the water was calm.

Ward needed help and there was nothing to lose by asking for it.

"Papa-Victor-Four, request you ask TSC to task a hot turnover for you. JDIA will authorize. It will take fifteen hours to clear the area and maybe weather will be better by then."

Pruitt listened to the sub skipper's voice. The guy sounded worried, tired, and beat-up. The pilot was glad he wasn't down there. Not that this bird was giving them a calm, smooth ride through the swirling clouds, but it wasn't the heaving and tossing the sub was getting.

"Roger, *Spadefish*. We'll ask," he answered. "It may take a little time. We'll drop SUS when we have an answer, then again before we go off station."

A SUS, or sound underwater signal, was a small bomb-shaped device the P-3 could drop into the ocean near the sub. Once in the water, it sent out a loud, coded, acoustic signal that a sub could hear on its sonar from a distance of several miles.

"Roger. Going deep. *Spadefish* out."

From the tremor in his voice, it sounded as if the skipper might be taking a punch or two in the gut as he spoke. Pruitt reached across and tapped Dalton on the arm.

"You take the bird. I'm going back to grab a cup of coffee and a sandwich. Want something?"

"Not right now. I'll get lunch in a bit. There's no point in offering those guys down there anything either."

He nodded downward, where the sea boiled angrily below the cloud cover. Pruitt shook his head sympathetically and headed on back to get his sandwich.

29

JOSÉ SILVERAS LEANED BACK AND SMILED CONTENTEDLY AS THE GRAY box on his desk hummed away. This new computer the *Norteamericanos* had supplied his department now made his job so much easier and his alternative pursuits so much safer

and effective. All he had to do was sit back in his desk chair
and sip strong coffee as he watched the computer do all the
tasks that El Presidente's government required of him. The
work for which he received the few pesos they paid him each
week. He had once labored away over files for days to perform the same tasks this machine accomplished in mere minutes. It was a marvel.

The computer ground away, digesting innumerable bits of
mundane data for the government bureaucracy. Hidden deep
in the microchips of its inner workings, the machine was
crunching away on another task. One infinitely more important and dangerous. What was it that pimply-faced gringo
computer technician had called it? "Working in background."
If the kid had only known what task Silveras's computer was
accomplishing "in background"!

While he moved boring government files around, the machine was searching cyberspace for specific and vital information required by El Jefe. It was churning, electronically sifting
through file drawers, rifling through bank records, reviewing
shipping manifests, doing all the work and taking all the risks
that Silveras once had to face in person.

An icon popped up on his screen with a faint *ding* sound. To
anyone watching, the innocuous little lightning bolt wouldn't
mean anything, and, unless they knew the special keystrokes,
no one would ever be able to find out.

Old habits die hard. Silveras looked around his cramped little office to make sure no one was anywhere around before he
touched the keys. He was all alone. With a few keystrokes and a
quickly entered password, he was looking at a long list of files
that contained any of the search words El Jefe had requested.

So, Señor Holbrooke was planning a little trip to Europe.
That was something El Jefe would be interested in. It looked
as if the banker was moving money—a great deal of money—
from his personal bank accounts. Very interesting indeed.

Silveras read through the files carefully, looking for anything else that might jump out at him, all the while committing
every detail to memory. Once he was certain he would forget

nothing, that he had gleaned all he needed from the documents, he closed the special program, stepped out of his office into the narrow hallway, and locked the door behind him.

He had developed quite an appetite. It was time for an early lunch and a special phone call.

Bill Beaman squirmed around in the web seat. He tried to find some reasonably comfortable position. The C-130's massive turboprops roared at what seemed to be just inches from his ears. He would rather bed down for a month in the roughest jungle, the most barren desert terrain, than have to ride for any length of time on one of these pregnant albatrosses. It didn't matter how many times he made these trips. There was no way to make the flight more endurable. Between the noise, the cold, and these damned seats, there was no way he could find sleep.

Beaman stared in awe at Dumkowski, seated across from him. The man was sleeping peacefully. A string of drool dangled at one corner of his mouth.

These missions all started the same. Unending hours of sitting on a C-130's canvas benches, facing his team, going over every detail in his mind, imagining everything that could go wrong. There were always the questions. Who would get hurt? Who wouldn't be coming back at all? What could he do to make it more likely that he could bring them all home safe? Would they accomplish the mission?

Impossible questions to answer, but impossible to ignore. And that's why they swirled about in his head the whole way as he tried to wiggle into some position that would give him some rest.

Chief Johnston plopped down beside Beaman. He had to yell to make himself heard over the continual roar of wind and airplane engines. As usual, he seemed to read Beaman's mind.

"Worrying yourself sick again, Skipper? How many times do I have to tell you, it don't help?" Johnston grinned and slapped the SEAL lieutenant commander on the knee. "Besides, this one is gonna be a cakewalk. Just a little stroll in the park."

Beaman managed a tired, wan smile and yelled back.

"Sure thing, Chief. I'm not worrying," he lied. "Just a walk in the park."

"Checked everyone's gear. Everything's ready. No last-minute glitches, so far. Talked to the air crew. Twenty minutes to the drop zone. Forecast for unlimited visibility. Winds over the zone are five to seven knots from the southwest. Be like dropping in at your mother's for dinner."

Beaman smiled a little more.

"Oh, so you've tried my mother's biscuits. Best secret weapon we have. Better'n depleted uranium. Those bastards are guaranteed to pierce any armor known to man."

Johnston grinned back and slowly stood, bracing himself against the slight sway of the aircraft.

"About time to roust the troops. We need to start getting saddled up for the jump." He walked down the fuselage of the plane, waking the other team members, mostly with the toe of his boot. There was a total of only six men this time. The vast cargo bay would have been cavernously empty if theirs had been the only mission for this bird. Instead, they were little more than a minor detour. The C-130 would continue on to Bogotá with a cargo of critical military supplies. That trip served as a nice cover for the SEAL drop. With the security leaks from the last trip down here and the resulting ambush, Beaman was mighty thankful for the cover story.

The jumpmaster tapped Beaman on the shoulder.

"Time to go!" he yelled over the noise of the turbines, and pointed aft toward the huge cargo door.

Beaman rose stiffly, stretched, then strapped on his equipment. He double-checked every piece. He cross-checked every piece of Chief Johnston's gear before Johnston inspected his, each man following the usual prejump ritual. Wouldn't be good form to forget to fasten the chute harness or to have the ripcord wrapped around a strap. That kind of thing was difficult to fix while plummeting to the ground like a dropped rock.

The six men walked aft and lined up in front of the cargo door at the rear of the airplane. The jumpmaster talked briefly into his helmet intercom, then pushed a button on the starboard bulkhead. The door slowly rattled down, opening the back of the plane to reveal a star-studded night sky above them. Beaman looked out and could see the ground ten thousand feet below them. There wasn't a light anywhere, only darkness, inviting them down.

The little red light high up on the starboard side of the cargo door went out and the green one came on. The jumpmaster signaled the SEAL leader that it was time to go.

Beaman casually walked out onto the end of the ramp and stepped off into nothingness. The rest of his team followed closely behind.

Once out and falling, Beaman held the altimeter on his wrist in front of his face, watching it as he dropped through the night sky. It rapidly counted down until he was only a thousand feet above the ground, about the height of a typical television tower. Only then did he yank the D ring to deploy his main parachute, and instinctively looked up to watch it unfurl above his head. The large, aerodynamically shaped canopy immediately filled with air, jerking him hard as it slowed his descent.

Beaman could just make out the dark shapes of his team stacked above him, their forms outlined against the field of stars. He counted. One, two three, four, five. Good, all five chutes accounted for. He yanked on the harness to turn and steer his canopy for the drop zone, now coming up to the northwest. The rest followed as if they were a choreographed dance line.

Beaman made a running landing almost precisely in the center of the little clearing. He tripped face-first into thick, juicy mud. So that was why this space was cleared and open. They were coming down in a damned bog. He climbed to his feet and pulled in his chute as Johnston landed right beside him. He fell too.

The chief rose, cursing roundly as the other four men dropped within a few feet of them. Johnston directed the team as they buried their jump gear and prepared to move out.

"Skipper, we're all ready to go . . . them that ain't been swallowed up by this damn mud. We don't need any camouflage. We look like we been rootin' around like a bunch of hogs." He slung away a handful of mud that he had scraped off the front of his suit. "I already sent the 'safe arrival' message and got a response."

"Okay, no sense hanging around here. We've got a mile of jungle to cross yet. And I'd like to get to those haunted ruins before daylight, just in case the damned ghosts around here get up with the chickens."

They were quickly lost in the thick overgrowth, leaving behind no signs at all of their ever having been there.

Commander Jonathan Ward eased down at the wardroom table. Joe Glass sat to his right, busily attacking a huge omelet. They were all by themselves, since the hour was still early. The rest of the officers were either on watch or still sleeping. This made it a good time for them to talk and turn over what was happening on the mission. Ward had spent the night in the control room, watching every move of the *Helena K*, as well as observing his own crew. Once he finished his big plate of eggs, Glass would spend the rest of the day in the control room while Ward worked and rested.

Ward sipped from his coffee cup while his XO labored on his massive breakfast.

"Sure you don't want to try one of these, Skipper? Cookie is a magician with these frozen eggs. Best cheese and mushroom omelet this side of the Hotel Del."

Ward chuckled.

"I see you got your appetite back once we got deep. We're lucky we didn't get somebody hurt up there."

Glass nodded, his mouth full of egg. He swallowed before he answered.

"Yep. We were lucky. What's happening with the weather by now? Any letup?"

"Sonar shows that it's backing around to the northeast. Looks like the front has passed. Sonar sea-state is down to a three or so. We went up a bit ago for a look around. Still choppy, but calming, or we would have likely disturbed your beauty sleep when we got up there. Our friend is still ahead of us, still heading to the northwest."

Glass took a swig of coffee.

"Good, we can get back to business. Our P-3 buddies still around?"

Ward shook his head.

"No, I sent them home about two o'clock this morning. Sonar returns are solid and we're clear of the fleet exercise area, thank goodness. I didn't figure we needed them any-more. No sense in making them miss their time in the rack if they don't need to."

"Any guess where that sleaze is headed?"

Ward shook his head.

"Not a clue. Only thing we know for sure is she's mani-fested for Vancouver. That almost certainly means that she's not headed there at all. Could be anywhere else. We'll just have to follow and find out." Ward looked around for a second then patted his stomach. "Where's Cookie? I think I'll take one of those omelets after all. Just half the size of yours, though. You trying to be the first commander kicked out of the sub service for obesity?"

Glass just winked and shoved another big bite of egg into his mouth.

Tom Kincaid cursed under his breath as a compact car darted in front of him, cutting him off, then blowing its squeaky little horn as if it was his fault for being there. Traffic was a swirling tangle, moving in fits and starts. He hated driving in rush-hour traffic, and it was even worse in this interminable misting rain.

A buzzing from the passenger seat snatched his thoughts away from contemplation of imminent road rage. He reached across the seat of the Chevy Suburban and grabbed the cell phone.

"Kincaid here," he growled irritably.

"Surprised you're up and about this early. I thought you DEA cowboys slept till noon and only got up for your manicure appointment."

Kincaid couldn't help but chuckle when he heard the gravelly voice of Ken Temple on the other end of the phone. His jokes might be stale but he usually brought information. Information for which Tom Kincaid was powerfully hungry.

"Yeah, that's true. But we're such political animals we keep D.C. time. Makes work out here tough. Have to be up by nine if you want any brownie points. I really feel sorry for those poor suckers out in Hawaii who have to . . ." Kincaid screeched to a stop as the light ahead of him changed to yellow and the compact's driver slammed on her own brakes right in front of him. "Damn stupid . . . Hey, Ken, what are you doing disturbing my Zenlike experience with Seattle traffic?"

"Our friends Ramirez and Rashad surfaced again. One of our beat cops over in Bellevue spotted Rashad's Beemer outside a bar. They don't get too many all-gold, low-rider Beemers in that neighborhood, I don't guess. Anyway, he smelled something and he ran a make on it."

Kincaid stepped on the gas as the signal changed to green, then slammed on the brakes again, barely missing a rusty pickup that was running the light from the right. Kincaid bounced off the steering wheel, shouting curses at the departing taillights that were almost hidden by the haze of blue smoke from the truck's exhaust.

"You want to run plates? Let me give you a set of plates to run! Then I want that asshole all to myself! Son of a bitch liked to have killed me!"

"Easy, Tom. Remember your blood pressure, big guy," Temple snickered, imagining the expression on the agent's irate face. "Anyway, as I was about to say, by the time the make got back, the Beemer was gone. The cop talked to the bartender. He positively identified the two. He was bitching about the big black guy who stole the tip off the table."

Kincaid listened, digesting the information, then asked, "Any follow up? Any idea where they are now?"

"No, we just know that they are back and moving about above ground again. We sent the make out to all the stations with orders to watch out for the pair but not to try to make any contact. They'll surface again. It's too hard for such a dynamic duo as they are to stay hidden for long."

Kincaid chewed his lip for a few minutes, lost in thought.

"Guess we'll just have to watch and wait," he finally answered. "If they're back above ground, they're probably getting back in business. My gut tells me we'd better squash those two cockroaches before they get a chance to do any damage."

Tom Kincaid's gut had always been a very dependable compass and it was comforting to know that all that had happened to him and his agency career had not deflected the needle a degree. All his instincts continued to scream that these two characters were the keys to deflating Juan de Santiago's deadly business plan. And now, even as the compact car's driver eased along for the better part of a mile at half the speed limit and with her blinker on the whole way, he found his anger with her fading. There was a far worse menace flaming up out there and he was dead certain now that he was in a prime position to stomp it out.

And he was certain that opportunity would be coming very, very soon.

Juan de Santiago sat behind the old mahogany desk in the hacienda office. The room smelled of old leather and cigar smoke and dust. The walls were lined with bookshelves filled completely with leather bound volumes of account registers documenting centuries of activities to carefully husband the soil and recording every peso touched by the rancheros.

De Santiago rarely used this room. The plush leather chairs and the heavy brass lamps were just not to his taste. What would one of his followers say if they saw him sitting here, in the master's office? Was he merely another master, intent on exploiting the peons for his own enrichment?

The room was perfect for the task at hand. The impression of wealth and power was vital if he was to get his point across.

The thick walls and the office's isolation from the rest of the house would serve well if the message was not well received.

There was a heavy knock at the deeply carved rosewood door. Guzmán entered even before de Santiago acknowledged him.

"El Jefe, the *Americano* is here. He demands to see you immediately."

De Santiago smiled and spoke softly.

"Invite him in then, Guzmán. Such an important man should not be kept waiting."

Guzmán looked at his leader, his face full of questions. He knew that El Jefe loathed the effete banker. He barely tolerated his presence, and would have cut his throat long before had he not required his intricate knowledge of international finance.

Guzmán knew one other thing. This quiet politeness was a dangerous thing. The bodyguard shivered and was thankful he was not in the banker's shoes this night.

Don Holbrooke shoved past Guzmán and stomped into the quiet room. He was livid, shouting and waving his arms wildly.

"What is the meaning of this?"

He shook his fist at de Santiago, the affected Harvard accent he so often adopted now forgotten in his rage.

In one quick motion, Guzmán reached behind his back and grabbed the hilt of the razor-sharp fighting knife he kept holstered there. De Santiago expected the move and motioned subtly for him to stop before he decapitated the fool banker.

"Señor Holbrooke, my friend. Why are you so worked up?" He gestured toward one of the wine red leather armchairs. "Come, sit. Make yourself comfortable and let us discuss your 'problem'—whatever it might be—like civilized men."

Holbrooke stomped his foot and glared at the rebel leader.

"I don't need to sit and discuss any damn thing! I just want my money back! The money you stole from me! Give it back right now or you'll be sorry!"

De Santiago repressed a chuckle at the sight of the little money-grubber so worked up. He found it droll that he had the effrontery to threaten him here in his own house.

"Would you care for a cigar? Perhaps a little cognac? We have a very fine Napoleon vintage."

Holbrooke was consumed by his rage and de Santiago's calm manner only made it worse. He flopped down into the offered chair, failing to see the sarcasm dripping from de Santiago's every word.

"Juan, cut the shit. I don't know how you figured out how to do it. I just know you did it. Now, give back the money you stole or I'll see that someone finds out where all the accounts—"

"But, Señor Holbrooke," de Santiago interrupted. "We seem to have a bit of a problem here, my friend. Thanks to Herr Schmidt and our friends in Switzerland, we have become aware of some rather serious thievery going on here. Remember, the revolution and I are far bigger customers of his bank than are you, and that appears to have earned us a certain loyalty from the Swiss. By my accounting, you stole this money from the revolution in the first place. Technically, I can't steal what was rightfully mine, now can I? We have discussed this many times, my friend. I was willing to overlook some of your thieving, so long as it was under control." As he spoke, De Santiago's tone changed dramatically. He began to chew off and spit out every word as he rose menacingly from behind the desk and towered over the seated banker. "But your greed knows no bounds. You steal from me at every turn, and even then you are not satisfied. No! The millions are not enough for you and your voracious appetite. Now, you have to sell my secrets to El Presidente! Señor Holbrooke . . . or should I say, El Falcone? You are one bird that will no longer fly."

Holbrooke dropped his jaw and stared blankly, wide-eyed, at the enraged face of Juan de Santiago. He almost seemed mesmerized by the snakelike eyes. He was too tongue-tied to deny the charge, too stunned to defend himself. He never saw de Santiago's next subtle gesture, or noticed Guzmán as he slipped behind the chair with catlike quickness, his fighting knife now unsheathed and flickering in the light.

In an amazingly quick motion, Guzmán grabbed the banker's long white hair in his fist and yanked his head back forcefully, exposing his neck, his frantically bobbing Adam's apple.

Holbrooke never saw the knife flash across his vision either. He felt a strange burning sensation encircle his throat. It was difficult for him to draw a breath.

He tried to speak, to try to convince El Jefe that he had no knowledge of El Falcone. All that came from his mouth was a gurgle of frothy blood.

"Now, Guzmán, get the pig out of here before his filthy blood taints my home even farther than has his very presence," de Santiago said.

Without even a glance back at the dying man, the leader strode out of the musty room and headed directly upstairs. He had a sudden irresistible urge to find Margarita, to tell her about his latest triumph, to proudly relate to her the unveiling and destruction of El Falcone.

And to have her writhing body once again working beneath him.

30

BILL BEAMAN SLIPPED SILENTLY THROUGH THE THICK, TANGLED JUNgle undergrowth, swimming his way through the grasping limbs and vines that seemed to want to grab him and keep him from making any progress at all. Dawn was breaking over the ridgetop to the east. It was getting late. The nocturnal jungle creatures were already bedded down for their day's rest. The daytime scavengers were just beginning to stir about. The SEAL team leader looked around him and could just make out the dim forms of the rest of his team as they fanned out beside him in the half-light.

The trek from the landing zone had been grueling but un-eventful, no sign of any other human beings. The six-man team had managed to trudge up the ridge and down the other side in the almost total darkness. Along about 0300, the sky darkened even more as storm clouds rolled in from the west, blotting out the stars. An hour later, the SEAL team was working its way through a full-blown rainstorm. They could barely see the trees in front of them as the driving rain relent-lessly beat down on them. They were soaked to the skin in minutes. They also knew that the sudden storm would help to keep them hidden from any probing eyes that might have caught sight of them, or would mask any inadvertent sound they might make. Beaman could only hope that anyone else out here was as uncomfortable as he and his men were.

The rain turned the thin jungle soil to slimy, oozing mud beneath their boots. Between the mud and the wet vegetation, the footing quickly became impossible. Every step upward to-ward the top of the ridge usually led to a half-a-step slide backward. The struggle up the slope was exhausting even for the well-conditioned SEAL team.

The rain stopped just as abruptly as it had started. A fresh, cool wind blew the clouds out to the east just as the men topped the ridge and began their drop down the other side. Even with the deluge over, it was impossible to see any dis-tance down into the valley before them. The dense vegetation, hanging low from its load of rainwater, hid everything.

Still, they made much better time as they slipped and slid down the slope with the assistance of gravity. They arrived at the edge of the clearing just as the sun broke over the top of yet another ridge that towered high in front of them.

Beaman raised his hand and pointed off in both directions, using hand signals to instruct his team on how he wanted them to fan out and scout the area. Before them, across a small clearing, bathed in the dim yellow light of the ascending sun, were the tumbled down remains of a burned out hacienda. The voracious jungle vegetation seemed to be hungrily gobbling up what was left before their eyes. Still, the scene looked exactly as it had in the satellite photos. This was the place they were looking for, but it didn't seem to be any sort of viable military target.

Nothing stirred. The place was eerily, ghostly quiet.

Chief Johnston and Broughton disappeared around to the right of the clearing, staying close enough together to cover each other as they slipped through the foliage while they used the jungle as cover in case the ruins had eyes. Dumkowski and Martinelli moved to the left and disappeared from view. Cantrell slid to a spot a few yards to the right of Beaman, then stopped short just before slipping out of the trees. He propped his M-60 in the fork of a huge mahogany tree.

Beaman reached into his haversack and pulled out the binoculars he kept there. He didn't need them at this range, but they helped sort out the details. Being able to see even the smallest thing could sometimes make the difference between success and failure, even life and death. There was nothing obviously out of the ordinary on his first sweep of the clearing. Then something over near the ramshackle shed caught Beaman's eye. Something that didn't belong there. He focused all his attention in that direction, carefully seeking out every single item as he fine-tuned the focus on the binoculars.

Finally he saw what it was that had caught his attention, something far up in the trees behind the shed. Almost totally hidden in the roots of an orchid was a small video camera, looking out over the clearing. Somebody was interested in watching what was going on out here in the midst of all this desolation, interested enough to rig and carefully hide a video camera, set to scan a lonely clearing in the middle of the jungle. Odds were it was not some nature lover hoping to see a tapir heading for water down by the river.

Beaman exhaled. The chance was remote that the camera would spy his team as they slipped through the shadows. That's why they had not blundered out into the opening in the first place. No, the greater concern was over what other surveillance devices might be hidden around the abandoned ruins. Pressure detectors, motion sensors, laser beams; there were dozens of ways to observe unwanted and unwary guests. They would have to be even more careful from now on.

The presence of the surveillance camera did confirm one fact. This innocuous-looking clearing was likely to be just as strategic as advertised.

Beaman continued a slow, careful, tedious search around the area. As much as he wanted to charge the shack and see what secret it held, he knew it was time well spent to make sure there were no more surprises out there. He could not find another trace of recent human habitation. He trained the glasses back up in the tree just to make sure he hadn't imagined the video camera up there. He found the orchid again, resting in the crotch of two limbs. It was a pretty flower, with white and golden blooms.

Beaman smiled as he had an odd thought. Bet Ellen Ward could identify that orchid right off, by common and scientific name. She always seemed to know those kinds of things. She had given him a guided tour of her garden the last time she and Jon had invited him over for dinner.

He zoomed the binoculars in to maximum power as he propped against a tree to steady himself. He looked at the roots of the orchid. There was the inhuman black glass eye staring coldly back at him.

Beaman slithered backward deeper into the shadows, hidden from the searching lens of the camera. He pulled the satellite transceiver from his pack and flipped the switches to bring it to life. The little green LED blinked to life, telling him that the machine was talking to the JDIA command center in San Diego. As he waited, he thought, *Sure would be nice to have a job where all you had to do was sit back in a comfortable chair and listen out for some slob out in the jungle some place to check in. Eight hours of quiet, safe boredom, then home to a hot meal and a warm, dry bed.*

Ward had been one of the ones who told Bill Beaman that he was born to be a SEAL, that if the SEALs had not existed, they would have had to invent the service for the likes of him.

He grinned as he pushed the little earpiece into his ear and tugged the tiny boom microphone around to the side of his mouth. He began talking quietly.

"Command, this is team. We are in place at the ruins. Be aware that this place is wired with video monitoring. Over."

Beaman heard Bethea's voice in his ear.

"Roger, team. Anything else?"

"Negative so far. Scouting the perimeter now. It took a little longer to get here than planned."

"Understood. Bill, be very careful. We believe this might be de Santiago's development lab. No telling what kind of force he might have there to protect it. But we need to know what's inside."

Beaman reflexively glanced around himself as he spoke.

"John, we don't know if there is an 'inside' yet. All we've found so far is that 'candid camera.' What do you want us to do if there is an 'inside'?"

"Just like we briefed. Get inside; find out what's there. Grab whatever you can and get out."

"You want this place taken down?"

"Use your discretion. If you can do it, and it makes sense, take it out. But be advised, we don't have any other assets to hit it with. Don't put your team at risk."

Beaman grimaced. He dreaded hearing those words. "Use your discretion." That was one of the things he had found it necessary to learn about working with JDIA. No simple going in, locating a solid target, blowing it up, and getting back out. So often now, they worked in gray, ill-defined areas. The bur-

den of the decisions was on his shoulders once they had taken
a look at and fully assessed whatever it was that they found
when they got there.

"Thanks, John. Appreciate your vote of confidence," Beaman commented dryly. "Just make sure you have the ex-
traction choppers standing by. We're going to need them at
noon, local time. Tell 'em the LZ may be hot. I'll keep you
posted. Team, out."

Beaman removed the earpiece and was stowing the transceiver when the two flank scout teams slid on their bellies
back into the little makeshift command post.

"Didn't see a thing," Johnston whispered as he opened
and began chewing on an energy bar. "Nothing but damn
vines, branches, and snakes. Especially snakes. Snakes
everywhere."

Nothing frightened the chief. Nothing but snakes, that is.

Beaman motioned for Johnston to follow him as he crawled
back to the tree line.

"Chief, let me show you something." He pointed at the
camera beneath the orchid, high up in the tree. "See that?
Someone is very interested in keeping an eye on this place."

"Yeah, I see what you mean," Johnston grunted as he
squinted into his own binoculars. "Anything else?"

Beaman shook his head.

"Not that I could find. Now, all we have to do is get over to
that shack and check it out without that camera seeing us. Any
ideas?"

Johnston carefully gazed out over the clearing.

"No way to slip past it that I can see. We can't wait until
dark and it's probably infrared-fitted anyway. I vote we follow
the true SEAL tradition and break the bastard, use the old direct approach."

"Can Cantrell hit it?"

"Skipper, that kid can hit FDR's nose on a dime at a thousand yards with that M-60 of his. Shot like that will be a piece
of cake. I imagine the folks who are watching the screen—if
any of the sons of bitches are awake—are used to it going on

the fritz out here. Out in the jungle like this, it has to happen
all the time."

"Okay, let's make it happen. As soon as that thing is out,
though, we move to the shack in one big hurry. Who knows
what else they may have trained on this clearing. Then we'll
see what's inside and go from there. Cantrell and Martinelli
stay out here to give us cover."

It was a bold plan, but the only viable one if they hoped to
accomplish their mission. There could be trip wires, booby
traps, land mines planted amid the jungle growth between
them and the shack. And none of them had any idea what
might await them once they entered the dilapidated shed.
They could only hope the camera and the sheer remoteness of
the place were its only protection.

Johnston slipped over to Cantrell's post in the mahogany
tree. Beaman watched as Johnston pointed up into the trees.
Cantrell looked hard, squinted, checked the wind, measured
the distance with his practiced eye, then nodded. He flashed
an "okay" hand sign to Beaman, winked, and smiled.

Johnston gathered Broughton and Dumkowski and slowly
moved around to the right, spreading out so they were about
ten feet apart. In a few minutes, four SEALs were crouched
and ready to move across the clearing as soon as Cantrell
poked the eye out.

Beaman pointed to the camera and nodded to Cantrell. The
SEAL gunner took careful aim with his M-60 and squeezed
off a quick three-round burst. The 7.62mm NATO rounds
ripped through the humid jungle air, angling upward, then,
with the effect of drag and gravity, arcing back down to the
target exactly as the shooter had calculated. The first jacket
round smashed the camera lens and shattered the circuit
boards behind it before losing energy and embedding itself in
the rear case. It had accomplished the job already but the next
two rounds crushed what was left of the case and tumbled to
the jungle floor.

The parts of the surveillance device hit the ground. Bill
Beaman ran across the clearing to the shadows at the side of

the tumbled down shack. The other three men ran zigzag courses across the open ground and flopped down a few yards short of the door. So far, so good. There had been no one firing at them yet.

Beaman glanced over his shoulder and pointed at the shack's door. Three H&K machine pistols were aimed in that direction.

Beaman stood to one side and gave the door a kick. The one rusty hinge that held the thing upright snapped easily and it fell into the shed, landing flat on the dirt floor in a billow of powdery dust. Beaman followed it in, moving low and fast, looking all about in the half-darkness, his finger on the trigger and ready to fire. He slammed his body backward against the wall and almost brought the rickety structure down with the force.

Nothing.

The small room was empty except for spiderwebs, a couple of sticks of rotted furniture, and a lonely centipede that scurried through the dirt, trying to hide from the sunlight Beaman had let in.

There was nothing at all in this place to threaten a SEAL. Mixed with his relief, Beaman had to deal with the disappointment. They had jumped out of that airplane, climbed a mountain, swum through what his grandpappy would have called a "young Noah," and all for nothing.

The other three SEALs stepped into the shack, their guns poised, and joined Beaman. Johnston shrugged.

"Not much here to guard, Skipper."

Dumkowski added, "And not a damn thing to blow up!"

"Doesn't look much like it," Beaman said, still whispering, as if he didn't want to disturb the spiders. "But why would they have that camera . . ."

The floor between Beaman's feet began to move. He jumped back against the wall, his gun barrel aimed where a trapdoor was opening up. Johnston and Dumkowski leaped out the doorway they had just entered and rolled to either side, the barrels of their own H&Ks just visible.

Broughton had nowhere to go. He was caught at the back of the shed and could only crouch down in the shadows and hope whoever it was wouldn't look his way. He would have to shoot before the newcomer did, no questions asked. There would be no hesitation.

The floor lifted fully and hinged back. Fluorescent light glowed from the entrance. A man climbed clumsily up the steps. He was half asleep. He was muttering barely understandable profanities about monkeys and cameras as he stepped out into the shed. The man stopped in his tracks, startled by the shape in front of him, hidden by the dark shadows. With a grunt of surprise, he tried desperately to grab the rifle slung across his back.

Broughton rose slowly, keeping the muzzle of his machine pistol pointed directly between the eyes of the fearful man. He stopped his attempt to get his rifle around and simply raised his hands, pleading for mercy. A dark, wet stain slowly bloomed on the front of his dirt-smudged khaki pants.

Beaman grabbed the rifle from behind and roughly ripped it off the guard, frisked him quickly for sidearms or a knife, then shoved the now-unarmed man into the far corner. The terrified man tripped and fell flat on his face in the dirt, raising his own cloud of dust. Dumkowski put his knee in the middle of the guard's back, grabbed his arms and tied them and his feet tightly, then gagged him to stop any attempt at a yelled warning to his compatriots. The man was crying and whimpering into the dust, any fight scared out of him.

At the nod from Beaman, Johnston pulled the pin on a flash grenade and tossed it down the stairway. An awful whoomph and a burst of bright, white light erupted back up the well. The four SEALs leaped down the steps before the noise had stopped reverberating or the smoke had begun to clear.

They found a shattered laboratory. The place was strewn with broken glass, damaged equipment, and unidentified liquids that dripped off bench tops onto the floor. Small fires burned in several spots, ignited by the grenade. Smoke and dust hung thickly in the cool air of the space. Three men dressed in lab coats, stunned by the concussion of the grenade, were slowly attempting to pick themselves up. They shook the fragments of glass and insulation and ceiling tile from their clothing and hair. One man in uniform khakis lay in a crumpled heap at the foot of the ladder. One leg was cocked at an odd angle and blood oozed from numerous wounds. He did not move.

Johnston dragged the dead guard out of the way, making sure their escape would not be hindered. The other SEALs tossed the dazed scientists back onto the floor and tied them securely. They offered no resistance. The attack team looked around them for any other signs of life, ears tuned for the sound of more guards that might be coming from farther back in a sizable underground bunker. Or for gunfire from above that might signal trouble approaching from the jungle.

Beaman yelled up the stairs at Dumkowski, telling him to bring his own prisoner down and to guard all four. The SEAL rolled the guard down the stairs like a barrel and took station where he could see them all. He was rewarded with four sets of wide, frightened eyes staring back at him.

Beaman led the other two team members farther into the underground compound. Rooms stretched into more rooms as they explored the amazingly large space, more labs, dorm rooms, even a rough rec room with a pool table and a bar stocked mostly with Russian vodka. Nothing showed above ground. Down here there was a fully outfitted research facility with all the comforts and capabilities a team of biochemists would seem to need. As they pushed through, the place was completely empty and silent now.

"There has to be more people here than the two guards and the guys in the lab coats," Beaman said.

He started to cautiously work his way around the edge of a doorway. He caught a flash of motion out of the corner of his eye. Without thought or hesitation he instinctively dived to the ground, shouting out a warning to his following team. The un-

mistakable staccato roar of an AK-47 on full automatic reverberated in the hallway. Chewed-up cement chips spattered
down on him as the wall next to where his head had just been
exploded from the impact of bullets.

Beaman rolled and fired several bursts down the corridor,
aiming as best he could at where he thought he had seen a
man's face in the near-darkness. From behind him, Johnston
tossed another grenade down the hall and yelled, "Fire in the
hole!" Beaman covered his head. The grenade burst rocked
the walls and blew a blinding swirl of dust and debris out toward the SEALs.

Beaman was hidden by rubble that fell from the ceiling.
Johnston grabbed him by his heels and pulled him back into
what little protection the wall of the hallway offered.

"You okay, Skipper?"

Beaman coughed and spat and wiped the dust and splatters
of blood from his face.

"Yeah, Chief. That was too close." When he noticed Johnston staring at him, at the blood he was smearing away, he
said, "Not mine."

Broughton went through the door low and fast, his H&K
sweeping around the room like a cobra ready to strike. Johnston followed a fraction of a second later. The room had evidently been the security office until minutes ago. The remains
of a smashed video monitor and two shattered radio trans-
ceivers were strewn about on the concrete floor. A rack with
four more AK-47s lay on the floor to the left of the table.
Three broken armchairs made up the only other furniture in
the room. The shooter lay in a heap against the far wall,
slammed back against a broken table by a considerable force.

Broughton prodded the corpse with his foot, rolling him
over so he was faceup. He had four bullet holes forming a
small neat circle in his forehead.

"Guess he thinks not giving up was a bad idea now," Broughton muttered.

Beaman looked around for more rooms or any kind of escape hatch. There was nothing left to explore. A small galley, a bunkroom, a library, and this command center they had just destroyed seemed to complete all the rooms leading off from the lab. De Santiago had assumed there was little chance this place would be located, much less disturbed. Its remote location, the surveillance equipment, the secrecy were all the protection this place needed. Only three guards? No back door out?

The arrogance made Beaman angry. He was aware they were deep in rebel-controlled territory. Who knew what kind of hell might descend on them once their presence here was known? And the noise of the first grenade had announced that loud and clear.

The three SEALs returned to the shattered lab. They made sure no one was hiding from them in a crevice or closet somewhere. The fires they had started with the first grenade had burnt themselves out now. The room was still filled with choking, thick smoke. Dumkowski held his weapon on the four prisoners who now struggled against their bonds. He had lined them up neatly and had them sitting on the floor, leaning against a lab bench. Now that they had gotten some of their senses back, they had begun to protest their treatment.

Beaman stepped in front of the four and growled, "All right, start talking. Which one of you bastards is going to tell us what's going on here?"

The towering figures of four heavily armed SEALs stepped menacingly closer, shoving a weapon in the face of each captive. They stopped squirming and tried to crawl beneath the bench.

Two of them muttered in some strange, guttural language. The other one, a mousy little guy with a decidedly Southern accent, began talking rapidly, his voice trembling but the words pouring out defiantly.

"Now, you looka here. You're American soldiers, aren't you? I'm an American citizen and you have no right to come in here and try to kill me or hold me against my will. I'm not breaking any laws, and even if I was, you have no jurisdiction here. I have my rights. Now, get me outta here. I wanna see a lawyer. Or somebody from the American embassy."

Beaman glared at him as he let him have his say. When the SEAL commander did speak, everyone in the room felt a chill from the tone of his voice, even as he mimicked the man's dialect. And the other two men in lab coats seemed to sense what he was saying even if they couldn't understand his words.

"No you looka here, Gomer Pyle. You're a damned long way from the US of A right now. Ain't no lawyer gonna be any help gittin' your miserable ass outta here. In about three minutes, me and my buddies here are gonna set off enough C-4 explosives to send fragments of this place all the way to Bogotá. You don't want to be right here for an up-close view of the fireworks, you'd better start singin' a tune I wanna hear."

With the last sentence, Beaman placed the snout of his pistol beneath the American's nose and gave it a hard, rude shove. There was the smell of excrement and all the color left the American's face. With a quick glance at the other captives, he bleated out, "It's all on that laptop computer, the one over by the wall. Everything's on it. All our work."

Martinelli stuck his head through the trapdoor.

"Hey, Skipper. We got company coming!" he hollered. "Looks like a whole bunch coming over the ridge on horseback, moving pretty quick."

Johnston looked over at Beaman.

"That ain't the cavalry coming to our rescue, boss. We better get moving."

Beaman yelled up at Dumkowski.

"Call and get the choppers in here quick as they can. We'll extract from the clearing."

"Cantrell's talking to 'em now. We sort of figured that's what we'd have to do. They say fifteen minutes. It's gonna be real close. I get the impression those Colombian pilots ain't anxious to come in to a hot LZ."

Beaman shrugged as if to say "Tough!" and yanked the little American to his feet, shoving him toward the ladder.

"You speak their language, Gomer?"

"Some."

"Then tell them they better go whatever direction we push them or they'll make real good bullet catchers for us up there."

The American said something that made the other captives' eyes go big.

Johnston was pulling two small packages from his backpack.

"We don't have enough C-4 to blow a place this big, but it'll mess it up enough they won't be able to use it for a long, long time. Add the rest of our grenades and it'll make a nice enough boom."

Dumkowski and Broughton set the charges and timers as Beaman and Johnston pushed the prisoners up the ladder. Beaman tucked the laptop computer into his pack, just in case the American was telling the truth. He leaped up the ladder.

The group ran out of the shed into the bright midmorning sunshine. They could see two H-60s clear the ridge to the west, heading their way. To the north, a group of thirty or so riders were barreling down the slopes as well. Coming their way in one big hurry. They would all converge at the clearing at about the same time.

"Cantrell, give them a few bursts with that M-60," Beaman yelled. "These squirt guns of ours won't reach up there."

Cantrell braced the machine gun against a tree and squeezed off several three-round bursts. Two riders at the front of the bunch fell from their horses as if yanked by wires. The rest pulled up their mounts and dove for cover. Cantrell fired more bursts as targets came into view. The riders scrambled for a place to hide. Several began firing back, their rounds kicking up dirt at the edge of the clearing.

Martinelli guided the H-60s directly down to the clearing, not a hundred feet out of range from where the rebel bullets were landing. They flared out and barely touched the ground as Beaman's team shoved the prisoners in and jumped in behind. Cantrell was the last man to leap into a waiting bird. The first of the rebels were back up on their feet and moving their way, firing again. Their shots made distinctive pinging sounds against the fuselage of the choppers.

Cantrell fired back from the doorway, chopping the legs out from under a couple of the rebels. The helicopter lifted away. He didn't let up until the bird had turned and churned away toward the south.

They were too far away and the chopper rotors were making too much noise for them to hear the boom when Juan de Santiago's vaunted additive lab blew, sending fragments of the rough shed that had covered it a good fifty feet in the air.

The rebels continued firing futilely at the helicopters after they had disappeared over the ridge.

31

JON WARD STUCK HIS HEAD INTO THE SONAR SHACK. THE DIM, BLUE fluorescent light barely illuminated the four men huddled in the closetlike space. Three of them sat in front of large CRT screens, intently watching the information displayed on them. The uninitiated would see nothing more than shimmering dots and squiggles, an interesting enough show but totally meaningless to anyone who was not an expert in interpreting the underwater noises detected by *Spadefish*'s sonar sensors. These men were experts.

Behind the three, Master Chief Mendoza sat on a tall stool, looking over their shoulders. He watched all three screens and listened to the sounds of the sea outside through his headset. He was the conductor, orchestrating every move his three sonar men made. He had over twenty years of listening and learning about the symphony of sounds in the sea, and especially the machines that caused the man-made noises. It seemed to Ward that Mendoza could eavesdrop on another boat and tell what it was going to do even before the boat had a chance to do it.

He was holding the earpieces tightly against his head, listening with deep concentration while staring at the middle sonar screen.

"What's he doing, Master Chief?"

Mendoza scowled in Ward's direction, annoyed at being disturbed while performing such a tedious chore. When he saw it was Ward standing there, he raised a finger to tell the skipper to wait for a second. He listened for several more seconds and nodded, confirming some mental evaluation he had made. He pushed one of the earpieces back off his ear.

"Damned if I know what he's doing, Skipper. He just stopped. We're still a hundred miles from the straits. No other contacts except those fishermen over at two-one-zero and they're at least twenty thousand yards away." Mendoza shrugged. "No reason I know of to stop way out here."

"Anything else?"

"Yeah, I just started to pick up some auxiliaries. That's what I was listening to when you came barging in."

Ward stepped over to have his own look at the center sonar display. Mendoza was very good, but no one got to command one of these boats without being pretty damned good, too. The operator handed Ward his headset.

"Here, Skipper. Analog broadband. It's on the bearing for that merch."

Ward held the earpiece to his head and listened to the noise of the ocean. He could hear the distinctive rising and falling tones of killer whales singing somewhere off in the distance. There was the unmistakable snapping of shrimp somewhere in that same direction. But through the background noise, the biologics of the ocean, he could also hear what sounded like water rushing from a pipe and the rotating beat of some kind of mechanical device. He listened harder. Whatever it was, it seemed to be a little out of balance. He could hear the frequency rise and fall a bit with each rotation.

"Sounds like he might be flooding down. I hear water. He has a pump running. The impeller bearing is rubbing. He needs to grease it before it seizes up on him."

Mendoza grinned.

"You haven't lost your ear, Skipper. Yep, that pump only has a few more hours to go and that's about all she wrote. What has me stumped are the chains. Hear them, real faint-like?"

Ward listened again, even more intently, if that were possible. He could barely make out the rattle. Or maybe he was only imagining it. It was so faint he couldn't be sure.

"Okay, Master Chief. I hear it, I think. Keep listening. We're going in closer and take a look."

Ward stepped out of the sonar shack, back in to the brightly lit passageway that led past his stateroom and into the control room. Joe Glass and Ed Beasley stood together on the periscope stand, staring attentively at the sonar repeater. Chris Durgan sat in front of the fire control computer, tweaking the dials, playing with the data, always watching every move the *Helena K* made.

"What you think, XO?" Ward asked Glass.

Glass looked up, startled by the skipper's sudden appearance.

"We were just getting ready to call you. You're supposed to be asleep. Looks like our friend just stopped." Glass stepped over to the plot table. The quartermaster was plotting *Spade-fish*'s position and their best guess of *Helena K*'s. The plot showed them at the mouth of the Straits of Juan de Fuca, the waterway that led to Puget Sound, Seattle, and Vancouver, British Columbia. They were right in the center of an area marked as fishing grounds. "May be time for him to send his little friend ashore if he really has one on board. He's in about the perfect place, in the middle of these fishing grounds, so he's away from other traffic. And he's far enough from Port Angeles harbor traffic control so they won't be tracking him on radar yet."

Ward stared at the chart and nodded agreement.

"Yep, perfect place. Time for us to get to work. Let's go take a look." Ward looked over his shoulder and ordered, "Officer of the Deck, proceed to periscope depth. Man battle stations silently."

Beasley reached into the overhead and snapped the scope control ring to the raised position. He squatted and waited as the greased shaft rose out of the scope well. When the control section emerged, he popped the black handles down, stuck his right eye to the eyepiece and slowly began walking a tight circle. Without moving his eye from the scope, he called out, "Diving Officer, make your depth six-four feet."

Chief Laskowski answered, "Make my depth six-four feet, aye," and turned, directing Cortez and MacNaughton while they brought *Spadefish* smoothly up from the depths.

"Chief of the Watch, man battle stations silently," Beasley called to Chief Lyman.

Lyman reached over to his left to a chrome-plated switch labeled "Emergency DC Lights" and flicked the switch on and off three times. Ward heard the soft pounding of feet as men rushed to their battle stations in response to the flashing lights. When submarine sonars became sensitive enough to hear the blast of the general alarm on another boat, submariners invented the silent method to warn the crew quietly. The reason for manning silently here wasn't to keep from alerting the *Helena K*. If the merch even had sonar, they likely would not be using it. Ward simply didn't want to disturb his people who were driving the sub up to periscope depth.

Ward watched the video monitor as it showed him an image of what Earl Beasley was seeing through the scope. The deep blue slowly lightened to turquoise as the sub came up. There were a few quick flashes of white as the scope broke the surface; then Ward was looking at the stern of the *Helena K*, no more than six thousand yards away. There was no telltale white wake behind her, no frothing, churning white water under her high stern. *Helena K*'s screw was not turning. She was dead in the water, not making way. There wasn't anyone on deck.

"Earl, come around to course zero-one-seven," Ward said quietly. "I want to slip up along her starboard side and see if there's anyone on the bridge or the main deck." The sub eased forward until Ward could see the bridge of the rusty freighter. "Earl, shift to twenty-four power."

Beasley snapped the periscope optics to its highest power. The view changed. Ward was looking into the door of the deckhouse, almost as if he was standing on *Helena K*'s bridge wing. It looked empty. There wasn't anyone there. The main deck was equally empty. The thing was all but a ghost ship.

Ward was satisfied that whatever was happening on the drug smuggler, it was happening below decks, down where they couldn't see.

"All right, Earl. I've seen enough. Let's drop down to one-two-zero feet." As the scope dropped below the surface, Ward stepped over to the plot table. Joe Glass stood there, intently studying the situation. Ward put his hand on Glass's shoulder. "What do you recommend, XO?"

Glass continued to stare at the plot.

"Skipper, he's got to be deploying that mini-sub. I can't imagine any other reason he'd be sitting out here like this. We should get in close and set up to trail that sucker. Something tells me he'll either be on a battery or maybe one of those new air-independent systems. That'll make him real quiet. We need to be close to make sure we find him right away when he gets launched. Otherwise, we're out of luck."

Ward chewed on his lip for a few seconds, lost in thought.

"The towed array is useless in this shallow water. Too much chance of snagging it on the bottom. With all the other traffic around here, passive tracking would be just about impossible." Ward paused for a long second before continuing. "I'm thinking maybe this is a place to use active sonar. He's not going to have an intercept receiver. As long as he doesn't hear the pings through the hull, we can keep tabs on him and he'll never know we're tailing him."

"But we still need to stay close, and to keep the transmit power down," Glass commented. "Even if that guy doesn't hear it, too much power will just blank everything with all the biologics this close to shore."

Ward nodded agreement.

"Okay, XO. Get *Spadefish* in a thousand yards astern of that rust bucket. I'm going to sonar and talk to Master Chief Mendoza."

Philippe Zurko reluctantly followed Rudi Sergiovski down the metal ladder through the little round hatch and into the *Zibrus*. The fat, obnoxious Russian plopped into the pilot's seat and plugged his headset into the communications system. Zurko was left to fend for himself, ignored by Sergiovski, as the pilot flipped switches, slowly bringing the little boat to life.

Zurko stowed his satchel and watched from a stool at the rear of the cramped space. He already felt the walls pressing in around him and they weren't even out of the boat and submerged yet. Only the thought of *El Jefe*'s anger if this mission failed gave him the impetus to crawl back into this fetid crypt once again. The ride out to meet the *Helena K* had been bad enough, at the very edge of his endurance. This trip would be over twice as long, each way. And they were sneaking into America, right past one of that country's most protected submarine bases. Even if they made the delivery successfully, they would have to come all the way back out to rendezvous with the *Helena K* once more, pick up Sui's heroin, and do the whole thing over again.

If they were found out anywhere along the route, they would surely be sunk. He would drown in this awful thing. But even that prospect was less frightful than facing the wrath of Juan de Santiago.

Sergiovski spoke into the headset.

"Captain Novstad, *Zibrus* is ready. Open the doors."

"Doors opening," Serge Novstad answered. "We will meet you at the rendezvous in five days. Good luck, Captain Sergiovski."

The doors in the bottom of the freighter opened, releasing the *Zibrus* to the sea. Sergiovski opened the vents for the mini-sub's ballast tanks, causing it to sink out of the bottom of the ship.

Zurko couldn't suppress a shiver as he saw the water lap up and over the small, thick viewing ports on the side of the little sub's sail. He stared while the picture changed from the black sides of the freighter's hold to the deep turquoise of the open sea.

"Philippe, my friend, we will sink to fifty meters and drive into the American harbor as boldly as we please!" Sergiovski shouted. "The auto pilot will drive us straight and true for the next several hours. Time for some vodka to celebrate the beginning of our little voyage!"

Philippe Zurko gladly took the offered drink, downed it in one gulp, and handed the cup back for another belt of courage.

A thousand yards behind the *Zibrus*, Ward stood in the sonar room next to Mendoza, listening to the mini-submarine's noises on a headset.

"Sounds like they're under way. XO was right. That sucker sure is quiet."

Mendoza nodded.

"Yep, it'll be hard to keep a bead on him when we get in the middle of the inshore traffic. We better map out all the noises this guy makes. When do you want to start active track?"

Ward answered, "Let's start now. I want to get his course and speed down pat, then move in closer."

Mendoza nodded and leaned over to talk to one of the sonar men. The operator began pushing a series of buttons arrayed around the screen. The screen picture changed to show a small sector of a circle and a couple of line graphs.

"Ready to go active, four millisecond, low-power twelve-degree sector pulse," Mendoza announced.

Ward nodded, his eyes focused on the screen.

"Go active."

The operator pushed a button. Ward heard the briefest

click. A curved trace moved up the sector on the screen. A blip appeared behind the trace and a peak appeared on the line graphs. The operator shouted, "I have a positive return! Range one-one hundred yards, bearing zero-one-three."

"Good, that's the bearing we hold the mini-sub on. Master Chief, let me know when you're ready to move closer. I figure we need to be about five hundred yards astern of this sucker when we get in the straits or we'll lose him in the clutter for sure."

"That ought to give us a little margin, Skipper," Mendoza commented. "But when we surface, active is going to get real hard. All that surface return will screw it up and I don't hold a lot of hope for passive broadband either."

"Well, Master Chief," Ward chuckled dryly. "That's why they pay me the big bucks. We aren't going to surface. We're going to run submerged until we run out of water."

Ward turned and headed for control. Mendoza swallowed hard as he watched him go.

A loud buzzer reverberated around inside the steel walls of the tiny space. Sergiovski roused himself, stretched, farted, and shoved the vodka bottle aside. He leaned forward and tried to read the autopilot screen through bleary eyes.

"*Da*, we are making good time," he rumbled, then belched deeply. "We are abreast of Cape Flattery. Philippe, my friend, we are now in the Straits of Juan de Fuca. We are going to drive right down the center of the traffic separation scheme."

The Russian turned a small knob on the control panel and watched as the digital readout right above skewed around to read "one-one-zero." He was steering the mini-sub to drive right down the median between the inbound and outbound lanes of the maritime superhighway that reached into Vancouver, Seattle, and Tacoma. This was one of the busiest ports in the world. The huge radar at Port Angeles, Washington, on the southern shore of the strait watched the comings and goings of ships steaming through the ten-mile-wide waterway. Controllers there directed the ships, spacing them out safely in their lanes, much like air traffic controllers.

"*Bueno,*" the Colombian said without conviction.

"Philippe, if you are concerned about the Americans, you can stand against that bulkhead," Sergiovski said with a crooked grin, pointing to his left. "You will be in Canada there. I'll sit over here in the United States."

The *Zibrus* cruised three hundred feet below the steel-gray waters of the broad strait even as the daily commerce of the world steamed overhead, oblivious of their presence.

Sergiovski yawned and Zurko could smell his foul breath.

"We have eight hours until our next turn. I'm going to take a nap."

Within seconds the fat Russian was once again snoring peacefully.

Zurko waited fifteen more minutes, watching the slobbering fool sleep. Finally he was satisfied Sergiovski would not likely rouse from his slumber. He picked up his little satchel and slipped through the hatch at the rear of the control room and entered the cargo bay. He opened the satchel and carefully removed the contents. Taking the first kilo package of cocaine, he inserted the hypodermic needle and injected a clear liquid.

Zurko calculated it would take four hours to dose all the coke with the extra additive. There should be plenty of time. The Russian bastard was sleeping the sleep of the dead. Still, he kept an ear cocked for the awful buzzing of the man's snores as he did his leader's bidding.

Five hundred yards behind the *Zibrus* and fifty feet deeper, *Spadefish* relentlessly followed her prey.

"You still getting good active?" Glass asked Mendoza over the sound-powered phone.

Glass was staring intently at the lines drawn on the chart in front of him as he waited for the reply. Dave Kuhn was busily drawing new lines and scribbling notes on the chart, recording every move the mini-sub made. Mendoza was looking at a screen that showed several line graphs slowly building in height.

"Yeah, XO. Still getting solid returns. We've been picking up a couple of good narrow band lines on the conformal array, too. LOFAR on one gives a blade rate for five knots. That equates to your solution, doesn't it?"

The conformal array was a series of sonar hydrophones mounted in a horseshoe shape around *Spadefish*'s bow, conforming to its rounded shape. The array was especially designed to detect discrete frequency signals, particularly those coming from propulsion equipment. Its results confirmed they were still tracking the same bogey, the target they suspected was a mini-sub launched from the *Helena K*.

"Five knots, course one-one-zero. Been doing that all the way in." Glass leaned over Kuhn's shoulder and looked at the chart. "He should be turning to the south-south-east, course about one-six-five in about ten minutes if he is going to stay in the middle of the separation scheme. Otherwise he's going to run into a twenty-fathom shoal in about three miles."

Mendoza pushed the earpiece hard against his head. He had just detected a noise there that he hadn't heard before, a noise that his instincts told him shouldn't have been there at all.

He grabbed the 21MC microphone and yelled, "Conn, Sonar! Chain rattle dead ahead and close! Come hard right, now!"

Earl Beasley jumped up, startled. He had been watching the sonar repeater as its waterfall display showed the varying sounds of the straits. The mini-sub painted a thin but distinct white line down the screen. Then he saw a couple of much brighter white dots show up right below the little icon for *Spadefish*'s course. Something new and loud lay dead ahead.

He yelled, "Helm, right full rudder! Steady course one-six zero! All stop!" Only then did he jump over to the chart table. "What the hell is that?"

Kuhn looked perplexed.

"Only thing nearby is the turn buoy for heading into Victoria Harbor. They must have moved the damn thing. We should be a couple of hundred yards south of it."

"Well, we ain't! We damn near hit it! That would've ruined our entire day," Beasley snorted as he slowly calmed down.

"Conn, Sonar. Report loss of contact on the mini-sub. We lost him when we came around. Don't hold him on any sensors. Commencing search."

Joe Glass felt his stomach sink. Jon Ward dropped his head for a moment.

The sonar team began the laborious process of trying to again find the quiet little mini-sub in the busy, noisy waters of the straits. It was like trying to locate the squeaky chair at a rock concert. Ward steered *Spadefish* around the confined waters while Mendoza and his team tried every trick they knew to make the swirling, noisy waters reveal the mini-sub once again.

Nothing worked. It seemed to have just disappeared.

After an hour's fruitless searching, Mendoza finally was willing to concede defeat.

"Skipper, I'm sorry. We just can't find it. He could be anywhere in a ten-mile circle by now."

Ward wearily ran his hand through his hair. He wasn't ready to give up yet. They had come too far to quit now. He stared pointedly at the charts before him. Finally, rubbing the two-day bristle on his chin, his face broke into an odd smile. Joe Glass looked at him questioningly.

Ward jabbed his index finger on a spot on the chart.

"Nav, broach to the surface, go to a full bell, and get here to this point as quickly as you can. Then get back down to a hundred and fifty feet."

Glass looked over the skipper's shoulder at the place where Ward was pointing. One leg of the strait narrowed into the Admiralty Passage between Port Townsend and Whidbey Island. The deep water was only two miles wide there. If the mini-sub came that way, *Spadefish* would have an easier time of finding it. But life wasn't quite that simple. That was a very big "if."

"Aren't you taking a chance?" Glass questioned. "There are

at least a dozen ways he could be heading. He could even be turning in to one of the channels to the north. He could be making for the Haro Straits, San Juan Channel, or Rosario Straits, trying to get to any of a thousand islands. Or he could even just be taking the back way around Whidbey Island."

Ward felt the sub lurch to the surface and accelerate as he answered.

"It's a risk all right. But, Joe, we have to try something besides just sitting here and hoping they sail by and tap on our hatch. I don't think they'd go to all this effort to smuggle coke into Canada. They'd still have to get it into the U.S. somehow. I'm betting they want to get to a nice quiet place inside Puget Sound to offload. We just need to find where." Ward stepped over to the radio. "We might as well tell JDIA what's going on. We'll want Bethea to tell Puget Sound Traffic Control we're coming anyway."

"Tell him one other thing, Skipper."

"What's that?"

"Ask him to tell those bastards to make a little more noise."

Spadefish waited.

Midchannel Bank lay a few hundred yards to port. Admiralty Bay was a little over a mile away to starboard. The sub hovered just above the bottom with her sensitive bow-mounted sonars pointed to the northwest, the way the mini-sub would be coming if Jon Ward had guessed correctly. The channel was shallow, no more than twenty fathoms at some points between Point Wilson and Admiralty Head. The mini-sub would have to come shallow then drop back down into the deeper waters once it was here in the bay.

Ward hoped to hear it then. That is, if it was even coming this way.

Time was running out. They had been sitting here for three hours now, more than enough time for the target to have caught up with them. Had it gone some other way after all? Had it slipped past them without their hearing it? Was it even a mini-sub at all?

Ward was beginning to worry. They had come too far, worked and sweated too much to be defeated here. Even if the mini-sub showed up again, it was going to be hairy. There wasn't any other way to track this guy except with *Spadefish* and her active sonar. There was no use in their going to the surface and banging away. The pings would just be reflected away from the target. That meant staying submerged, down in the same medium where the target was operating. If the min-sub went much farther down the Sound, it would get very tight. Ward knew the water was plenty deep enough, but the steep vertical walls closed in quickly to a very narrow slot.

Mendoza's voice boomed over the 21MC.

"Conn, sonar. We're picking up tonals on the conformal array. We've got our boy back! Bearing three-five-one."

Ward wiped the sweat from his forehead and took a sip of coffee. Damn stuff was cold but he didn't mind one bit.

"Okay, we're back in business. We'll let him generate past us then slip in behind him. Watch the water depth from here on out. It gets shallow and the channel gets narrower. Nav, launch the slot buoy."

Quietly, the old boat moved out into the center of the channel. A small red cylinder floated up to the surface behind it. When the cylinder reached the surface, a thin antenna popped up and a coded radio message bounced off the P-3 airplane that circled overhead, letting them know that the hunt was on again.

The strange little convoy moved south down the Admiralty Inlet Channel, past the entrance to the Hood Canal, past Useless Bay, and on into Puget Sound. Here the channel deepened considerably, down to over a hundred fathoms. *Spadefish* followed the mini-sub as it sank deep into the dark, cold water. The bustling city of Seattle was only a mile to their port and the lush green hills of Bainbridge Island were a mile to starboard. Had they been on the surface, they could have waved at the tourists in the Space Needle.

There was no time for waving and precious little for breathing. Putting the big sub into such a narrow, granite-lined channel was a treacherous operation.

And it had only just begun.

32

JUAN DE SANTIAGO SLAMMED HIS FIST DOWN ON THE DESK IN FRONT of him with painful force. His face was purple with rage.

"Damn that big *Norteamericano*! He has thwarted me for the last time!"

Guzmán backed further into the corner of the small office, trying to blend in and hide among the bookcases and furniture. He had dreaded telling de Santiago of the destruction of the laboratory, of the escape of the American SEAL team, of the death of Jorge Ortiez and the capture of his well-paid scientists. But there was no one else so he had done his duty.

Margarita Alvarado stood behind El Jefe, kneading the taut muscles of his shoulders.

"Calm yourself, *mi amor*," she sweetly implored. "Such rage will certainly cause a heart attack. Just one *Norteamericano* cannot stop a revolution so powerful as yours."

De Santiago shrugged her hands away brusquely.

"Leave me alone, woman. You don't understand. This bastard has cost me . . . has cost my people . . . billions of pesos. He must be eliminated!"

He stood and turned toward the window, almost knocking her down with the back of his chair. The small frame of glass looked out across the courtyard to the stables. On beyond, he could just make out the tops of the mountains over the stable roof, out there where they tried to hide from him in the clouds. Several of his soldiers were in the courtyard below, cleaning weapons, doing chores, or simply lounging in the morning sunshine, awaiting the command of their leader to go and fight a battle for the revolution.

The view out his window was lost on de Santiago. As his anger cooled, he was quickly deep in thought.

Finally he turned and shouted "Guzmán!" as if he had forgotten that the man was right there in the room with him.

"*Sí*, El Jefe."

"This meeting with El Presidente you have mentioned to me? The report says the *Norteamericano* is going to meet with him Thursday afternoon to report on the mission that destroyed our lab?"

"*Sí*, El Jefe."

De Santiago grunted.

"Good, that gives us three days to get ready for a moment that will be written about in the history books of our country for generations to come. Gather a hundred of our best men. We will rid our homeland of two vermin at once and finally return our country to the people." He smiled smugly, satisfied with his sudden momentous decision. "We should have removed Guitteriz the instant his presence became more than a minor bother to us. Now, with the help of the gringos and the blood money of the *Americanos*, he has become intolerable. And the soldier? I welcome the opportunity to show him how powerful the people are in our country when their cause is just. He will soon see what a fine soldier El Jefe is!"

De Santiago excitedly outlined his rudimentary plan to Guzmán. Neither man noticed Margarita Alvarado quietly slip from the room. She had heard all she needed to hear.

It was time for El Falcone to rise from the dead and send one more warning.

"Where's the bastard going, Skipper?"

Dave Kuhn had been sweating over these charts for almost twenty-four hours now. The ordeal was starting to show on his face, in the break in his voice.

Ward glanced around the control room. Kuhn wasn't the only one nearing exhaustion. They were all beaten down by the constant crushing tension. Ward wasn't sure how much longer his crew could hold up under this strain before someone made a mistake. And even the smallest mistake in such close quarters could be tragic.

The mini-sub had led them far into Puget Sound. The sides of the deep, narrow channel were nearly vertical granite walls. There would be no give there if they strayed even slightly.

"Don't know, Dave," Ward answered. "He's running out of choices, so I expect we'll find out soon."

Chris Durgan looked up from his computer screen.

"Possible contact zig. Solution tracking off."

"Conn, sonar. Contact is changing course. He's coming right," Mendoza sang.

"Conn, aye," Glass answered, loud enough for everyone in the control room to hear him. "Expected maneuver. He's coming around to head down the Maury Island reach toward Tacoma. He should steady up on course two-four-zero."

Glass stepped over to stand beside Ward. Together they looked at the chart. Finally, it was Glass who spoke.

"Skipper, if he heads through the Tacoma Narrows, we're screwed."

"Why's that, XO? Water's deep enough. I know it looks a little narrow, but so what? We've come this far."

"XO, new solution," Durgan called out. "Range six-one-zero yards, course two-four-four, speed five."

Glass reached over and patted Durgan on the shoulder. The new course the mini-sub was taking was exactly what he expected.

"XO, we'll keep following this sleaze until he crawls into a hole or we run out of water," Ward said quietly. Then, in almost a whisper, he added, "I can't wait to find out which happens first."

Glass nodded and went back to work.

The mini-sub led them through the Dalco Passage to the west, then turned south again, entering the Tacoma Narrows.

The deep water of the narrows was only a few hundred yards wide, and only thirty fathoms deep at that. It made a slow curving arc, first to the southeast, then around to the southwest before opening into a myriad of coves, inlets and bays.

The granite walls seemed to close in on them as Ward brought his boat slowly and carefully around the curve of the Narrows. They were cruising a hundred feet under the surface now.

Only forty-five feet of water separated the top of *Spadefish*'s sail from the afternoon sunshine. Some of the tankers that plied these waters drew more than ninety feet.

There was only forty feet of murky black water between her keel and the hard, unyielding, rock bottom of the Narrows.

Rudi Sergiovski called out happily to Philippe Zurko.

"We're almost there. I'm taking a shortcut up through the Hale Passage. See it there on the chart, between Fox Island and Fosdick Point?"

Zurko shook himself awake. He had been huddled uncomfortably in the back corner of the cramped space, dozing off, resting from the tedious task of dosing all the bags of cocaine with the additive. He glanced at the chart with no attempt at showing interest.

"A little shallow, isn't it?"

Sergiovski nodded.

"*Da*, it is. We will use the caterpillar tracks. This way will save us an hour and we will arrive just after darkness." He reached over and flipped a switch. "Stopping the engines. Pull that lever when I tell you to," he said, pointing to a little blue handle a few feet forward of where Zurko sat.

He flooded a little water into the mini-sub so that it sank to the bottom while it slowed its forward progress. It settled down onto the floor of the sound. Sergiovski turned on a video camera mounted on the bow that gave him a picture of where they were going. The light filtering down through the cloudy water was just enough to enable him to see a few feet ahead.

He motioned to Zurko, and the Colombian pulled the lever as instructed. The caterpillar tracks started to turn. The little sub crawled forward through the shallow water of the passage, creeping its way closer and closer to its rendezvous.

"I don't know what happened, Skipper," Mendoza explained. "One minute we had solid contact, the next he was gone. No sonals, no broadband, and no active return. He just disappeared."

Ward slammed his fist onto the table. The pencils and coffee cups jumped and clattered.

"Damn it! We were so close! There's no room here to search for him, that's for sure. I guess it's time for us to turn this over to someone else." He turned to Earl Beasley and ordered, "Nav, surface the ship. Let's head back for open water before we get her stuck up to her ass in mud."

"XO, get on the horn and tell JDIA we lost them." The burning sensation Jon Ward had been feeling in the pit of his stomach had just grown noticeably worse.

The *Zibrus* crawled through the muck around the north end of Fox Island, hidden in water too shallow for *Spadefish* to enter, even if she stayed completely on the surface. With their eyes looking ahead, straining to see where they were headed, neither man on the mini-sub saw the huge black shape rise to the surface several miles behind them and slowly steam back in the direction from which they had just come.

Jason Rashad restlessly paced the length of the pier. Where was that damn sub? Carlos had said it would be here tonight. Sometime tonight. No other details. Well, now it was already two hours after sunset and the son of a bitch had not popped its ass out of the drink yet. Maybe they had stopped for a siesta.

The night was being wasted.

The low, misty clouds blowing through alternately hid and revealed the star-studded sky from him. The cool breeze and the glorious view of pine forest and water were wasted on the drug pusher, though. He was here for a purpose, and the quicker he got the job done and got back to Seattle, the better he liked it.

He pulled a smoke from his pocket and lit it. The flare of the flame from his solid gold Dunhill lighter blinded him so that he didn't see the ripple start a few yards out on the glass-smooth inlet. The tiny sail of the *Zibrus* was already above the water before he noticed it, and even then, he wasn't sure he was seeing what he was seeing.

"Jesus!"

With its black skin, the thing looked almost alive, like some tubby primordial beast emerging from the depths. Slowly, the mini-sub slid alongside the pier, its sail barely coming to the level of the pier deck. At his signal, two of Rashad's hired thugs jumped down onto the slick, rounded deck of the sub, as if to try to bulldog the creature into submission. One promptly slid off the side, yelping painfully as he splashed into the cold water. The other man managed to hold on to the sub's skin and slip lines over the cleats, securing *Zibrus* to the pier. He threw his comrade a line and pulled him from the water.

The hatch popped open and Philippe Zurko jumped out, sucking in all the cool, damp air as he could manage.

"Who is in charge here?" he finally demanded of the man who was struggling to pull the other from the drink. "We must get to work and unload quickly."

Rashad stepped to the edge of the pier and took another drag on his cigarette before answering the demanding Latin.

"I am in charge here," he called down to him. Zurko looked up abruptly, surprised there was someone up there that he had not noticed. "And we will unload you as quickly as possible. Come on up and stretch your legs while my people start to off-load."

Zurko could just see a large, brown panel truck backing toward him down the pier as he climbed the ladder up to where Rashad offered him a hand up. The vehicle didn't have any lights showing at all, not even its brake lights. The truck

ground to a halt with its back door right at the ladder. Six
more men, dressed in black and wearing sidearms, jumped out
the open back door.

Zurko shivered. If this was an ambush, he was a dead man.

Rashad, with a friendly enough grin on his dark face,
pulled a silver flask from his jacket pocket and handed it to
Zurko.

"Here, you need a drink. Macallem thirty-year-old Scotch.
Takes the chill off a fine Seattle evening."

Zurko gratefully accepted the container, unscrewed its lid,
and carefully wiped the rim with the tail of his shirt. Only
then did he take a healthy swig and hand the flask back to
Rashad. It was cold and damp for one accustomed to the trop-
ics. He would gladly take whatever this rather wild individual
was offering if it would warm him up.

"*Gracias*. It is good to be back on land, my friend. So good
I cannot express it properly." He turned to watch the men line
up from the spot where the sub was tied up to where the truck
waited. "How long will it take you to unload our cargo? It cannot be safe here."

Rashad glanced down at the mini-sub, to where a rather
large man stood in the hatch yelling orders in a thick Russian
accent.

"It'll go a helluva lot faster when your fat friend gets his ass
out of the hatch. Probably tonight and most of tomorrow
night."

"*Madre de Dios!* Tonight and tomorrow night? Can't you go
any faster?" Zurko implored. The longer he was stuck in this
place, the greater his chances of the *Americanos* riding in as he
had seen them do in the western movies he had watched as a
child, capturing him, seizing El Jefe's shipment. The shipment
for which he was ultimately responsible. The thought of jail
frightened Philippe Zurko even more than entering that seago-
ing coffin again. He knew that even there, behind heavy bars
and thick concrete, he would not be beyond de Santiago's wrath.

Rashad snorted and sucked his cigarette for a moment before answering.

"Do a little math. You have thirty-five tons of coke down there in that soup can, all in kilo bricks. That's thirty-five thousand bricks we have to hand up through that little hatch and put onto a truck." He paused for effect, then added, "If you think you can do it faster, my friend, go ahead. We'll find us a comfortable place and watch your ass work."

Rudi Sergiovski pulled his bulk slowly up the ladder to the pier as the thugs started passing bricks through the hatch and up to the waiting truck. Rashad handed the man the flask for his own welcome snort. The Russian did not bother to wipe the rim and finished most of the Scotch in a single gulp.

Sergiovski bragged of his prowess in guiding the little submarine into the inlet without detection. Rashad pretended to listen as he watched the group loading the first truck.

One thousand bricks, twenty-two hundred pounds per vehicle.

Just a little over thirty minutes passed before the first brown truck was filled and headed for the warehouse at the head of the pier. Then the second one was backed into place and the first brick stacked inside it.

Rashad shook his head as he blew smoke out his nose. At this pace it would take nineteen hours to off-load, even if his men could maintain the pace. That was about three full nights' worth of work.

Lots of time. Lots of exposure.

He decided not to tell Zurko. The stupid Latino would figure it all out soon enough on his own.

Earl Beasley called up the ladder to Ward on the bridge.

"Skipper, got the message boards. Permission to come up?"

Ward was enjoying the night wind blowing though his hair, the cool air on his face. It didn't relieve the frustration of this final mission of the *Spadefish* but it helped. The submarine had steamed back up the Puget Sound, traveling all the way on the surface while most of the crew rested. Ward stayed up on the bridge with only Seaman Cortez at his side, making sure they got through all the hazards of these busy waters.

Like this old boat he loved so much, he would have plenty of time to rest soon. Another two hours and they would be back out in open water. They would get *Spadefish* submerged once again, back down there where she belonged, then he could sleep.

"Come on up, Nav. Anything interesting on the boards?"

Beasley handed the aluminum clipboard up to Ward.

"I think you'll want to read the top one." He clambered up the last short length of ladder, nodded to Cortez, and stood beside Ward. "Nice night. Wind's kicking up but it's good to get some fresh air."

Ward squatted down so he could read the messages without the brisk breeze blowing the papers about. He held a small flashlight equipped with a red lens close to the board. It gave just enough illumination to make out the words without blinding anyone nearby.

"Damn, they lost that rusty bucket," he muttered. "*Helena K* headed almost due west and disappeared in a storm. No satellite. No air search. He just went away."

"Yeah, I read it," Beasley said. "Of course, you gotta know that they want us to go find him now."

Ward slapped the board shut and handed it back to Beasley.

"Why didn't he wait there for the sub to come back? Where could he be going?" Ward turned to Beasley. "Nav, tell the XO we need to dive and move as fast as we can. Find me a hole to dive in and find it quick."

As Beasley slid down the ladder he heard Ward's voice over the 7MC already.

"Helm, bridge. Ahead flank."

It was time for this old submarine to resume the hunt.

Spadefish surged ahead as she rushed to meet the long rollers of the open ocean. They moved to sea and picked up speed. The waves broke higher and higher on the sail. A huge wall of water broke over the top of the sail and before he could grab hold of anything, the wave's surge swept Cortez out of the tiny cockpit. If not for his harness tied to a stanchion on the bridge, the hapless seaman would have been washed over the side and disappeared far astern. The sub would have had to turn about and try to find a very small dot in a very big ocean.

As it was, he was tossed over the side of the sail and slammed brutally into the hard steel when the lanyard pulled taut. He hung there, helpless, barely able to find the breath to call for help.

"Skipper! Help! Help! I can't get back in."

The motion of the boat threw him hard against the sail again, knocking the wind from his lungs.

Ward quickly reached over and grabbed the lanyard with both hands. He pulled with all his strength, trying to haul Cortez back inside before he was hurt worse by the relentless crashing of the sea.

Inch by inch, he managed to pull the lanyard up. Using every ounce of muscle he could muster, he hauled away on the rope, knowing he couldn't let go long enough to call for help. He would have to pull the man back out of the grasp of the ocean.

He managed to haul Cortez back to the edge of the cockpit, to where he could cling tightly to the combing. Ward was able to rest a moment, to gather the strength he needed to reach over and pull his man back in to safety.

"You okay?" Ward asked as he gasped for air.

"Yes, sir. Bruised some." He winced when he tried to draw a deep breath, but there was unmistakable gratitude in his eyes when he looked up at Ward. "Thanks, Skipper. Thanks."

Ward motioned toward the ladder.

"Can you get down by yourself okay?"

Cortez nodded.

"I think so. I'll sure try."

He gingerly slid over to the hatch on his backside, then made his way down the ladder one slow rung at a time.

As soon as Cortez was safely down, Ward yelled down on the 7MC.

"Shift control below. Captain coming below."

He started down the ladder. Another big wave washed over the bridge, sending a cold column of water down the hatch with him. Ward spat and sputtered then slammed the hatch shut and dropped down to the control room.

It was time for *Spadefish* to return to the deep where she belonged, to resume the hunt for which she was born.

The *Helena K* steamed steadily westward. The raging storm had stopped as suddenly as it had started. One minute the rusty freighter was pitching and bucking in towering seas. The next it was rolling gently in only moderately choppy waters. Weather was like that sometimes up here in the North Pacific, a thousand miles west of Oregon. When a major front blew through, the back wall was often sharply defined. The difference of a couple of miles could mean being beaten by an unmerciful sea and sailing placidly under a star-studded sky.

Serge Novstad grabbed a pair of binoculars and stepped out onto the bridge wing.

That Chinese scow had to be around here someplace. Novstad had gotten his boat at the rendezvous spot and on time. Never could trust those little Orientals. They'd be late and try to blame it on him. Then they would have to do the transfer in broad, bright daylight. That would allow those damned American satellites to have a perfect view of the whole thing. The storm had hidden them so far and the clouds lingered. Now would be the perfect time to do the transfer, if only the damn Orientals would show.

The radio speaker crackled to life.

"*Helena K*, this is *Malay Messenger*. I hold you on radar, range ten miles, bearing zero-seven-one from me. Request you come to course two-four-nine."

They had arrived on time. Novstad watched the bow of his ship swing slowly to the southwest. He replied and shut up, keeping radio traffic to a minimum.

He trained his binoculars ahead, but still couldn't see the Chinese ship. If they were really only ten miles away, it would

be but a few minutes before the white masthead light would
pop over the horizon.

The wait seemed interminable. Novstad spied the glimmer
of a white smudge on the horizon. He could see the red and
green running lights below and flanking the white light. The
shape of the huge container ship slowly took form in the
night, a darker black shadow against a dark sky.

The two ships stopped abreast of each other, with a couple
of yards of open sea between them. Someone stepped out of
the wheelhouse of the Chinese ship and began talking into a
loud-hailer.

"Ahoy, *Helena K*. Glad to see you."

"Ahoy, *Malay Messenger*! How do you want to do this?"

"Have your men stand by, Captain. We will be sending lines
over. Recommend we tie up port side to port side. My deck
cranes will easily reach your main deck that way."

Novstad saw several men rush out onto the main deck of
the *Malay Messenger*, each of them armed with a shotgun.
They spaced themselves out along the deck and aimed their
guns high over the *Helena K*. When they fired, small rubber
projectiles arced up and over the *Helena K*, trailing a light line
behind each one. The deck crew on the *Helena K* grabbed the
lines and pulled them in. Attached to those lines were heavier
lines, and then still heavier ones, until finally the crew was
winching the massive hawsers needed to secure the two ships
together in the open sea.

They made quick work of it. In less than an hour, the two
ships were firmly tied together. The giant deck cranes on the
Malay Messenger began to move. A container was selected
from the hundred or more stacked on her deck and it was
lifted effortlessly, moved out over the *Helena K*, and lowered
gently. In minutes, it was chained and bolted securely in
place.

The procedure was repeated two more times.

Novstad watched wide-eyed as the crane returned to lift
something else, something not a cargo container. It was a

dozen men in a large basket. He had not expected this, and he didn't like the looks of it. Even from a distance, he couldn't help but notice the hardness of the men, the weapons they carried. Even as the men swung in the air in the basket, crossing the short distance between the two ships, Novstad was back on his own loud-hailer, yelling across at the *Malay Messenger*'s captain.

"What is this? I can't take so many people. We don't have provisions. This was not a part of the arrangements."

"Captain, I'm afraid Master Sui insists. They are only joining you to help you guard Master Sui's valuable property."

Novstad bit cleanly through his cigar and angrily spit the tip into the ocean.

A cold shiver ran the length of his spine.

33

JON WARD FELL BACK INTO HIS BUNK, COMPLETELY EXHAUSTED. GOD, it felt good to lie down! Maybe he could finally get a good night's sleep. The tension of trailing the mini-sub into shallow water had taken a greater toll on him than he knew. And the bumps and bruises from the rough time on the bridge, from wrestling Cortez back aboard, still ached some, but the hot shower had helped ease that.

Gratefully, the word on Cortez was good. He had only suffered a few bruises. No cracked ribs as Ward had feared. Doc said he should be good as new in the morning.

For the resilience of youth again.

He lay there and tried to find sleep. Ward felt the subtle vibrations of the sub. They told him the boat was running all out, at one hundred percent power, smooth as silk, performing as well as she had the day she was commissioned. They had been running at flank, a little over twenty-five knots on this girl, since they dived a couple of hours before. This is one time when a *Los Angeles*-class would be nice. Better, one of the new *Seawolf*-class boats. Their better speed would cut hours off this race. Still, he was proud of this old girl. *Spadefish* would get where she was going, and she would deliver when she got there, too.

Half an hour later, Ward still lay there, flipped over on his stomach, still wide awake as he reflected on the last few days. He couldn't help but worry about the next couple. The run down Puget Sound had been exciting, a thrill for him and his crew to be doing something they knew was useful. It had been taxing, too. To have it end with the bastards getting away just didn't seem right. In fact, it grated.

He sure hoped Bethea could get word to Tom Kincaid in time for him to find where the son of a bitch surfaced. The DEA agent would turn the entire Pacific Northwest upside down to find those drugs. If anybody could, Kincaid could. The man was on a personal mission.

When the chase collapsed, Ward's first thought was that he could finally go back home to Ellen. He was wondering how he would feel when he disembarked from this old boat for the final time, what words he would say to the men who had served her so courageously.

The message came from JDIA that they had to run out into the North Pacific and once again locate the *Helena K. Spadefish* had a reprieve. Another task, another challenge, another opportunity for the submarine and her crew to prove themselves.

Ward rolled back over onto his back, found a position that didn't hurt quite so bad, and fell into a deep slumber.

Bert Jankowski had always loved fishing. There was nothing he enjoyed more than being out in an open boat, his line in the water even before the sun peeked over the shoulder of Mount Rainier and painted the spruce along Carr Inlet with a golden glow. Nothing better than seeing the world come alive from a spot where his boat bobbed gently in the morning calm and big salmon longed to gobble up his hook.

That's why he headed out here every chance he got. If the truth be known, that was the real reason he had settled here when he retired from the navy twenty years ago, instead of going back home to the family farm near Topeka. Martha was under the impression that it had been the job at the little shipyard in Tacoma. He never tried to explain that there were no fishing spots like this one back on the plains of Kansas.

Jankowski carefully stowed his equipment in the little outboard. Too many years serving as a chief boatswain's mate had made him a creature of habit. Procedure was firmly imprinted on his psyche. Every bit of gear was stowed in its place and lashed in proper enough to pass any inspection. That even included the SAR buoy that Martha insisted he carry anytime he was to be out in the boat. She read some *Readers' Digest* story about survivors of a sailboat sinking in the South Pacific, of how they were rescued when satellites pinpointed the location of their SAR buoy. Ever since, she insisted he carry one, along with the big thermos of hot coffee she always climbed out of bed to fix for him. Never mind that he was in Puget Sound and would never be more than a couple of miles from land. Or that he could easily stop by Miranda's Bait and Grub and fill his thermos with the thirty-weight java they sold there.

He stowed the buoy and the big thermos and smiled. Bless her. She had waved bye to him from plenty of piers and wharves all over the world. The least he could do was humor her nowadays when he left her for only a few hours, instead of for a few months.

He paused for a moment, as he always did, to admire his boat. Jankowski had built it himself, carefully selecting the oak ribs and cedar hull planking one piece at a time. The teak brightwork was his particular joy. It reminded him of the brightwork on the *Missouri*, the pride of the fleet when he served aboard her. Yep, she was a beauty all right.

It was still totally dark as Jankowski cast off the lines to the pier and headed out from East Cromwell, through the Hale Passage, into Carr Inlet. Three hours to sunrise. He should be able to get in some good fishing before the sun came up. His buddies back at Miranda's reported the salmon fishing was especially good up by the old navy sound lab on Fox Island. He decided he might as well try there first. At least it was deserted and nobody would shoo him away.

He pointed the boat that way and reached for Martha's thermos of coffee.

The air temperature inside *Spadefish*'s reactor compartment was normally 160 degrees. That was too hot for anyone to go inside there to work on anything. The space was locked shut anyway. The radiation levels would kill anyone who spent any time in there with the reactor critical. Thirty years of such intense temperatures and high radiation had taken their toll on the equipment. Metals weakened, plastics hardened, insulation broke down as a matter of course.

With the old girl running all out, heat and radiation inside the compartment were at their highest. If something were going to fail, it would happen then. The main coolant valve position sensor that Dave Kuhn had repaired weeks earlier had been manufactured five years before the engineer was born. It was installed in *Spadefish*'s reactor system the same year he learned to walk.

The shellac insulating the transformer had done all it could do. A final bit of the stuff melted away and the coils of wires shorted together. There was a brief puff of smoke and the indicator failed.

Bert Waters, the reactor operator, saw the green "valve open" light flicker out a millisecond before the siren blasted in his ear. The red "reactor scram" light flashed brightly in his face, demanding his attention. Every needle on the myriad of gauges in front of him started moving chaotically.

Waters jumped up and shouted, "Reactor scram! Loss of

open indication in the port loop! Shifting main coolant pumps to 'one slow' in starboard, shutting port steam stop."

His hands moved wildly across the reactor control panel as his eyes took in every bit of information he could glean from the rapidly dancing needles in front of him.

Scott Frost had been taking a swallow of coffee when the alarm blared just inches above his left ear. The cup fell to the deck and rolled out the maneuvering-room door, instantly forgotten. He glanced for the barest instant at the reactor control panel and saw lights flash on, telling him the control rods were all on the bottom of the reactor. The reactor was shut down. It wasn't making any more heat but they were still drawing steam at an alarming rate. Steam that would be vital to get them started back up again.

Frost grabbed the big chrome ahead throttle and spun it with all his might. The howl of steam roaring down the twelve-inch pipes just overhead to satisfy the demands of the wide-open main engine throttles was silenced. Frost reached over and flipped the engine order telegraph to the All Stop position.

Chris Durgan jumped from his seat behind Waters and stared wide-eyed for a second, startled by the sudden noise and activity. He knew what he had to do. With his heart in his throat, he reached up and behind him for the 7MC microphone. He keyed the button and yelled his command.

"Reactor scram! Answering 'all-stop'! Request casualty assistance team lay aft."

The reactor temperature had been dropping unbelievably fast. It slowed some, but it was still cooling too fast. The electrical operator turned a couple of large rheostats and shifted electrical power to the battery. That helped some.

Steve Friedman grabbed the 1MC microphone behind the periscope stand.

"Reactor scram! Rig ship for reduced electrical! Casualty assistance team lay aft. Prepare to snorkel!"

Watch standers in the engine room scurried around, frantically turning off equipment that wasn't vital for their survival.

Other technicians were busy already, trying to figure out what caused the boat's nuclear reactor to shut down in the first place.

Bruce Hendrix charged through the reactor-compartment tunnel door into the engineering space, leading a team of ten more technicians, running aft to help their shipmates. Hendrix was the senior and most experienced nuclear electronics technician onboard. Finding the problem and fixing it was his task.

Frank Bechtold, the senior enlisted watch stander in the engine room and the chief machinist, met Hendrix at the base of the short ladder at the forward end of the machinery space. He began his report even as people streamed past him in the narrow corridor between the massive electronic panels.

"Bruce, the engine room is shut down. I need charging and discharging station watches." He paused when he saw Dave Kuhn jump down the ladder, still zipping his poopie suit. Bechtold went on, but now both Hendrix and the engineer were listening intently. "We lost open indication on the port loop. The reactor protection system sensed no flow in that loop and scrammed the reactor. The reactor temperature dropped like a rock. We can still do a fast recovery start-up, but just barely."

A fast recovery start-up was a special procedure developed after the *Thresher* disaster back in the early sixties. It allowed the submarine operators to start the reactor and get power back in an emergency at sea, but only if certain safety limits were satisfied. If the limits were exceeded, a much longer and more controlled procedure had to be used. Having the reactor temperature above the minimum was one of the most important limits.

Below their feet, the three men could hear the *chug-chug* of the coolant charging pumps as they strained to put water into the reactor system to make up for the contraction of the rapid cooling. They had to keep the core covered with water. The water removed the heat generated by decaying fission fragments. An uncovered core would melt, and that would be a true disaster. It was all a well-choreographed dance to keep the reactor safe yet still able to get power back as quickly as possible.

The sub rolled violently, tossing the three against the side of a panel, then, just as viciously rolled the other way, sending them tumbling to the other side of the compartment.

"Jesus," Kuhn grumbled. "Looks like we're up at periscope depth and the storm's still going on up there. That's gonna make this damned interesting."

One of Hendrix's electronics technicians rose from the panel where he had been squatting. Sweat trickled off his forehead, dripped from his chin, and already soaked the back of his poopie suit. Having no air-conditioning in such a cramped space that was already filled with hot pipes had already allowed the temperature to soar.

"That ties it, Chief. Definite open circuit on the valve position indication. We can't fix that from here."

Kuhn looked at Hendrix. He knew what was needed.

"Chief Hendrix, break out your equipment and the procedure to replace that indicator. Get your team ready. Chief Bechtold, get ready for an emergency reactor compartment entry. I'm going to talk to the Skipper."

Another roll hit them, smashing them into the switchgear. The 1MC speaker blasted: "Commence snorkeling."

All the way forward, in the lowest level of the bow compartment, the diesel operator twisted himself like a pretzel to reach all the controls he simultaneously operated. With his right hand, he shoved the shiny brass quadrant-valve handle forward, forcing compressed air into the cylinders to make the machine roll over. With his left hand, he held in a button that overrode the diesel safety circuit so the diesel could come up to speed. With his right foot he held open the kick drain so that water in the induction piping could drain out.

The lovingly preserved, bright-red machine growled and groaned in protest as it came to life. Deafening noise, diesel smoke and the smell of fuel oil filled the little compartment. The "rock crusher" was ready to do its job, giving *Spadefish* a source of emergency electrical power.

It was limited but vital. Otherwise, they were dead in the water.

Durgan stood and watched the battery amps click away. The maneuvering room was almost silent once the initial flurry of activity was completed. The race now was to save the very limited power still available to them from the battery. If they conserved all they could, it would provide a couple of hours' worth of electrical power. Power needed to restart the reactor and to supplement the diesel once it was ready. Every click of the amp-hour meter meant that much more had been used already.

The operator released the switches, grabbed a microphone and yelled to be heard over the deafening din.

"Diesel on the governor, ready for emergency loading!"

Durgan didn't waste any time loading the diesel generator. He quickly shifted as much electrical load as he could to the "rock crusher." The machine seemed to groan and squat down like a tired but trusty plow horse as more electrical load was shifted its way, but it was ready to handle the work.

The snorkel mast, sticking out of the churning waves just behind the periscope, sucked in the great quantities of air the diesel needed to run. When the sea surged over the mast, the snorkel valve slammed shut to keep the water out, just as it was designed to do. But every time that happened in this raging sea, the diesel sucked on the air inside the sub. And when it did, it popped the ears of every man on board.

Kuhn grabbed an MJ phone to talk to Ward and heard him answer groggily.

"Skipper, we lost the port open VPI. There's nothing to do but go into the reactor and fix it. Chief Bechtold is setting up for an emergency reactor compartment entry. Chief Hendrix is getting the tools and parts out."

Ward listened to his engineer and felt his stomach drop. He knew how difficult and dangerous this procedure was. The reactor and its radiation weren't the problem. Radiation levels dropped off almost as soon as the reactor scrammed. Heat was the problem. It would still be over 160 degrees in there. Most of the pipes were heated to over four hundred degrees. With *Spadefish* pitching and rolling in this storm, people were going to get burned if they went in there. It was only a question of how badly.

To add to the misery, there wasn't time to ventilate fresh air into the compartment. The space had been sealed tight for weeks. There was no telling what noxious gases waited inside. Whoever was brave enough to go in there would have to wear air-fed breathing masks.

There was no choice but to face the heat. It would take weeks for the reactor to cool on its own. And it would be impossible to force-cool it at sea with the limited power available from the battery and diesel, and even that would take several days. Meanwhile, they would soon be without any power at all, unable to restart the reactor as they bobbed helplessly about on a treacherous sea.

Besides that, there was a dirty ship out there somewhere. If the mini-sub filled with killer cocaine made it in and out of Puget Sound, it would surely be coming back to its mother ship and that would be their only chance to stop it. If it got away, who knows where it would deliver the poison next? And how many would die then?

They had to get power, had to get moving.

"Who's going in?"

"Chief Hendrix and I," Kuhn answered without hesitation.

Ward wasn't surprised.

"All right. Dave, be careful in there."

"Piece of cake, Skipper. Don't worry."

Jason Rashad had found himself a comfortable spot atop some gunnysacks out of the way of the men who were unloading the sub, but close enough so he could make sure every brick found its way to the back of the brown van. He had rolled himself a big joint and was halfway finished with it when heard the staccato beat of an outboard motor from somewhere out there on the water.

"Shit!"

The bastard was coming their way, but it was several minutes before he could make out the little white boat breaking through the predawn mist.

"Shit!" he said again.

They were almost finished off-loading. Another two hours and they would be out of here, the job finished. Rashad couldn't wait to be back in Seattle, back in his warm apartment, all wrapped up with some white pussy and sailing on some non-doctored blow. Mostly, though, he wanted desperately to be rid of that whining Latino and the fat, obnoxious Russian.

Not even rounding up more help and speeding up the off-load had made this watch any less miserable. And now, when they were so near its completion, here comes a severe complication, putt-putting their way.

There was a big man standing in the stern of the little boat, waving a flashlight and yelling at him.

"Ahoy on the pier! What you guys doing? I thought this place was abandoned. You boys having a problem?"

Rashad stood stiffly and watched as the boat drew closer, still sucking on his smoke but not answering the intruder's questions. The men passing the cocaine up to the pier stopped working and watched.

When Bert Jankowski was close enough to assure a kill, Rashad raised his Mac 10 machine pistol and fired. The first burst caught Jankowski squarely in the chest and threw him sprawling over the transom of the boat. He was dead before he hit the water.

With a cruel grin on his face, Rashad continued firing into the little boat, splintering the carefully finished brightwork and shattering the wooden hull. Slowly, the cold waters of Carr Inlet filled the boat as it sank ever lower in the water. Finally, it slipped beneath the surface and sank past the floating body of the dead fisherman.

Rashad shouted back to his thugs who stood there, staring wide-eyed at where the boat had just disappeared.

"Hurry up! Show's over! We're gonna have to get finished

and get out of here before somebody misses that bastard and comes looking for him."

As he watched his men work even more feverishly to load the bricks in the last truck, Rashad promptly changed plans. No way now to slip the trucks out of here one at a time over several days. They would all have to go at once and just hope no one noticed them. Once they were over the bridge to the mainland, he would split them up to find different routes to the warehouse up by SEATAC airport.

As they worked, no one on the pier noticed the small orange buoy float free from the sinking wreck and rise to the surface. They were too busy loading cocaine, mumbling to each other about what they had just witnessed.

The buoy was water-activated. As soon as it reached the surface, it went to work, sending its coded signal, telling any listener that someone was in the waters of Carr Inlet and needed help.

Dave Kuhn and Bruce Hendrix looked a bit like moon-walkers, dressed in yellow anti-contamination coveralls, welder's gloves, and emergency air-breathing masks as they waited in front of the door that led into the sub's nuclear reactor. Bechtold fitted a large spanner wrench on the massive nuts holding the iron strong-backs across the door, then smacked it with a hammer again and again until the nuts were loosened. He lifted the heavy red I beams out of the way. Air whistled past the thick, heavy steel door as it slowly swung open.

It felt as if someone had just cracked the trapdoor to hell.

The two yellow-clad figures stepped inside onto a small metal grate and slid down a ladder to the deck, ten feet below. The heat hit Kuhn like a blow to the chest. It was a powerful force, a malevolent presence that seemed bent on forcing them back out of the compartment.

There seemed no way they could tolerate this heat, much less try to work in it. It simply was beyond human endurance.

Both men knew there was no other way. It had to be done.

They gathered their strength and resolve and tried to put the intense discomfort out of mind. The valve was right there in front of them, only a step away.

Hendrix pulled a pair of wire cutters from the tool bag and snipped the wires that held a pad of insulating lagging in place over the VPI. He pulled the pad off and dropped it to the deck. Heat radiated from the hot metal as if from a red-hot fireplace poker.

Sweat already poured from their bodies. The masks were covered with perspiration and salt, making seeing almost impossible. Both men already felt faint, and had to concentrate on keeping their footing as the boat rocked beneath them. They did not want to fall against the superheated metal. It would instantly sear any exposed flesh.

Kuhn grabbed a screwdriver and went to work, removing the cover, carefully catching each piping hot screw before it got away. They couldn't afford to lose one and have to try to fish around this furnace for it.

When the cover fell away, they saw that their diagnosis was confirmed. The sensor inside the indicator was a charred mess.

Kuhn removed the terminals and slid the molten mass out onto the deck. Hendrix slid in the new sensor and tried his best to hook up the terminals. He couldn't grasp the tiny screws with the clumsy welding gloves. It was just too delicate an operation.

He glanced over at Kuhn and shrugged as best he could in the suit. There was no choice. He slid off the bulky gloves and dropped them to the deck.

Barehanded, he grasped the screws and began replacing them. Kuhn grimaced, holding his breath as he watched Hendrix work. He was able to get the screws in and tightened down this way, but there was no way to avoid the burning hot metal. The flesh on his fingertips reddened, then blistered. Kuhn could hear the faint sizzle of charring flesh and the grunts of pain from the nuclear technician. Tears rolled down Hendrix's cheeks as the pain became overwhelming. Still he fought back the urge to drop the tools and howl in agony.

The last screw slid into place and was tightened. Hendrix dropped his tools and fell back, clutching his charred hands and moaning in pain. Kuhn grabbed him, threw him over his back, braced against another roll of the boat, then, when the deck beneath them stopped bucking, scurried up the ladder. He pushed Hendrix through the door into the tunnel then fell through himself, collapsing on the deck, rubber-legged from the heat and exertion.

"He's burned bad," Kuhn rasped. "Get him up to Doc quick." He gasped for air and drank deeply from the bottle of water Bechtold handed him. The compartment ceiling seemed to be swirling and he was afraid he was about to lose consciousness. "It's fixed. Start the alignment."

Replacing the VPI sensor was only the first step. Now there would be several hours of testing and adjusting to make sure it worked. Fortunately, that was done outside the reactor compartment, back in the instrument alley where the temperature was merely stifling by now.

Kuhn attempted to stand, but he was too wobbly. He sat back down on the deck and allowed two of the crew to help him remove the yellow coveralls. He tried to stand again, pulling himself up by grasping piping. Finally, he was upright, but still holding on for support.

"Where's Chief Hendrix?" he asked.

"Don't worry, Eng," Bechtold said. "Doc has him. He'll be okay. Now where do you think you're going? You need to lie down and rest a bit."

Kuhn started down the ladder heading aft toward the engineering spaces, still grasping pipes for support.

"I got work to do. We gotta get this thing aligned and the reactor started up."

He stumbled through the hatch and headed aft.

"Admiral, I told you that old bucket would never make it." The gloating in Pierre Desseaux's voice was obvious. "She should be razor blades and that crew of Ward's should have been sent home so they could find a job they're capable of doing. Maybe in city sanitation."

Tom Donnegan was doing all he could to keep from biting

through his cigar. Desseaux was normally insufferable, but when events went his way, he was positively impossible to stomach. Still, Donnegan began in a low, calm voice.

"Captain, you've said your piece. We all know how you feel on this subject." Donnegan clutched the red phone in a vise-like grip. "But we've got sailors in trouble. Your sailors. Get a team up to Port Angeles ASAP. The Coast Guard will helo them out to *Spadefish*. They're sending a patrol boat out to cover the mission."

Donnegan slammed down the phone before he said something in anger that he might later regret.

"Skipper, where we going?"

The helmsman looked out through the rain-streaked windshield of the patrol boat's wheelhouse. Coast Guard Commander Barry Jones braced himself against the pitch of the sea.

"Heading out to intercept a suspected druggie. Some garbage scow named the *Helena K*."

The bow of the *Cyclone* disappeared once again under the green water of the storm-tossed sea. The bow rose back up dutifully, seawater running down the deck and over the side. She slapped back down hard, tossing foaming white water from either side of her bow.

Jones was proud of his new ship. The *Cyclone*, a sister of *Hurricane*, had been built for the Navy Special Boats Unit to deliver SEALs to wherever they needed to go. She now sported the broad orange diagonal stripe of the Coast Guard.

"Weren't for this storm, it'd be a cakewalk. Just go find this slug and tow it home," Jones commented. "I'll be in my cabin if you need me."

He stepped aft and into the little closet that served as his cabin while the helmsman held the ship steady, plowing on in the heavy seas.

Bert Waters glanced over to where Dave Kuhn sat. He rested on a toolbox at the end of the narrow alley between the rows of instrument panels. Waters shook his head.

"Eng, it ain't workin'. We've been at this for six hours now. I've tried everything I know."

Kuhn angrily threw down the thick tech manual he was reading.

"Damn! Damn! And double damn! We know that VPI worked before we went in. It bench-checked fine. We know it was wired right. I watched and checked every lead the chief put on."

Tears welled involuntarily in the engineer's eyes as he remembered the awful sight of Hendrix working on despite the horrible pain he must have been suffering. Doc Marston had reported that he would heal okay but his hands would be permanently scarred. He was in his rack now, heavily sedated to ward off the pain.

Waters nodded. He knew just where Kuhn was for that instant.

"There has to be an explanation. Maybe 'MES' . . . 'magic electric shit.' "

Kuhn tried to force a smile in response to Waters's attempt at humor but it wouldn't come.

"All right, let's go through the procedure one more time. Maybe we missed something."

He reached over to pick up the discarded tech manual to go back to the beginning. Then the engineer noticed something. The book had fallen open to the description section, the part of the manual that gave a simplified explanation for nontechnicians. That section was many pages in front of the troubleshooting and repair sections they had been using.

There, at the bottom of the page, his eyes fell on an innocuous little note: "If the VPI sensor is manufactured by TRW, the terminal numbering is reversed from the drawings and procedures in this manual."

Kuhn looked hard at Waters.

"Bert, who made that sensor?"

Waters sorted through a bag of trash and pulled out the box the part had come in. He held it up so Kuhn could see it. Prominently stenciled across the top of the box were the words MANUFACTURER: TRW, INC.

"There's the problem!" He paused for a moment as the realization of what had to happen next hit him. "Bert, we have
to go back into that reactor compartment."

Kuhn pulled himself erect and walked back up into the reactor compartment tunnel, his legs still wobbly beneath him.
Waters followed him.

"Eng, let me go do it. You're still zapped from the last time."

"No, Bert. I know how it's laid out. I've been in there. Besides, I need you to be able to do the alignment. You wait here.
Chief Bechtold will come in with me."

The engineer pulled the coveralls and gloves on again, then
disappeared down the ladder, followed by the burly machinist
chief, moving awkwardly in the protective gear. Kuhn stepped
up to the sensor and immediately tossed off his gloves. Taking
a deep breath, he grasped each lead, switching them around to
the right order. The flesh on his hands sizzled and popped. He
cried out, screaming from the pain, the tears almost blinding
him. Still, he worked on. It took him twenty awful minutes to
complete the task. Bechtold could only stand there, staring in
disbelief, unable to do anything to assist other than helping to
brace the engineer against the continual rocking of the boat.

Finally the last lead was in place and tightened. Like Chief
Hendrix before him, Kuhn fell to his knees once he was finished, clutching his charred hands. He stumbled, half-
crawling to the ladder, shaking off Bechtold's attempts to help
him. He clawed his way up the metal ladder and fell heavily
through the doorway and onto the tunnel deck.

"It's fixed," the engineer gasped, then, mercifully, he
passed out cold.

In another four hours, *Spadefish* was once again under way.
The diesel was cooled down and quiet again. The battery was
being recharged. The ocean water four hundred feet below the
surface was calm and she slid smoothly through the depths.
Most of the crew members were resting, exhausted from the
ordeal of the last twenty-four hours, the steady hum of the
boat helping them sleep.

Jonathan Ward was wide-awake, though. He sat in the quiet wardroom with Joe Glass and the corpsman.

"How are they, Doc?" he asked, his concern for Kuhn and Hendrix etched on his face.

The buffet along the inboard bulkhead was still stacked high with piles of medical dressings, stainless-steel trays of surgical equipment, and the other paraphernalia of an emergency operating room. The operating table lights still hung from the overhead above the wardroom table.

Doc Marston took a swallow of coffee.

"They're both sedated now. Their hands are going to hurt like hell for a while. You know how painful burns can be. Both of 'em have deep third-degree burns over most of both hands. They'll have scarring when the burns heal. I'd say they'll both need to have a good bit of reconstructive surgery." He looked at his own hands, lost in thought for a long moment. "Infection and shock are our biggest worries right now."

Glass looked over at the corpsman.

"Do we medevac them right away?"

Marston shook his head.

"They're stable now. Treatment isn't life-threatening."

"Thanks, Doc. I agree," Ward said. He pointed upward, toward the ocean's surface above them. "And that storm up there would make any medevac a dangerous proposition for everyone involved right now. Doc, do whatever you can do to make them as comfortable as possible. We'll get them off the boat when the storm blows out. By then we should have found that lousy rust bucket for John Bethea." Ward rose to leave. As he walked out, he added, "XO, tell Chris Durgan he's acting engineer. He's certainly proved he can handle it."

"Aye, skipper."

"Now, let's go find us a mad dog and put it out of its misery."

The skipper of *Spadefish* was gone.

34

KEN TEMPLE REACHED OVER TO TAP TOM KINCAID ON THE SHOULDER, trying to get his attention. It was impossible to talk inside the noisy Bell Jet Ranger helicopter without an intercom. The one at Kincaid's seat didn't work. The Seattle Police Department bean counters had been cutting cost on maintenance again.

"What's next?" Temple grumbled, though he knew Kincaid couldn't hear a word he said. "They gonna ration bullets? Only three per shoot-out allowed?"

The two cops had requisitioned the chopper when John Bethea called for a search for the missing mini-sub and its suspected load of coke. When they mentioned Bethea and the JDIA, the paperwork was approved instantly and they were airborne before they knew it. They spent every minute of daylight flying up and down the hundreds of inlets and coves along the lower Puget Sound. They had only sore butts and ringing ears to show for it.

Kincaid lowered the binoculars and leaned back in the open window to hear what his friend had to say. Temple yelled to be heard.

"Tom, Coast Guard called. They got an SAR beacon activated over on Carr Inlet. That storm out at Cape Flattery has them all tied up pulling fishermen outta the drink. They want us to swing over and take a look."

Kincaid nodded. He had seen his share of the SAR buoys on the Coast Guard boats he had ridden. He had even tracked one druggie who had a habit of tying them to the mangled body parts of informants and leaving them floating in the Gulf of Mexico for the DEA to find. Still, he doubted there was anything to this one. Not that far down in the narrow waters of the sound.

"Probably just one fell over the side. Some party boater kicked it overboard reaching for the beer cooler."

"Yeah, but it's only five minutes over there with this thing. May as well see what's going on."

Kincaid felt the Jet Ranger bank and tilt as it gained speed, heading to the north. The sun was up and already beginning to burn off the early-morning haze, even though it still lingered lazily among the towering spruce trees. They had been flying fruitless circles for over two hours now. It was almost time to head for SEATAC to refuel and grab some breakfast. This little detour was almost directly on the way.

"What's that?" Kincaid asked, pointing to the buildings hiding in the trees along the shoreline in the cove they were approaching. Temple read his lips.

"Some kind of old navy lab. Been closed for years. Abandoned."

The pilot watched his GPS as he brought the chopper to a hover fifty feet above the exact coordinates the Coast Guard station had sent them. Kincaid and Temple leaned out, searching for any signs of the SAR buoy. The pilot started to move the chopper in a slowly expanding spiral search pattern around the coordinates.

Ken Temple saw it first.

A red plaid shirt floating just beneath the surface. The detective had pulled enough bodies from the drink in his day to recognize what this was.

There was no accidental SAR activation.

Someone had died here.

Barry Jones watched the *Cyclone*'s radarscope intently. Another contact, bearing two-five-seven, range twenty miles. Could this one be the *Helena K*? The patrol boat had stopped ten ships so far this morning already and raised the hackles of a captain or two. None had matched the pictures Jones held, though. He would be happy when they had that ship in tow and were heading home.

There were worse places to be than out here on a morning

like this one. The air was cool, the sea calm now that the storm had blown to the east.

Jones picked up the microphone.

"Suspect contact. Man the small boat boarding party."

He watched as some of his crew ran out on deck to take stations at the two 25mm Bushmaster cannons. There was no reason to expect they would need to use them. Even drug smugglers gave in quickly when they saw how well armed *Cyclone* was. Her guns commanded respect.

The speaker above his head blasted a reply.

"Skipper, XO. Small boat party manned and ready. I'm leading the party. Ready to lower the RHIB on your order."

Everything was going according to the book. Jones liked that. Keep the surprises to a minimum. Follow procedure. Complete the mission.

Then go home safely.

Ray Mendoza leaned back after staring hard at the sonar screen for a full five minutes. His mind was made up. He reached for the microphone.

"Conn, Sonar. Contact sierra-nine-two is definitely our old friend the *Helena K*. We've listened to that trash hauler enough that I'd recognize her in my sleep." Mendoza watched the traces on the screen for a few more seconds. "Now, the other guy? Contact sierra-nine-three is running four five-bladed screws. My guess is it's a *Cyclone*-class PC. He's moving pretty fast. I'd say turns for twenty-five knots. Oh, and the traces are converging."

Jon Ward glanced over at Joe Glass and allowed himself a small grin. The XO had his team busy tracking the two contacts as the dimly lit control room buzzed with activity. Glass looked up from the navigation plot and nodded in Ward's direction.

"Skipper, we have a solution. Confirm what sonar just reported. The two are definitely converging. Estimated range fifteen thousand yards. Looks like the PC is dropping in for a bite of lunch with our old friends on the *Helena K*."

"Well, Joe, why don't we just go up and watch? I'd like to

have a good seat so I can see this sucker go down." Ward turned to Beasley, standing by the periscopes. "Nav, make your depth six-two feet."

The *Helena K* sat there on the horizon, just coming into view from the bridge of the *Cyclone*. No doubt about it. She exactly matched the picture Barry Jones held. Jones grabbed the marine band radio microphone and checked that its dial was on channel sixteen. He pushed the key and started talking.

"*Helena K*, this is the United States Coast Guard. Come to 'all-stop.' Stand by to receive a boarding party. Over."

Jones waited for a moment. No response. He repeated himself.

The freighter's bow swung around sharply. Black smoke belched from its stack as it picked up speed. The crazy son of a bitch was going to attempt to outrun the *Cyclone*.

Jones smiled. That was a very foolish thing to do. He figured that he had at least a fifteen-knot speed advantage on the freighter. The skipper of that old bucket was only delaying the inevitable.

He reached down and pulled the throttle control to All Ahead Flank. The *Cyclone* jumped ahead obediently as her four screws bit into the sea and propelled her forward.

Jones spoke into the microphone again.

"*Helena K. Helena K*. This is the United States Coast Guard. Heave to or we will fire."

Jones could see the furious churning of the *Helena K*'s single screw as she tried vainly to push the old tub faster. He punched the station selector button on the intercom for the forward gun mount.

"Forward mount, fire a warning burst off her bow."

The gun trained around to point in the direction of the fleeing merch and promptly barked. The air tore as the shots whistled over the freighter. A row of three geysers erupted two hundred yards ahead of her.

The freighter's screw stopped and she coasted to a halt. Jones heard a deep voice with a northern European accent on his radio. The man was trying to sound outraged, but Jones doubted the tremble in his voice was from anger.

"Coast Guard, this is the *Helena K*. What is the meaning of this? We are in international waters. This is a Russian flagged ship under charter to the People's Republic of Korea. Why are you attacking us? You have no jurisdiction here."

"Captain, stand by to be boarded," Jones answered. "We will search your vessel. I request your cooperation, but we will search you without it if necessary."

There was no reply.

The *Cyclone* closed the distance between the two ships quickly and glided to a stop with the *Helena K* five hundred yards off the patrol boat's starboard beam. Both Bushmasters swung out to train on the unarmed ship.

This was nothing new. Jones and his crew had done dozens of these boardings up here in the Northwest. It was rare to have to fire off a shot across their bow as they had this morning. It was only necessary to pull up alongside and show them their teeth. No one was ever foolish enough to try to run. Or open fire. Most of these guys were merely hired hands, more than willing to take a little jail time rather than face the wrath of the Coast Guard's guns.

Jones glanced aft to see the RHIB slide down the boat ramp with the boarding party. Its big twin outboards roared to life and it shot toward the *Helena K*, the XO sitting up in the bow like the painting of Washington crossing the Delaware.

The eight Chinese men fanned out from behind one of the cargo containers on the merchant ship's deck. They pointed their shoulder-fired missiles directly at the *Cyclone*.

The last thing Commander Barry Jones saw was the burning trail of the missile flying directly into the wheelhouse of the *Cyclone*. The blinding flash tore the wheelhouse apart.

Two other perfectly aimed missiles tore into each Bushmaster mount and exploded. The other three missiles ripped into the superstructure of the *Cyclone* and turned her into little more than a burning hulk.

The XO stood in the RHIB with his mouth agape, disbelieving. His ship was now burning from a dozen fires back there where he had just left. He could make out dead or wounded shipmates hanging from the wreckage while others tried to drag themselves clear of the fires. He turned to yell to the coxswain to get them out of there.

He was a second too slow.

Two more of the Chinese opened fire with a 23mm machine gun. The cannon slugs tore through the XO's back and exited his chest before exploding into the bottom of the RHIB. Other bullets ripped through the rest of the defenseless men on the craft.

In ten seconds, the boat was sinking.

Serge Novstad watched the savage attack in horror from the ship's bridge. This wasn't supposed to happen. It was a simple smuggling run. If they got caught, so what? His money would be in his Swiss account gathering interest while he served a pittance of jail time. Then he'd be out and back in Stockholm, living the good life until the next job came along.

"You stupid sons of bitches! What have you done? You've just killed us all."

The leader of the Chinese gunmen looked up from the main deck, a chilling smile on his face, and shouted up to the captain.

"We have done our duty. We have protected Master Sui's property, just as he directed!" He turned and ordered his men to reload their weapons. Turning back to Novstad, he yelled, "Now, Captain, I suggest we move closer so we may ensure there will be no survivors to tell anyone what happened here. Then we'll steam on to the rendezvous with the mini-sub as planned."

The Swede took another big slug from the bottle of Scotch he held in his hand. He tried to wash away the images he had just witnessed.

Earl Beasley walked *Spadefish*'s periscope in a slow circle, watching the water of the blue Pacific flash past. The only sound he heard was the COB calling out the depth change.

"One-one-zero feet . . . one-zero-five feet . . . one hundred feet . . ."

Then he heard words that sent a chill up his spine.

"Conn, Sonar. Picking up loud explosions on the bearing of sierra-nine-two and nine-three!" Mendoza's voice echoed around the quiet control room. "Sounds like sierra-nine-three's engines have stopped."

Ward shouted, "Nav, get us up quick! Someone's shooting up there!"

Chief Roddie Macallister dragged himself from the ruins of the after deckhouse on the *Cyclone*. His legs didn't want to work. He reached down to brush away whatever it was that was stinging his left thigh. His hand came away covered with something wet and sticky. Macallister stared in amazement at the bright red blood dripping from his fingers. There was a gaping gash across his thigh, his leg almost severed. He had seen wounds like this before. The only way to keep from bleeding to death was to apply a good, tight tourniquet. He ripped off his shirt, wrapped it around his leg just above the wound, and twisted it as tight as he could manage.

The bleeding slowed. He felt woozy, dizzy, but he would make it. He'd seen worse. Now, he had to figure out what the hell had happened.

Then the deep, low rumble of a heavy machine gun drowned out the crackling of the fires that blazed all around him. Macallister stuck his head around the corner of the deckhouse. He could see the machine cannon on the merchant's main deck firing into the *Cyclone*. He stared in horror.

Then Macallister understood. They intended to sink the *Cyclone*, to make sure there were no witnesses to this cruel ambush.

He ducked behind the meager cover of the aluminum deckhouse.

He remembered the bridge-to-bridge radio in the other RHIB. If he could just get to it.

Macallister slithered along as best he could. He headed aft

across the unprotected deck to reach the boat well. He prayed they couldn't see him. He made it, hiding behind the bullet-stitched remains of the second RHIB. The splintering gunfire moved on past him. He reached in and fished around until he found the radio transceiver. It wasn't damaged. It didn't have much power output, but it was his only hope.

He switched it on and verified that it was on channel sixteen.

"Any ship, any ship. This is the Coast Guard ship *Cyclone*. Mayday! Mayday! We are under attack. We are under attack by an armed freighter. Our position is approximately one-three-one west longitude, four-seven-point-five north latitude. Someone please help us. They're machine-gunning the survivors. We're defenseless."

He was having trouble finding breath. He repeated the call. He said a silent prayer that someone . . . anyone . . . was close enough to hear the radio's weak signal.

The radio behind Ward's head crackled as the scope broke the water. He could clearly hear Roddie Macallister's desperate plea for help.

He could see the *Helena K* slowly circling the burning wreckage like a bloodthirsty shark, the machine cannon on her main deck firing viciously into the defenseless hulk. It was an image he would not soon forget. Nor would he be able to forget the agonizing appeals of the wounded Coast Guardsman on channel sixteen, the sounds of machine gun fire in the background.

There was only one thing to do and he knew they had to do it quickly.

"Snapshot, sierra-nine-two, tube one!" Ward shouted. "Set surface settings, high speed, Doppler enable in."

What he was about to do was a calculated risk. The two ships were only a hundred yards apart. The torpedo could easily hit the wrong one. The weapon was set to go for the moving target; the one whose sonar return showed a Doppler shift. It was a risk Ward had to take. The pleading voice on the radio would have convinced him to go ahead even if nothing else had.

Stan Guhl's fingers danced across the torpedo-firing panel as he talked to Chief Ralston down in the torpedo room. To Ward, watching the scene unfold above, it seemed to take forever. Twenty seconds passed. Guhl shouted, "Ready, snapshot tube one."

Glass nodded and shouted to Ward, "Solution set."

"Shoot tube one!" Ward ordered.

He simultaneously felt and heard the surge of high-pressure air as the ADCAP torpedo was flushed out of the tube.

"Normal launch, running in preenable!" Guhl shouted.

"Conn, Sonar. Hold own ship's unit running in high speed."

The ADCAP was on its way.

The freighter was steaming across the stern of the *Cyclone* now, hiding it from *Spadefish*'s view.

"Good," Ward muttered. "Just stay like that for a minute, you son of a bitch!"

At this range, the torpedo had four minutes to run before it reached its target. Nothing to do but watch and wait. There was nothing Ward could do to make it get there any faster. He watched the computer simulation play out on the screen and looked through the periscope.

He decided there was no sense in wasting any time. The closer *Spadefish* was to the wreck when the torpedo arrived, the quicker they could begin pulling survivors from the water and off whatever was left of the PC.

"Ahead full. Make turns for fifteen knots," Ward ordered.

The periscope started to buck against the force of the sea pushing against it. Ward looked aft and saw the scope was kicking up a high, white rooster tail. Normally that was a definite problem, but right now he really didn't care if the murderous scum saw them or not. His blood boiled as he thought of that cannon pounding away at the helpless sailors on the deck of the damaged boat.

"Two minutes run time," Guhl called out. "Torpedo in active search."

The torpedo activated the sonar hydrophones in its nose. The active sonar pulses were tuned to search the water in a cone sixty degrees wide in front of the torpedo. It was essentially a fast, deadly bloodhound on a very long leash.

Ward turned to Beasley and ordered, "Nav, have the search and rescue party and four riflemen stand by at the ops compartment hatch. And a gunner ready to go to the bridge. Get sidearms for you and me." Beasley looked quizzically at the skipper. "As soon as that SOB is on the bottom, we're going to rescue all the survivors. I expect a few of the ones from the *Helena K* may be stupid enough to resist our help."

The torpedo started receiving returns from its active sonar. The pulses were matched in its memory processor to the ones it expected to see from a surface ship. The returns showed Doppler, telling the torpedo its target was moving.

It was satisfied. This was the target.

"Detect! Detect!" Guhl yelled as he read the signals the torpedo was sending back to his computer screen. "Acquisition! Weapon is homing! Coming up in depth!"

Ward pressed his eye to the periscope. Everyone else watched the video monitor.

"Final arming sequence!" Guhl called out.

Just seconds now.

The torpedo ran up to a depth of thirty-five feet. The active sonar in the nose was pinging rapidly now. An electronic switch armed the electromagnetic detector. It tried to sense any large metal body nearby. A small, upward looking hydrophone listened for any sonar signal from directly overhead. When the torpedo was eight feet directly under the freighter, both the metal detector and the hydrophone saw what they were searching for. An electric pulse flashed through the firing circuit to the warhead detonator.

As if in slow motion, the sea beneath the *Helena K* appeared to rise up, improbably lifting her midsection. Then the ocean fell out from under her, leaving her supported only from the bow and stern. An orange flash shot up the side of the dying drug runner. A tear started down by her keel and shot up either side. In the blink of an eye, the freighter broke in half and the bow and stern rose high in the air. The containers on her deck broke free of their lashings and plunged heavily into the water, heading for the bottom. The ship's huge bronze screw still turned slowly as the stern section slid into the sea.

The bow floated for a few more seconds, pointing almost straight up and bobbing gently like a huge cork. Slowly, it slid backward, disappearing beneath the surface of the Pacific Ocean with barely a splash.

A loud cheer broke out in the control room as soon as the torpedo detonated. It stopped almost immediately as the warriors watched the death throes of their enemy. Witnessing the demise of a ship, even one as evil and odious as this one, was a terrible thing. Good or bad, people were dying up there. Ward's crew instinctively sensed it was nothing to cheer about.

When the bow disappeared, Ward shouted, "COB, broach the ship! Chief of the Watch, line up to put a low-pressure blow on all main ballast tanks."

Ray Laskowski turned to Cortez and MacNaughton.

"Full rise on the fairwater planes. Zero the stern planes." *Spadefish* shot upward, held on the surface by her speed. "All ahead flank."

She strained to race at top speed to where the sea battle had taken place, to rescue any survivors. Ward waited as the low-pressure blower forced air into the ballast tanks and shoved the seawater out. Laskowski was satisfied.

"On the surface and holding, Skipper."

Ward strapped on the holstered 9mm Beretta that Beasley handed him and rushed up the ladder to open the bridge hatch. Beasley and the rifleman followed.

Ward slowed the sub as they approached the wreckage, coasting to a stop once they were almost touching the remnants of the *Cyclone*. The bullet-stitched hulk was barely afloat, streaming smoke from fires that were still burning inside. Bodies lay where they had fallen during the ambush. A battered group of ten men, beaten and stunned at the ferocity of the ambush, stood on the fantail waving wearily at Ward.

"Search and rescue team, lay topside," Ward commanded.

The hatch opened on the main deck a few feet aft of the sail and ten sailors poured out. Four stood watching the water with their M-16s at the ready. The rest pushed equipment up the hatch and laid it out.

The last man up the hatch was Joe Glass. Ward shouted down to him.

"XO, I'll bring us alongside. Get those men onboard and send a party over to search for any more survivors and to retrieve the bodies."

Chief Macallister was the last one lifted over. There were no more. From a crew of twenty-eight, only ten would be coming home alive.

Doc Marston had his hands full tending to the wounded. The wardroom and the mess decks once more became the emergency hospital. Cookie Dotson helped suture wounds and clean burns while Doc worked on Macallister's leg. His seemed to be the worst injury and no one could imagine how he was able to crawl the length of the deck and reach the bridge-to-bridge radio.

With all the remaining Coast Guardsmen, both living and dead, aboard, Ward cast off the *Cyclone* and moved over to check the debris left from the *Helena K*. One of his crewmen spotted someone floating, clinging to a piece of wreckage, calling drunkenly for help. He was big, blond, and had an obvious Swedish lilt in his voice. Captain Serge Novstad offered no resistance as he was plucked from the water and rudely shoved down the hatch.

They found no other survivors from the *Helena K*.

The bridge announcing system speaker squawked.

"Bridge, radio. Request the captain pick up the JA."

Ward reached over and grabbed the handset.

"Captain."

"Captain, this is Chief Lyman. We are in contact with Coast Guard Station Port Angeles. They have a C-130 on the way out. ETA one hour. Cutter getting underway from Cape Flattery, ETA in twenty-four hours. They request we stand by here."

"Chief, tell them we have wounded on board who need hospitalization. We will be making best speed to Cape Flattery. Also, tell them we have the captain of the *Helena K* in custody. Name of Serge Novstad. Claims Swedish citizenship. They can have the slimeball just as soon as we get back."

"Aye, sir."

Ward looked down at the main deck. Everyone was below and the hatch was swinging shut. He turned to Beasley.

"Well, Nav. Looks like we've done all we can do here. Let's head for home."

"Aye, sir."

35

TOM KINCAID WATCHED AS THE POLICE LAUNCH GLIDED THROUGH THE mist back toward the spot where he waited on the pier. It stopped alongside, its exhaust burbling gently in the clear water. Ken Temple was standing in the after cockpit and tossed Kincaid a line. He wrapped it a couple of times around a cleat on the pier.

"What did you find?" the DEA agent yelled, even before the detective could get off the boat.

"The guy was on the receiving end of some kind of automatic weapon. He had at least ten holes in him. The medical examiner's man says it doesn't look like he's been in the water very long."

Temple hopped up onto the pier while Kincaid reached out and grabbed his arm, giving the big man a lift up. Temple shook the rainwater off his bright yellow poncho, then reached into a pocket and pulled out a Ziploc bag that held a water-soaked man's wallet.

"He had this on him. It says his name is Bert Jankowski and lists an address in East Cromwell. That's just across the bridge, a couple of miles to the east. Nobody's reported him missing so that sorta backs up the opinion that he's only been in the drink a little while. I called from the boat and had 'em send a black-and-white out to the address to give somebody the bad news, maybe see why he was out here in the first place." He laid the wallet on the top of one of the pier pilings, flipped open his notepad and studied what he had written there. "Also says he's a retired chief from the navy, aged sixty-five. Tommy, I don't think this guy is one of your druggies at all."

Kincaid nodded his agreement.

"Probably not. I'll bet you he stumbled up on them before they got the shit unloaded and they took him out."

Before Temple had a chance to agree, they were interrupted by a shout from one of the uniformed officers waving to them from the head of the pier.

"Hey, Detective, over here. You might want to see this."

The two men walked quickly to the end of the pier and stepped onto the abandoned blacktop road, now cracked and broken from the elements, weeds and small trees growing through in spots. The officer led them toward an old metal warehouse. On the way, Temple pointed at the ground.

"Looks like there's been a good bit of traffic over this area in the last several days," the detective said. "See how the grass and weeds are trampled down?"

"I noticed that, too," the officer said. "And there are plenty of truck tracks in the mud around there, too."

They walked on to where the sliding door to the warehouse stood open. The inside was dark and empty, the air stale and dank like any long abandoned place. There was also the faint, unmistakable odor of tobacco smoke. Even a hint of marijuana.

Temple looked sideways at the young patrolman.

"Any of your guys been sneaking a smoke in here out of the rain?"

"No, sir. This is what I wanted you to see. It's not like the navy to leave a building unlocked when they leave it." He held up a large padlock, the hasp cut neatly in two. The lock was rusty, but the cut metal was bright and shiny. "We found this over there in the brush next to the building. The door was standing open when we got here. Somebody's been here. Lots of somebodies. But it looks like they left here in a hurry. See the tire marks over there?"

He pointed to several pairs of black skid marks on the concrete floor inside the shed. Temple nodded.

"Good work. We need to send some officers out to question the locals. See if anybody saw anything unusual around here lately. I don't hold much hope, though. Fox Island is pretty secluded. People move over here for their privacy. And this place was out of the way, even for Fox Island. Still, if there was this much traffic down here, maybe somebody noticed something."

"Or heard something," Kincaid added. "Somebody made a lot of racket plugging our poor navy man out there."

"Yessir. Maybe we'll get lucky, Mr. G-Man."

"Yeah, maybe. And it'll be about damn time."

John Bethea rested his head in his hands and rubbed his eyes hard with his fingers. Things were moving way too fast. No surprise there. That's the way these things usually happened. Like traffic in Southern California, things would creep and crawl for a ways, then it was all zoom zoom.

First there had been Tom Donnegan's call from Hawaii to tell him that *Spadefish* was operational again, but at the price of two badly injured crewmen who had heroically done their duty, no matter the consequences.

Then there was El Falcone's report, the word that de Santiago had finally flipped and was planning an assassination of the president of his country.

Next came the angry call from the Commandant of the Coast Guard, giving him mortal hell for sending the *Cyclone* into an ambush that ultimately cost the lives of eighteen fine young men and a good ship.

That was the worst blow. Bethea had been disconsolate enough about that tragedy already.

He also knew this was war, and a shady one at that. A war that claimed victims just as all wars do, whether they were sailors manning gun positions on a patrol boat or stupid kids looking for a thrill and a high.

They had successfully kept the details of the ambush from the media so far. *Spadefish* was not mentioned. It was just an attack on a Coast Guard patrol boat by an especially vicious group of drug smugglers, the patrol boat able to sink the ship with return fire, an unknown number of smugglers lost, the contraband cargo gone, but the ship's captain captured.

The real question that nagged at John Bethea was how in hell the *Helena K* got herself so well armed without him knowing about it. They had boarded the bastard and inspected her while she was steaming off Colombia. Then they had tracked her and kept her under surveillance from underwater, from the air and from space for days on end. The only time the freighter was out of their sight was during the storm when she had moved west of where she dropped the mini-sub. She must have met up with someone out there then. And Jon Ward had reported noticing freight lashed to her deck just before he blew her to smithereens, containers that had not been there before.

They'd never know now what was in those containers. Or who the *Helena K* might have hooked up with out there in the middle of the North Pacific. Whoever it was would have long since been gone.

Now, to top off his perfect day, here was Tom Kincaid on the line, reporting that they had pulled an innocent civilian out of Puget Sound, an apparent victim of Ramirez and de Santiago and their malignant commerce. And Kincaid said that there was no sign of the mini-sub or the smugglers other than tire tracks, tobacco smoke, and the dead man they had left behind. That meant the whole lot of deadly coke was loose somewhere in the country and there was nothing they could do now but try to find yet another needle in a much bigger haystack.

This war could quickly turn into mass murder if that dope was as deadly as the last stuff had been.

This was not a good day.

Bethea had been around long enough and had been hit by enough bad news to know what to do. He had said it often enough that one of his daughters had made a plaque with the words on it as a craft project at summer camp years before. It was right there on his desk, just as it had been ever since she first gave it to him.

"Fix what you can. Feel bad about the rest when you have time."

He managed some semblance of a grin as he reached for the red secure phone and punched in a series of digits. When the call was answered on the other end, he launched into his message immediately, without any of the customary pleasantries.

"El Presidente Guitteriz, I have important information. Please listen carefully."

Ken Temple searched his pockets, trying to locate the cell phone. The damned thing's annoying buzz was interrupting his thinking. He found it in his raincoat pocket and flipped it open.

"Temple!" he growled.

He and Tom Kincaid were hitching a ride back over to SEATAC with a black-and-white squad car to pick up their own vehicles. The DEA man complained mildly about being stuck in the backseat, in the cage, but it was the quickest way to get back. The helicopter had to go on back without them while they inspected the abandoned navy site. Now, they were high over the Tacoma Narrows on the broad span of the bridge, watching uncomfortably as it swayed noticeably beneath them in the wind. It didn't help any to remember that this bridge's predecessor had collapsed in a breeze no more pronounced than this on the day it was first opened to the public.

"Detective, this is Officer Watson," the voice on the phone said. The name didn't ring any bells with Temple until the caller added, "You know, the patrol officer over on Fox Island."

"Oh, yeah. The one who found the warehouse lock. Good work, Officer Watson. That was very observant."

"Thank you, sir." The young patrolman sounded pleased. Praise from Detective Temple was hard to win. He had the reputation as a cop's cop. "The reason I called was to give you some more information we came up with. We canvassed all the residences on Fox Island like you asked. One of them turned up something." There was a pause. Watson was probably reading from his notes. Temple held his breath and gave Kincaid the high sign. "A Mrs. Vasquez. She lives down by the bridge, One-oh-one Fox Island Drive. She told one of our guys she was up early this morning to let her dogs out and that she saw a whole bunch of UPS trucks leave the island. She counted a dozen altogether, like they were in some kind of convoy, and they seemed to her to be driving pretty fast for the narrow road."

"Dozen UPS trucks, huh?"

"Yes, sir. Mud-brown panel trucks with UPS right there on the side. She said she didn't think a whole lot about it at the time. She's been noticing two or three trucks coming in every day for the last week or so. She just figured they were doing something out there at the old navy lab, maybe working on them or something. But all of them leaving at once, just about daylight, and them driving that fast on a back road? That got her curious enough to remember it anyway."

Temple nodded and scribbled away on his notepad with his free hand.

"Okay. You got more?"

"Yes, sir. I took it on myself to call UPS. They say they've only made one delivery out here this week. One truck. And that was to an address a good two miles from where that lady lives. They haven't had anything going on out here otherwise."

"Got it. Good work, Officer Watson. You got the makings of a good detective someday, you ever want to give up the glamour of writing speeding tickets at radar traps."

Temple disconnected from that call and punched in more numbers.

Kincaid raised his eyebrow. Temple held the cell phone to his ear and listened to the throb of its ring.

"Could be our break! Tell you in a minute."

"Police Central Dispatch."

"Central, this is Detective Temple, badge two-five-four-eight. I need an APB on any UPS trucks in the area. I'm especially interested in any that might be traveling as a group. They are to be reported and followed at a distance. They are not to be approached."

The operator on the other end of the phone sounded as if she was having trouble believing what she heard.

"The area?"

"From Tacoma up past SEATAC, all the way to Bellevue and Everett."

"Let me get this straight, detective. You want us to report sightings of all UPS trucks just about everywhere in the Pacific Northwest? There are probably a thousand or more of them on the roads around here at any given time."

"I know that. The ones I want are bogus. And get the state to keep an eye out on I-ninety and I-five, too, in case they head south or east." He paused a moment. "Oh, one other thing. I also want you to call UPS dispatch and tell them to pull all their trucks off the road right now and keep 'em off until further notice."

"Yes, sir. I'm to tell UPS to go out of business until we tell them they can go back to work someday. And exactly whose authority do I use for this?"

Temple looked at Kincaid and grinned broadly.

"The authorization comes from Rick Taylor, director of the

DEA, who reports directly to the president of the United States. And it's a matter of life and death. Young lady, this has National Emergency Precedence. Understand? National Emergency Precedence."

Kincaid smiled as Temple hung up.

"That was good, using my boss's authority without bothering to consult with the bastard."

"You mind, Agent Kincaid?"

"Not in the least, Detective Temple. Hell, he'll probably try to grab credit for this whole operation anyway if we bring this scum down. We might as well let him earn his part of the glory. And if it goes bust, both our asses are grass anyway." The cop driving the black-and-white grinned along with them. He knew about bosses, too. "By the way, what exactly is National Emergency Precedence, anyway? That's a new one on me."

Temple chuckled and said, "No idea, but it sure sounded good, didn't it?"

Kincaid laughed out loud, then said, "Now, tell me what the hell's going on."

And Ken Temple did just that as the black-and-white wound its way around to the junction with Interstate 5.

Jason Rashad met Carlos Ramirez at the sliding door, moving it open wide enough so he could drive in. The warehouse sat on the backside of SEATAC airport in a section of commercial storage buildings and light industrial installations. Most of the warehouses were on short-term leases to companies engaged in various types of Asian trading. One of the advantages of leasing here was that no one seemed to take much interest in whatever that business was. Most of them were doing perfectly legal business. It was the perfect place to hide a bunch of trucks for a few days before trans-shipping the stuff on out. There were comings and goings in this neighborhood at all hours of the day and night, plenty of truck traffic. No neighbors would raise an eyebrow if there were deliveries leaving out from the building down at the end of the row, the one right next to the high chain-link fence that marked the far end of the complex.

Carlos gunned the powerful engine of his black 911 Targa as he steered it through the door, then slammed on the brakes and hopped out as soon as he had screeched to a stop.

"So, how'd it go down there with the mini-sub? Any problems?"

Rashad's face barely shifted, but ended up in a wicked, self-satisfied smirk.

"Nothing I couldn't handle. The other three trucks are on their way to the warehouse in Portland and the rest of the stuff's all here. And that damn little sewer pipe of a submarine is bottom-crawling its way on back to the rendezvous point. We'll have the other part of the cargo back at the sound lab in a week." He nodded toward the line of trucks along one wall of the building. "We're almost ready to start distribution. We're working on repainting the trucks and we'll send them out in a bit. I thought we'd make them bakery delivery trucks this time. How does 'Snow Bakery' sound to you?"

Ramirez didn't share the large black man's sense of humor. He grunted.

"I don't really give a shit what you call them. Just get the stuff out to our customers so I can report to de Santiago that everything is done. And we damn well better make sure he never finds out about the stuff we skimmed off the top. You screw up and that crazy bastard will cut off our balls and feed them to us."

Rashad shook his head. He cleared the thought of what the rebel leader might do if this part of the plan failed. He looked over at one of the trucks, its windows covered with paper, already getting its first coat of paint.

"Give me a day, boss. It'll take that long for the paint to dry in this damned wet weather."

Ramirez slipped back into the sports car. He leaned out the window.

"First shipment from here leaves Thursday at the latest, Jason." He cranked up the engine. "No slipups."

He spun the car around and disappeared in a haze of exhaust and burned rubber.

Vancouver, Washington, motorcycle officer Kevin McCoy had found himself a nice, sneaky niche between a bridge abutment and a chain link fence alongside I-5. Traffic barreling down on him along the last straightaway before the bridge over the Columbia River to Portland had no way of seeing him there. They showed up on his radar gun well before they had a chance to hit their brakes and get themselves legal. Today the fog had most drivers behaving. He was taking it easy, leaned back, resting his perpetually aching sacroiliac, listening to the jabber on the radio.

Three UPS trucks running nose to tail right at him. A light went on his head. There had been something from dispatch a few minutes before about watching for packs of the brown trucks. The readout on the radar gun said they were doing better than seventy-five. That cinched it.

He turned on the blue strobes and took off after the convoy.

The last truck in line slowed at once and pulled obediently to a stop at the side of the interstate. The other two sped on as if they had not seen him at all. Ticket one guy and somebody else would see the others if they didn't slow down.

He parked the bike on its kickstand. The officer walked toward the delivery van. Something wicked whizzed past his ear. He swatted at whatever it was. Another something took a bite out of the shoulder pad of his leather jacket and shattered one of the mirrors on his motorcycle behind him.

"Jesus!" he yelped and dove for the cover of the rear of the van.

The cop slithered beneath the van and got his own service revolver unsnapped out of its holster. Whoever was inside could easily back up and run over him if he wanted to. He could bend down and let him have it while he cowered under

there. He looked around. There was a culvert about thirty feet
to his right. But then he saw a pair of legs hop down from the
driver's side of the van and run toward the rear of the vehicle.

Halfway back, the man realized the cop was not lying back
there bleeding. He dropped to his knees to look beneath the
truck. McCoy saw the glint of a pistol. He didn't hesitate. He
let loose four quick rounds.

The gunman went down hard, writhing on the asphalt, his
gun skittering into the middle of passing traffic. McCoy
scrambled out from beneath the truck. He slid along the opposite side of the van from the wounded gunman. Easing
around, he held the gun out in front of him with both hands.
He had to see if there was anyone else in the vehicle, anyone
with a weapon.

Nobody else in the cab of the truck. He climbed inside and
stepped through the doorway into the cargo area.

No one there either. Only white bricks wrapped in cello-
phane and stacked high down each side.

The shooter was still lying there when he got back outside.
The guy's eyes were shut. He squirmed in pain. A small pool
of blood formed beneath him. McCoy stood over him, his gun
pointed squarely at the man's forehead.

"What the hell is going on?" he finally asked.

The man's eyes burst open in wild panic.

"Don't shoot don't shoot don't shoot!" he begged. "I'm
only a driver. I tell you everything I know. I tell you everything I know."

McCoy kept his barrel directed at the man's head, trying to
keep his hand from shaking while he reported, "Shots fired,
suspect in custody, send an ambulance," via the two-way radio
microphone on his shoulder.

"Okay, while we wait for my buddies to show up, why don't
you just tell me everything you know before my finger accidentally squeezes this trigger?"

Ken Temple and Tom Kincaid sat staring at each other across
Temple's desk. The cramped little cubicle had just enough

room for the desk and two straight-backed chairs. Temple
hated paperwork and it showed. The stuff filled the IN basket
and toppled over to litter the desktop. Several of the buff-
colored folders were stained with coffee rings. A telephone
and two coffee cups sat amongst the litter. Neatness was not
one of the detective's virtues.

"Ken, you ever do any admin?" Kincaid asked, looking in
disbelief at the size of the paper stack.

Temple shook his head.

"Nah. I give everything six months. Anybody asks about
something in six months, it goes in that stack," he said, pointing at one corner of the desk. "If they ask again in another six
months, I might consider doing it. If no one asks three times,
it gets trashed. So far, it all gets trashed."

The phone started to jangle and Temple grabbed it. As the
person on the other end talked, he rifled through the pile of
folders. A bunch of them fell to the floor, joining many others
that had already ended up down there. He found the legal pad
he was looking for and started to take notes, scribbling around
the residue of a jelly doughnut left on the page.

"What? Damnation! Okay, what's the address of the place
up here?"

He wrote something else on the pad. Kincaid tried to read
the scratching but couldn't decipher what it was. He could tell
the big detective was excited. Maybe their luck was continuing to get better.

Temple turned the notepad around and showed Kincaid the
address he had scrawled there. The DEA agent walked to the
large map tacked to the cubicle wall and tried to find the street
while Temple continued his conversation. There it was, down
by the airport.

"Okay, you say there were three of the trucks down there?
The rest should be at the warehouse here?" Temple nodded.
He flashed a huge grin at Kincaid. "Thank you, Detective.
You've been a tremendous help."

Temple returned the phone to its cradle and rose to leave.

"Sometimes it's better to be lucky than good. Come on,

slowpoke. Time to go to work. That was a cop down in Vancouver. One of his traffic officers stopped a UPS truck running in a pack of three down there. He heard the APB go out on the radio. One of them pulled over and the bastard driving the thing started taking shots at him. The cop took him down. He says the driver started singing like a songbird when he thought the cycle cop was going to plug him between the eyes. The other trucks should still be at that warehouse up here, but if they get word we caught one of their guys, they'll get out in one hell of a hurry, I bet. The other two trucks down there have already failed to show up where the perp said they were supposed to be going. I guess they knew their buddy would spill his guts if he got caught, so they went somewhere else."

Kincaid couldn't believe his ears. He ran to keep up with the amazingly fast moving detective.

"They have any idea how many people might be baby-sitting the trucks up here?"

Temple reached to hold open the elevator door.

"He didn't say. But get this. It'll really pique your interest."

"I'm biting."

"The guy said we should watch out for a mean-ass black son of a bitch in a gold Beemer."

Jonathan Ward stood on the bridge of his submarine and watched as the Coast Guard boat pulled alongside. It looked like a forty-footer, a good boat for these waters. It was a little cramped for the short run back to the pier with the survivors of the *Cyclone* ambush. Ward wished it could be far more crowded, that there were more men that had survived the attack.

Still it was good to be back in the sheltered waters by Port Angeles. The storm had blown out, the sky was blue, and a light breeze stirred a little chop in the straits. It was altogether a nice day.

He would be very happy when *Helena K*'s captain was in Coast Guard custody. Ward had turned him over to Chief Ralston to handle. The chief had kept the Swede shackled and under armed guard down in the torpedo room. It couldn't have been very comfortable, but Ward didn't care. The bastard could complain all he wanted about the bad food, the lack of booze, or whatever else. Ward couldn't get the picture out of his head of the freighter circling the helpless Coast Guard vessel, pounding her mercilessly. On the trip back, he had been tempted to mete out a little old-fashioned maritime justice, but he knew the authorities would take care of the bastard. And learn more about the whole operation in the process.

Ward watched the coxswain of the Coast Guard boat speak into his radio. Ward's walkie-talkie crackled to life.

"Good afternoon, Captain. Permission to come alongside?"

"Permission granted. Come alongside, cleat three, on the lee side. I'm making three knots, course zero-eight-six."

The coxswain spun the wheel around and the little boat swung around to pass astern of *Spadefish*. He brought it up along to port side, matching the sub's speed. One of the Coast Guardsmen jumped onto the fo'c'sle of the boat and tossed a line over to the sub.

The radio crackled again.

"Ready to transfer the dead and wounded when you are, sir."

Ward looked down over the back of the sail, aft of the protruding fairwater plane. The white boat bobbed gently in the calm waters of the sub's lee side. The injured crewmen from the *Cyclone* slowly climbed out of the sub's hatch and were helped across to the boat. Chief Macallister, strapped to a stretcher, was the last of the ten. He waved and called out "Thank you again, Skipper!" as he was lifted over to the boat.

"You're welcome, Chief," Ward shouted back. "Don't go chasing any nurses until that leg's healed."

Next came the bags that held the bodies of the men who had died aboard the *Cyclone*. Even the wounded men stopped, stood at attention, and saluted their fallen friends as the two craft rocked gently and the gulls circled overhead in the warm sun, as if they were paying their own tribute.

Finally, Hendrix and Kuhn climbed out of the hatch, each with his hands heavily bandaged. Kuhn stood at attention and saluted the ensign flying from a staff extending from the top of the sail. He yelled, "Captain, permission to go ashore!"

Ward saluted the engineer right back.

"Permission granted. I expect you two on the pier when we get to San Diego."

"We'll be there. We'll bring the beer."

"Deal."

Jonathan Ward could hardly get the single word out past the sudden lump that had appeared in his throat.

He ended the salute by deftly wiping away a tear.

"See anything?" Kincaid asked.

He and Detective Ken Temple squatted together in the brush, fifty yards from a chain-link fence. The back wall of the warehouse rose up high only a few feet on the other side of the fence. Temple was squinting through his sniper scope, peeking out from under the branches of a thorny yew bush.

"Nothing since the gold Beemer drove up. That's been an hour ago now."

Kincaid glanced at his watch. Its luminous dial said it was a few minutes after four A.M. Two more hours until sunrise. He shivered in the light mist. It certainly got cold out here at night, the chill seeping right through the black Gore-Tex rain suit.

The continual warmth. That was just one more thing he missed about his old life in South Florida. Still, it felt good to now be here, doing something. Something that would make a difference, save lives.

Now he worked at picturing the bad guys, how they were out of the drizzle and nice and warm inside their dry warehouse. They had plenty of hot coffee in there, too. His own thermos had gone dry about midnight. He used the images and his own discomfort to further stoke the white-hot anger he was kindling.

"Okay, we go when Ramirez shows," he said. "Everybody in place?"

Temple chuckled. For a cool DEA operator, Kincaid could be one nervous Nellie on a stakeout.

"Tom, for the hundredth time, everybody's ready. You sure you want to wait around to see if that slime shows up? They may be planning on leaving before he drops by, you know. Or what if he's gone on to meet them wherever they're taking the shit already? They gotta know by now about the other guy getting busted downstate."

"We'll move if that happens. I just can't believe they'll move out without him here to see it happen, though. Besides, I want him on the premises when this thing goes down so we'll have a stronger case." Temple could hear the angry trembling in Kincaid's voice. "And I just hope those two bastards want to put up a fight so I can save the government of the United States a little money and time."

As if on cue, headlights pierced the darkness at the far end of the street. Whoever it was, he was moving quickly.

Temple's radio squawked: "Black Porsche coming."

He grabbed the microphone.

"Heads up, everyone. As soon as we ID Ramirez, we move."

The black Targa materialized under the dim light at the warehouse door. A short, dark-haired man hopped out and entered through a side door.

Temple focused the sniper scope and squinted into it.

"That's him. People, move! Move! Move!"

Two dozen heavily armed men dressed in identical black uniforms rushed out of a pair of buildings farther up the street, moving quickly toward the target warehouse. A dozen more armed men rose from the brush around Temple and Kincaid and rushed the chain-link fence. They cut through and charged the warehouse from that side. Two helicopters rose from the landing pad at SEATAC and were circling overhead, playing large searchlights on the scene below while Seattle

PD squad cars, their blue lights strobing, blocked all entrance
and exits to the complex.

All that activity outside didn't go unnoticed by those inside
Someone started shooting from the door, firing blindly with a
machine pistol. The staccato ripping sound and bright muzzle
flash tore through the night and one of the DEA men who
were approaching went down with a sharp yelp, clutching his
calf.

A single shot answered. It was the deeper bark of a
Wetherby .308 Magnum sniper rifle. The machine pistol clat
tered to the ground, and its owner tumbled from behind the
doorway and crumpled lifelessly to the pavement.

A bullhorn blasted: "Inside the building! This is the DEA
You are surrounded! Give yourselves up!"

Defiant gunfire erupted from several windows around the
building. It was answered by return fire from the SWAT
teams. The smugglers were badly outmatched. Their volleys
were random and poorly aimed. The return fire was accurate
The futile shooting from inside the warehouse slowed and fi
nally stopped completely.

Two dark figures burst out of the back door, trying to make
it to the fence. Both carried machine pistols, firing randomly
as they ran toward the hole in the fence near where Kincaid
and Temple still lay watching.

"Halt! Drop your weapons or we'll shoot," Temple yelled.

Both escapees made the mistake of raising their gun barrels
in the direction of the two lawmen. Kincaid's Beretta barked
at almost the same instant that Temple's Glock fired.

The two thugs fell.

The firefight was winding down. It was time to go inside
and pick up the pieces. Temple and Kincaid reloaded and
slowly approached the building's large sliding door from the
side, being careful not to expose themselves to anyone hiding
in the darkness inside. Anyone who might still have a bit of
fight left.

There was the sound of an automobile engine roaring to life

inside. The gold Beemer crashed right through the door, its
tires squealing. Kincaid jumped to the side, barely clearing
the rocketing car. Ken Temple, ten years older and fifty
pounds heavier, wasn't quite fleet enough. The right front
fender hit him solidly, a powerful blow to his legs and midsection. The force of the impact sent him sprawling awkwardly,
flying through the air, tumbling to the ground in a heap, one
leg bent at an odd angle. The Beemer's rear end skewed
wildly, the rear fender striking the detective one more time before its driver got it straightened and headed down the service
road.

Tom Kincaid rolled on his shoulder to his feet and came up
shooting. The car's rear window shattered with a loud pop,
disintegrating into a shower of glass pellets after the first two
shots. Someone fired back at him but Kincaid didn't let up. He
emptied the Glock into the fleeing vehicle. It veered to the
right and crashed hard into the concrete wall of a building further down the line, its horn a continuous mournful wail as
steam and smoke billowed from the crumpled machine.

Kincaid allowed a couple of the assault force to check on
the driver of the car. He suspected what condition they would
find him in. He reloaded his Glock once again as he ran back
to his friend's still body. The big detective lay where he had
fallen and did not move. Kincaid dropped to his knees and felt
for a pulse at Temple's throat. He couldn't find one. Desperately hoping, he tried again. There it was. He was still alive.

He yelled as loudly as he could.

"Officer down! Get medical help." There didn't seem to be
any bleeding. Internal injuries, a head wound. "Get me a
chopper! We've got to get him to a hospital!"

He spied a police helicopter touching down in the field on
the other side of the fence. Kincaid used all the strength he
could muster to gather up his friend in his arms, drape him
over one shoulder, and run toward the chopper.

A police captain in dress uniform with a lot of braid was
climbing out. Showing up now that the shooting was over so

he could join in the glory as soon as the media arrived. Kincaid brushed him aside to lift the inert body of his friend into the cabin of the chopper.

"Get him to the nearest hospital as fast as you can!" he ordered the pilot.

The captain stepped up. He grabbed Kincaid and gave him a shove away from the helicopter.

"Just a second, agent. I'm in command here. There are other wounded in that warehouse we will have to triage and see who needs help first. We'll take them all when we have a load ready to evacuate."

Kincaid glared at the short, rotund little man. Several chins hid his collar devices under mottled flesh.

"Any other cops hurt?" Kincaid growled.

"I don't know, but several of the suspects are wounded. We have to assess which ones are the most seriously—"

Tom Kincaid was near explosion, and when he interrupted the cop, his voice was loud and menacing, his lips inches from the fat captain's face.

"I don't give a damn about them. They should have thought of this before they started. While you're taking the rectal temperatures of a few bad guys, this brave officer is dying!" He turned to the pilot and bellowed, "Get this piece of shit off the ground before I throw you out and fly it myself."

The pilot didn't wait for a second invitation. He was on Kincaid's side. He saluted smartly, pushed the throttle forward, and pulled back on the collector, lifting the helicopter off the ground and dusting Kincaid and the captain with dirt and debris.

The captain still blustered, yelling things about civil rights and liability suits and chains of command as Kincaid turned and purposefully walked back over to the warehouse.

The SWAT team was just emerging with a dozen men in handcuffs. Carlos Ramirez, his expensive designer suit dirt-stained and torn, led the prisoners.

"You won't believe how much coke they have on those trucks in there," one of the officers said.

"How many trucks?"

"Nine."

Kincaid fell into step alongside Ramirez.

"Mister, I count at least a dozen counts of murder, terrorism, drug smuggling, and probably a few other charges I haven't thought of yet. My only regret is that I won't get to throw the switch myself when they burn your sorry ass."

Ramirez managed an insolent smirk.

"You're barking up the wrong tree, DEA. My lawyer will have me out before the sun's up. And I'll have your sister before lunch."

Kincaid stopped, looked at him sideways, and fought the almost overpowering urge to stick the Glock to the bastard's forehead and pull the trigger.

Instead he turned and walked slowly toward the side street and his own parked car.

He was tired. Very, very tired.

36

JUAN DE SANTIAGO DEMONSTRATED HIS USUAL IMPATIENCE AS HE waited.

"Are you certain everyone is in place?"

Antonio de Fuka sighed as long and loudly as he dared and looked back across the little room at El Jefe. The leader paced back and forth, his boots raising little clouds of dust from the dirt floor. He glanced out the room's lone paneless window, out onto a squalid street in the midst of the worst shantytown in Bogotá.

"Street" was a misnomer, bestowing more grandeur than the nameless dirt track deserved. It wandered at odd angles among tin-walled shacks and was barely wide enough for a motorized vehicle to squeeze through. Dirty, half-naked children played there, oblivious of the raw sewage coursing through the mud, while grownups napped in the shade of the doorways or huddled together on the corner. De Santiago felt as much at home here as he did in his beloved jungle. Much of the early part of the revolution had been spent here, using the squalor and poverty of this place as the catalyst for the rebellion.

"Everything is ready, El Jefe," de Fuka assured his leader yet again. "Our men are in position. The ordnance is poised as you directed. They will attack on your signal. We will not fail."

De Santiago merely grunted. The waiting this time was especially difficult. He was well aware that his staff considered him a man of most limited patience. The past three days had not detracted from that image. They knew how momentous this occasion would be. There was no room for error. That's why they had taken such unusual precautions in rounding up his most trusted fighters, his most battle-tested soldiers, their most sophisticated weapons and shooters, and in slipping them into Bogotá undetected. Even with his well-positioned intelligence gatherers, gaining information about the debriefing Guitteriz would be holding with the *yanqui* soldier was more difficult than anything they had ever done.

Security had been unusually high around this meeting and that raised de Santiago's antenna. Even José Silveras, the most valuable of spies, could find out little other than the location and the time. Luckily, Silveras found enough details in the many databases to help them piece together a plan, but only at the last possible minute. Now it had been confirmed through two other sources, so de Santiago and de Fuka had given the order to proceed with the plan. This would be the best chance they would have to get revenge for the damage the *Americano* had done. And it was a fine opportunity to remove El Presidente and throw the government into chaos.

This was a move born of desperation, but it would be just as effective nonetheless. It was a glorious day for the people, for the revolution.

There was one other distraction: the troubling lack of information from the north. The first shipment of dosed cocaine should have arrived at the secret off-load south of Seattle, and the second load of freight, Sui's heroin, should be well on its way down the Straits of Juan de Fuca via the mini-sub by now. And de Santiago should have heard from Novstad, Zurko, or Ramirez with some kind of update.

They had been silent. It was not a good omen.

Perhaps they were only being very cautious. It would be a most inopportune time for the DEA or the JDIA to get wind of the potent product he was sending into America. They would know how serious El Jefe was about his revolution, about his plan to capture the American market, about how adept he was at breaking their pitiful anti-drug barrier. How eager the customers were in their country to try his mix.

There might be another reason why he had not heard anything yet. Perhaps they were merely derelict in their duty. For that, they would eventually answer. De Santiago hoped for such a simple explanation. He suspected deep down in his bones that another disaster had struck. His masterfully created plan was already in shambles here at home.

El Jefe knew something else, and it was the most disturbing realization of all. His people were beginning to doubt him. Word of all the setbacks had spread among his supporters. Many were beginning to question his ability to lead the revolution.

With this ultimate bold move, he would show them he still had the power to lead. Very soon, he would finally control his country, once and for all. Those who had betrayed him would pay, right along with the *yanqui* bastards.

Guzmán stepped through the doorway from the street.

"El Jefe, the car; it is ready," he grunted as he checked his wristwatch.

De Santiago glanced back at his lovely Margarita, who sat quietly in the far corner of the rustic room.

"I will come back for you soon, my dear. And when I do, you will make love to the new president of our country."

She smiled beautifully, her face seemingly lighting up the dark, dank room, and she blew him a kiss.

De Santiago strode purposely out the doorway of the shanty and stepped into the open rear door of the black Land Rover, ready to witness firsthand the long-overdue grand climax of his revolution.

Rudi Sergiovski tried one more time. The underwater telephone seemed to be working fine. The signal was going out all right. He could hear his voice reflecting off the ocean surface fifty meters above him.

So where was that damn Swede and his rust bucket of a ship?

Sergiovski checked his navigation again. He was right where he was supposed to be, precisely at the rendezvous point.

"Hey, Philippe, my friend. Check my navigation. Make sure I have it right."

Philippe Zurko reluctantly roused himself from the stool where he was dozing. He moved over to look at the navigation console.

"Looks okay to me. What's the worry?"

The fat Russian was beginning to sweat and his voice had involuntarily risen an octave.

"The worry, my unlearned companion, is this: Our fuel cells only have so much capacity. We have about two hours' power left right now. If Novstad doesn't show quickly, we are out of luck. It will get very dark and cold in here."

Zurko wished he had paid a lot more attention when the garrulous Sergiovski had explained to him how the *Zibrus* worked.

"Is there nothing you can do?" he gulped. "Surely you have backups! A battery? A diesel engine? Something!"

The Russian took a swig of vodka from his bottle then wiped his lips with his sleeve. Zurko suspected the man was getting near drunk by now.

"It works like this, Señor Zurko." Sergiovski didn't even try to hide the derision in his voice when he spoke Zurko's name. "The fuel cells give us all our power. *All* our power. That means power for propulsion to drive back to shore, power for light, power to clean the air, and power to pump water." He took another belt of the vodka. He was exasperated at having to waste effort explaining their predicament yet again to this thick-skulled Latino. "The fuel cells need hydrogen and we are almost out of hydrogen. The *Helena K* has our resupply. Without it, we are stuck out here, dead in the water. You want to ask the U.S. Coast Guard for a tow to shore?"

"Surely we have emergency systems that we could—"

"There was no capacity for any emergency systems. They were removed so we could carry more cocaine, remember? I warned you about this when we designed this piece of shit. You insisted. You and your beloved El Jefe. You said another ton of cocaine was much more important than a 'smelly old diesel,' I think you called it."

Sergiovski belched and jerked upward on the sub's control yoke. The little *Zibrus* angled sharply for the surface.

"What are you doing?"

"We will surface and try to radio that stupid Swede," Sergiovski muttered, more to himself than in answer to Zurko's question. "Maybe he is lost, looking for us."

The mini-sub bobbed to the surface, its tiny sail barely clearing the wave tops. Zurko stared out through the thick glass porthole to see the choppy gray north Pacific. Waves lapped up and over the little porthole and he felt himself getting queasy.

"But Señor Sergiovski, we should not be using the radio out here because—"

The look on the Russian's red face stopped him cold. Sergiovski fiddled with the dials of the radio, then he spoke in English in his thick Russian accent, his words further slurred by the effects of the mostly empty bottle of vodka.

"*Helena K*, this is *Zibrus*. We are at rendezvous. Where are you? Over."

The Russian repeated the phrase over and over, listening vainly between transmissions, desperately hoping the freighter would reply.

There was nothing but static on the little speaker.

In the sky a thousand feet overhead, a United States Coast Guard C-130 turned in slow, lazy circles. Its mission was a mostly hopeless one, to assist in the recovery of the *Cyclone* and the search for any more possible survivors. The search was futile and the crew knew it. They were tired now after hours of looking at nothing more than miles and miles of wavetops. They were angry over the vicious surprise attack on one of their own that had brought them out here in the first place.

Even this soon after the ambush, the name *Helena K* was infamous throughout the Coast Guard. When the pilot heard the name of the ship in his headset, he was immediately alert.

He listened carefully to the repeated transmissions, the seeming desperation in the voice. Whatever craft the *"Zibrus"* might be, it seemed frantic to contact the killer ship. The C-130's pilot continued to listen while his copilot used the other radio to contact the rescue cutter that was towing what remained of the *Cyclone* slowly back to Port Angeles.

The cutter made a small course change and headed in the direction of the radio call. It would be six hours before they could get there.

The C-130 had already located the source of the radio transmissions and soon slowly orbited above it, watching the tiny black shape far below, bobbing on the ocean's surface.

The fuel cells on the *Zibrus* held out almost an hour longer than Sergiovski predicted. As they gave out, the lights on the mini-sub darkened. The only illumination inside was the sunlight through the two tiny portholes. The air inside grew thick and heavy. Within an hour of the failure of the cells, it was already getting difficult for the men inside to breathe.

Sergiovski fell into a drunken stupor and was practically unconscious. Zurko, struggling to draw breath, reached up and opened the hatch to let some fresh air in. Waves swept over the sail and poured frigid seawater down the open hatch, drenching both men.

Sergiovski was revived and screamed in anger.

"You idiot! You will sink us! Don't you understand? There are no pumps to get rid of this water."

He shoved Zurko aside and slammed the hatch shut just as another torrent of cold water spilled down the opening.

By the time the Coast Guard cutter eased alongside the tiny mini-sub, the two occupants were more than happy to see any rescuer, even the U.S. military.

They climbed out onto the cutter's deck and into custody. Zurko even fell to his knees and kissed the deck of the cutter before offering his wrists to be handcuffed.

SEAL Lieutenant Commander Bill Beaman sat at the austere metal table across from the commanding general of the Colombian Army. Chief Johnston fidgeted in his seat on Beaman's right. Both men looked uncomfortable. The truth was, they would have rather assaulted a hostile enemy beach fortification than spend time in a room full of government VIPs like these. El Presidente had insisted on this personal debriefing and it was hard to turn down the personal invitation.

Beaman gazed slowly around the stark room. It was typical of the military briefing rooms he had seen all around the world. The only way to tell that this wasn't Oman or Vadso, Norway, was to look out the window and see the tropical foliage out there. As was typical, maps dominated the walls around a table filled with mostly empty Styrofoam coffee cups. The folding chairs aligned around the table were occupied by Guitteriz's senior military staff, each wearing their dress uniforms with rows of ribbons and plenty of brass, evidently to show off for the *Americanos*.

President Guitteriz finally entered the room, greeted the

Americans warmly, and returned the salutes of his staff. He cleared his throat and began speaking in near-perfect English.

"Señor Beaman, once again my country is in debt to you and your brave men. We owe you our everlasting gratitude for ridding us of Juan de Santiago's laboratory. You saved many lives through your skill and bravery." El Presidente glanced around the room then continued in a lowered voice. "Although the next time we would prefer if you asked us first before you jumped into our country and shot our citizens."

Beaman reddened and protested.

"But, El Presidente, we had reason to believe . . ."

Guitteriz smiled and raised his hand as he interrupted.

"We understand perfectly your security concerns, especially considering past tragic events. I am happy to report to you as well as to my staff that we believe we have taken care of the major leak. Colonel Perez is in charge of our internal security forces. I believe you will be interested in what he has to say."

The swarthy colonel at the far end of the table rose and strode to the center of the room. His crisply starched khaki uniform and spit-polished boots contrasted sharply with the SEALs' torn and frayed "cammies." They only had the outfits they had with them in their packs when they parachuted in. This meeting had been called before they had time to find anything else to wear. Beaman was still not sure why it was so important for them to be here.

Perez stood in front of a small-scale map of the city at the front of the briefing room.

"El Presidente, Lieutenant Commander Beaman, when you expressed concern about our security procedures after that awful ambush of your men in the jungle, we began an intensive search for leaks." He nodded toward the SEAL. "Due to our sources inside de Santiago's organization, we knew we were looking for a spy who was very well hidden and very careful. But one who had access to very sensitive information." Colonel Perez allowed himself the barest crease of a smile. "Fortunately for us, he was not careful enough. The computer system your JDIA gave us made him very lazy and allowed us to catch him. Hidden in the many programs on each machine was a monitoring function that reported every file that each machine accessed. No one knew of this except two computer experts we imported to conduct continuous audits on the units."

"Most ingenious," Guitteriz commented.

Perez nodded an acceptance of the president's praise and continued.

"We found a relatively minor bureaucrat, a man named José Silveras, in our military communications department. He was taking an unusual interest in many files that were outside his authority. We have been feeding him misinformation now for the last two weeks. We are certain that this information is going directly to de Santiago and his staff. If events unfold as we suspect they will in only a short time from now, we will no longer need Señor Silveras in place and he—along with de Santiago—will pay for their betrayal of the people of our country. And, of course, for the lives of your brave men, Lieutenant Commander."

"Thank you, Colonel Perez," Beaman said with a nod to Perez. Then he turned to Guitteriz. "Mr. President, I only request that I be allowed to be there when you capture de Santiago."

Guitteriz smiled.

"I understand perfectly, Lieutenant Commander. But it will not be necessary. We have our best men set to spring the trap on the bastard once and for all."

"But I don't think you understand at all, if you'll pardon me for saying so." Beaman stood and leaned on the table with both hands. "It's not only for the men who died in that ambush. They were soldiers. Good soldiers. They died doing what they were trained to do. I want to be there for all those who died because they were stupid enough to snort de Santiago's cocaine. Stupidity shouldn't carry a death sentence. And for the others who have gotten hooked on his shit. And all those who would eventually become his victims if he's allowed to keep exporting that crap.

"You know the real reason I want to be there? Because I hate hypocrites! I hate a man who kills and maims and pretends it's all for the good of his people, when all he really wants to do is capture the keys to power, to enrich himself through the blood of his own people as well as mine.

"Mr. President, I want to be there to see the look on the bastard's face when he realizes the gig is up. When it dawns on him that no amount of his rhetoric can rally enough support to prevent him from spending the rest of his miserable days in some especially nasty prison somewhere.

"Mr. President, I want to be there with my men to see him go down hard!"

Chief Johnston was watching Beaman with wide eyes. He'd served with the man for four years and he had never before heard him utter more than a few sentences at a time. He certainly had never heard him make such an emotional speech to a sitting head of state.

The president rubbed his chin and glanced at his assembled military staff around the metal table. Each man gave a slight nod.

"Thank you, Lieutenant Commander. Permission granted. I can now tell you that your presence here today is part of a trap that we are laying for de Santiago, and this meeting is part of the bait. Now, Señor Beaman, this is how we propose to deal with him once and for all time."

Juan de Santiago stared out through the dirt-smeared windshield of the Land Rover as it squeezed between the hovels and through the crowds of ragged urchins who rushed to see the odd vehicle as it passed. They stopped at the end of a street that allowed them a view of the place where the debriefing was supposed to be held.

"Antonio, are you quite sure they are meeting down there?" He gestured toward the small military compound a few hundred meters below them. It was little more than a couple of hastily constructed tar paper–covered barracks, with a low earth berm and chain-link fence around it, and a helicopter landing pad in the middle. It had been built here on the out-skirts of Bogotá only in the last few weeks. It hardly seemed like the kind of place the president of the country would use for a military briefing.

Antonio de Fuka nodded vigorously.

"*Sí*, El Jefe. That is what Silveras reported and he has been without error in the past. El Presidente apparently felt that se-crecy was his best protection and this unlikely meeting place would be safest."

They watched as a few government troops lounged around the doors to one of the barracks. They were mostly out of uni-form as they smoked and played cards. Their weapons were carelessly tossed aside. They were seemingly unconcerned about any possible rebel attack.

De Santiago snorted. His troops would never be so slovenly, so careless.

"How long now until El Presidente arrives?"

De Fuka spoke into his cell phone, listened, then answered de Santiago.

"His helicopter just left the presidential residence. It should be here in ten minutes at the most."

De Santiago nodded and smiled. The revolution would be over in ten minutes. His dream of freeing his people from the despot capitalist would be realized. And he would finally be El Jefe in more than name only. Once the president was re-moved, he could assemble his troops from the jungles and overrun the capital.

All the land would be his! And God only knew how much of the rest of the world would open up to him.

"Good," he said, punching Guzmán on the shoulder. "Drive closer, my friend. I want to feel the heat when El Presidente begins his journey to hell."

Guzmán slipped the Land Rover into gear and slowly drove down the winding road toward the compound.

"Everyone is in place and ready?" De Santiago continued

to question his lieutenant. "You are quite sure?"

De Fuka spoke into the cell phone once again and nodded.

"*Sí*, El Jefe. As I have reported, everyone is ready. The missile shooters are all back on the ridge over there waiting. They will shoot down the helicopter when it is directly over the compound. The fighters are ready to crash the gates and shoot anyone who moves. The missile shooters will shoot anti-tank missiles into the buildings and will annihilate any vehicle that tries to escape. No one will survive. Of that you can be completely sure."

De Santiago smiled.

"*Muy bueno, mi amigo*. You will soon have your own cabinet position in your country's new government, Señor de Fuka. Now tell me again in detail how El Presidente will die."

Merely hearing de Fuka's words caused a powerful tingling in his loins.

Soon. Very soon!

The lone Black Hawk helicopter cleared the ridgeline to the east and fluttered lazily on a course directly toward the compound. It flew along straight and level with no attempt at a treetop approach, or any other combat maneuver for that matter. The pilot seemed to have no concern at all about being detected or attacked. It stopped in midair, hovering a hundred meters above the landing pad before slowly beginning to settle down like a fat and happy gull.

Stinger missiles rose from the ground with a *whoosh* from four different locations around the ridge that overlooked the compound from the west. The heat-seeking missiles had no problem at all finding their intended target as they streaked directly toward the Black Hawk's hot jet exhaust as it made its deliberate descent to the pad. There was no place for the chopper to escape.

The helicopter exploded brilliantly in an orange and black fireball and with a boom that reverberated off the ridges. The twisted metal, rendered incapable of flight, fell heavily onto the pad and burned furiously. Thick black smoke billowed up into the sky and was visible from most of the city in only moments. No one inside could have possibly survived.

As soon as he saw the missiles rise and begin their flight toward El Presidente's helicopter, de Santiago screamed at Guzmán that it was now time to crash the front gate. The Land Rover had pulled in directly behind a bright yellow school bus. It was a touch suggested by de Santiago himself. Anyone guarding the gate of the compound would hesitate to fire in the direction of a school bus.

The school bus barreled down the road, the big black car following closely. It crashed hard through the small barrier that attempted to block the entrance to the compound, then pulled to a halt inside. Rebel fighters poured out the bus's side and rear doors, guns blazing wildly, scattering a hail of bullets.

Guzmán swung the nose of the Land Rover past the bus and headed directly for the burning remains of the helicopter where the president had just died horribly. De Santiago checked his MAC-10, making sure there was a round chambered. He looked back at his brave fighters who were already pushing El Presidente's routed troops back into their barracks.

The attack was going exactly as planned.

The fighting was so intense that no one noticed a small black globe that was hovering, just peeking over the opposite ridgeline, the hills to the east. Stinger missiles blasted into the air and headed for the president's chopper. Sensors inside the globe of the OH-58 Kiowa scout helicopter locked onto the missiles and calculated the trajectory back to their launch points. The rebel troops poured from the school bus. Six Apache helicopters leapt over the ridge and hovered there briefly. The data link between the scout chopper and the Apaches automatically downloaded the target coordinates to the Apache pilots' heads-up displays. Hellfire missiles were launched from the Apaches. On the far ridge, four pickup trucks, their store of spare Stingers and anti-tank missiles, and their rebel crews were obliterated from the face of the earth in less time than it takes to draw a deep breath.

Without pausing to watch the result of their attack, all six choppers then skittered above the compound, their chin-mounted cannons darting back and forth, spewing death and destruction on the shocked rebel fighters. Many died without even knowing where the bullets were coming from.

The government troops halted their carefully choreographed retreat. They turned as one and opened fire on what was left of their pursuers. Hundreds more troops joined them, shooting from heavily fortified positions inside the barracks. More government troops poured out of shacks and buildings outside the compound, catching the rebels in a deadly vise of concentrated crossfire.

Guzmán saw the nature of their predicament. There was only one thing to do. He spun the Land Rover around and stomped on the throttle as hard as he could, trying all the while to place himself between the rain of gunfire and the wide-eyed leader of the revolution who was in the seat behind him. Antonio de Fuka, in the passenger seat, braced himself against the dash, and gritted his teeth.

The machine's powerful engine rocketed the car away from the gate, back toward the fence that formed the compound's perimeter. It gathered enough speed to shoot up over the protective earthen berm and slam down in the middle of the razor wire–topped chain-link fence. The weight of the vehicle crushed down the fence. Guzmán never let up on the accelerator. The car fishtailed in the dirt but shot forward, dragging a strand of the fence with it as they tried to escape from all the hell that was breaking loose inside the barracks compound behind them.

One of the Apache pilots spied the escaping vehicle through all the smoke. He looked directly at the Land Rover. The chain guns, slaved to his heads-up display, automatically slewed around to aim at what he looked at. He opened fire.

The first shells slammed into the car's front end. The engine was destroyed in an explosion of fire and steam. The heavy car careened forward from its own momentum, slamming hard into a cement pillar. The impact drove what was left of the motor all the way back into the driver's compartment and sent Antonio de Fuka hurtling forward through the windshield.

Juan de Santiago ended up in the back floorboard, standing on his head. He pulled himself up, shook himself off, and wiped hot blood from his forehead. He checked himself for wounds. Wasn't his blood. He looked up through the smoke and steam and saw Antonio de Fuka's shattered, lifeless body, rammed halfway through the windshield. An ugly gash on his throat no longer gushed blood. His heart had stopped.

On the other side of the front seat, Guzmán moaned and pushed his way back from the steering wheel, struggling to free himself from the mangled mass of metal that captured his legs.

"Help me, El Jefe," he said with surprising calm. "My legs. They are caught."

Juan de Santiago squeezed through the crumpled frame of the side window and dropped to the ground outside. He crouched there for a second and looked around. The Apache had gone on back to circle over the compound, looking for other targets. Three or four government troops were running across the landing pad toward the hole in the fence, heading for where they had seen the car crash.

He did a double take. A familiar face led the troops. The big *yanqui* soldier. The one from the jungle ambush.

In the midst of all the death and destruction around him, Juan de Santiago's face split into an evil grin.

He had been right. They would meet again in battle. This was not the place. Not just yet.

More smoke poured from the wrecked Rover and wicked tongues of flame now licked from where the engine had been. There was a strong odor of leaking gasoline.

"Help me, El Jefe. I don't want to burn. I want to be here to protect you when you take the capital, my leader. Remember how I carried you on my back at the Alverado hacienda when—"

De Santiago turned to him, looked him in the eye, and spat squarely in his face.

"It was you all along, wasn't it, Guzmán? Only you knew enough to be El Falcone. I should have known. I should have known."

He raised his pistol and pointed it to Guzmán's forehead. He noticed the hungry flames already boiling into the passenger compartment of the car.

De Santiago laughed.

"Fire. Is it not the worst death imaginable?"

He turned his back and scurried across the street, away from the blazing vehicle, ignoring Guzmán's screams of agony as the first flames reached his trapped legs.

The leader of the people's revolution disappeared into the rat's maze of rough buildings and shanties.

Bill Beaman watched de Santiago's back as he disappeared into the narrow alley. He leaped the fence and ran after him as hard as he could, but the chase was nigh unto impossible. This was de Santiago's territory, as much as the dense Colombian rain forest was. He knew every twist and turn of these slums. Beaman had the distinct feeling that he was following a rattlesnake right into its den.

There was no choice. He had to try to run the bastard down.

He caught another glimpse of de Santiago as he darted down another alley fifty feet up the narrow street and to the left. Beaman waded through a pack of street kids as he ran all-out to the alley's entrance.

He stopped short to peep around the edge before he entered. No sense dying in an ambush today.

There was de Santiago again, still fleeing, turning another corner a block ahead. Beaman looked back over his shoulder. Johnston was a hundred yards behind, running to catch up but being hindered by the same bunch of begging kids.

Beaman couldn't wait. He darted down the alley, almost slipping down in the slimy muck of wastewater, mud, and human feces. He rounded the corner, trying to fight the feeling that the rebel chieftain was leading him along on this chase, staying just far enough ahead to avoid capture, but allowing him to continue the pursuit.

Down another alley he ran, up the hillside, across another narrow street, fighting his way past a clothesline full of clothes and wading awkwardly through a vendor's pile of woven baskets.

No doubt about it. He was gaining on de Santiago.

The rebel, looking back, ducked down yet another dark, shadowy alley. When Beaman got to the corner, he scooted around without pausing this time.

De Santiago was nowhere in sight.

The SEAL caught a deep breath and charged blindly down the alley, looking for a doorway or nook where the bastard might have gone to ground like some jungle varmint. There was no way out that he could see.

The son of a bitch couldn't possibly have sprinted to the next corner that fast.

Realization hit him an instant before he sensed more than heard the slightest movement in the alley, above and behind him. The SEAL stopped short, coiled, ready to spring around and confront the rebel leader.

From above, on top of a narrow tin-roofed overhang that stuck out over the alley, de Santiago snarled down at him.

"Buenos dias!"

Beaman turned around slowly. He saw de Santiago on the little eave, an evil smile on his face, his MAC-10 pointed directly at Beaman's heart.

"At last, we meet in person, *mi amigo Americano*. Drop your weapon and keep your hands where I can see them."

Beaman's H&K fell in the muck. He raised his hands as he desperately looked back down the alley, hoping against hope that he would see Chief Johnston, covering his back.

The rebel leader hopped down from his perch, landing nimbly. He was still quite agile for someone his age. With the barrel of his gun, he motioned Beaman to step around the corner at the end of the alley and open the door to the nearest shanty.

"Inside, *por favor*. I don't think it would be good to stand out here and compare notes on being a brave, strong warrior. Do you?"

Beaman did as he was told, knowing already that once inside, he was a dead man. He blinked to adjust his eyes to the dark interior. The dirt-floored room was empty except for a dilapidated table and two rickety chairs. There was a small, rough, wooden crucifix hanging on the wall.

His eyes adjusted. A woman who had been standing back in the corner of the room came into focus. She stood quietly, her hands at her side, watching him and de Santiago, making no effort to flee. It seemed as if she was expecting them. His eyes finally came around. Beaman could see that she wore a simple peasant skirt and blouse, a humble outfit that only accentuated her stunning beauty.

He could only think of the Angel of Death, that this lovely creature was here to collect his soul once de Santiago separated it from his body.

She moved slowly over to stand behind de Santiago, to touch his forearm, a gesture so familiar and easy it confirmed that it was no accident that de Santiago's flight had led to this particular shanty among all the ones in Bogotá. The SEAL now knew for certain that he had only moments to live. He couldn't help but notice that the woman's movement had the grace and beauty of a ballerina, that there was no malice in her amazing eyes as she watched him.

"Margarita, my love, let me introduce you to the *yanqui* soldier I told you about. The one whose skill and bravery I admired so much when we attacked his troops in the mountains. Now, here he is. Imagine that! Only moments ago, he was so convinced I was finally defeated. He and his helicopters and the troops of El Presidente were close to destroying the revolution. Their ambush was so nearly a success. Many of our troops are dead. But not El Jefe. El Jefe lives to continue to lead his people to freedom. But not El Presidente. El Presidente has finally paid for his sins against the people of the country he has raped for so long. He is on his way to hell.

Margarita, this is the most glorious day of our revolution! The
helicopter of El Presidente is burning down on the field."

He gestured toward the window of the shanty with the barrel
of his MAC-10, his eyes shining with tears as he spoke. "Wonderful Margarita, it is a glorious day. You can see the smoke of
El Presidente's funeral pyre from here. And before the ashes
of the wreckage have cooled, my army and I will take the capital and return the government to our people once and for all."

Beaman pursed his lips and shook his head. If he was to die,
he was at least going to get in one good dig.

"Juan, my man, you don't know how wrong you are. So
very wrong. That chopper your missiles took down? That was
nothing more than a radio-controlled drone, a decoy to draw
out your gunners. El Presidente is still very much alive. Safe
and sound. And you, my friend, are finished."

De Santiago eyes went wide, his mouth opened, and he
screamed in rage.

"Noooooo!" But then an eerie calm seemed to sweep over
his face. The evil smirk was back as he bowed his neck in defiance. "No, it is not that simple, *mi amigo Americano*. As
long as El Jefe lives, the revolution continues. I am very much
alive, *mi amigo*. The rest of the revolution begins as soon as I
have the pleasure of killing you, just as I killed your traitorous
spy, El Falcone. It's a shame in a way, though. At least you are
a soldier, a brave soldier, your loyalties sincere and uncom-
promised, and that I admire. You are not like the bastard coward El Falcone, who would steal from me all the time he was
stabbing his leader in the back. All traitors must eventually
die. I took special pleasure in seeing his life end. But you? It is
a shame that we had to fight against each other and not serve
side by side." He raised his pistol to eye level, the muzzle of
the MAC-10 two inches from the bridge of Beaman's nose.
"Still, it is now time for you, too, to die."

The SEAL tensed.

De Santiago sighted down the barrel. He could not see Margarita Alvarado reaching behind her and pulling the needle-

sharp stiletto from the belt of her skirt. She cooed sweetly into de Santiago's ear.

"You are right, Juan my darling. It is time for all traitors to die. And this is for my father, Enrique Alvarado."

A puzzled look crossed de Santiago's face as she aimed the point of her knife to a spot just above his collar. She shoved it sharply upward.

Beaman dropped instinctively and rolled frantically through the dust of the shanty's floor to the minimal shelter of the rough wooden table. He didn't have time to see the sweet smile on Margarita Alvarado's face.

El Jefe was probably alive just long enough to hear the next words from the full lips of his love.

"I am El Falcone. I have my revenge at last."

The blade broke through his cerebellum and into his cerebrum. He felt a sting, saw a blinding flash, then there was nothingness.

El Jefe and the revolution were dead.

epilogue

SUI KIA SHUN SAT ALONE IN STONY SILENCE. THE GARDEN THAT WAS so calming, that brought him so much joy, was now dark and foreboding. A thundercloud blocked most of the late afternoon sun. Even the songbirds seemed to sense his mood and were oddly silent.

The young woman slipped out the glass doors of the house and walked quietly across the stone patio to stand before him. He did not acknowledge her presence. She cast her eyes downward, staring at the ground, and finally spoke.

"My father, I have bad news to report. We have been informed that the American Coast Guard sank the Colombian's ship. All our shipment was lost. Almost an entire year's production gone. The guards we placed aboard have perished as well."

Shun showed no sign he had heard her words as he picked up an exquisite jade carving from the granite table next to his chair. The delicate little bird, fashioned from the finest white jade, was over fifteen hundred years old. Artisans living during the T'ang Dynasty had spent years fashioning every minute detail. The priceless artifact warmed in Shun's hand, and normally, it would have brought him much comfort.

He suddenly smashed his hand down on the table, shattering the carving into a thousand fragments.

His eyes burned like embers as he raised them to the woman. His voice roared when he spoke.

"You have brought great shame and disgrace on this house. This mission was yours to complete. It was your responsibility to assure its success. Leave now. You are no longer worthy to be my daughter."

The young woman, her head still bowed low, nodded once then shuffled out the door. She knew that she could never return to her home nor speak with him again.

A low rumble of angry thunder reverberated off the mountains as she quietly slid the door closed behind her.

Tom Kincaid stepped off the elevator into the intensive-care unit. He hated hospitals, the sounds, the smells of the places. Every time he stepped into one, he couldn't keep his thoughts from rocketing back almost twenty years. He had rushed to the emergency room at Angel of Mercy Hospital, only to be told he was too late. That his beautiful sister had just died of a massive drug overdose. And that senseless loss had left him all alone, with no one else. It was a gaping hole in his life he had never been able to fill.

The feeling of frustration and helplessness was still with him. He had used it to his advantage, to steel his resolve to do all he could to prevent other bright lights from being snuffed out.

The nurse at the monitoring desk warned him that Temple was sleeping.

"Your friend is doing as well as could be expected given the extent of his injuries. He had massive injuries. We didn't think he would make it when he first got here. Another five minutes and he likely wouldn't have. It was touch and go for the last couple of days. He's a fighter, though. And strong as an ox."

Kincaid thought about the big cop who had become such a close friend in such a short time. The nurse was right. He was a tough old so-and-so, but the last time he had seen Temple, the detective was unconscious and barely clinging to life.

"So he's going to make it?" he asked pensively.

The nurse smiled and nodded.

"He should be all right, barring any complications. Rehabilitation is going to be tough, though. He'll have to relearn a few things, like how to walk." She checked her wristwatch. "We're not supposed to let any visitors into ICU except during visiting hours. But I know what you two just went through together. You can go in for a few minutes now."

Kincaid followed her into the little curtained-off enclosure. Temple lay there on the hospital bed, connected by a maze of wires and tubes to bottles of clear liquids dripping into his veins and machines monitoring every function of his battered body. He looked deathly pale and not nearly the robust cop he had been a few days before.

"How come we can't ever find a cop when we need one?" Kincaid asked, almost whispering.

Temple's eyes blinked open.

"Hey, Tommy," he croaked. "We get 'em?"

Kincaid smiled.

"Yep. All except the two trucks that got away. We don't know where they ended up. Rashad won't be a bother to anybody anymore, though. Ramirez is going away for a long, long time, too."

"Good. Good."

Kincaid's smile grew even broader.

"Guess what else. Rick Taylor called. Wants me to come to D.C. Take over all enforcement for the DEA. Make him look good. He's too busy doing press conferences to try to run down any druggies anymore."

"No kiddin'. What you tell him?"

"Told him where he and his political cronies could stick his job. Besides, I got a better offer. Detective Temple, you're talking to the new Deputy Director of the JDIA. I work for John Bethea now. And I'll need somebody I can trust to head the Northwest office. Know anybody who might be interested in a cushy government job in . . . say . . . six months?"

Temple tried to smile, but even that slight effort made him groan from the pain. The nurse touched Kincaid's arm.

"He needs his rest. You'd better say good-bye for now."

Kincaid grasped his friend's hand.

"Ken, get better. And hey! Don't be playing grab-ass with these nurses around here. I can't have you facing a sexual-harassment charge first thing on the job. I'll be back tomorrow."

"Hey, Tommy."

"Yeah, big guy?"

"Enjoyed taking down some bad guys with you."

The party was in a fashionable two-story apartment, just up the hill from Berkeley. Some of the attendees were students, mostly women, but most of the rest worked together at a software publishing company down in Oakland. They had already watched the sun as it dropped below the skyline of San Francisco to the west. Now it was time for the first of the powder to be brought out.

"You're not going to believe this," the host, a tall, long-haired man, bragged. "The guy I got it from says it's really rare stuff, a special Colombian blend. Once you try it, you'll never be satisfied with the regular thing again."

"Oooh, Juan Valdez lives," one of the college girls giggled. She was pretty, dark-eyed, with lively, mischievous eyes. "Give me the first toot."

"You sure you can handle it?"

"Try me!"

"Maybe I will."

She cuffed him on the shoulder playfully, then bent over to try the rare, special-blend cocaine while the crowd cheered her on.

Spadefish lay tied to the pier, quietly at rest. The fresh coat of black paint glistened in the morning sunshine. Her commissioning and unit awards pennants snapped sharply from the staff mounted to the after edge of the sail. A portable stage rested across her back a few feet farther aft. It was decorated with red, white, and blue bunting, and a large *Spadefish* insignia hung on the back wall.

The crew, all in dress uniforms, stood in ranks on the pier, alongside the old black ship they loved. They faced a sizable crowd of invited guests, all seated to listen to the speakers for this occasion.

Ellen Ward sat in the front row with her children, Linda and

Jim Ward, seated on either side of her. She couldn't help it. She brushed away tears from her eyes as she listened to what each of the speakers had to say about what she had always called her husband's "mistress." John Bethea sat behind Ellen, next to Bill Beaman and his SEAL team.

Up on the stage, Tom Donnegan and Pierre Desseaux had each spent ten minutes extolling the virtues and proud history of *Spadefish*. Desseaux's remarks, though, sounded forced. He detailed the actions of the submarine and her crew during her last mission.

Jon Ward stepped up to the microphone.

"Admiral, it is with great regret that I request permission to inactivate USS *Spadefish*."

Admiral Donnegan rose and gave the order.

"Captain, inactivate USS *Spadefish*."

Ward saluted smartly and turned to Joe Glass, who was standing beside the commissioning pennant.

"XO, haul down the commissioning pennant."

Glass slowly lowered the thin wedge of cloth that signified *Spadefish* as a commissioned ship. Further aft, Earl Beasley slowly lowered the Stars and Stripes.

Admiral Donnegan and Captain Desseaux rose and walked off the sub and onto the pier. Jon Ward turned to Glass one more time.

"XO, secure the watch."

Ward led the last of *Spadefish*'s crew slowly over the gangway onto the pier. To a man, they each looked back at her, as if they wanted to say a final good-bye, but the words simply wouldn't come.

Ward stopped and stood there for a moment, watching the way the current tugged at the old submarine. Out there in the harbor, way beyond where *Spadefish* now lay tethered, another sub was just pulling away, the *Cherry Two* tug at her side, headed proudly out for the open sea. For a moment, as the wake of the other sub rocked her, it almost looked as if Ward's old boat was tugging at her moorings, straining to steam back out there where she belonged, too. But then, she seemed to settle down once again against the pier, content to stay right where she was.

The brave old girl was going to her final rest at last.